Plays Well with Others

White People

Oldest Living Confederate Widow Tells All

Allan Gurganus

THE PRACTICAL HEART

Allan Gurganus lives in a small town in North Carolina. The title novella of this book won the National Magazine Prize. His other honors include the Los Angeles Times Book Prize, the Southern Book Prize, and the Sue Kaufman Prize from the American Academy of Arts and Letters.

THE PRACTICAL HEART

FOUR NOVELLAS

ALLAN GURGANUS

VINTAGE CONTEMPORARIES

VINTAGE BOOKS • A DIVISION OF RANDOM HOUSE, INC.

NEW YORK

First Vintage Contemporaries Edition, September 2002

The novella *The Practical Heart* was first published as a chapbook
by the North Carolina Wesleyan College Press in a signed edition
of 1,000 copies. *Harper's* magazine presented Section One as a
folio in 1993. The Jewish Museum featured Section One in its
catalog *John Singer Sargent, Portraits of the Wertheimer Family* in 2001.
   Preservation News appeared in *Conjunctions* and in *Preservation*,
the magazine of the National Trust. It was subsequently reprinted
in *Best American Gay Fiction* (Little, Brown, and Co., 1998).
   He's One, Too, commissioned by Patrick Merla for his 1996
anthology, *Boys Like Us*, was later published in *Granta.*

The Library of Congress has cataloged the Knopf edition as follows:
Gurganus, Allan [date]
The practical heart : four novellas / Allan Gurganus. —1st ed.
p. cm.
Contents: The practical heart—Preservation news—
He's one, too—Saint monster.
ISBN 0-679-43763-0
1. United States—Social life and customs—
20th century—Fiction. I. Title.
PS3557.U814 P73 2001
813'.54—dc21   2001032665

Vintage ISBN: 978-0-375-72763-4

www.vintagebooks.com

Printed in the United States of America
10   9   8   7   6   5

For Jane Holding,
friend, sculptor, mother of sons,
gardener and garden

The first obligation of a gentleman is to dream.

—OSCAR WILDE

This census is the first to let U.S. citizens choose from among seven racial categories: "White," "Black," "Asian or Pacific Islander," "American Indian or Alaska Native," "Multiracial," "Hispanic," or "Other."

   823 Americans checked all seven racial boxes.

—*USA Today*

Q: How do you get to Carnegie Hall?
A: Practice, practice, practice.

—OLD JOKE

CONTENTS

ACKNOWLEDGMENTS

I am honored to thank my generous first readers: Mona Simpson, Joanne Meschery, Erica Eisdorfer and Dave Deming, Daisy Thorp, Charles Millard, Andrea Simon, Danny Kaiser, George Eatman, Michael Pollan and Judith Belzer, Helen Miranda Wilson and Timothy Woodman. Terry Smith was the gifted small-press publisher who first offered my novella *The Practical Heart*. Like so many other important presses, his has been closed because of fiscal crises. I was honored to work with him. Cecil Wooten, Latinist and friend, gave invaluable help to *Saint Monster*.

I'm indebted to my brave grandmother and great-aunts, The Fraser Girls, who first inspired (and then demanded) *The Practical Heart*.

All my books have been designed by two wizards. Peter Andersen guides all the interior decisions with a reader's heart and an artist's eyes. Chip Kidd has done my covers with psychic skill and a seeming ease Mozartian. I thank them both for having the wit to read those books they help to shape. Increasingly a rarity, I believe.

My assistant, Mona Sinquefield, has braved the no-man's-land between caffeine highs and technophobic lows. Her belief and company proved essential.

My agent, Amanda Urban, has shown such immediate and long-range faith in my work. Her genius for detail can rival any novelist's.

And, finally, my editor, Gary Fisketjon, granted me his clarion judgment, long patience, and consoling presence.

Thank you, friends.

THE PRACTICAL HEART

For Michael Pollan,
and
for Jack Fullilove
(1917–2000)

At last, the distinguished thing.
—HENRY JAMES, final words

THE EXPENSE OF SPIRIT

I

Oh, did I mention that John Singer Sargent painted my great-aunt? No?

—Yes, Muriel.

What led to the portrait? A streetcar accident.

What led to the streetcar? Her professor father's low appetite for cowboy novels written by Karl May. May (1842–1912) was a German high-school teacher nabbed for petty theft. In prison he taught himself to write. His narrow cell's subject? Galloping Indians of the Great Plains, palominos, buttes. He saw America only after writing sixty books about it. And yet, to this dreamer con man I owe my American citizenship, my lack of a trust fund, and, I suppose, the Sargent portrait.

My great-grandfather, Professor Donald Fraser of the University of Glasgow, was tenured, landed, married, surrounded by four adored if never-quite-beautiful daughters. A gardener pruned his vista. Three intelligent maids realphabetized his library. Professor Fraser had inherited the seven-acre compound with its orchard, with the sixteenth-century stone house, big and old enough to warrant a name—Sunnyside, naturally. (Oh, to have a dollar for every lost homeplace once called Sunnyside.)

Fraser was forty-five, boasted a lustrous white beard that seemed a dividend on his distinction. He'd published four books, two about Robert Burns and one concerning lotus imagery in world literature. (All this is all true, I swear to God.) His most personal work, *The Bagpipe, Some Reminiscences,* chronicled his own collection of ancient nearly museum-worthy pipes.

But local happiness was not enough. No, his venturing spirit led him to those cheap, gallant, faintly autoerotic Westerns by a German jailbird jewel thief. And the Professor believed those tales. Then he learned of a teacher exchange program. And without really consulting his family, Donald Fraser chose to transport them all to a university in Chicago for a year. He thought Chicago was The West. Turns out it was, but not "The West" he'd planned.

History is not just lived; it's also wished, isn't it? Maybe Art is history most livingly wished. Oh, to break in now and shout back to him, ambered in the 1870s, "Great-Grandpapa, stay home. Perfect Sunnyside's rock garden. Marry off your smart daughters to the smug and titled local gentry. Save to buy more Mackintosh furniture. Get fat. But don't read trashy books for boys. Great art always offers troubling adult portraiture. Bad art offers easy lies and makes for bad decisions. Stay. Stay there."

But I can't. And he couldn't, and if he hadn't, Singer Sargent wouldn't enter into it, and you might not be interested.

Professor Fraser, his ladies, and their nineteen trunks (packed with one year's art supplies for the daughters) arrived, unheralded, in the mythic Chicago of the 1870s. The town had a cowboy novel's mules and dust. After rain, it became a Venice made of mud. Painted women, revealing entire inches of dead-white ankle, loitered under gas streetlamps in even the best neighborhoods. Civil War veterans, their blue uniforms emptied of legs and arms, begged, aggressive, on street corners. No building looked more than six months old. To the stately Professor's four virgin daughters, workmen muttered personal ghastly things. Stockyards brought the scent of reality into the most elevated thought. Everything seemed omen.

One afternoon, to cheer five womenfolk, Donald Fraser squired them toward high tea at what, one heard, was the best hotel. It featured Chicago's first revolving door. But a crowd stood pressing noses to the portal's fanning glass. One clever brown hen had escaped a passing farm cart. She then dashed toward safety but chose a door like an upright threshing machine made of mirror. Professor Fraser could see the chicken in there, still alive and flapping against tile floor, her head twisted beneath the rotating black rubber flange, her red wattle seeped out from underneath like black rubber's own red rubber blood.

"Don't look, Muriel," the Scotsman told his eldest girl and confidante, who looked. Nobody could push the door without killing the bird. Her free wing beat so, trying to lift a ten-story building nesting on her spine. The crowd of city swells in fur, velvet, and cashmere seemed unconcerned about one chicken's life, but everyone acted embarrassed that a single country fowl could block entry to so fine an establishment, and at teatime. Muriel, having peeked, her face a stark white vertical beneath its tweed bonnet, now tried to hold cupped hands over three younger sisters' eyes. "It's a hurt one," she explained. "If you see it, you'll remember, so don't . . . please." The youngsters peeked; crying resulted. Muriel already understood: This sight had entered her forever, a hen was lodged there in that door and the sight was in her now.

The family soon discovered: homesickness meant just that—sickness, a stubborn flu of longing. Sometimes the sight of a letter's pink Scottish stamp could send any of them unto nausea itself. The girls did sketches of Sunnyside's apple orchard. Muriel, the astute eldest, Papa's favorite, portrayed Sunnyside's foyer. She showed its William Morris laurel wallpaper backing forty frames of Piranesi's classical ruins. She even added the yellow ceramic umbrella-stand, crammed with hawthorn walking sticks and houseguests' orphaned umbrellas. Her drawing made the container seem so avuncular a jumble that, according to Papa, it looked the very portrait of Mr. Holmes's squat, companionable sidekick, Dr. Watson. "I see that." Muriel nodded, smiling.

The visiting Professor taught classes in an accent his students joked about; they asked for repetitions. Two months before the Frasers' planned return to Glasgow, the whole family began packing. Overpreparing, Fraser brogues thickened to butterscotch density. The day before departure arrived, the Professor's wife—pretty, plump—hurried to Marshall Field's, buying gifts for Scottish relatives, tablecloths and matching napkins. Laden with goods, happy, rushing, she was one block from the store when a streetcar jumped its tracks. It came at her. It was striking her. It had pinned her underneath it. Already, her pelvis had been crushed like some

Sèvres teacup trod upon by boots. Kind treatment she received on the street was later attributed to eleven scattered bundles in Field's gift-wrapping. Those, if not her dreadful screams, had marked her as a lady. Four doctors, overpaid, the best by all accounts, told Donald Fraser, "Scotland? Any travel would be fatal. She would die on the train to New York." The accident rendered the daughter of Lord Kilkairn an invalid for life. She could not walk, would have to be carried, forever moaning, from bed to bed.

And so the Professor's employment ended. (The teacher he'd traded places with came home wearing a touristic tartan vest, and amicably evicted the clan.) Fraser's own university was an ocean away, unable to continue his salary or tenure. Donald Fraser was forced to move his brood to ever-more-modest lodgings. Educated by live-in tutors at Sunnyside, the man was skilled in Greek and Latin. To quote all the poetry he had by heart would take him three days. He could draw serviceably, could sing in a decent tenor the popular Italian arias; his bagpipe collection was considered somewhat comprehensive. He'd known Rossetti, had entertained Ruskin. He had shared a childhood mathematics coach with that other gifted, charming nomad susceptible to boys' literature: Robert Louis Stevenson. But not one of Fraser's skills/languages/friendships warranted five dollars of ready Chicago cash.

Stranded here, Professor Fraser sought a permanent job at the university, but he'd been a guest, a novelty. So he ran a newspaper ad, the cheapest four-word minimum: "Can Tutor, Most Subjects."

With the house exchange over, shelter for a family of six must be paid for out of pocket by a man who'd never known the heartache of rent. The Frasers' leased house now stood between a busy firehouse and a busier liquor store. Servants at Sunnyside wrote for their salaries. The professor began contributing articles to a local sporting paper. As his waggish, tragic pen name, he chose "Raffles." *The Racing News* complained he too often mentioned lotuses, Greek gods. Donald Fraser considered taking in a lodger. He tried the public schools, but his Scottish credentials were not respected here. Soon the word "Professor," written before his name, seemed as dubious as the "Doctor" he saw scribbled on calling cards tacked to doors in the dark halls of the latest boardinghouse.

He was forced to telegraph a land agent in Glasgow. He sold Sunnyside via mail—his furniture, his library, everything at a loss. His wife's bills were terrible, and he, so eager to get the poor woman home (mistaking this for Cure itself), consulted doctors who made promises they could not keep. Instead, they gave her drugs she came to need too much, even as the prices rose.

Four daughters performed their usual Friday musicales on a rental Chickering upright, not the homeplace's signed Bechstein. In a small if overdecorated parlor, maroon hangings flanked the mantel; pennants showed a peacock to the right, a peahen to the left, both worked in metal threads, placed there, in part, to hide the plaster's cracks.

The Sisters Fraser attended crowded slumside public schools. A head-lice epidemic made even their curls suspect. Their mama had been the forceful utilitarian, humoring Papa's whims, standing guard over his writing hours. Whenever he acted swaggering or impractical, she had smiled at their daughters, saying as he listened, "Spare wee Donald his illusions, girls. They're our only real capital." But now—without her help—how loud and under-rehearsed poor Papa sounded. The girls soon lied to protect him; school was fun; this flat was "cozy"; America was friendly. Mrs. Fraser needed attending round-the-clock; her bedside table seemed an opium den's as she reverted to baby talk, lived banked in pillows, gained weight, looked pale and round in her daytime nightdress. The girls pampered Mama with chocolates and mustard plasters; they sang to her. If left alone even a minute, she cried. Mabel, the youngest, chanted to herself, "All the king's horses and all the king's men could not put poor Mama back together again." But Mrs. Fraser—second daughter of Lord Kilkairn—would live, a victim of stupefying good health, for another thirty-five years.

One evening while his wife slept her laudanum sleep, the Professor called his daughters from their narrow rooms, walls pasted with photogravures, inspirational poems, and their own accomplished sketches. Into the hands of Muriel, Ethel, Jenny, Mabel, he placed gold coins, $200 apiece. "Hide these," he said. "It's what ye'll have from our selling the dear homeplace. Your mother will never travel again. This must be your dowry. No matter what awaits us on ahead, I will never ask you for it. And if I somehow do, you're never to surrender it, ye hear me?" Then Fraser quoted his correspondent and onetime houseguest, John Ruskin, " 'The greatest thing a human soul ever does in this world is to SEE something, and tell what it SAW in a plain way. Hundreds of people can talk for one who can think, but thousands can think for one who can see. To see clearly is poetry, prophecy, and religion—all in one.' Girls, continually SEE yourselves. Know you were born to be more . . . than mere Americans."

As the sisters, arms around one another, sat watching, Papa overwound his pocket watch while reciting Bobby Burns in roiling Gaelic. It was a language the daughters had already most cleanly forgot. Weeping, the gentleman feigned a coughing fit, then rushed out for a walk along a great lake he pretended, late at night, to be the surging River Clyde.

The more fuddled Professor Fraser became, the louder did he praise his eldest girl as "the son I never had." To Muriel he ceded household accounts once kept by her mother; to Muriel he confided his daily shame; he told every fact learned belatedly about the imprisoned author of those Westerns that'd tricked him into sacrificing his wife and virgin daughters to some idea of an American future. "One assumes a writer knows whereof he speaks, that he's traveled farther than some atlas copied in a jail cell," Donald Fraser complained about Karl May's deception. But the more gossip he collected concerning the writer's woes (May had been blinded from birth until age five by nothing worse than malnutrition), the more allied he felt with a fellow victim. Untenured, Donald Fraser—alias "Raffles" of *The Racing News*—could only envy May's speed, his caliber of well-paying pulp.

Within too few years, Fraser had sent all his girls into the world to earn their keep; for him, this tragedy outweighed the accident itself. To fare badly in Scotland was unseemly if melancholic, familiar; but "Perfesser" Fraser, as they called him here, soon understood that in America there was no curse, no comparison to lowly body parts, no blighting word as wicked as plain "failure." It rendered you and yours prairie Untouchables.

One girl would become an executive secretary, one a private tutor in French, and, saddest, the youngest and fairest found work wearing a starched mobcap and frilled apron selling Belgian chocolates in a lovely little mirrored shop on Michigan Avenue. Muriel, the talented eldest, a child-prodigy performer in Glasgow some years back, now taught the children of the rich to play piano presentably.

Before the accident, she had entertained at afternoon parties for Mrs. Armour, who then hired her to train the little Armours. The heiress lectured Muriel that she must always use the mansion's side entrance marked with a bronze plaque, DELIVERIES AND STAFF. Miss Fraser arrived wearing a black dress; the garment itself required costly benzine cleaning, but its detachable white lace cuffs and collar could be laundered daily and at home. Muriel understood from the start that a cheap black dress looks better longer than a cheap blue dress. In her carpet satchel, she always brought: her family's own dependable fruitwood metronome, the difficult Czerny exercises annotated with her decisive script, an apple as her usual lunch, and slip-on gold ballet slippers to make pedal instruction easier.

Mrs. Armour liked her children to take their lessons while she held large teas for small women in distant rooms. She liked the sound of cultural betterment. She once sent Muriel a note, via the butler's gold tray, *"S'il vous plaît? Fewer scales, more melody pour mes chères amies?"* When Muriel herself played a little Bach two-part invention, she heard the company ooh-aah. Muriel guessed the heiress must've claimed credit for her child; our heroine could not resist sliding into a passage from Pergolesi, one of great difficulty, as the ooh-aahs soon muted to silence. Mrs. Armour, the famous auburn-tressed beauty, had been Miss Sophy Brophy, a novelty dancer in the Varieties. She now insisted on being called "So-*phie*-a." Her pretension was legendary, as was her cruelty to overeducated underlings like Miss Muriel Fraser. "Must you forever drag your scuffed carpet 'clutch' right into our Venetian Room?" Muriel's Roman nose was perhaps too bold, her Norman chin a bit too shy, but her black suit and knowing smile troubled even Mrs. Armour.

Maybe it was above some massive Bösendorfer grand, maybe in just such a lakefront palace, perhaps while listening to an eight-year-old millionaire bed-wetter punish the keyboard up and down, then down and up, maybe there Muriel saw her first Sargent. She discovered another fine example at the new Art Institute. Miss Muriel Fraser, a chaste girl, nineteen, then, suddenly and unfairly, twenty-seven, now somehow edging toward her thirties, Muriel—in her fitch-fur collar and matching muff dyed to seem mink—studied one of Mr. Sargent's early improvements on a local meatpacking heiress. In the picture, Muriel found something auto-biographical. Not in the silly woman herself, no, but in the heiress's hastily rendered white satin, her ropes of all-too-real pearls rendered as globules of cream-colored oil paint that, at a distance of six feet, became pearlier than any oyster's best try. It was exactly the upgrading of reality to which Muriel, as pianist, expatriate, and practical dreamer, subscribed. If you could not be a great artist yourself, then you drew near the best one alive. This, perhaps, was as close as any uncourted piano teacher and former prodigy could come if not to love, then at least to honor. A close second, surely. And the Master you knew enough to choose? He saved you, and, with you, redeemed your clan's tarnished dignity. For how long? Merely Forever.

Muriel, being eldest of the daughters, best remembered the stone manse full of bustled servants and amateur theatrics. She recalled the scent of blossom from the apple orchard when Papa claimed the whole seven acres were "under full sail." One entire attic room held costumes, ancestors' greasy periwigs, snuff-stained red brocade frock coats. Muriel remembered shopkeepers dropping half-curtseys to Professor Fraser's daughters, now reduced to bowed shopkeepers themselves. Looking up at the yards of canvas still so lushly painted that they seemed eternally wet, transitive, maybe Muriel first phrased the notion, "Might this not constitute a knowingness to stave off losses? Is this not a baffle against such renters' sadness as we now live in? Could this not be, at last, the dis-tinguished thing?"

Over the mantel of the Frasers' railroad flat there hung a mammoth gilt-framed mirror. Of no value, it was intended to lighten a dim room too prosaic with its sooty airshaft view, too sobered by crackled varnishes, too earnestly poetic with its wistful peafowl hangings. Imagine the restitution performed by a Sargent of some loved one. Set in the simplest silver frame, it would replace that heavy, ugly, hopeful, empty mirror.

Muriel decided: belonging to Sargent's own moneyed set was not required. No, perhaps distinction rested more precisely in having first recognized the single major portrait artist of your own epoch; and then simply "arranging" (oh, what a sinking void our stalwart spinster felt at that term "arranging") to be portrayed by that very painter. His immortality was assured, and yours with it, your tradition's with it, and his, with Art's own. Securing such an image would mean reinstating your family into that framing proscenial reality where it so plainly belonged, from which it had so cruelly toppled. One artful image would prove to the Sophy Brophy Armours of this world that your loved ones' single mingy tragedy had been, if not averted, then transcended. It would reveal that there are deeper beauties stretched beyond one's incidentally absent Physical Beauty. A Sargent portrait might tell you who you might, most favorably, have been. It would prove that your accustomed entrance remained the marble-arched, unnamed, Palladian front one—not the side alley's green door under its wall-bolted bronze interdiction: DELIVERIES AND STAFF.

Such a quest for portraiture, permanence, might also offer some of the rushing pleasure that accompanied absolute usefulness. Muriel most longed for use; even the indignities of daily piano lessons were eased when she told herself, "I do not teach Armours. I teach Music." All that practice, practice, practice. And then to leave behind no justifying performance! Surely that would be a double death.

And so, unusual for anyone on either side of my family, Muriel, the musical one, the practical one, gradually and then suddenly knew exactly what she wanted.

Past that, she began to understand all that she must sacrifice to get it. Nothing seemed too difficult. No social slight, no skipped meal, no finery forgone could compare with having glimpsed the justifying Eternal at the center of her dignity daily betrayed. Here in exile, in an Elba called Illinois, around the single silent chance, Miss Fraser's life soon organized itself.

. . .

Maybe Muriel overheard a covey of local ladies, not quite rich enough to imagine being portrayed by Mr. Sargent, spell out a few facts concerning this well-placed American born abroad. His Boston mother inherited so much money, she forced her doctor husband to give up his patients and decamp forever to Europe's best hotels. Mrs. Sargent, herself a clever watercolorist, took her boy John on picture-making excursions up many a hotel's own alp. Young Singer Sargent, born a prodigy, was soon training in Paris, making teachers jealous. He soon painted the respectable, then the notable, then the brilliant. His vigorous brushwork brought American energy to portraits of the tireder crowned heads. His Van Dyck technique and marble certainty gave America's newly mon-eyed the suavity of pedigreed beauty they most craved. And Sargent was not just a civilized man but some new specimen of genius. Now living in England, he'd already painted forty English lords and their ladies, had depicted Mr. Henry James (by subscription). Sar-gent never even saw the States till he turned seventeen. And Muriel, a loyalist expatriate herself, would later admire the way he turned down a knighthood in order to remain American. After all, "Sir" John Singer Sargent had a certain destined ring to it. She learned that he'd befriended Gabriel Fauré, that he loved the man's music as she did. At the main branch of the Chicago Public Library, Muriel perused (for free) the literary reviews in hopes of seeing some tiny oleographic copy of Sargent's latest picture. And she commenced to save.

Even after she paid Papa her board and offered her share of Mama's growing drug expenses, even after she helped rescue her baby sister from working in the chocolate shop to stay home with Mama, Muriel still economized with an inner rigor Scots are famous for. But her daily concessions were rendered the easier by vulgarities and harshnesses around her in what Papa, ever more embittered, called the Land of the Cuspidor. To make her own apple-a-day luncheon feel a bit more Roman-noble, Muriel befriended the young fruit vendors. She collected their proud, spotty lore, becoming an expert on the ideal characteristics of today's two-cent pippin, tomorrow's two-cent Winesap. If sadness be one's lot, then one became a connoisseur of sadness. Muriel made a cult of walking everywhere (incidentally saving fares). After Mama's mishap, all Frasers hated the grind of streetcars' tracks, their useless bells, but no Fraser could afford the costly horse cabs. Cabs were only for emergencies and—everyone agreed in a show of hands at a family council—only for temperatures of at least fifteen below. Miss Muriel's fine black buttoned shoes were re-re-re-repaired. Soon she no longer needed to wear the ballet slippers to teach pedal work—so sensitive a second skin did her worn soles make.

In Scotland, the spoilt girls had been invited to complain about this and that. It was a rite of refinement to find trifling fault with some of what Papa provided: a blouse rendered scratchy by zealous overstarching, the birthday cake too overtly chocolate—and Papa liked that, there. He called his girls "my pea-fearing princesses." But now, but here, the girls must praise everything, and Papa complained. He railed—some bearded bourgeois whose fortune would be returned to him one paycheck at a time by his four day-labor Cordelias. Sisters slipped the landlady rent supplements, begging that she understate the true amount to save Papa's feelings. Some nights, in a rare good mood, he made his usual toasts. Candlelight at table softened and enlarged the flat to almost seeming Sunnyside's beamed dining room. In the saving half-light, he requoted mottoes said a thousand times before: "Baby Mabel, please pass the salt dish, my beauty? As Chazal wisely tells us, 'Salt is the policeman of taste; it keeps the various flavors of a dish in order and restrains the stronger from tyrannizing over the weaker.' " His girls smiled, as did Mama, propped nearby. But Fraser's declamations seemed to mean far less at this mended rental table, its two shortest legs made steadier by the dominoes Muriel had wedged underneath. Papa's next epigram was now upstaged by a sudden fire alarm next door, by some stranger's marital dispute out on the landing. "Why is it no one ever *listens* to me here?" And Fraser slammed his fist upon the tabletop.

Salt leapt so.

Muriel found a way to attend the second halves of symphony concerts, slipping, with terrified authority, into an empty orchestra seat just as gaslights died. Sometimes gruff latecomers banished her, in sight of two thousand observers. Once, Sophy Brophy Armour, presiding, bosomy in white, from a similarly bosomy white stage-side box, nearly witnessed such a humiliation. One elder lady usher had commenced to recognize Miss Fraser, to save her. If, in public places, young mothers half-smilingly acknowledge one another, nodding, then so do the Single sniff out and respect one another's dignified solitude. The visibly unmarried usherette, silent, officious in uniform and pedantic in dispensing programs, soon beckoned Muriel Fraser from the "Will Wait: Standing Room" line (cheapest of all). The usher then guided Muriel down front to an exquisite aisle seat, creating a silent flourishing fuss that our piano teacher hated enjoying as she did.

It was Miss Fraser's particular genius to see herself exactly as she was. A mixed blessing, surely. Not actively homely, she still had little to endear herself to a stranger's eye. Though a gifted musician, she knew that those pianists taken seriously in Chicago's music circles were all young men with massive profiles, manes of hair. These youths had foreign-sounding names often invented to improve on monikers straw-plain as Sophy Brophy's. These boys all enjoyed society sponsorship, meaning older lady admirers, interested in a pretty fellow's genius, or more. Muriel had received a few excellent notices for her own early concerts: "In the Brahms, we heard an emergent soulfulness that far surpasses her technique, which is already merely perfect." But, as with her prospects for a worthy suitor, Muriel understood precisely what "someone like Miss Muriel Fraser" might, after all, expect. "Miss" came to seem both her noun and verb.

It was this double vision that marked her as the least likely person ever to desire a portrait from the world's leading society painter. And yet that very contradiction helped fuel Muriel's resolve: To believe that history—even if merely assigned as, say, one's face is assigned—could be partly saved and sweetened by the wish, some wish, any wish enacted, a wish obeyed.

Sir Osbert Sitwell called Sargent's portraits "guardians of the Edwardian shrine." As a boy, Sitwell "sat to" Sargent; the child whined and wandered till the painter was driven to quote distracting limericks. Sitwell wrote, "[Sargent's subjects] loved him, I think, because, with all his merits, he showed them to be rich.

Looking at his portraits, they finally understood how rich they really were. . . ." What then had Muriel to anticipate? Might not the Master reveal her essential poverty? Or would he hint, past the fortune lost, at some present interior wealth? Must Miss Fraser hurl herself upon the Master's charity, his professionalism, or simply his social knowingness? Surely one's sustaining spiritual well-being would prove harder to depict than mere white satin and real pearls. And yet Muriel felt half ready to entrust herself to Genius's hands as to some surgeon's. Was this not simple common sense? You found the single specialist who might save you, at whatever price. Past that, was there a choice? Art becomes your own history most livingly wished. Seeing clearly can constitute your poetry, prophecy, and religion. How sensible, plain faith in beauty. How practical, Art.

Times, Muriel wondered, was her own Scottish lineage worth her stark nunnish loyalty in preserving it? She reread Papa's four books and knew, despite great hope, their charming limitations. Perhaps she owed her truest allegiance to the line's more illustrious future, some chronicler to come? Her "sort," after all, was no more than the bourgeoisie that keeps its womenfolk engaged with fireside stitchery and punch-making, its men collecting volumes of military history, supervising the yew topiaries' progress, refortifying the garden house. Her mother's father, though technically Lord Kilkairn, was famous, if at all, for his precocious gout, his impassioned grouse-hunting, for his touching if finally ruinous moneylending to a favorite shooting companion, the then-young Prince of Wales, eventually King Edward VII, a wag who lived far beyond the reach of any bill collection.

Muriel, bundled in scarves, clutching her carpetbag, out here in a wind that cut across a thousand miles of prairie unimpeded, stood at a railroad crosswalk studying another hundred cattle cars bringing animals to slaughter, to use. The lowing beasts, breaths smoking, gaped out at her—as if to ask her help from History, assigned. Their cuds' white spittle still showed chopped greenery from one last home-meadow meal. And as Muriel watched another ten thousand rattle toward their predestined date with the plates of

Delmonico's, she felt herself to be the eldest heir and protector of so forthright and distinct, so pleasant and useful a tradition.

Muriel knew—with rank unsentimentality—what she herself could forevermore expect: a further succession of often lazy, always indulged students, facing the open copy of their assigned "Für Elise" and admitting, quite insolently, that they hadn't practiced since last week, all the while daring plain Miss Muriel Fraser to find a punishment strong enough to interest them in art while remaining mild enough to prevent her being fired.

In the Armours' kitchen, the butler paid her from a macaroon tin marked HOUSEHOLD PETTY CASH. In those days, dollars came in coins, and, having had her weekly salary flipped at her, she learned, defiant as any apple-peddling street urchin, to snag it midair with one pale, expert palm.

Every six weeks, Miss Fraser was summoned to Mrs. Armour's boudoir reception room. Red-haired, dressed in a spillsome Empire manner, Sophy Armour reclined upon a chaise almost Pompeiian. The chamber was bone-color with green piping that reminded our reserved if irreverent Muriel of one word: spearmint. Mrs. Armour made carelessly certain that the strict-looking teacher, pointedly not invited to sit, glimpsed the title of a book she held. Golden script incised *Ruskin—"Sesame and Lilies"* on a leather binding crafted from one fetal calf who'd made the ultimate sacrifice for the stockyard heiress.

Muriel stood being grilled about the junior Armours' gathering musical skills. What were the odds against a possible concert career for one if not two of them? The practical truth ran counter to Miss Fraser's own best interest. And yet her standards would permit no outright lie. As Muriel recounted small if building victories in keyboard competence, she studied Sophy Armour's Ruskin. The great man had been a Fraser family acquaintance, after all; and Muriel adjudged this edition thicker than the inscribed copy her papa still refused to sell. A butler summoned Mrs. Armour: some visiting Parisian decorator needed a consultation as to the proper citrus yellow for an impending sorbet of a Yellow Room. The florid lady rose, wedged her book into a little Louis XV glass-fronted case, and, in rustling past Miss Fraser, gave one stern daring glance that piqued the teacher's interest.

Only a person this disciplined at intellectual curiosity, only someone with very good hearing—lest Mrs. Armour return—only someone ruddered by a certain wily nerve, would have risked padding over as Muriel did now. Unfastening the case, she lifted Ruskin. Out of him fell a brown paperbound "novelette."

"The Upstairs Maid's Impractical Heart;
or, A Cautionary Confession"

Muriel, biting her own lip with nearly sick-making pleasure, felt shamed at how much sly and racing joy she felt. Odd to picture suddenly a dun hen's wing beating, odd to picture cattle staring from a slow train toward the skyline of Chicago, maybe taking that distant form as some mountain suitable for grazing. All while Miss Fraser's right forefinger—tapered, nearly aristocratic from being so long for hire—skimmed a sample page:

> *My window-cleaning requiring my mounting the library ladder was now interrupted, as I posed helpless above him. His bedampened lips, then the bristle moustache of the devilishly handsome young master pressed, violent as a bee sting, then melting as bee honey, against my left knee and, no, please, oh up suddenly beneath the confines of my best white apron. What to do? Just one room away, his mother dictated bread 'n' butter notes. A regretted yet flooding warmth suffused, then seized me with its wanton hypnotism, just where HE did, between my own strong working-girl's legs. "Please, sir, stop, for the sake of my employment, for the sake of all that's . . . oh, ooh, sir . . ."*

Miss Fraser replaced the book(s) exactly, then negotiated many hallways; exiting through a hotel-sized kitchen, she snagged today's coin. On her long walk home she wondered, might she have mentioned once playing two John Field nocturnes for Mr. Ruskin himself? He had been not uncomplimentary. The great man's admonition had been to "see," then plainly to "say." But this edict did not include the gloating irony of having seen happily more than certain others; such comparisons were odious, undignified.

The temptation to feel superior toward one's employer was really too demeaning. And yet Muriel, during the three-mile hike toward home, her carpetbag swinging at arm's end like some glad school-girl's, felt the lash of pleasure, of overbroad amusement and delight. History had ordained that she herself must hide a genuine association with Ruskin beneath this, her own plain wren-brown wrapper, whereas History lathed Sophy Brophy's pulpy brownish heart in gilt, calf, sesame, and lilies.

Stopping to speak to her usual apple-boy, Muriel found herself noticing one nearby doorway's hidden denizen. A prostitute pre-pared herself for business, for night. The woman already wore a shopgirl suit but, from her purse, she pulled a few final properties. This happened at six-thirty or so. The great male working force came pouring onto Chicago's streets; unnumbered black bowler hats made an antlike carapace of bent advancing heads. Here came featureless husbands and bachelors blindly seeking some prof-itable use for the little energy not squeezed from them all day at office desks, counters, stools—such warrens, a kind of human stockyard. The far end of the street showed the great clear lake; the shadowed buildings made a blue-black trough, and down it, in this direction, poured the mass of ruddy faces, tonsured moustaches, white celluloid collars. In their buoyant voices—joking about beer and sporting wagers—Muriel heard a closing-hour longing she well knew. But, watchful, one hand idly touching apple stems, Miss Fraser tried imagining which of these men might be lonely or nearsighted enough to hire that woman yonder.

The whore was nearly Muriel's age, though an overbold gift at face-painting made that easier to miss. Miss Fraser, shielded by the pyramid of apples, red and green, watched the woman square off with a doorway's full-length mirror. She was plain, uncomplicated-looking, her hair the color of rust. From her black handbag she withdrew two handkerchiefs, folded them into triangular com-presses, wedged these into her bodice. The whore posed, fluffing and resettling this side, then that. Her head cocked, judging in a way quite likable. By finding this mirrored entry to a bankrupt shoe store, she had secured such public privacy. For Muriel, this lent the scene its odd outlaw allure. The woman, without stealth, with a fatalistic kind of raptness, now daubed on rouge. The gesture looked as joyless and factual as medicating some paper cut. Then came the comedy of lipstick application: overriding a series of large flexed faces, this grimace comic, falling into a wide-mouthed comi-tragedy mope, then back to neutral-tragic.

But it was the bawd's cloth violets Muriel found most amusing, then arresting. Flowers were moved several times about the jacket, now tucked behind one big ear, then withdrawn with a shy laugh. Pressed to left shoulder, lower, no, up. False leaves showed a bitter green—blossoms, the correct velvety purple. Once the posy was safety-pinned to just the right spot, the whore tried freshening it a bit. At best, this nosegay had been a ten-cent ornament. Now it was stiffened and dirty, moistened by drizzle under sundry street-lamps. As voices of workingmen boomed nearby, her fussing with the violets grew more frantic. Hundreds of potential clients were getting past. First the prostitute squeezed flowers, one hand primp-ing, tickling in a manner most encouraging. Her attempts to communicate beauty to this lifeless sprig of wire and gauze became—for Muriel—first familiar, then spirited, finally endear-ing. It made Miss Fraser believe that, once this woman touched some man's coat sleeve, she could convince him of anything; could even transcend her overadvertising. For what might one say to some hefty office manager who'd paid hard cash for handling ample breasts? Could such artless padding be made to seem but a flirtation, some courtesan's high art? The violets resisted; so now the young lady bent over her own chest. Rough hands cupped around the purple and—with a force of hope that caused the watchful Miss Fraser to emit a low involuntary groan—the girl huffed. She breathed into such shelter as her red hands made, hoping to plump the lifeless flowers. She stood there, flexed for-ward, consulting the mirror, but, no, the things just drooped. So—a realist—the woman struck the mirror one halfhearted blow, then pushed violets back into her deep black purse. She straightened her hem and turned toward the street's ninety thousand men in ninety thousand suits as black as hers. She turned just as Muriel rushed off, not daring to be seen, not knowing how to hide the look—whatever it be—haunting her own stricken face.

Chicago, drawing its countless mules and cows and hogs and chickens, constituted a kind of glamorous death-wish. Miss Fraser, darting through the crowds, pleased at all the blank and hatted bustle, wondered: What herding sadness had lured her father here, in quest of what? His own Buffalo Bill–ness? Some forty-five-year-old's last chance at being wild? To come clear here from Glasgow. But, if Miss Fraser had ever wavered in her resolve to go ahead, risk everything on having a picture made—*her* picture made—then those three minutes changed that. Her watching the artifice of a plain smart woman seeking to improve herself—that woman, fighting with her every trick and frippery, with all her wiles and animal instincts, to appear necessary for some one man tonight—this helped Muriel understand afresh: how impossible the beautiful gesture in a world so commercial, grinding, dimmed. Walking home very fast, she felt yet more determined. Slung between odd emotional half-tones, not laughter yet not quite a scream. These swings seemed to resemble those huge masklike grimaces that underwrite a little lipstick's practiced application.

And Muriel determined she must see it through.

II.   A Portrait of the Portrait as a Young Woman

It took Miss Fraser seven years to collect nearly enough. She earned from sixty-five cents to one dollar per house-call lesson of an hour. Muriel had made inquiries through friends in Glasgow who knew people in London who might know the sort of folks who'd know the amount you must cough up for a Sargent oil sketch of just your head, or your head and torso, or a family grouping in some characteristic room of the home, either with or without a dog. The more surface inches of you and yours included, the more you naturally paid.

When Muriel announced at last her plan to sail to England in hopes of securing a meeting with Singer Sargent on the chance that he might do a painting of her that she could, in turn, afford, her father threw a red glass pipe-rest against the hearth. Bouncing, it did not break. He vowed to disown her. Muriel might have wondered which legacy the old man threatened to withhold, but she did not embarrass him with the mere facts of their assigned lives. Papa announced that this Mr. Sargent was, despite his clientele, just a rich American doctor's son who'd got above his station. "He is, after all, notwithstanding a certain flair and facility, no Lord Leighton. And, to quote my acquaintance George Moore, if you'll forgive my saying so, my dear, 'Cruelty was the vice of the ancients. Vanity is that of the modern world. Vanity is the last disease.' "

Muriel, inhaling once, explained that she had long since made arrangements, fares paid in advance. If her papa could endure this seeming vanity, he would, she believed, eventually thank her. The Professor finally stated his worst fear: "Are you by chance planning to use yer dowrrry? Not that, Muriel. You're only thirty-eight. Till now, ye've always been so practical." He took her elongated white hand. She nodded. "This I'm doing is extremely practical, Papa. Great art always is. You told us to *see* something and then *say* in a simple way what we'd seen. I regret your pain, but you swore the dowry was mine. I will write you, every day."

On April 2 of 1888, aboard the SS *Georgia*, Muriel and her taller, prettier younger sister Ethel (eventually my grandmother) sailed second-class toward Southampton. In Muriel's possession, a note to Sargent from a former student, now daughter to the American under-ambassador at the Court of Saint James's. Using a teapot, Muriel steamed open the letter, to Ethel's embarrassment, in plain view of the ship's steward. It said, "You will wish to welcome Miss Fraser, who is quite the musical personality in her area." Of the recommendation, Muriel told her sister, "It is either too kind or not kind enough, but I will take it." And smiled.

The crossing proved stormy. Their first night out, the Fraser girls—for so they called themselves as if to stave off age—sat watching their assigned dinner companions go silent, go green, go running. A silver serving-cart on castors slid away from the waiter, and here it came rattling past, overturning gilt chairs, reeling comical as a stage drunk. Ethel's face showed a sleepy unhappiness, and when Muriel saw her sister tasting her own mouth and swallowing too often, she said, "That kind of silliness is no' for the likes of us. Mama has been ill enough long enough for all of us together and for good. We didn't purchase this quite decent food in order to stay below holding on to basins, did we, dearest Ethel?" "No," Ethel smiled, and that was all, they were fine. By the end of their rough eight-day crossing, only the Frasers appeared for meals during first sitting at their end of the second-class dining room. Waiters congratulated them and flirted with Ethel, taking Muriel, if not for her mother, then for her chaperone. Not getting seasick was what these sisters had in lieu of large tips, viable jewelry, visible social distinction. That, and their mission.

Muriel had allowed herself this single seeming vanity. Though she knew that any of her three younger sisters surpassed her in graceful appearance, she somehow refrained from inviting them to pose. Being depicted was her reward for having imagined depiction itself. Putting aside the fee for Singer Sargent, Muriel had spent nothing beyond it on new clothing to soften the all-too-factual angles of her face and figure. She deduced that Frans Hals must be a favorite of Sargent's; she assumed that her customary clothing—black, with the cuffs and collars of white lace (even if machine-made)—would speak to Sargent's racial memory of the Dutch masters. She knew, relentlessly, yet lightly, how she looked. And that can, at the right moment, constitute a power nigh onto the power of beauty itself. Her bearing, her pride, her self-knowledge almost scientific: these became a form of distinction visible only to those equipped to see it. (And those were all she cared to know.) Muriel had saved her coins for this one purpose and, plainly now: the painting would be, however plainly, not of Ethel, not Jenny, and not pretty baby Mabel. But, yes—of plain, pure Muriel herself.

She knew that if she achieved the distinguished thing at last, it might someday permit her family—always known as vaguely "artistic"—to perhaps claim one member as an eventual and actual artist. She half-guessed, she of the good but bold nose and shy chin, that this future kinsman might—blessed with the correct sex and the right leonine profile, buttressed by highborn female support, innocent or no—push her own great sacrifice to the Great Plains, where she most wished it, casual, to dwell: the realm of easy assumption, the freedom of his tossing off in passing, and with an air so entitled as to be but half conscious, "Oh, did I mention that my great-aunt posed for John Singer Sargent? No?" And how easily she could then imagine his bitterly pleasing, tonic little fillip, "Yes—Muriel."

On landing, they proceeded to the Cotswold village of Broadway, where Mr. Singer Sargent summered. The buildings were made of a yellow local stone, and, come evening, the sisters held hands, for the town glowed golden as some candy-tin litho-chromium of Jerusalem, but with foxgloves. Having settled at the Lygon Arms and sent, via messenger, their note of introduction and a short letter explaining a desire to meet the artist, the Fraser girls awaited a reply. Muriel and Ethel, paying full price at the village's best hotel (knowing they would need the added respectability its notepaper afforded), waited eleven days. Mr. Sargent would then return from Italy. In her letter, Muriel found herself unwilling to mention wanting to be depicted; it surprised her how she hesitated between saying "I wish to be painted" and "portrayed." They sounded both too formal and too personal, pathetic as the shopgirl with her violets, presumptuous as Sophy Brophy. So, instead, Muriel merely asked leave to pay a social call.

What I admire in recalling this now-famous family account of my great-aunt's quest (a sensible and scrupulous woman and, from all reports, the possessor of a surprisingly louche sense of humor), what I admire is precisely her middle-class persistence as she stormed the citadel of international connections, of aesthetical hauteur. She and Ethel concocted ambitious walking tours of local country churches, their red Baedeker guide suspended before the pince-nez they were both forced to wear around small print. On the ship, they'd noticed that better-traveled Americans' Baedekers were worn, sun-faded or ringed with Burgundy-wine stains. So, in the Frasers' tiny stateroom, giggling, they'd taken turns stepping on the cover, wearing it to tatters that suggested, first, experience, then an extreme sophistication that finally verged upon world-weariness. They began to economize, taking only the provided breakfast scone and tea, then hiking abroad. They returned from one such stroll, April 19, to find a note at the desk: "Tea at four then? Here only briefly, I fear. Courteously, JSS."

. . .

Need I say that, wearing fine black hats, they arrived when all the church bells, all the village mantel clocks, were gonging in uneven agreement of the exact hour? The sisters were greeted by a young Italian manservant of distinguished appearance but seemingly no common language. He simply pointed to the proper room. The house was all windows and looked out onto a garden abounding in several potted lilies, lilies they guessed to be props for Sargent's masterwork of the Academy show two years previous. The sisters were left seated alone so long that Muriel explored a bit. The chamber in which they waited had the overutilized air of a first-class train-station waiting room, and in the corner she noticed two stray calling cards, one announcing Lord and Lady Rocksavage. But Ethel soon hissed that someone was coming and Muriel dove for a chair.

In strode a man who seemed the hired and presentable fellow who would, in turn, introduce some eccentric disheveled artist. Muriel felt relieved to recognize, via a self-portrait reproduced two inches square, Mr. Sargent himself. Austere, tall, and impeccable as some bank trust officer in a three-piece black suit, he wore the simplest of watch chains. And yet he seemed to have pop-eyes and a beard that claimed too much of his neck; he was not nearly so handsome as her papa. Singer Sargent spoke in a ripened Anglicized American accent. His manners were exemplary, if a bit glassy and automatic. Muriel had warned her less experienced sister not to let on that they'd sailed precisely to beseech Maestro for a sitting. And when he perfunctorily asked what had brought them abroad, Muriel answered a bit too loudly, "The churches."

"A worthy pursuit. —I am expecting, I fear, a German couple to join us. Perhaps they've been delayed. Was your crossing difficult?" And you felt he had asked this of more than a few other, earlier Americans.

Muriel was candid in explaining about the runaway silver serving-cart that, in dancing a sickening reel from table to table, had sent the few remaining diehards herding to the rail. "We determined not to be sick and, in deciding, seemed to make it so." She wondered if she'd been too explicit when the painter saw fit to

quote a limerick he admitted had become a recent "craze" of his, a
ditty employed to amuse such fidgety children as sat for him.

> There was a young lady of Spain
> Who often was sick on a train
> Not once and again
> But again and again
> And again and again and again.

There was laughter, relaxation. "I am especially susceptible to
your watercolors, sir. And it is, I believe, for that medium, as well as
your oil portraits, that posterity will note you. Do you use both
mediums in a single studio? Might I be bold enough to see where
you manage all you so wondrously manage?"

He nodded and led them down a series of dark halls. "Chicago,"
he said aloud. "There's a Mrs. Armour whose picture I believe I
once did."

"Yes, I see Mrs. Armour now and again. And—come to think on
it—again and again and again."

He laughed, half-turning to reconsider his visitor. "I believe she
was in the theater, before?" and his tone was so assured and invited
such fun.

Muriel, quite primed to use Fauré's celestial *Requiem* as her
impending topic, could hardly believe she was gossiping with
Singer Sargent about the woman who paid her one dollar per hour.
"Not to put too fine a point upon it," Muriel set forth, "but Mrs.
Maitlandt Armour was, one hears, Sophy Brophy of Gerhardt Ray-
mond's Variety Beauties. I'm afraid there's a slightly malicious story
about her, not that she's fully to blame. You doubtless know about
her inviting Paderewski to play after dinner?" If John Sargent had
heard, he was gracious in pretending otherwise.

It took Muriel's fullest concentration to rattle out her tale while
arriving in the mammoth studio—the three easels, the Steinway
concert grand, the upended mahogany-and-ebony steamer trunk
with its heavy bouquet of peonies. The room revealed a wealth of
reflecting surfaces wherein it was impossible to know which detail
was painted and which actual, and which, actually, both.

Yes, backstage at a Paderewski concert, it seems the pouter-
pigeon Mrs. Armour invited the great musician to play at "my man-

sion," after dinner the following evening. In plain hearing of every-one, she asked what his fee would be. "Fifteen thousand dollars, forty minutes' music of my choosing." "That in itself," she replied, "will present no difficulty. But I feel I must needs warn you to use the staff entrance and that, after playing, I will not sanction your speaking to, or in any way mingling with, my distinguished guests." "Ahh," he smiled, "in that case, madam, TEN thousand dollars."

The painter, chuckling, asked Muriel to repeat the precise phras-ing. Seeing he planned to use it, she felt she'd already been, in some small manner, portrayed by him. To be useful: that was all Muriel had ever wanted. To practice your lifetime's Czerny lessons but for the sake of a final performance, not more mere practice. To be of such thorough Use made you so richly mortal that your spirit residue remained, luminous, of continual compasslike use to oth-ers. Art gave your poor life the ultimate utility. Muriel Fraser did not teach Armours; Music taught itself through her. Yet, having arrived here, having determined a way to accomplish both eternal use and eternal pleasure—how, now, to ask?

She did not mention having learned through intermediaries that watercolor portraits, though rarely done, could be had for less than $350, while oils began at upwards of $800 to $1,200. In the wall safe at the Lygon Arms, Muriel had left her best jet-beaded reticule. It now contained but $600, and yet from that sum she and her sis-ter must return to Southampton and then take the long train ride from New York to boomtown Chicago.

"I'd begun a little watercolor, just to get my hand in again," and he gestured down at the broad white page marked with traces of those pink flowers set on the upmost end of the sleek trunk just opposite. Muriel decided against stepping over too suddenly. And now, having achieved his studio—her dowry long since spent to get here, her life savings dwindling fast—Muriel found that, the more familiar and relaxed she felt with the great painter, the less likely it became that she might state just why she'd come. "Yes," he said, leaning on the table where the watercolor rested, "I believe Mrs. Armour is the first I painted among a group there known to some, I am told, as 'the meat people,' " and he gave a grin as noncommittal as a grin can be. Muriel recalled the portrait itself, remarking inwardly that he'd at least paid Mrs. Sophy Brophy Armour the compliment of elongation.

The artist mentioned how glad he was to be in the Cotswolds again, how he regretted having to rush off the very next morning. And Muriel paused in patrolling the studio; she felt her sister's eyes upon her. "Is it customary"—Ethel herself intended to try something—"for you to accept appointments from those who might wish to 'sit to you' for a portrait?"

"Months and years in advance. 'Doing mugs,' I call it in the slang. I should soon like to get beyond that. . . ."

He seemed to dare Muriel to state her history as wished, not assigned. The fabled Seeing would be hers; but perhaps, she now saw, the Telling of the vision was not to be. . . .

In order to save a few pence, she had not eaten lunch, believing this might further enhance her pallor. Now Muriel regretted that. She felt dizzied at being so near her hope and yet finding herself too unlike the Sophy Brophys of this world to just come out with it. Ethel, stricken, kept staring at the older sister, bobbing her head in a manner touching if a bit grotesque, as if to say, "Go ahead. Ask now."

"Mrs. Armour"—Muriel held fire—"at least has the distinction of having been set down by you. Tomorrow you leave?" He absently nodded, staring at the floppy peonies and the highly polished trunk that reflected flowers' glowing aura; and, taking up a brush, he dispersed the slightest wash and soon seemed utterly lost to mere conversation. Did the Fraser girls distract him from his work or inspire him to go on with it? He was not much noticing them. He had two thousand visitors a year.

Outside the immense window, Muriel noted one yellowed leaf fall from an elm, spiraling to the lawn, its descent modest, perfect, final. There came the childhood memory of one brown hen's translucent wing beating beneath a door's black rubber blade, murdered by a glazed entrance that seemed welcoming but was, being mirror, only the sky disguised. And all at once the impossibility of her mission broke upon her. She saw that precisely what gave her more inward stature than the meat people was just what would prevent her coming out with it, asking him to "do" her, "save" her, even for a fee. Even if she'd somehow assembled the correct secret amount. A wing-whipped lightness set to roaring in her ears. Trembling seized her calves, both knees locked, but instead of her feeling stricken, an unearthly clarity settled. Some flooding white intelligence claimed her. "So," was her thought. Finally—Muriel Fraser had proven to herself (yet only to herself) her possession of it, of the distinguished thing, at last. And this very distinction prevented her naming that which she most wanted, wanted for reasons too urgent to state, for motives far beyond mere personal vanity, from an impulse as steadying and noble as any she'd encountered on a five-line musical staff or occupying any carved gilt frame. It would only come to pass in her imagination. But THERE it had been seen, then plainly stated, and therefore it was true, forever.

Maestro liked to talk, during. Deft, half absently, he applied water paint. The Italian activated a phonograph with a bugle like a mammoth celluloid morning glory. Mixing bowls dripping with dried pigment occupied a sleigh-shaped daybed parked in one swagged corner of the glassy room. Behind a door loomed one headless mannequin wearing a dress beaded in a poisonous green, the costume in which Ellen Terry had been painted by the master, setting a crown upon her own head, in her role of Lady Macbeth. Maestro took up the theme of churches. He recommended ones in the neighborhood worth visiting and then ranged farther afield, mentioning hideous overrestorations of otherwise perfect *a capella* jewels in his adored Tuscany.

As he spoke with fluency of his brush technique, he squeezed conversational dots of tubed watercolor paint upon a white glass to his right, blending these easily as he recombined casual spoken topics. The Italian appeared and disappeared, bearing clean white rags and bearing carafes of clear water. These he arranged and dispensed around the man in banker's clothes, the servant performing his sacramental duties with an acolyte's half-bored, half-awed matter-of-factness. By means of frequent recranking, he kept the tenor aria endlessly repeating. The late daylight seemed to coat the studio's carved chairs, brass helmets, the Chinese screen backing one mammoth bouquet of disintegrating peonies set atop the handsome trunk. The chamber turned a tint now pink, now gold, soon both at once.

Just as my great-aunt understood she could not ask; just as she understood that seven years' savings, the daily plan, the apples had been in the service of practice, not performance, of getting here, not getting painted; just as she halted, giddied, alongside the trunk that Sargent idly if intently painted—just as she most wished she'd eaten both lunch and breakfast, as she stood wondering if all the postponed seasickness were about to strike, there came an insistent, indeed heart-stopping pounding on the front door. "That," he sighed, "will be the Germans. Only Germans can knock *comme ça*." And he had set aside his brush when he chanced to look her way.

Feeling light-headed (she really should've eaten, she really should've been born a genius, rich, or beautiful, or all three), she had leaned upon the trunk, to prevent a crude stagger forward or perhaps even a fall (the disgrace of that, here!). And the slight pressure of her pianist's hand caused the petals of the lowest peony to drop, with half a humid sigh, around her tensed white forefinger and thumb on which all weight now pivoted. The chin was lifted, accidentally displaying the long pale neck that her crippled mother had mercilessly and often described as, "along with Muriel's hands, her one distinguished feature." The painter saw the face set atop a neck tilting back for breath till it accidentally craned toward seeming almost swanlike, and something, something in the woman's fortitude at trying to hide her vast disappointment, to hide her vast distinction (which was of the self-same Chartres size), something in the fading light, maybe even something obdurate and half attractive in the bone structure of her sinewy ridged side-face, something there revealed a respect for art so surrendered, so complete, it could not be ordered on demand. And one felt in the artist's straightening spine, in a bracing almost alarmed, that something had annealed him. It made his habit of social lightness go briefly grave as, reconsidering, he paused, then barked four syllables of Italian at his manservant. One heard the front door open, a low explanation, a grumbled guttural protest, then the door most quietly closing.

And the lifted dampened brush returned to motion!

"Miss Fraser, stay, please, as you are. Just so. May I impose on you. There IS something. And, with watercolor, we shall soon know. You are quite well?"

"Quite," said she. "Well," she, superstitious, added.

Muriel stood facing the light, her long fingers supporting her, fingers strengthened into beauty by simple work—the infinite pressings over smaller hands, the countless virtuoso demonstrations with which she ended each lesson. This veteran hand was now bordered by supple ticklish petals that had made their only sound in falling. The servant arrived just as the aria wound, ratcheting, down; knowing the signs, he did not renew its spiraling blare. The paper where Sargent ministered was secured against its board by common mailing tape. The paper was of excellent nappy texture and was the size of, say, the Declaration of Independence. With music stopped, you could hear his brush now press, now stutter; and Muriel could feel his gaze upon her, warming like the mustard plasters poor Mama liked. There was something therapeutic, being so *in* the gaze one had just so totally forsworn. Popular journals claimed that Singer Sargent sometimes played his studio piano to cheer and refresh his famous subjects; and Muriel had come to occupy the useful pleasure of posing for fourteen minutes, just long enough to let herself wonder what he would play when and if he played. She was just deciding how to work into impending talk her admiration for his admiration of Fauré when "There," he said.

"Beg pardon?" Muriel offered. And instantly regretted this common little phrase, wishing she'd merely turned and lifted one eyebrow, but there it was.

"I have taken the liberty," Singer Sargent said, "of enlarging your hat brim. No criticism of the hat itself implied, you understand, Miss. But only for compositional purposes."

Muriel stretched slightly (her neck would be stiff during most of the return crossing, so concentrated a pose had she so briefly

taken). Ethel meekly rose, then sat again, then stood like a concerned relation called in from the doctor's antechamber to hear
the verdict on some loved one's life.

"It's the merest suggestion of you, naturally. However . . ." And
he squinted, stroking the right side of his moustache with the
thumb of a hand still holding its brush's long maroon handle. It
was Ethel, clutching her handbag as if yet braving the wooden side-
walks of some dangerous prairie metropolis, who first took a place
beside the somber man in black. "Oh, *Mur*-iel," the sister cried.
And the painter smiled, as with a belief that if the first witness of a
portrait exclaimed not to the artist but to its subject—it must be a
fair likeness indeed.

"But, Maestro," Muriel herself ventured, stopping behind him.
"However shall I . . . ? You see, it is 'I' as I feel, as well as 'I' as God,
alas, saw fit to somewhat carelessly make me." She'd not planned
the statement. And it, Muriel admitted later, helped make up for
that dreadful tartish Middle West "Beg pardon?" Though not
completely.

"Shall we finish our tea here," he asked and told them. And soon
they all sat in the carved chairs they would later see in portraits of
prime ministers, royal couples, august artistic eminences, and milk-
white moonflower ingenues.

They did not speak further of the picture until Muriel stood to
leave. Maestro offered, "Shall we have it shipped to you, then?"

"What a bother that must cause you. If the paint is quite dry and
if it might be rolled, perhaps I could venture to do something so
simple as take it . . . with me? That, don't you find, remains one of
watercolors' many merits—their portability, so to speak."

Again in insurmountable yet, one felt, idiomatic Italian, he
ordered that a pasteboard tube be brought, and, before becoming
hidden, the picture was studied again. "Are you averse, Maestro, to
signing your works? Or does it interfere with the overall design, or
whatever?" The "whatever" she would later rue, but at least it was
less bad than that beef-jerky American "Beg pardon?"

"No." He took up the brush and bowed forward, left a trace of
name not unprominently placed.

"About my homage, your remuneration, or what have you . . ."

she began, dogged, Scottish, stifled but determined. And really, now, for the first time in the seven years since she first labored toward this, Miss Muriel Fraser felt embarrassed at her half-coarse daring; it was like some pastor's pious eldest daughter unaccountably choosing the traveling career of a juggling comic actress. She was briefly confused as to her motives in all she had attempted. But now Muriel could not imagine returning home without having achieved this one distinguished thing via fate's own patronage. The prospect became such a sadness, it belatedly weakened her.

There was a louder knocking at the front door, which somehow made them all laugh. This time he seemed to order his servant to refrain from even answering. So, the signature blown until quite dry, Maestro rolled the picture with a wrenching matter-of-factness and popped it—no other word would do—into its tube.

And then, jovial as a mayor, he was walking them to the door. "This has been quite refreshing, spending time with two of my countrywomen who've remained so utterly unstudied. You would not believe the pretension of certain Americans who seek one out here."

"It can be a little frightful," Muriel offered, and then Ethel, the door now opened, saw fit to risk, "Though they doubtless mean well and are merely nervous in your presence. It is clumsiness is all, perhaps." And smiled.

He seemed pleased enough, but as the door was nearly closed, they heard him cough some orders to his servant, or indicate social relief, going on to the next thing. And they felt no doubt, as they strode arm in arm back to the hotel, that Maestro had, for all his courtesy, already largely forgotten them. Maybe the Germans must now be dealt with? Maybe he needed dinner? Surely he had moved on to persons more significant and more lovely and with actual money. But the Fraser girls, their hen-brown mailing tube held before and against them, they did not mind.

The two drifted past the front desk, failing to acknowledge the greeting of the bellman. Only when alone together did they embrace. Then unexpectedly they sobbed. They could not stop weeping. "Poor Mama," Muriel said, as if explaining everything. The sisters seemed to cry for injustices endured. And not only by their loved ones. No, by everybody. The whore's belief that her own breath might resurrect cloth violets. To be paid, in flipped coins, from a macaroon tin. The difficulty of quite literally every day on earth. How very odd that achieving some small token of justice should release in you not license toward a pure lit joy but descent into such careening blackened rage. The Fraser girls were both so wracked by heaves and bleats, they soon commenced laughing. They pointed to each other's tear-painted face. It was only after ordering a full cream-tea, served in their rooms (an additional expense), only then did they dare turn up the gas lamp, and take out the picture, and look at it.

Still holding on to each other, the sisters agreed it had the grandeur of his massive oil portraits but the intimacy, the atmospheric jeweled flash, of his best watercolors. It resembled Muriel but made her look, if no prettier, thank God—for flattery per se was her worst fear—then better. Just "better"—not overly elongated but more distinguished because, quite simply, more visibly herself than ever before.

Come morning, Muriel would send, by messenger, the jet-worked black purse containing American bills in the amount of $400. Along with it, a three-sentence note: "I know the Caravaggios and have been painted by Sargent. I can now say I have experienced the ultimate. My thanks, and my sister's, for your hospitality. Muriel Fraser."

(Her original note contained the postscript: "Have the Germans re-stormed the citadel?" But, after consulting her sister—an executive secretary, after all, who had used three years' future vacations to come along—Muriel reconsidered and—wisely, I believe—copied the lines afresh, without that overfamiliar aside.)

By return, their messenger brought the artist's simple vellum notepaper, "The pleasure was all on my side, I assure you. JSS," and the reticule. When Muriel glimpsed the money still folded inside, she had a sinking spell. It was only after her sensible and better-looking sister got her seated and wrapped a blanket round the subject's legs, that Ethel thought to actually count the money. Maestro had seen fit to keep back $200 but had returned the rest and, of course, the handsome little beadwork bag itself.

The boat fare, the cost of boarding for three weeks, the travel within England, and the return trip to Chicago—added to the price of the portrait—cost my Great-aunt Muriel nearly $900. Her dowry and savings gone, she would—without regret—take on years of additional night pupils to help justify and offset the single great expense of her life. But, she was later told, those with four times that amount to spend, those with pedigrees and ambassadorial letters of a magnitude far beyond even those wangled by Wrigleys, Armours, Palmers, and Fields, even those persons failed to achieve an audience with the great man, much less a picture.

Framed in the thinnest of stark silver frames (Muriel believed that gold smacked of stockyard owners' carnivorous pride), a glass-fronted watercolor replaced the mantel's heavy mirror. The crowded little parlor benefited from the picture's style, force, and lightly distinguished presence. Younger sisters sometimes said they missed consulting the central looking-glass, but Muriel's mother asked to be carried in and propped before the painting, hours at a time. It soothed her as nothing else did.

They decided to take down the peafowl hangings that flanked the fireplace. True, the crackled plaster showed, but now it seemed more eccentric, less pitiful. Though Papa was terribly critical of those boys brave enough to court his girls (such swains all proved to be mere Americans!), two sisters did bring home nice young men to see "the family Sargent." Three boys' genteel mothers came to pay respects. Muriel was asked to lend the picture to an exhibition in New York. She consented. Two Chicago papers reproduced Sargent's portrait of her. One caption referred to her as "the distinguished local pianist and sometime coach to the finest of our youthful Lakeside keyboard talent."

III. REWARD

The painting now hangs in the Art Institute of Chicago. The woman shown looks, if not beautiful, then doggedly high-minded and, far better, a bit mischievous. Her expression contains qualities associated with the Scottish national character. Like the bagpipe's wailing tone, her smile combines pagan playfulness with a mournful Nordic solemnity. (Golf, the major export of Scotland, with its elaborate strategy for a dubious end, might offer another example.)

Arranged in profile against a pearl-gray suggestion of window panes and drapery, one hand's tripod of tensed fingers rests among the scattered petals as she stands confronting daylight; she seems between appointments, lost in some personal rewarding reverie.

She is pale but fixed, and the one depicted corner of her mouth shows something gleeful, as if the subject is plotting or, indeed, achieving, at the very moment of depiction, a goal, a comeuppance, a sweet payback fervently sought. Is the joke that an unwed, unrich, quite smart, forward-looking piano enthusiast from the Middle West has just attained something so long wished for? It is an expression that might be termed "intellectual happiness"— that joy some feel must be a contradiction in terms but which, made flesh here, quite plainly is not. Here use and pleasure, practice and performance are joined at last and for all time. The distinguished thing, intact and, via clarion water-clear understatement, preserved, preserved.

The wide dark hat and a hastily rendered lace collar on a black black dress, all this could have only been done very fast, in speedy watercolor, by a genius of some sort, between other obligations, all at once, by accident. His accident, her plan.

At the Art Institute, this is the single watercolor in a room of six massive vertical oils. These others limn department-store heiresses and meat ladies. The oil portraits sometimes seem more intent on flattering the costly Worth dresses than ladies' dashingly rendered local faces, their supplemental chins hastily euphemized but nonetheless suggested. One lady confronts us from alongside a Great Dane dog, obviously borrowed, and she holds a riding crop. But there's an unfortunate assumption that she is about to hop sidesaddle onto the beast and whip it into service as an unwilling form of transportation. Just this April, I myself loitered in the echoing chamber of white marble. For forty minutes, I listened with feigned detachment as talkative gallery visitors discussed the museum's cluster of its choicest Sargents. I swear that, a hundred-odd years after the picture was done and forty-some years after its subject's death, the picture's freshness still seems to grow.

After being overawed (even somewhat enjoyably snubbed) by the nine-foot oils, the more diligent lookers often come to rest before this, the smallest painting of the seven. I love to see viewers linger here longest. We find a woman vertical beyond an upturned steamer trunk, as if some household is in transit, and yet a still life has been improvised atop the trunk where one outstretched and elegant hand pivots. A wash of cobalt blue fills that hand with quick implied blood. What best distinguishes this picture from its mannequin companions is the way it presents a person plainly meditating on something, some fact or idea visibly satisfying. Simply put, it is a watercolor of a woman not handsome, not hideous, but shown, under her overhanging eave of a black hat, *thinking* something.

I can imagine Muriel, just before she surrendered her small masterwork to the Institute. I see her just prior to achieving her clan's (and her own) permanent detour past the squat alley entrance marked DELIVERIES AND STAFF. Easy to picture her just before yielding to History as she somewhat wished it. Muriel is seated at the parlor's rent-to-own Chickering upright, an instrument long since rented unto ownership. A slow, sweet snoring from one room away means Mama, resting well. Outside, some roving street vendor cries, "Nice and sharp, let me put the edge back on those knives and scissors. Cut into anything. Get 'em nice and sharp for you today?"

Over that and alongside it, I hear Muriel, retired, playing a favorite Field nocturne, at noon. Notes accumulate under and around her like brush strokes, like paychecks; like all the pinfeathers required to make one airworthy wing, angel-white or hen-brown. She touches keys while studying the mantel's picture that, through the saving mystery of Art, is notable because it is not merely herself, and yet somewhat is, herself. Muriel plays today, for free, for joy, for no one but herself.

The museum affixed a gilt label to Muriel's own simple silver frame and dove-gray silk mat. The museum adjudged her choices unimprovable. It reads: " 'Portrait of a Lady, in Black'—watercolor. Subject: Miss Muriel Fraser (American)—by John Singer Sargent (American, 1856–1925). Executed, April 19, 1888. —A Gift of the Sitter."

. . .

So all this, you see, underwrites her permission, her blessing on my artful offhandedness in finally remarking to you, with a carelessness oh so hard-won, as if to almost make light of it—the distinguished thing, our one distinguished thing, at last:

Oh, did I mention that John Singer Sargent painted my great-aunt? No?

—Yes, Muriel, our practical one.

THE IMPRACTICAL
TRUTH

Fact is is is Fable.
—JAMES MERRILL

I.   PASSPORT

I did have a Great-aunt Muriel. Also true how one misguided
streetcar stranded her whole family for life. By 1890, Muriel's dashing father, author of the out-of-print *Lotus Images in World Literature:
A Reflection,* debarred from university library privileges, fired from
being "Raffles" of *The Racing News,* impatient at teaching holy
English to mere Asia Minor foreigners, was forced at last to under-
take full-frontal "trade."

In a literary irony no sane writer would go near, he ended his
career selling tablecloths and matching napkins at Marshall Field
and Co., the very items from the same store that had accessorized
his wife's tragedy. With his groomed white beard and Longfellow
grandeur, the man was put to use as a nine-to-five visual aid for
women hoping to make their tables appear respectable as he.
Ladies naturally gravitated toward a gent almost distinguished-
looking enough to pose as some Scottish professor who'd published four books, who'd inherited a nineteen-room freehold
house worthy of a name. Donald Fraser appeared, in fact, someone
distinguished enough to have lost everything, and survived.

Maybe that—and not a family Sargent—becomes the lasting, ultimate Distinction? To have forfeited all your class trappings, but to
remain somewhat standing. Here's hoping that counts. It might be
my own unlucky family's single chance at amounting to anything,
at getting on record. And might that matter? I have no choice,
given our history, our story, but to believe it does. —Odd that "His-

tory wished" should be so much easier to tell than "History merely
if bravely lived."

In your own life, don't you find that?

For Donald Fraser's sixtieth birthday, daughters gave him a pair
of lively English water spaniels. Dogs soon accompanied him everywhere except Field's "Fancy Linen Goods." The esteemed Professor, long deprived of his property, his classroom audience, finally
stopped saying, "No one ever list-ens to me." Now his dogs did. He
named them Sonny and Sadie. Muriel was quiet in noting how
much these names, uttered all together, recalled the word "Sunnyside." He'd say, "Come Sonny/Sadie, my poor landlocked creatures. Shall we stroll our bit o' lakefront and see what erosion's
left us since last night?" In spaniels' unwavering respect, the old
man seemed to recover some of his sense of home, of honor, even
humor. The pretty animals, flanking him, rendered this once-
forbidding patriarch picturesque. Fraser became less a skulking
fugitive of the lakeside park, more an official greeter on this estate
he did not own. He indulged the pets just as his young daughters—
without his ever quite suspecting—had shielded him. To Sonny
and Sadie, he quoted Gaelic poetry that they alone seemed able to
enjoy. Ears perked, heads tilting, they stared up at him with a helpless trust unseen for decades from his kin merely American.

My actual Aunt Muriel wore a pince-nez all her life. She possessed a beautiful contralto speaking voice. It seemed richer than
her face and wider than the fragile partridge neck. Her Glasgow
accent still lived—a cushy burr—beneath the Midwest's layered
brass. Aunt's hair went gray when she was twenty-some; she wore it
pulled back in a bun to "keep it out of the way." She had one good
friend, named Jewel. A family joke, how Muriel carried a tight-
furled black umbrella even on days half sunny. As a child, I recall
Aunt Muriel's always smelling clean yet clerical. It was a minty, neutral scent, like the glue on a good business envelope. If she was agitated, her aroma could upgrade to that of Twining's English
Breakfast Tea steeping after being violently at boil. One personable

widower called on her during the entire summer of 1908, but either he was married or lost interest or moved, or all three. His name, it is recalled with a bitter retentiveness peculiar to poor literate families, was "Stan," "Stan" Something.

After trying, as a young woman, to teach piano, Muriel Fraser found her pupils no more lucrative or socially notable than the twin daughters of a Bengali hemp-importer and the handsome son of her own Presbyterian pastor. Thanks to the secretarial pool of her sister Ethel, she finally took a day job. Quickly accomplished at the new shorthand, being blessed with a most avid intellect, Miss Fraser spent the next forty-seven years serving as executive secretary to a fifth vice-president of the International Harvester Company, the fellow charged with manufacturing bailers and crop-binding twines. —Musical yet hardheaded, trim yet faintly asexual, cheerful if not visibly ecstatic or excessive, blessed with the ripe speaking voice but a thin singing one, Muriel never married, devoting herself to her difficult, wounded, attractive parents.

My question is: Why her? Of all the family members held up to my kid brother and myself as excellent American examples, Miss Muriel Evangeline Kilkairn Fraser was never cited once.

I came of age in eastern North Carolina but often wrote to my favorite of "The Fraser Girls." Savoring such exclamatory illustrated childhood bulletins, Muriel determined I could draw, or was trying hard. So, in the margins of her own terse letters, she started sketching quarter-notes with faces, wispy stick figures playing drums or horns. She assured me, age eight, that artistic genes coursed, wild, through our family. Muriel prepared me for the onslaught of my own latent brilliance—brilliance at doing what, she didn't yet say. Maybe she preferred not to limit me? Aunt saw predictive traces of my good mind everywhere; and who was I to contradict her? She foretold Prizes, in much the way my parents hinted at a cruel Puberty waiting dead ahead. I preferred Aunt's verdict.

Kids along our suburban North Carolina street were force-fed lessons in ballroom dancing, dressage, and piano, even the boys. I endured three years of dreary Czerny exercises. One of Aunt's notes told me, with what seemed glossy sophistication, "Czerny has few great supporters, no? The very word 'Czerny' means, of course, 'black' in Czech." This fact I tried, with uneven success, to wedge into conversations at grammar-school marble games. Nobody had the slightest idea what I meant. Looking back, I see that happened often. It helps explain how much, between trips North, I longed for the snobbish certainties of a brisk, unlikely woman my father called Miss Mouse.

Mother caught me admiring one of Muriel's little illustrated notes and said, "How dear. She's like our own Beatrix Potter, isn't she? Only without the talent." Christmases, Aunt might send my younger brother a ski sweater or some cowboy wallet—his name burned there in lasso script. But, upon me, Great-aunt Muriel lavished the most exquisite of art supplies. The expensive candy of Winsor Newton tubed watercolors, paper so rich with rag no frame was needed to help it stand. Such supplies were always beautifully gift-wrapped by Marshall Field's. (Our family's fate seemed as bound to that emporium as some clans to, say, the Roman Catholic Church.)

In Falls, North Carolina, you could only buy artist's equipment in one corner of our better hardware store. On sale beside a tray of pink bathtub-plugs, such local paint smacked less of art than carpentry. —Just before Christmas, I would roll the best of my whole year's work into a brown mailing tube. (She never didn't like my efforts!) Her gifts led me to check out art books from our local library. I found one, *The Underappreciated Singer Sargent,* and, applying the idea of being underrated to her and to myself, renewed the book and renewed it. Muriel insured my love with her annual bundle, the finest art supplies mere money could buy. I swear, with those, she half-created me. And this.

I *felt* related to her. There was something in how Muriel, though cohabiting with family, lived so visibly alone. Something in her own appetite for study, her faith in the "National Geographic Society" (whose expeditions she hinted she helped fund). Something in her morbid breath-mint fear of imposing on others. Something in her gluttonous eyes, her Museum memberships, her relish for facts, her extraordinary memory and its companion, sympathy. All these drew me, like predictions.

Masquerading as a boy, I weakened with gratitude whenever Aunt—recognizing one of my emerging qualities—mailed me some sketch or playbill. My local teachers worried I "exaggerated." They claimed I was cursed with a "perhaps morbid and surely over-vivid imagination" (a direct quote). Short of driving you to criminal acts, can the Imagination be too vivid? Can a wish have too much ballast, too much invented History? Can a person's life be over-alive? And to Whom should we apologize for too much Seeing?

My parents fretted: Miss Mouse was overstimulating me. "Something here from one of your more elderly girlfriends," they held her good blue stationery in their big oily paws. Such jealousy bewildered me. But then I could lock my room's door, could settle on my bed in stocking feet, could plant the reading glasses on my snub freckled nose, could study both sides of the envelope before tearing into her fresh packet of lore.

Muriel had a nickname for me. It was based on one of my infant mishearings: she'd planted me in her bony lap while perusing pages of the *Geographic*. At a picture of some jowly black-robed Caribbean judge, she read the caption, "His Honor," but I somehow heard "His Owl." This delighted her, not as a lapse, but an invention. She reported this to strangers till my parents began to look at each other.

Soon—inside each Muriel letter—she abbreviated me "H.H. H.O." "His Honor His Owl." By the time I was eight, these endearments began to fill me with a strange half-sexual charge. Such intimacy came, after all, from a woman, a grown woman, and one so adult and alone, so marginal to all but me—she seemed either half dead or half invented. I knew I would provide the rest. I volunteered for that, I'd be her sixty-eight-pound avenger. A battle was coming, one I must prepare for. What my parents considered Muriel's plain sadness, I saw as the Tragedy of Everything Taken from Her, and "Our Line." Morbid perhaps, I asked Mother many ghoulish questions about her grandmother's streetcar accident. Did the trolley actually climb actually right on top of her? And just sit there? For how long? To my lurid little mind, the family tragedy had sexual overtones—a pretty woman on her back, pelvis crushed, surrounded by costly gifts still safe in their white tissue paper.

At eight, I ordered encoder rings off the back of cereal boxes ("Boys, Nobody Will Crack YOUR Secret Messages, Ever"). Muriel's letters seemed encrypted, and sweeter for that. I felt a tenderness whose by-product was a kind of enraged defensiveness. When my parents made jokes about a Northerly nest of chilly Scottish spinsters, I left the room with a silent grandeur so discreet I sometimes wondered if they noticed.

Aunt sent me office gossip and not-that-riveting neighborhood news flashes: "Guess what? Someone at church left ten Presbyterian hymnals outdoors in the bushes last week. Certainly nobody knows why. But, H.O., they were very nearly ruined by the rain!" She wrote explaining about sentences that spelled the same things backwards and forwards. By return mail, I scored: "Madam, I'm Adam." Aunt retorted: "Eve." She offered fabric swatches: "Which is best for the parlor's wingchair, H.H. H.O.?" Magazine articles were marked only "Made Me Think of You, of Course."

I begged to go visit her. "In six or eight months," they told me. I saved my dimes. I planned for this one distinguishing thing that set me apart from other routine kids on Country Club Drive.

My parents provided the shelter, the food, and schooling. Taking care of us, they sometimes seemed too busy to note precisely who they'd drawn from the genetic sweepstakes. Mother provided a new set of maroon encyclopedias and the coarse newsprint for Bradley and me to sketch on. Brother and I were expected to be self-sufficient, uncomplaining. To clean up after ourselves regarding both hygiene and emotion. In our lipless Presbyterian realm, grime and emotion were considered equally annoying, similarly susceptible to strong soap, fierce bristles, and "the silent treatment." My father never once tossed a ball to Brother and me on our two-acre lawn (which appeared designed for exactly that). If we strolled the yard with him, it was to follow his massive back and the faceted arm pointing out some spot we'd missed while trimming the endless hedge, a tourniquet that stanched our unused yard from others adjoining it.

Our parents' kindnesses seemed present-day precautions against some future litigation. "Don't ever say you didn't have the very best encyclopedias, plus the yearbook updates," Mother encouraged whenever she found us scanning a volume. "I hope you appreciate the steak you boys get every Saturday night. Look at them, wolfing it down, T-bone this tender." —Appreciation cannot, I think, be actively solicited.

Awaiting the Chicago trip, I remember marking my bedside calendar. Beyond my aunt, there was an added expectation. Since Father liked to "get the jump on" Falls, North Carolina's 1956 rush hour, he always packed our Buick Super the night before. At dawn, I would hear the dark house come alive with Christmassy draggings and knocks, paper rustlings. Once the car was humming, last thing before leaving, our father would pad into the rooms of his sleeping sons; he always lugged me out first. This meant his lifting me in footed blue pajamas; this meant his carrying me, still feigning weighty dreams; this meant his settling me inside a nest of quilts he'd made for us on the Buick's back seat of pearl-gray flannel broadcloth. As Dad rushed back indoors for Bradley, I remember scouting through the car window. I'd never been awake this early. Our yard, the neighbor's roof were wet, all silver-blue and gold, and looked brand-new. When I heard the front door open, I konked over in some faked adorable attitude. Mother brought along our daytime clothes. And only when we got a few miles clear of the city limits, listening to the folks' usual dull list, "I turned off the stove, didn't I? We canceled the paper delivery, right," only then would Brother and I sit up. Pretending to wake, we yawned, "But where ARE we, Daddy?" Like so much in our stiff, attractive lives, all of it was simulated. This little ritual, this being carried— last luggage—to the car, might seem trivial, but it filled us with an unexplainable excitement. All year, we waited. It was the one part of our Chicago treks my kid brother liked. Only later, only recently, did Bradley and I, seated at the end of a dock on his property at Venice, California, figure just why this had always been a favorite memory. Because: only while loading us into his sedan, only then— apart from shaking our hands, or slapping us, or sometimes pulling on our snowsuits—only then did this rangy man feel free to touch us once a year. In our faked sleep, how we curled against him, our arms around his solid neck. —Why this enforced coldness that fathers saw as their job description then? Why were we kids seen as assured slackers, latent beatniks, who must be kept in line like some miniature militia? Why, if you work yourself blind for your own children, should you be scared to squeeze and tousle them with the sweet rough-housing they so crave? Such were the mysteries surrounding that oddly more comprehensible mystery: Muriel's patronage and fascinated attendance on one bright child. I tell you all this other so you'll see why I really needed her—Muriel, who couldn't keep her hands off my brother and myself. And for that, was considered "strange."

In the usual order of succession, father passes lore to son, mother to daughter. Great-aunt to great-nephew has, I'm told, some precedents in certain Oceanic tribes. But she broke rank, she came at me and barked, "Follow," and I just did. Muriel had decided that talent skips a generation—which left us both in the clear! And, weary, from the sidelines, my parents watched with equal parts amusement, pity, dread. If Muriel had controlled the family fortune—if we'd had one anymore—my tie with her might have been more seriously promoted. But I'm thankful to my parents. They were social, handsome, well-meaning, exhausted. Unlike Muriel, fifty years their senior, they seemed, as I recall them, always very, very tired. Only in retirement would they find an almost childlike vitality I had never witnessed. But during those gray days of their youths, Muriel came forward, asking, thanking, assuming. And my parents mostly let her have me.

The only time I felt sick with readiness to say, "I do, I do appreciate this," was on being hand-bundled into our Buick headed North. My parents saw these trips as a duty; my kid brother considered them hell; I literally pined for my great aunt.

Someone should eventually write the truth: there is always something embarrassing about love. All of it. That's because there's always something wrong with the beloved. Because one's motives for loving are never pure as love itself. It's too good for us. That's why our hearts stay broken.

Between sightings, my image of Muriel evolved and faltered and improved. She lengthened, stood straighter, dressed better, and took on qualities like Shirley Temple's stern yet rich stepgrandmother seen on the late show (probably Edna Mae Oliver?); this old girl finally revealed her good nature with a game try at doing the Charleston. Sometimes in memory Muriel made atypical hostess-entrances. She acted kindly toward the servants, who, on account of this, did even more for her. And her home's polished white halls were wider than those in your bigger Yankee hotels. First glimpse of Muriel Actual always shocked me. She'd both shrunk and wizened. I'd forgotten her medicinal bifocals and how she forever appeared faintly powdered, hair and arms and face. (I was already a secret late-show fan, and it seemed strange to me that my Rebecca should be played by Mrs. Danvers.) But as soon as this toothsome hag bent down before me (there wasn't far to stoop), soon as I smelled her documentary file-drawer scent, soon as she put her knotty hands upon my shoulders and said, "Here His Honor and Owlness is, at last. I have planned it to the minute and all of Chicago knows you're here," that pretty much did it.

I don't think I just imagined that sexual charge. I still own her insinuating, cryptic letters. They are charming. And like so many charming things, they can finally seem pointless. But they do hint: whatever Muriel had saved of her romantic erotic restlessness, she offered me. If my father and mother ASSUMED me, Muriel SAW me—observed me with a lavish spendthrift joy it troubles me a little to recall.

These days, parents would never let their eight-year-old go off on unsupervised day trips alongside an adult so obsessed with such a pretty, pretentious, innocent, and eager child. "I believe that if Miss Mouse told him to jump off a building he would," my father said. And I sat listening, already choosing which of Sullivan's Chicago towers Muriel might consider most beautiful.

My great-aunt's hard life often made her squint as if recovering from one affront while preparing for another. It was a family joke, Muriel's morbid fear of public toilets, her ability—if need be—to wait for days (sisters' private nickname for her, "The Camel"). She did her necessary job for International Harvester; she allotted herself the weekly "girls' night out"—sipping a single cordial with her beloved Jewel while they discussed office politics and upcoming holidays—then she retreated, spent the rest of her time hiding at home. There, framed and propped on the mantel, was a citation from International Harvester dated 1921. "For Innovation in

Bailer Feeder Design That Saved the Company Untold Funds, and for General Excellence." She had buzzed her boss, asked permission to enter unbidden, then silently placed a sketch on his green desk-blotter. She let the drawing explain itself: it proposed that a three-pronged reel, designed for its nineteenth-century attractiveness and not seriously reconsidered since, be reduced to a two-head reeler. "I believe fewer snags might result. I have, in fact, sir, given it some thought." To his credit, though her boss smiled, he thanked her. He immediately cornered someone to redo Auntie's drawing, then he took it elsewhere, upstairs; upstairs he was soon promoted, from fifth to third vice-president. Muriel got her two-hundred-dollar bonus and a handsome brass plaque preserved at home in a thin silver frame. Executives intended to make her stand and accept this at the staff Christmas banquet, but she outfoxed them, faked a dreadful cold, stayed home.

Only her laughter preserved what Muriel might've become if left in state at Sunnyside in Scotland: her chortle lurched out raucous, startling and indolent, selfish. Muriel's sense of humor was, like mine, drawn to dumb broad jokes. "I have a Roman nose," she told me honestly. "It roams all over my face!" Her sisters and my folks would sniff as we two clutched each other, hollering with laughter of a depth that hurt, most wonderfully hurt. We saved up "absolute killers," not trusting these to letters. Our jokes concerned misplaced bloomers and hideous funeral-home mishaps. "Hey, Joe, switch those heads around again," ran the punch line of one. It sent her running for the ladies' room, she of the cast-iron bladder. Sometimes we could not look at each other without cackling.

My father privately hinted: Muriel was one of those virgins who, in having preserved her own "factory seal," was eager to protect her every surface inch from puncture, rain, or insult. He teased, "I think the Mouse Woman's idea of a good time is to come home from a long day's work and just haul off and spend a couple hours reorganizing her purse." Her sketchy, unassuming body seemed furled and inwardly spiraling as the habitual umbrella. In those days, every souvenir shop offered cheap shot glasses and playing cards printed with old-maid jokes: these pistol-packing single ladies were shown traveling in pairs like nuns. They were depicted as

gleeful on discovering a burly masked burglar (male) beneath
their bed. This thug always sported a blackjack, a dark turtleneck, a
flat cloth cap, a massive jaw that needed shaving. The caption ran:
"Looks like we caught us a big 'un, Effie, but I seen him first!"

My actual Aunt Muriel's own aesthetic was developed, if not, perhaps, as developed as I hinted earlier. Her mama was now dead,
and then Papa, and she and her two unmarried sisters—the French
teacher, the retired chocolatier—shared a small bungalow at 1200
Home Avenue in Oak Park. Only the vivacious Ethel, my mother's
mother, had hurt Papa's feelings by marrying American and moving out. The remaining Frasers were set in their ways, devoted to
their childish rituals like the Sunday cookie-baking. They left the
long-dead Sonny's and Sadie's wicker baskets flanking the hearth,
a tribute to Papa. The Fraser girls still lived with one drawing of
Sunnyside in every downstairs room. Any child's headcold or
twisted ankle brought from them the grim solicitude of people
who've grown up tending some larger-than-life invalid in a smaller-
than-adequate apartment. They'd never quite got used to brash,
material America. They called their former apartment "the old
flat." People were still "in hospital" or "going down to university."
As if to prove that money'd never mattered to them after fifty years
as wage slaves, it sometimes pleased these granddaughters of a
minor lord left broke by uncollectible loans to a triple-chinned
future king of England to make charming mistakes with American
currency.

My father was a war hero, a Bronze Star winner, a very sound and
pleasing-looking fellow. When he visited Muriel, I noted his tolerant, pitying grin. His upper lip curled out from his good teeth.
These days, I might call that sadness at his being near a woman
never once opened, entered, by a man. I'd call it unease that his
usual long-legged charm never quite worked on her. Back then, I
mistook Daddy's gaze for some curious attraction he must feel for
her, as I did. There was no jealousy. Oh no, I was too secure for
that. His interest in her flattered me. For—admit it—there was
something shaming about a floury old aunt, about my overvisible
love for her, a love I couldn't figure how (or why) to hide. Did I say
that she was in her eighties then?

. . .

Certain heiresses of this world can hire their own biographers, can print the books privately on vellum that outranks in quality, in rag, the parchment of our national documents. But what of the others? What of the real people? Who will praise the ones who lose fortunes and never regain them? Who will praise the ones who work to eat and eat to live—and live to . . . what?

II. ONE TRAINING SESSION: VERNISSAGE

Now we'd finally arrived in glamorous Chicago—a town that seemed my own lost homeplace—Aunt whisked me off for secret daylong expeditions. She never offered an address where we might be found. Why does it still embarrass me a bit to tell you some of this? Is it our grotesquerie—Aunt's and mine—as the Loving Couple, hand in hand? Does our culture so fixate on that handsome young heterosexual pair you see, arm in arm in ads, the teeth, so normative a wedding-cake ornament—that the rest of us feel we must abstain from public affection? Or do her poverty and homeliness still trouble me? I felt such blind faith in her worldliness, her eagerness to show me all that she found beautiful and therefore useful.

Toward my brother, Bradley, Muriel condescended. She adjudged him to be merely "all boy." So her sisters rushed in to make him their favorite and to loudly say what an adventure they'd all have at the Brookfield Zoo, now wouldn't they? But their "adopting" him was too generalized, too late, and everybody knew it. I felt sorry for Bradley, though not enough to actually include him. That, after all, was beyond my control.

Muriel's preparations seemed so elaborate—the umbrella, maps of the city and all major museums—her purse a-bulge with thermoses, three spare hankies for us each—these must have reassured my folks. "Your purse, Muriel," Dad once joked, "could've saved the Donner party." "I'm sure nobody ever expected ME to save anyone's party. I don't in the least catch your reference." Leaving the house, I had to endure my baby brother's tearful glare, my parent's confused (and oddly auntish) hurt feelings. "Well, you all have a lovely whatever," Mother would say. Muriel squatted before me, strict in straightening my blond tweed cap that matched the coat. Auntie muttered, "Do we ever not, His Owl?"

Off we set, hands linked, a very old and somewhat dusty hurrying lady in widowy hues, she all groomed and talcumed and gloved and hatted, and smelling of good envelope glue, pulling along this scrubbed kid, our eyeglasses one form of bond, and both of us too short for other folks, though not for each other, and often talking at the same time. People sometimes smiled. I took this as a good sign; I had no choice. Besides, she'd told me that Chicago knew I was now here. I nodded to strangers just as I'd greet familiar natives of downtown Falls, North Carolina. And many Yankees nodded back but appeared troubled, as if their not knowing me filled them with guilt, a doubt. As if they should.

Today Aunt wore her navy-blue, its hem long, white crocheting curled, a salad, at her cuffs and collar. On one shoulder, cloth violets she saw as part of her uniform. She sometimes referred to them, only half apologetically, as "perhaps somewhat gay, no?" ("Gay" used, of course, in the original sense of that word.) Muriel viewed the flowers as some badge of her bohemian credentials, so easy, at first glance, to miss in such a person. Her dark tailored suit was downright postal in its many pockets that buttoned; these contained coins, breath sweeteners, a pen-flashlight, one silver mechanical pencil, lilac sachets the size of tumors. She always carried a British halfpenny brought over when she was a girl, its denomination too small to merit exchange into dollars when the Frasers had most needed those. "For luck," she sometimes showed it to me, smiling.

Certain of our yearly rites attracted other of the town's frayed-cuff gentility. "Ignore them," came Aunt's cold advice. They also loved the free Christmas organ concerts played on Marshall Field's mammoth instrument. At our good table in the tearoom, music made the store seem even more a shrine: with English breakfast tea and scones as our silent Eucharist, clothes dummies posing as holy statuary. We pretended not to see the often Irish family groupings, also splurging, faking naturalness here. Adjacent old ladies made much over little hair-bowed girls or, worse, other small boys. One such red-haired kid put his tongue out at me, then pointed to his crotch. I whipped my head aside with a nose-in-air grandeur that seemed, to me, suitable for the great-grandson of one Lord Kilkairn.

Sometimes, for no reason, Muriel would rise and come around the table to wipe my nose with unnecessary roughness. Using one of numerous hankies ironed for that, she'd audibly spit onto the thing, then rub my nose or forehead till it squeaked. Aunt seemed pleased when others saw our ritual contact; I sometimes felt that she was literally polishing me, some heirloom object she toted around just to "finish" in public view. Odd, her cloudy old-lady spit did not quite horrify me. Once in Field's I made a gaffe: I asked to see the historic counter where my great-granddad had sold fancy linen goods. His daughter gave one snarling little wince. She replied, her full spiteful brogue fanning forth, "That is a moment of our lives we willna be needin' to recall today or iver, thank ye, sar."

Aunt admired my skill at painting but didn't share the knack. No, Muriel explained, she was less the Art Institute, more "the archeological, practical, and applied arts." She dragged me, almost galloping ("Too few days," she said. I blamed my father's short vacation, not Time itself). Nothing seemed beneath her ruthless scientist's attention. If, during one of our long walks down Clark Street, we passed some young smudgy beggar urinating against an alley wall, a dirty boy wearing bright street-assembled clothes, Muriel would stop. She'd nod and say, "See, dear? People make do. —Sad, no?" And she watched me—a child from the semi-posh Southern suburbs—try to understand that people peed where people could, that people wore what people found. I remarked on the man's brilliant tatters, "He's like a kite's tail, but all over."

"Yes, you've just made me visss-ualize. Excellent." Aunt led me away before the fellow caught us staring. " 'Kite Man.' Yes, I'm seeing a distinct improvement over last year." But she spoke through clenched molars. Aunt squeezed my hand with so much glee it made my decoder ring pinch. The better I talked, the deeper she breathed, the higher her color rose beneath its muting powder. My every metaphor, however crude, filled her with an enraged, encoded pleasure. The anger scared me but was, in fact, familiar as her eyeglasses to mine. She seemed to be grooming her Owl, first for articulation, then for revenge. But revenge on whom? And was articulation automatically revenge? All armored in her wishes and my kite tails, whom would I fight? Few schoolchildren are ever told what they're being educated *for*. But I knew I had a will and aptitude for getting even. —I was, after all, a child who understood how it felt to be slapped full across the face by a sodden, jealous, moody father, half articulate and aptly sick of clever backtalk. I knew what it meant to be considered odd by neighbor kids; in a town like Falls, "original" is the synonym for "weird." Aunt Muriel's low-grade weekday rage drew forth mine. Rage at unfairness, at sloppiness and cruelty. Hers incited and schooled a little starter-culture rage all my own. I would guard her. By describing her. If need be, doctoring this or that. "Yes, 'Kite Tail Man.' Ever sharper, Owl. There's no saying where-all you'll . . . Limitless I should think. Yes," she gloated.

I knew that whizzing beggars would never do as "Show and Tell." I knew my parents would drive blocks out of their way to screen Brother and me from any unfortunate, much less a young one and in splashing distance. But Aunt, walking fast, urging me forward, felt enlivened by the joy my sixty-eight pounds gave her ninety-four. Muriel's right hand—the one ungloved, kept bare for me—was dry and hard around my own. Mine sweated as with stage fright. Hers felt very callused. Fearing my disloyalty, I could shut my eyes and pretend I walked beside a pet, an animal, but something like a chimpanzee, trained up as nearly human. (I later asked my brother why he thought an executive secretary would have such a toughened grip. "Probably from all the time the old girl spent whacking her fat bald boss off," he told me with gloomy pleasure. I think I left the room. It's not clear he noticed.)

Always insist on seeing some of Chicago from the elevated tram. I soon learned to call it, with great insouciance, "The El." Sometimes we rode for half the day, an unspecified part of my education.

Given what a Chicago streetcar had done to Muriel's poor mama, I felt how brave we were to risk it, forty feet above the pavement. I'd seen King Kong lift such a streetcar, like finger food plucked off a tray, its screaming passengers dangling. This ride seemed designed by Lionel to delight any eight-year-old. It skimmed near the tarry roofline of the silver city. It took us eerily hideously close to strangers' kitchens.

For me, no ride in Disneyland (then under mythic construction) could rival privileged glimpses into Yankee strangers' squalid apartments. Plaster walls were painted bright as my tubed paints, so unlike the dull beige bandaging every WASP interior at home. "Today," she said close by my ear, "we're bound to the museum and I intend revealing their centerpiece, no less a treat than something called the Human Heart. All right with ye? Well, I should think so. But till then, mine Owl most Honorsome, please tell me just what it is you're presently a-seeing." Aunt's command. And, oh, to do that!

Kneeling on the rattan seat, I pressed my forehead to the window, sticky and corrupt but clear; and there came forth a narrative. It was apparently almost always good. At least it made her laugh as, planning our grand day's learning, she unfolded her museum map, used so often, I saw, the creases were worn suedey. My telling pleased a few adjacent strangers. Odd, even the toughest black people—wearing ushers' red uniforms or carrying dry mops in empty buckets—seemed amused at the sight of us together; they would watch us with a fond kind of idle sarcasm. I now think my Southern accent made people chuckle. At the time, I assumed it was my insights or the joy I took in chronicling this fine slum. It all looked like slum to me. Every building appeared six hundred years old, crusted with soot, carved garlands, pigeon tributes. Aunt, map opening ever wider, was just a head that nodded, nodded, some metronome I sang to. —Plus, today I'd get a free ticket to the Human Heart, whatever THAT was.

Hailing as I did from mere suburbia—margins of lawn privacy framing each family—I felt ashamed at how much you could see of city people's lives. Throw pillows, crucifixes. It was Muriel who sensed I was embarrassed—not of staring, but of being caught. "If you can see in and spy something of interest, then I say go ahead and Look at it. And if you can look hard enough long enough, you can maybe learn what you see by saying what it is. If you try all of that, believe me, you've gone a long way toward helping to justify such . . ."

"'Peeping'?" I laughed. "As you like. 'Peeping,' then, my sweet Peeper Tom." She pretended to squeeze my nose off, then showed me her own thumb's pink tip. She tilted forward, listening to all I described as passing, trust me, just behind her back. Aunt claimed she "didn't care a fig" what other passengers thought. She'd said she'd told them I was coming.

As I knelt here, describing, enlarging, my shoulder touched hers and I was enveloped in her cleanly scrubbed and punitive Scottish smell. Being (among other things) a boy of eight, I admired the great bronze spears holding the chains supporting an old theater marquee where pigeons the color of carbon paper socialized. A woman in a slip, canting forward at a sink, washing her hair, blinded by suds, patting for a towel and missing, missing it. On somebody's stove, a red pot boiled three white eggs (it appeared significant because framed by the first and greatest of all picture frames, a window in the house of living people).

Everything seems wondrous omen when looking is encouraged.

Muriel laughed while I explained how a really fat man was bent double on a couch, was cutting his big toenail with the concentration of a brain surgeon. Muriel gave off her spoilt, cruel laugh that hinted at some unknown former beauty. "A big *fat* one," I said, feasting on the word, "so *fat,* and all his pinkies stickin' out! He's home at noon because I bet he is . . . a baker who's retired." She checked over at me, her mouth tightening with . . . pride? She turned back to her map with new vigor; and I glimpsed a bed—it was passing us backwards, seemingly going faster than our streetcar—and two nude pinkish-yellowy adults of no particular sex, pushing at and into one another. One of them wore a single black saddle oxford. That is all I know. I said nothing. Instead, I turned and sat there, stunned, posture-perfect, my legs too short to reach the floor, staring straight ahead, commentary stalled. I still thought Dogs were the Boys' Ones and Cats the Girls'. For all my show-off guesswork, despite my art and mild precocity, I did not yet know where babies came from. Now I leaned into her tea-at-office scent, I watched her long white forefinger tracing encrypted red floor-lines: "Birds of Paradise, stuffed, various: See 4-C." What, oh what, would Aunt have told me of those two human thrubbing lumps, framed in so speeding a bed deciphering into each other's middles? Everything, probably. And simply, probably. Oscar Wilde wrote, "One is no less good judge of a thing for not having done it oneself."

But I didn't dare ask.

Today's goal, the Museum of Science and Industry; how grand a title that yet is for me, perfect Deco phrase. Our parents sometimes took Brother and me to dusty state museums in Raleigh; but after forty minutes, we grew fretful; or, rather, Bradley did. By then the entry's official turnstile looked more intriguing than those plaster cavemen lummoxed around a campfire (one red Christmas-tree bulb under crushed tinfoil). If we didn't read labels and follow the arrows, our parents went crazy. They would jerk us to the parking lot as soon as we started "acting funny." Dad would "pop" the crowns of our heads and then say to shush up or he'd REALLY give us something to cry about. Mother grew more serene and pretended she noticed nothing and would never really help us against him. —But with my great-aunt and in holy, knowing Chicago—anything I pronounced either interesting or dull, that interested her.

Just now, in "Gems and Fossils," I pointed out how sad it was that the black silhouettes showing a man and a woman standing on arrows should mean nothing more than where the nearest bathrooms were. Aunt nodded. "Fine point, Owl. I expect you've just made me notice that forever." Was I playing on her own aversion? By now, how could I tell where her wishes ended and my assignments began?

"A bit later, when the crowd shrinks, I will be showing you what I've saved back till ye were of an age. . . ."

" 'The Human Heart'?"

"You get a goodly checkmark, sir. I'll give a hint, you with the High Owl Q. You can walk right into this one." As usual, I kept trying to picture.

Muriel always seemed calmer in the deserted parts of a museum. Here red fire extinguishers hung undisguised and seemed part of the Pre-Cambrian detail. Fire hatchets were framed behind "Break Glass Only for Emergency." Sunlight swarmed with specimens of dust motes spelt out in tweedy, milky blocks. In such still vaulted afternoon chambers, the day itself seemed trapped, and then capaciously exhibited. Radiators clanged with a zoo's fitful pounding. In the late and silent sunlight, one glass case, one clear side of it, would bring into focus all the sun's off-color energy. At the far end, beyond the Hall of Birds, a single pane of brightness burned, and soon that winning pane, with its Latin label on the lifted tail of some stuffed extinct rodent, was so attended by stray spectator brilliance, it seemed about to burst, most wonderful, to flame.

The only other people you ever saw here were either lost or scary, hidden by choice. You heard their rubber soles long before they appeared, and there was often something wrong with them. (How must Aunt and I have looked to them?) They'd come past carrying too much luggage or hiding birthmarked faces or walking with brave rectitude on some squeaky built-up shoe. They were other avoiders, seeking contact with a world made just a little safer by the art of taxidermy, by glass, by frame, by art.

I would stare at Aunt through the foyer-sized showcase. Between us, "Birds of Paradise" posed. They were South Sea creatures, stuffed now, their tails unlikely, iridescent, as exaggerated as bad afterthought fibs. Aunt told me that their brown glass eyes were fake, but those seemed the realest of anything. Their topknots were impractical as tiaras, but actual as my own stubborn cowlick.

"One sees such wonders." Muriel pointed to a bird particularly cursive. "But one doesn't always know what to *do* with them, quite. I myself have never mastered all of this. Still, I can imagine how it's done. You will, though. The details are everything and more. *You* will know, won't you, His Honor His Owl?" My shoulders rose as my head came down quick. I both shrugged and nodded. Yes, Muriel.

· · ·

We had a quiet game, and harmless. We—the energetic crone consulting three outdated guidebooks, and a little boy with a bowl haircut his father administered like a standard "pop" every six weeks—described each other to each other via artifacts, stuffed things. We even did it before display cases containing minerals that, when you pushed the button, lit up with nuclear smirky colors. We each said which rock looked most like the loved one. "There you are." I pointed, and she smiled as if caught at the end of hide-and-seek. Nodding, she accepted my every valuation as the truest, latest portrait of herself. Alone together in this untrafficked part of the world's museum, our thoughts seemed permanently set on "Rhyme." I never felt smarter than when I was admiring my great-aunt's great underrated intelligence. Her dad had been a full professor, but she never even got to go to one half-day of college! She knew that my mother would make sure I attended good schools. And Aunt was only glad for me. Compared with her utter lack of jealousy, I felt narrow and petty. But I would try—would try to be more like her.

At the Fowls of Paradise, she said I most resembled that bird, the lyre bird. But I heard "liar." So I was the little liar bird, hunh? True enough. But I hated being called that. After all, my lies exaggerated Muriel into someone very beautiful, and rich, and all but winged. I knew what the truth was; I knew you only break that for Emergencies.

Our innocence attracted erotic aggression. I remember three separate times, after I struggled to open the door of "MEN'S" (male in silhouette), as Aunt stood guard, ineffectually, outside. I remember the tile floors and the urinals almost too tall to achieve. And, I recall, there was some man, mostly a younger one, who posed at the farthest urinal, looking over at me, right at me, smiling, openmouthed, clearing his throat. I felt accused. And, ever eager to learn the forks, I gave this young man a quick look, as if to apologize for some botched unknown Yankee urinal-etiquette. Today's young blond guy said, "You seem like a pretty inner-rested little boy. Lookee here, what'll we do 'bout all this?" And it seemed that "inner-rested" hinted at some calm I falsely showed. Here was a new exhibit; stuffed-looking, it filled me with revulsion, fellow-feeling, grief, yet admiration, and a numbness that made me limp a bit as I scuttled back out to Aunt, still there. Her holding her umbrella with such martial zeal had not prevented my seeing maybe more than I really should.

I sometimes caught her, waiting there, slumped against a wall. I came to understand that, at eighty-some, Aunt's rushing pace was not natural to her. It was Muriel's imitation of me, of what she felt a boy my age would like. Her fear of holding me back forced her to bustle and lose breath. And it was exactly this rush-rush state of Auntie's that my parents and my brother liked to imitate. But it was really *me* they "did"—*her* me.

His Owl was now to enter this museum's walk-in model of a promised major organ. "You might well be as awed as I first was by the sheer scale of the Human Heart," she coaxed or threatened. I was wearing the little chesterfield coat she'd praised two years ago, even though the sleeves were suddenly short, and I kept pulling them down. I was eight, after all, a small-town kid. And this igloo heart thing's loud thumping, the shifting of its sleek red roofing ventricles, scared me. There was a line of people waiting to get in; they held their coats and scanned brochures; and they looked so sad. Among them, the throat-clearing young man from upstairs. He seemed nervous to see me out and about. "Do we know what we're getting into?" I asked, and Aunt smiled, believing I'd been joking; I had not.

Here was a livid practical organ larger than a revolving door. You were expected to mount a gangway servant's entrance into/ through/out of its pumping hollows. I acted chicken till Muriel, clutching her umbrella in one hand and my wrist in the other, dragged me through the thing three times. "There," she said, "you get the idea." (I'd like to believe that even as a kid I understood: no act is ever riskier than entering another human heart. Auntie gave me my first guided tour.)

I agreed to stay within its gory walls, to study backlit educational pictures there; Aunt settled herself on the bench circling the rotunda. There, tired parents waited till kids had learned some-thing. When I peeked out, Aunt Muriel waved, but pointed I should go back in and study further. She did this while surveying other adults, maybe hoping to be taken for my mother, or at least

Grandma—not just the chaperone. She wore a black cloche hat so out of fashion it forced people to do double takes, then judge, then look, quick, away. I decided that, by now, her style was almost chic, almost—or so I told myself to make our outings seem less observed and feel more fun. I saw how she held her umbrella upright, metal tip set firm on the white tile floor. But Aunt kept its wooden swan-crook aimed outward and, I noticed, pivoting back and forth, as if letting it, some camera or pet, have a good look around. Was she talking to herself? Who had done this to her? What had? Living too hard, or maybe having wished too hard? Or work? Stan? Stan's running off? Or just plain Time? Had I?

Aunt appeared finch-sized tucked out there waiting, nervous, a bit odd. Now, from the Human Heart, I watched her with a concern half amused, half protective. My great feeling for Aunt Muriel confused me. If boys of eight admit to feeling love at all, they tend to see its weakening brunt as their own fault, a lapse to stifle. I feared it was both bad luck and sissified to show too often my unlikely attraction, a mystery especially to myself. But how to encode and obscure our love's immense comfort in a world of slapped faces, trolley beds, and young men making museum displays of their lower bodies' private science and industry? She once told me that, as eldest, she would've inherited Sunnyside. She said as the oldest boy, I would've got it all direct from her—its orchard, library, and art. If only her papa hadn't read the impractical cowboy art of one Mr. May. If only . . . I were hers. . . . If only . . . Years later, I understood: nobody ever wondered, aloud or not, if poor Muriel failed to marry because she was a lesbian. That, I saw, would have implied much more curiosity than our family ever showed her. Did I make this woman up to serve some need of mine—support, respect, an audience, and, incidental, love? How much of my own family life was I overvividly inventing? And how much of it, assigned, not wished—daily, badly, and morbidly—made me up?

After our pilgrimage to the habitable heart, aortas for its chimneys, Auntie beckoned me into the Museum Store. She would now buy me some little souvenir. But I mustn't show my sometimes jealous baby brother, all right? Here was a glass case I called "a glass case," and she called "vitrine." On it, adult veined human hearts, scale models in high-grade impact-resistant ruby-colored plastic. They half-reminded me of that rude young man upstairs. You could disassemble them; you could learn from that. With the greedy memory of a vacationing child denied, I recall how these models cost $4.98 plus tax. Seeing the price, Muriel turned away from me. Umbrella clamped between her knees, she leaned nearly headfirst into her opened handbag, she pried open a black brass-jawed nylon coin-purse. Aunt swiveled from her cash to the counter's gleaming heart, and back to fiscal reality, back, then back.

Beyond the expensive model, I noticed a big postcard depicting other children—strangers to me, Yankees—entering and leaving the heart's exhibition. Stapled to each card, sealed inside a clear cellophane sack, was a one-inch plastic heart—not shaped like any-one's actual organ—but symmetrical, designed, mere valentine—that artful and oversimplified. Each card costs 89¢.

Now Muriel spied those too, I felt the click. I understood: my small aunt's spirit was enormous, her ambitions for me were even more vast; she saved to splurge on these luxurious outings and on my Christmas paints. But what a tight-boned corset her retiree's budget made! She turned and smiled apology my way. The "beg pardon" in her lifted eyebrows told me, if I made a scene or sighed hard—then, yes, she'd buy me a real-looking heart, not just the chintzy, tiny false one. I saw what I must do. I saw what I must plainly say. It killed me, behaving.

She knelt toward my height, giving at the knees, her umbrella a cane. And as she grinned discolored teeth my way, I knew to beam right back. Bifocaled pince-nez made her eyes subdivide: shields of magnified mineral gray-green. Though I felt betrayed, less by expe-rience than by my great-aunt herself, I said exactly what my parents would've wished. I said what I had been taught by nine hundred years of cringing, genteel, bent-backed manners.

"Ma'am? The card's just as nice. It'll probably help me remem-ber just as well, probably. —Really."

"But you're sure? Only if ye're absolutely certain."

"Yeah. Really." I knew to answer with bright forced conviction.

Is this not our bitter heritage? Trading away the Pleasures we most want, in hopes of scoring Duty Points to win some greater credit up ahead and via Suffering's rebates? Sick. And surely sad. But, ours. —I am forty-five years old. I live alone and basically like it. But I am personally so tired of

*enforced self-denial. Of being considered just a fragment-fraction of some
family not founded yet. I'm tired of restaurant hostesses reaching for menus
while looking over my shoulder to say, "Just you? Only the one?" I recall
Muriel's stubborn traction, her willingness to constitute a crowd of one.*

    But there it is. Call it pain. Or call it our tradition.

Then "poor Muriel"—for so my parents named her—thanked
me as she rose to face the clerk. Onto the glass case she emptied
her change purse's secret compartment. While the checkout girl
made a mouth at the four customers waiting behind us, Aunt said
she'd just be getting rid of these few pennies here, all right? And
Muriel's elegant, tapered, pianistic fingertips counted groups of
five aloud, counted aloud the 89¢, plus tax.

The museum's logo being on the brown paper bag, that made
my loss a little easier to bear. Hand in hand, we silently endured the
long elevated-streetcar ride home. She'd bought the item meant
for people smart enough to want some keepsake, but too poor to
expect the finest.

I wanted the expensive heart.

III.   REWARD

Aunt spent her last year in a rest home south of Evanston. Her
two surviving sisters had died within ten days of one another.
Family loyalty had become, of necessity, our tribe's low-cost form of
recognized nobility. Muriel, the oldest of them, was miffed at being
left behind and said so. But to whom? Only at the end did she
reveal some of the outlaw mischief I alone had felt bulking there
beneath her breath mints and "gay" violets.

A letter arrived in North Carolina for the executor of Aunt's trivial estate, my mother. It was from the home's director: "Muriel is
fast becoming one of our all-time worst incorrigibles." "Well, high
time, and good for her!" Dad laughed. Mother said, "Great, go on
and chortle, you ox. But this is the third place, and if they chuck
her out, she's on the street, Richard. Or, worse, down here with us."
That sure shut Dad up.

—See, Aunt kept running away. Armed only with her change purse and umbrella, she would leave a note on her good blue paper: "Food Dreadful. Consider This My Two Weeks Notice. It's Inadequate. Do Not Follow Me." Then she simply wandered out into traffic. Aunt either thumbed or stood there till the car of someone tenderhearted or citizenlike stopped. Muriel told strangers that the Presbyterian Home badly abused her; she said that Presbyterians were "secretly mostly prostitutes, Papist villains, and frequent doo-doo heads." "They hurt my wrists," she told me when I saw her last. Auntie sat there in bed, long fingers of her right hand braceleting the wrist of her left, rubbing, testing, till I almost believed her.

My parents, merciful, had given me plane fare. It was my first air trip alone. They themselves felt little urge to rush up here to see her. At our local arts center, I had just sold eight paintings from my first one-boy show. I was half sick with an adolescent's joy at recognition: I told myself I'd "done it all for her." It pleases many men to claim this of their wishes. Two newspaper notices were folded in my pocket. But Aunt hardly listened, she seemed restless, irked.

When I arrived, she'd confused me by asking if I had attended "the College of Cardinals." . . . This made an image of red birds wearing mortarboards. "I'm in junior high, Aunt. 'The College of Cardinals'? That doesn't make any sense," I told her, plain, with the strength of love. I saw her suspect she'd revealed too much; she lowered her head, slightly ashamed at being caught.

To soothe her, I described the opening, catered by Mom mostly. Aunt hinted, wasn't the show a bit too local to matter much? "It's not as if it were being held someplace real, inside the Loop," she spoke while staring at the air vent over her bed. Inside my blazer pocket, I clutched thirty photos of the opening I now feared I'd never get to show her. Strange, I hadn't thought to bring her a real painting—instead, just snapshots of the things hung on the gallery walls and quietly for sale. Her room could've used some help. It was in a turret, had no windows, and was partly round, not much bigger than a hotel's entry breezeway.

After her last escape, the rest home took to tying her in a rocking chair. My parents had signed the release—"For her own protection, really." The one nurse strong enough to manage Auntie was a heavy young black woman. Muriel now complained about her. Oddly enough, she was named Muriel too. Aunt told me how, once both her arms had been lashed to the chair, once a shawl had been tucked around her so that others' visitors would not be disturbed by the sight of "restraints," Aunt's chunky jailer had bent over to pick up bedclothes mussed during the latest thrashing struggle. "Then, you see, by accident, she showed her whole backside to me, His Owl, and it just proved too much for resisting. My hands were bound but, you understand, she'd foolishly left my feet quite free. One good swift kick sent her flying face-first flat onto the floor. She made quite the undignified grunt, going down. Sounded a perfect pig, she did. Must weigh three hundred easily. 'Uugahh!' like that. Rome will give me hell for doing it, but, oh . . . extremely satisfying, I must say. Then she was very slow to turn around but she looked back up at me, still tied. She said, 'Does you really hate me so damn much, ole lady?' And I said then, 'It's nothing personal. But I'm afraid I must admit that, dear me, yes. Yes, "Muriel." I fairly despise you.'"

I brought the topic back, of course, to me, my painting. Aunt acted peeved as some person tied up all day. I might have seen that I was asking for it.

"You know?" she started. "I expected you to get better at your pictures considerably faster, I fear. There's something terribly flat about your figures. It appears they aren't so much painted as carved. They seem to have no choice. No 'inner fire.'" Muriel's brogue now sounded dense as some new immigrant's; her sentences flecked flying spittle. "Really?" I studied my long white hands. "Not enough 'inner fire,' hunh?"

"Well—I believe back then I claimed that you were quite the little masterpiece, am I no' right? I'm saying that any lack of progress is not due to any lack of encouragement on *my* part, now, is it, now, Owl?" "No, ma'am," I agreed, but explained that I'd only just turned fourteen in June and, to be fair, the week before I'd made— what?—$457.30 from my painting. "Now he's onto the money of it, is he? Because we lost everything, this generation thinks it's going to show up in the cash drawer or none of it is real, am I right? Don't you dare bring money into this. You have no idea. Fourteen might sound young to some, but you're presently a-speaking to the person who's been expecting something from you, and I mean daily. Now in he waltzes with cash receipts. We needed art, you little ribbon clerk!"

I knew this was meant as punishment. But even at that age, even considering the fortune my earnings seemed—I saw that no amount would ever make it up to her; I mean, the debits. I noticed with horror that her nightdress was misbuttoned, that she wore no underclothes. And just by sitting here, I'd have to see her flat tire of one breast and some portion of a nipple gray-brown and cracked-looking. She didn't know. She was pert and frazzled and she kept smiling. "Good you've come," she said now. I wanted to rescue her from this narrow room. I wanted to rescue her from History—so bad at assigning, so good at misplacing. Such a slob, really, History. Muriel's grandfather was asked to give crippling amounts (irretrievable loans) to the porky future King of England. Finders keepers, losers weepers. . . . Was there not some way to help her, even now? Some intuitive science, some practical bill-collector's art? The more cross she acted toward me, the more I felt I knew her, and the more unworthy I felt. I sat here, winded and confused, so glad they'd let me come alone. Nobody need ever know she'd scolded me like that for being too slow, for my mentioning the money. Nobody would know. She least of all. But, I didn't count on my own habitual remembering, a gift so enhanced in me by Muriel Evangeline Kilkairn Fraser.

"Was I wrong?" she asked, half aware she might've bruised my feelings. "No, ma'am," I said. "I don't know how to do portraits yet. They're harder than people realize. Portraits matter more than people think, I think."

She nodded, but toward the air vent.

Aunt's white hair, tugged free of its bun, appeared a witch's, thin on top, wild wings out the sides. Her eyes seemed strained and blockish in their pouches. "But, what'd they do with your glasses?" I finally asked. She pointed to a drawer. I found them, lenses filthy. Glad to be useful, I cleaned these, my own spit on the back strand of my first silk necktie (bought with profits from the show). "Can you see now?" I set them on her long nose.

"See WHAT?"

I was glad my parents hadn't found her like this. I believed they might hold it against me. Sitting here, I felt the first round of some strange guilt. The place smelled unclean. Staffers kept staring through Aunt's open door, all wearing glum expressions, as if expecting to find her on her hands and knees, or maybe strangling me. I touched her bedclothes and gave off my best guardian looks to the wheelchaired corridor. Even here and unattended, Aunt's clerical good-envelope-glue smell held on, as if baked into her by routine, a last gift. On the wall beside her pillow hung one framed girlish drawing of Sunnyside . . . a gate, a stone wall, the hollyhocks. On her bedside table, a brown celluloid radio, one side melted by tubes' heat; today it was set to a gospel station, spitting quiet static. Atop a bureau missing its oval mirror, a single favorite doll of hers still safe under one clear glass dome. Beside it, a Bible concordance published in Glasgow in 1840, but no Bible here. One dog-eared copy of *Forever Amber,* a best-selling bodice-ripper historical romance from the forties, the nineteen forties. And, in its dainty silver frame, that brass plaque from International Harvester (now in Chapter Eleven) praising Muriel for saving the company so much bailing twine, "and for general excellence." —All the sixteenth-century homeplace's lore and trappings come down to this. The only thing still beautiful, her familiar battered black umbrella tilted against the curving wall, the umbrella alone somehow witty and intact.

I sat wondering, could I ever help make things up to this old woman by—at least—making things up?

Whenever authorities caught the impenitent runaway, Aunt never seemed headed for Oak Park. The bungalow at 1200 Home Avenue was long since sold. Authorities always found her aiming for the lake. Maybe some memory of ocean? safety? true escape?

Now she interrupted my renewed saga of several good Carolina families who'd wisely added my oil paintings to their collections. "They hurt, they hurt me. They listen, too." She nodded toward the air-duct's grillwork, shreds of dust shuddering there. It did look sinister. I took her small rough hand. Turning it over, I found the bruises. Old ones fading greenish under newer navy-blue.

"You see now? My, but your face certainly just changed, it did. Well, good. Son, nobody ever listens to me anymore. The Presbyterians, I find after a lifetime's loyalty and tithing, turn out to be secretly 'in with' the Pope. I see that now. Rome knows you're here. Everything we say, they keep it all in Gregg dictation. Once you're gone, they'll take it out on me. You could sleep in the chair. They won't try any further funny business with you in here. Please tell your mother, won't you? Oh, how they treat me. If you have spirit in this place, they monitor that. They'll monitor whatever little spirit the person has left in her, His Honor His Owl. Remember everything, son. How pretty you really are. There's no telling what trouble it'll get you into, being the kind of boy that looks like that. Where are the dogs? I've often thought a dog would help in here. It could go for things. Papa's did. You look like Papa in a portrait he had taken at your age. Such a voice did he have, the arias of an evening. I played well then. Even Mr. Ruskin was not uncomplimentary. They sold the piano. And the stool. For nothing. A song they got. I'd like a dog, would be nice. The director complains about it when I must go off places on my own. But I have been independent right along. —They take you down in shorthand. Then they use it on you, they send that, duplicate and triplicate, to Rome. —I can only go on like this, I think, because I HAVE gone on like this."

Then she laughed that wild spoilt-rich-girl laugh, she nodded once, placed her long forefinger vertical against her lips: "Shhh, His Honor." Aunt signed above the bed toward the humming heating vent. Next, midair, with one crabbed hand, she made a puppet gesture of human legs sneaking away, big slow comic tiptoe steps. Such a hoarse, aristocratic, likable whisper against my face: "I plan leaving again Tuesday, noon. They'll never find me this time. —Besides, Owl, tell me, what're they going to DO to me now? What's there left to DO to your wild Muriel?"

Call my earlier inventions a revenge on behalf of the smartest hen to escape a farm cart, only to accidentally enter a guillotine disguised, a door made out of mirror. History assigned. For my exaggerations of the real toward the beautiful, I will not apologize.

Say I am getting even with those cowboy novels that led a man who should've known better to travel someplace new and dangerous, exposing his children (and great-grandchildren) to robbery. For years, I felt a snobbish shame at how the books that brought my people to America were not great literature but junky Westerns. And yet, would life have been made easier if Shakespeare had engineered my great-grandmother's appointment underneath the rutting streetcar? —I did research to help my actual and would-be history seem more real to you (and incidentally to me). I discovered the following heartening passage about my half-blind German jewel-thief ancestor-in-art. This is verbatim from *The Encyclopedia of Frontier and Western Fiction*, by John Tuska and Vicki Pierkaski:

MAY, KARL (1842–1912) Phenomenally popular author of travel and adventure novels, many of which were set in the American West, was born at Hohenstein-Ernsttahl, Saxony in Germany. May's vision was impaired as a child because of malnutrition. He spent his youth in the shadow of the great famine that swept Central Europe in the mid 1840's and the economic dislocations which led to the tragic weavers' rebellion of 1844. But he was a gifted youth. The sacrifices of May's family and the largesse of the Church enabled him to finish school and enter a teachers' training college. Soon after graduation in 1861, however, he was arrested for stealing a watch and sentenced to a prison term which ended all possibility of a teaching career. May claimed throughout his life to have been innocent of this theft. After several months' imprisonment, the depressed and bitter May swore vengeance on bourgeois society and began a life of fraud, swindle, and larceny which lasted twelve years and sent him back to jail for stretches from 1865–1868 and 1870–1874. While incarcerated, he read voraciously in the prison library, devouring travel memoirs and adventure stories of distant lands, particularly those about the Arab world and the American frontier.

The chastened May began his literary career writing village tales and cheap adventure stories for an unscrupulous publisher of family magazines and trashy short novels. Although he had never traveled outside Germany, he produced his first two books on the American "wild" West, "Jenseits der Felsengebirge" (Beyond the Rocky Mountains) and "In Fernen Western" (In the Far West).

Over the next thirty years, drawing mainly from atlases, ethnological studies, and travelers' journals, May published a spate of similar books, the best and most popular of which was the trilogy "Winnetou" (1893–1910). Set in the plains and mountains of the West and Southwest at about the time of the Civil War, it chronicles the deeds of a knightly band of heroic "men of the West" surrounding a young German adventurer, "Old Shatterhand" and his blood brother, Winnetou, the noble chief of the Mescalero Apaches. In this band were "Old Fire-hand," "Old Surehand," "Sharpeye," "Old Wabble," and Sam Hawkens. Themselves men of untarnished integrity and valor, they are nevertheless constantly being vilified, double-crossed and ambushed by an assortment of white scoundrels and mis-led Indians. And yet, there are no truly bad Indians in "Win-netou," only angry and naive victims of the whites' cruelty and greed. May compared Winnetou to a "deer that . . . (now) sees and hears with its soul" and contrasted the Indian with white men who are as "docile domestic animals." Upon his death, Winnetou acknowledges Christ and requests that an "Ave Maria" be sung for him. Despite the gross lack of realism and moralizing sentimentality, these stories still abound in hair-raising surprises, outrageous comedy, unforgettable characters.

May's years of anonymous toil as a hack writer were fol-lowed by two decades of success which made him a bestselling writer in Germany, particularly among the youth. Responding in part to demands from his growing public, May gradually began to pretend that he was, in fact, characters from his books. He had photographs taken of himself in Western garb and Oriental costume which he signed and sent to his fans. But wealth and fame had the disadvantage of making his life a matter of public curiosity and malice. This led, in 1904, to the scandalous revelation of his early years of crime and imprison-ment and to the even more damaging discovery that he had never been to the United States at all (much less experienced the adventures narrated in his Westerns).

The pose had been a relatively harmless fraud. But in light of his criminal record it appeared yet another episode of a long history of swindle and moral hypocrisy. Humiliated by these disclosures and his own attempts at denial, May made a three-month tour of America in 1908 but traveled no further West than Buffalo, New York. In his last years, he wrote two justifications of his life which some critics consider his finest literary works. Abused in the press and defeated in the court in his suits for defamation of character, May died a broken man.

Until recently Karl May has been considered beneath contempt by most literary critics and historians. At best he was recognized as a master of juvenile adventure stories and a popular writer of escapist fiction for the common man. His novels were, for the most part, hastily written, uneven, and inconsistent; his stories, tangles of unlikely coincidence and improbable action. . . . Indeed the renewed interest in May's work is principally an outgrowth of contemporary interest in their symbolic element, their joyous outwardness, their religiose nearly dream-like quality.

May was praised by men as diverse as Albert Einstein, Hermann Hesse, Albert Schweitzer, and Adolf Hitler. During World War II, Hitler sent 300,000 Winnetou novels to German soldiers as recommended tactical reading. Asked about early mentors, Einstein once commented: "My whole adolescence stood under his sign. Indeed, even today (May) has been dear to me in many a desperate hour." Hermann Hesse wrote, "His is a whole new kind of work. I shall call it The Fiction of Wish Fulfillment."

After May's death in disgrace, German readers and loyalists took up a large subscription and created a Museum in his honor. That Museum does not, however, directly concern this fantasist's unhappy biography. The Karl May Institute remains open today. It contains one of Germany's foremost collections of genuine Plains Indian weaponry, art, and religious artifacts. Many have seen this as the highest praise, perhaps even a belated exoneration, of an imaginative man pilloried for his popular falsehoods.

Insofar as I know, of course, my Great-aunt Muriel, though a very real person, a churchgoer (Second Presbyterian), and an excellent cook by all reports, showed no interest in Singer Sargent and was never painted by him. Despite being born in Scotland, she spent so

much of her salary on Mama's drug bills, on her museum memberships and the National Geographic Society contributions, on her
niece and then her great-nephews, Muriel never managed to feel
quite rich enough for a return to the homeplace. Ethel discouraged her, having found Sunnyside's former orchard a development
of cottagers' stuccoed houses. The stone homeplace was now a
roadhouse; yellow placards advertising Kodak film were bolted to
its front. I made up that other.

I've made so much of it up, you see. And then, having invented
it, I transform the fiction into a curious pedigree. The story itself,
the will to believe the best of my own—that becomes a credo. It's
an article of faith I find that I can live by.

John Ruskin actually told my actual great-grandpapa, who, in
turn, told his mute and practical daughters, "To see clearly is
poetry, prophecy, and religion—all in one. The greatest thing a
human soul ever does in this world is to SEE something, and tell
what it SAW in a plain way."

If only somebody could paint Muriel, fancy and plain, both ways.
In light, and in shade. As wished, and then as History merely
assigned. But you don't get both, do you? Not in one frame.

—And, maybe for people like me, for clans like mine, the tender,
the face-saving lie *is* our art form—our distinguished thing, at last.

"I have taken the liberty of enlarging your hat brim. But only for
compositional purposes. No criticism of the hat itself implied, you
understand, Miss."

> *My people's pose has been a relatively harmless fraud.*
> *In their economizing, find my actual inheritance.*
> *In kindness to each other, find one pure form of love.*
> *And in our lovely necessary lies—find the truest story of my life.*

Preservation News, being a publication dedicated to saving historic structures of North Carolina, funded by the National Endowment for the Humanities and generous donors just like you.

For Elizabeth Matheson, and for Myrick Howard

AVAILABLE FOR RESTORATION: ELKTON GREEN
Located: downtown Falls, NC,
Person County, 2.4 acres

Elkton Green is the pre-eminent bracketed Victorian gingerbread mansion in north-eastern North Carolina. It will be leveled by wreckers if some fairy-god-purchaser is not found by April 1. Help us, please?

Preferably somebody with plenty of good sense, mad about history, alive to the finer nuances of strong-armed social pretense, and with a discretionary income to sort of match. Pretty please? Little family foundations are always nice. We just know you're out there.

Fact is, we have got two extensions from the very cooperative Falls Town Zoning Board. But even with a treasure like Elkton Green, this, my friends, is our literal last chance. Already bids have come in for the pearwood-and-mahogany parqueted spiral staircase, for all the stained glass; but these are bids from a chain restaurant that will perform a mastectomy, that will then wedge bits of the mansion's exquisite features into separate franchises where people order their quite bad beef awfully overcooked. Large portions of too-buttered "garlic bread" are intended to distract them. It makes us swoon, the thought. Perish it.

Built in 1856 for the Penner-Coker family, this high Victorian "pile" seems to have been inspired by the minarets of the Prince's "Folly" Pavilion at Brighton. Elkton Green retains its Tudor rose medallions and endearingly redundant cornices. Even its brackets are bracketed. A gracious, indeed show-off, home in the downtown Historic Summit District, we are talking 24 rooms; we're talking porches enough to accommodate every banished smoker left alive in Falls, NC. Lavish plantings survive, including a mature box maze (needs work, as mazes, alas, tend to).

The lawn, rolling clear down to the River Tar, is a fine acre and a half. We speak now of a lawn so suitable for croquet, I'll throw in my own best 1920s Wilson set, and just leave it up for you to look at, and get vague credit for.

Elkton Green's West Wing features a faux-Romanesque capital set directly beside one that might be called "Adirondack Carnival Ecclesiastical Ecstatic." Our "righthand person," the inimitable Mary Ellen Broadfield, said, "This home is like some lady from a very good family who's had entirely too much coffee and feels forced to try on every hat in a third-rate shop, all at once." There are sane people who consider the house overornamented. But for us, the mansion's gingerbread detailing represents Elegance pushed—testing—clear to the edge of Comedy. (Which is just where some of us most long to live!)

Elkton Green's 14-foot ceilings boast heavy, indeed luscious moldings; there are faux-marbled baseboards and grained doors and a dining-room mural (oil on leather, 10 × 21 feet). Its subject seems to have been suggested by Judge J. V. Coker's extensive collection of American Indian artifacts. Coker's brilliant early acquisitions—however dubiously gained from those rough-hewn grave-robbing bounty hunters known even then as "New York art dealers"—formed the cornerstone gift to what is now the Smithsonian's impressive horde.

The mural shows a band of fruit-carrying Indians, generically bare if genitally unspecified. They greet one paunchy Quaker-looking gent smiling from beneath a probably hurtful black tricorn hat. (There is an eerie similarity to Edward Hicks's later *Peaceable Kingdom* series.) The fat white guy is said to resemble the great-great-grandfather of Elkton Green's builder, one Judge Josiah Vestry Coker (1670–1749). He remained on fine terms with his Native American neighbors even through the Tuscarora War of 1711. He negotiated the release of certain English lady settlers taken as hostages. They were freed through his personal diplomacy and an anonymous donation of "many sovereigne of the King's coinage, meetly dispatched by His Own horses." The mural is of museum quality and unique in the state.

Some people have complained that I tell too much about the history of each house. That is not possible.

For the record, the man who built Elkton Green inherited a goodly fortune via this very Judge and arts collector. But plump Caleb Coker soon handsomely supplanted his patrimony through naval stores, pitch and rope and turpentine, sold along the state's then-bustling steamship coast. Coker's own King Cotton holdings—taken collectively—equaled half the land mass of Rhode Island. It was he, Caleb Hunstable Coker (1812–1891), who conceived of Elkton Green as the site for his beautiful daughter's wedding. This, prior to his actually having a daughter. (Such is the energy and optimism of our America!) The mansion's stained-glass skylight-lit staircase was designed to make stunning the choreography of one girl's white-veiled descent.

Concord, Coker's only child, was born just three years after the home's completion. Her mother died in childbirth. Fortunate for herself and her father (and his architects!), Concord proved to be the beauty a 51-step staircase preordained.

It was Concord, at age 18, who founded the first Falls Public Lending Library for Ladies. She furnished it with her cast-off novels. (She is said to have read two a day since age 10. Her father saw this as proof of her refinement, and incidentally his own.) When Concord finally wed at the age of 31, she chose a future Chief Justice of the State Supreme Court. By her day's standards, Concord Coker was already middle-aged. This last-minute reprieve from spinsterhood and a threatened end to the Coker line further piqued her father's extravagance. It had already been expressed, perhaps too malely, in this house that, for all its feminizing frontal gingery lace, remains blessed with a Grover Cleveland girth of solemnity, not to mix metaphors or, worse, periods. Elkton Green's builder swore it must now fulfill its destiny, must now become the stage for what Caleb Coker announced, in print alas, would be "the wedding of the century."

The bride's proud poppa, nine-term mayor of Falls, imported a 60-piece string orchestra from (not Richmond but) Philadelphia. Through his naval connections, he chartered one of the last for-lease four-masted schooners, the *Reliance*. It brought all instruments, the three requested extra harps, and distinguished Yankee visitors south to Wilmington's harbor.

But Mr. Coker was too ambitious and too rich to stop there. He soon stage-managed a single decorative touch that even now gives him an ongoing life in local Falls legend. (Who could ask for anything more?) With help from a railroad-owning friend and later business partner of the Barnum and Bailey Circus—Caleb Coker imported spiders, yes, specialty spiders, from South America. I don't pretend to understand all this, but the eight news clippings here—long since turned brown as cigars—all vouch for the insects' unlikely presence. The exact species has been lost to us, despite our tireless research. It grieves us, this lapse; my fondest hope was to offer the species' exact Latin name. I fear there's no time left before our present Issue # 14 must be "put to bed." However, I *have* discovered that these creatures were brought to Falls by rail.

Thanks to a bibliophilic fellow preservationist, I own the somewhat comic shipping invoice. Under "Descrp. Laden Goods:" some shaky hand has written, "Spiders, large, South American, keeper was well-spoken & aware of poss. passnger discomfort. Paid first class fare for each cage. Kept crates draped excllnt. All steps taken." Spiders arrived in steel containers described by one witness as "little metal safes with wire-mesh-covered breathing holes." The insects' trainer released them at night into Elkton Green's water oaks and camellias and over its then-young box maze on the south lawn. Spiders soon spun gossamer at a rate almost unseemly, till now locally unknown. Two dawns later, they had overshot even Christo, wrapping Elkton Green entire. Silver webbing was said to cover every shrub and bracketed spindle. According to a newspaper account, "one wheel-barrow, a tall ladder left in the wrong place, and glassy results of the milkman's visit soon needed freeing from sudden gauze." Mounting even taller ladders, slaves now sprinkled real gold dust over all the webs. The whole place then got strung with 6,000, yes, white Chinese lanterns. For an evening wedding, the grounds were lit with "over 20,000 white tapers, of the finest."

At 6 a.m. the Coker retainers began lighting the white lanterns. Now, to our jaded eyes, this light-show might seem a pleasing sight. But for Falls, of the period, where one oil lamp per kitchen table was considered a luxury, such display shone without parallel. It took 21 servants 12 hours to light and relight every wick, avoiding the still-busy spiders, by now themselves turned gold. Come sunset, two counties' fire departments stood by, so stoked with rum toddies that their utility was undercut, but luckily never needed. It was reported how, by evening, the glow could be seen fully one and a half miles away.

A chronicle of the day inevitably mentions Midas. The *Falls Herald Traveler* called the nighttime sight of Elkton Green "locked within the powdered gold candleglow casts over finest webbing, a spectacle from pre-Christian myth, in its excess both offputting and yet wondrous as some children's book's occurrence. A strange idea, so perfectly implemented that it shall not be soon forgot by any of the over 1,000 uninvited guests allowed and even encouraged to stand outside Elkton Green's cast-iron gates and stare. Each onlooker was provided a gilt packet of rice to shower upon the handsome escaping bridal couple. It must be noted that, while the bride appeared almost starkly beautiful, Elkton Green itself, a home easily accommodating the exceptional string orchestra of 60, plus unnumbered guests, glowed with a fond pride that seemed cordial, aware, and all but human in its joy. Many onlookers remarked the impression of a house come utterly, as it were, sentiently and watchfully alive."

Elkton Green now stands, somewhat startled it must be admitted, in downtown commercial Falls, NC. It is within easy take-out distance of both a Hardee's and a Colonel Sanders, alas. Three years back, we personally planted fast-growing Leyland cypresses to screen out such blight. The mansion rests on 2.4 acres of its original 880. It is just around the corner from the White-Rooker–designed Gothic Revival courthouse. (Would it be immodest to mention our organization's having saved this masterwork in January 1983?) Elkton Green still holds a place of honor along Summit Avenue, a street lined with other Victorian mastodons and the magnolias planted by Falls's "Betterment Committee" in 1891. Why the four-car garages, aluminum outbuildings, and easy parking for 500 (count 'em) cars? Genteelly put, . . . Elkton Green was, during the late 1950s, transformed into Falls's finest white funeral establishment. I say, there must be life after embalming for Elkton Green! Pul-lease?

Falls is located just off I-95 and I-40, the main byways linking Miami and New York. This certainly helps give Elkton Green, with its extensive leaded windows, arched interior doorways, Vermont-marble rose-and-lotus-carved hearth facings, its commodious rooms and ingenious still-working system of dumbwaiters, great potential as a going Bed and Breakfast. (If that is what it takes to save it.) Anyone who has seen and loved Orson Welles's *The Magnificent Ambersons,* anyone who has ever nursed a fantasy of issuing one's own white-draped daughter from the head of a great staircase featuring the period's requisite bronze of bare-bottomed Mercury (he's there), needs to see (then save) this brave survivor.

It's a very big house built to edify, impress, and perhaps slightly terrify this little town. For a moot $210,000, it's yours to use—as gently or as bullingly—as you see fit.

Square Feet: 6,899. Lot: 2.4 acres. Zoning: B1 (central business). Revolving Funds available immediately. Plus ample parking for your next garden party of 650 guests, for your own (second or third?) wedding, or hygienic facilities befitting your (first) funeral! Everything's ready. We know you're out there. It's yours, please.

The history (& the croquet) come free.

Celebrating the Life *of*
Theodore Hunstable Worth
volunteer interim editor: MARY ELLEN BROADFIELD

You have just read the last "Available for Restoration" note actually written by our much-missed leader, gadfly, and inspiration, Theodore "Tad" Worth. I was just one of the many people touched by him. I am but one of the countless fortunates now living in houses Tad saved from the bull-dozer. I feel I must make a few remarks. Some will be statesmanlike and formal (as is our wont, we preservationists!). Others will, no doubt, prove utterly uncalled-for, and therefore of a sort I think he'd like.

I.   A Perhaps Too Personal Reflection

First I only knew Tad Worth socially, as everybody did. But I can't say I counted Tad a close friend.

Our deeper contact commenced six years ago. It was just after my husband died. I was sitting in my Hillsborough kitchen, feeling more than a little sorry for myself. My children had flown the coop for college, perpetual grad school and, at long last, jobs. The game of bridge, eventful and statistically challenging though it can be, had begun to let me feel a bit abandoned too. Nothing seemed enough. Nothing actually meant anything. Tad had a curious way of being at the right place at the right time. Or as someone later put it, "at the right time, for the right place." Right for the salvation of noble houses and their sometimes mopey occupants.

This gift of timing secured, for our grandchildren and for theirs, the continuing presence of churches, two of them African Methodist Episcopal, one major 19th-century courthouse, the German-carved carousel at High Point, and an entire downtown district slated for destruction only 10 days after Tad's first inquiries to save it. (Few of us will forget a 24-hour vigil that felt like getting the heroine untied from the railroad tracks!)

I was not the only old "widow woman" in Tad Worth's Morocco-bound, paint-splattered address book. There is a natural law that allows us, the ladies, I mean, to have an extra decade or three. There is some justice in that, I believe. Even so, many of these widows confess to feeling like ramshackle old "historic" homeplaces themselves. I felt myself to be some house suddenly emptied of all its occupants and, despite possessing fairly decent dentil moldings, fallen into disrepair beyond the help of Elizabeth Arden, the National Trust, or the Holy Spirit!

The moment my husband died, I became such a crumbling "prestige property." Well, imagine the pleasure of this old homeplace upon being turned, half against her will, into an office, then upgraded into Action Central till, through being an unsalaried Bed and Breakfast, I finally found myself having become, to quote my Trekkie children, "The Mother Ship."

All on behalf of Historic Preservation, and all on account of this extraordinary, very down-to-earth type of person who gave me "the call." Like that Caravaggio depicting the tax collector's being summoned from his counting table to Duty, to Care, and to, at last, a Cause.

This "number" of our periodical must be different from any other. We must all reflect some of what we've lost in a person of Tad's moral and artistic talents. This issue will offer you, our loyal donors and supporters and readers, Tad's fellow carpenters and archivists, snobs and friends, something like his own last will and testament.

Tad's housemate, Patrick Trevor, can tell you how much willpower Tad, as the strength lessened, gave to writing his parts of this, Issue # 14. There were several new properties Tad planned to describe more fully, hoping to intrigue a latent buyer. (He was at work on a love poem to Shadowlawn Plantation when he died. But Elkton Green was the only home Tad managed, from his bed, to fully "portray.") It must be admitted, in his hospital room on March 28 we told Tad that we'd found the long-awaited "fairy-god-purchaser" for Elkton Green. We invented certain details—a family foundation funded by a carpeting concern—a newly retired Connecticut couple looking for some getaway, etc. We told Tad that Elkton Green had been saved, thanks to a faxed copy of his seductive history! We lied to him. What good, by then, to let him know we'd lost the place?

It was just one of the properties Tad had worked years to "wrestle" onto the registry. (He had bought and planted those cypresses three years before the place was even listed with us. It took a whole Saturday and the lad did it all "on spec.") If we sacrifice any more of these exquisite plantation and small-town homes to the wrecking crew, so much remaining beauty will be taken from our state. It meant everything to Tad, sketching out these farms and houses as only Tad Worth could. His room at Duke Hospital was stacked with deeds and court records, with wills in Xerox, slave rosters, an antique leather "elephant" folio marked "Characteristic Non-Poisonous Spiders of Central and South America, depicted in native circumstances," architectural and decorating sourcebooks from the 18th century to the present. There were six potted orchids. Somebody had thrown an old paisley shawl over the curtain rod circling his bed. A new nurse walked in one day and said, "So—who lives here? Merlin?" We all laughed and, though weak by then, Tad, never one to miss a comic opportunity, spoke up, "More like Merlin's maid, honey."

Tad died on the night of April 1. (He'd once stated he was aiming for that date, intending some final confession of foolishness.) He perished believing Elkton Green had been spared. With some difficulty, he told us just where his prized croquet set was stored, ready. We found the mallet stand already tied with a grass-green satin bow.

. . .

May I, as editor emeritus (that is, the only local person "tetched" enough to even try and edit this thing), permit myself the luxury of trying to set down a few memories of Tad? "For the record," as he would put it. Tad Worth was a great believer in "the record." No one ever did more to keep our dear state's record legible or longer "in print."

Though he's a person sure to be remembered vividly by those who knew him, Tad is someone oddly apt to disappear. He planned that, you see. He was very quick at giving others credit, perhaps too quick. Tad seemed eager to blend into the heaps of deeds of his library research, into the lives of his "lieutenants," into the very timbers and planks of those properties he saved. I cannot bear anonymity for this boy of ours—and though he'd reached his early 40s, "a boy" is what he'll always seem to me, to someone my age. You will find his name on no plaque at any of the over 57 homes and public edifices he helped us spare. Just the names of original builders, of founding farmers, mayors, owners, and, of course, the time-tested family names of those prosperous, bored "widow women" who became Tad Worth's funding and phoning army. But on what marble tablet do we find Theodore Hunstable Worth's moniker engraved?

Let that start here. Call this "a personal indulgence," but telling Tad's particular truth also presents a chore of excruciating difficulty. I was once asked to speak—extemporaneously!—at the funeral of a woman who had worked for my family for 49 years. All I know is that I managed to say something. That in itself seemed feat aplenty. Here, at least, I have the blessing of silence, shelter, and revision. So I am going to take my jolly good time if that's all right. It's odd, but I feel my whole life has been a preparation for doing just this. Which is maybe why I feel so nervous about overstaying, overstating. Tad inspires overstatement, and perhaps demands it! If only I could find a prose style as modest, upright, and human in scale as the Federal architecture Tad loved best. That's what I intend here: to make one little Doric temple on a hill for him.

For the record, Tad gave me the first job I ever had, apart from Wife and Mother and Friend, and all that those massive duties entail. Such tasks were precisely what women of my generation expected. But certain energies always went untapped. Precisely in not being asked after, many skills remained undescribed, and therefore went unknown. Tad believed in my "structural integrity" at a time when this rickety old structure sorely doubted she would stand for one more day.

He walked into my house without knocking. I had not been able or willing to even answer my front door. I was so out of sorts and thought so poorly of myself after George died. I felt responsible for that, I guess (the way we poor WASPs will). Until Tad's helpful revision, Saint Sebastian had always somehow been my idea of a life, a search for further sharper arrows! Yikes, but it's true. So, actually saying "Knock knock," into my kitchen walks this chunky, agreeable young man with high color, long blondish-red hair, a blue Oxford-cloth buttondown, and chinos whose knees proved he'd been down on all fours checking some ancient building's footings (not that I would've used that term back then). From his alligator belt, a jingling eight-inch key ring. He wore Topsiders, at least they had the outline of Topsiders, but they seemed created by Mr. Jackson Pollock, so paint-and-plaster-swirled were they. In one hand, he held a little note that I myself had scribbled to him after some recent party. I'd mailed it six days prior to George's being found in his fishing boat. It was a thank-you note for something or other, a joking little teasing little letter I'd jotted, nothing really.

"You can write, Mary Ellen," so Tad said. "You slipped up and showed us that. This thing had us all doubled over, laughing. And it cracked us up three hours prior to drink time. I don't know if you understand what a rare and negotiable skill writing simply and persuasively is! No? I thought not. A skill useful for my purposes, of course. But now you've tipped your hand, you simply have to come on board. You owe it to the rest of us. I'm going to have to hold you to your word. You *are* a person of your word, aren't you, Mary Ellen Broadfield?" I had not the foggiest idea what young Tad Worth was talking about. I expressed this aloud.

From a deep pocket of his nasty chinos, he pulled out a folded wad of papers, blueprints, statistics. They concerned a certain property he believed he could get his hands on for the Register. Scraps of inspectors' reports, Polaroids of glum interior details and, I believe, a matchbook from Sanitary Fish Market with room measurements jotted there amongst traces of Tabasco sauce. He told me: First, this home needs saving from the razing crews that have been instrumental in making so much of our state look like Ohio or anywhere dull else on earth. Then this home must be put up for sale, Tad explained. That particular day, he wisely assumed nothing (given my grieving state and likely appearance). He spelled it out: The house, once sold at subsidized prices, would be restored. "Not just pickled and 'museumified' but inhabited, returned to its function. Providing shelter, comfort, and incidental joy." That's a direct quote. Still, peeved, I sat there blinking.

Tad settled beside me at my own kitchen table. From his country doctor's bag of a briefcase, he eased forth the sheaf of photographs he'd taken with his similarly paint-scarred Pentax. He said the house was called Sandover. Toward me, he then pushed a jotted list of people in the town where this ignored domestic masterpiece had stood since 1803. People who could help. "I just know you must know about three-quarters of the hard-drinking gentry down Little Washington way," he tried flattering me back into life. I knew that trick well enough.

I told him I didn't maintain contact with all that many people really. I also told Tad I'd just had kind of a shock, with George dying alone on the Neuse River, right after I had pronounced such fishing trips "a big fat bore." I had made my husband go by himself to drift around alone in a deceased condition. It took the Coast Guard five long days to find our boat. I swear the wait nearly killed me. I said I needed time.

My own address book was buried under some Erle Stanley Gardners and the answering machine I'd just installed to fend off universal sympathy and gossipy well-wishers. There was a grand total of 21 unreturned phone calls flashing on the thing. One rumor I'd been allowed to overhear claimed that my late husband had been discovered face-up in our boat, features half consumed by seagulls (not true). Such tittle-tattle can challenge a person's sense of dignity and value, not to mention shaking her accustomed social standing.

Three of those waiting calls would turn out to be from Tad Worth here. He now said, "You need a martini is what you need, girl, and then you need to go get your address book over there out from under those cheap paperback mysteries. I assume that Gutenbergy Bible-y humongous-looking thing is your address book? And then we need to compare the names on this list with the names in yonder tome-ette, and then you need to get your excellent sinewy ass in gear, girl. I hear you don't even answer your phone no mo'. You've already quit coming to the door. I know what that means, Mary Ellen. I've been there, gir'friend, and I'm telling you, get with the program. And while you're up, I could use a martini too. But, look, just show the gin a vermouth bottle, just scare it by maybe whispering the word 'Vermont'—that's vermouth enough—and then you need to come back here and focus on something past the tip of your fine Hollingsworth nose. I don't reckon you have any 'snack items' or cheese or anything around, do you? Not that my Gothick saddlebags need it, Heaven presarve 'em." I stared at him as if he were speaking Serbo-Croat. I finally said, "Does the phrase 'over the top' mean anything to you, young man?"

"Mean anything? It's my goddamn credo!"

So, before Tad would even consider leaving, he made me, after two goodly drinks, no more, telephone three girls I'd known at Saint Catherine's. One of them was married, as it happened, to the longtime mayor of Little Washington. If I had ever known that, I'd forgotten. Everybody in Washington, NC, will tell you their town is years older than our nation's copycat capital, and therefore should be called "the Original Washington." That's where Sandover, the Meade-Ulrich mansion, was located, a 20-room late-Georgian palace about to be done away with—so that public servants at City Hall would have better parking opportunities each morning. I ask you! Tad left me with this list and other homework, plus he scheduled a return appointment, said he'd come back in three days, no later. To see how I'd done. I believe three days has certain precedents as an ideal resurrection time. He knew I'd need that long to get out of a green chenille—yes, chenille—robe I'd taken to sulking around in. (I still don't know how that got into my closet or where it's got to since.)

Reached a point where I did not remember actually formally volunteering. He'd left behind the spooky photos of water-stained heart-pine Adam-paneled parlors, of fanlights shaped like yard-wide scallop shells, of English boxwoods about the size of the planet Pluto (his line, not yours truly's). Here I was, not even a dues-paying member. All the paperwork was disfiguring my kitchen table. I felt put upon. And yet somehow, by the following Thursday, I had talked the mayor's wife (Deedee Pruden, darling girl, always so good in art class at "catching likenesses") into heading a task force that would make the Meade-Ulrich mansion a Hospitality Center for the city of Little Washington. In other words, I felt like I had somewhat helped to start to save an antebellum jewel that'd taken three years and 40,000 1803 dollars and untold day laborers—slaves and Boston brick masons—to build.

By the following week, Tad and Patrick were right here cooking softshell crabs at my own till-lately seldom-used (except for coffee) stove. And it was only when I heard myself say, by phone (while they eavesdropped as planned), heard myself say somewhat flirtatiously to a boy from Shelby that I used to date, "Honey? Reeve? Are you listening? Because if you and the other so-called pillars of Shelby sit around there sipping your 'Jacks and water' while some nouveau Atlanta yahoo takes his tractor to that Osage House's bracketed cornices given an Italianate flavor by the square porch posts and those heavy corn-patterned pilasters in our beloved region's finest Greek Revival idiom, why, the ghost of your sainted Grandmother Spruill (who always liked me, God rest her soul), she's going to put a serious hex on your golf game, Reeve. Now, *think*."

And it was only when Tad and Patrick laughed, then covered their mouths (afraid to mess up a hard deal I was driving with a little of my late husband's serious financial flair, if I do say so myself!)—it was only then that your Mary Ellen Broadfield here understood how Preservation might, if approached correctly, prove . . . well . . . preservative.

II.

I mention that last part only because, this now being my newsletter (ha ha!), I simply chose to mention it. But in the above incident, I represent just one of hundreds, or maybe a thousand or two other people he is forever rescuing. You see? I keep falling into the present tense when speaking of Tad. I expect we all will for a long time yet. I must say, it's unbelievable he's dead. My husband perished of natural causes at age 71. (Is this too personal? I'll leave that to my closest friends and second-readers to decide later). When my husband died, I felt I could not go on. George had provided such a definition of my life. I was suddenly a single-owner home with no history but his. It seemed so unfair, his perishing at 71. Then Tad died at a bit more than half George's age, died of causes I cannot call natural (though nature, I reckon, contains them). And "unfair" took on a whole new kind of meaning. Fact is, I simply cannot believe Tad Worth is dead. You keep waiting for the voice, then you keep waiting for its echo. This must be what it's like to lose your own child. Downtown, you see resemblances in perfect strangers glimpsed from behind. You actually go up to them. They turn around and their faces look hideous, only because the faces are not his. But you all know all this already.

Well . . . Tad was, as we can attest, a jack-of-all-trades. Having been so philanthropic with his smallish trust fund so early on, he fairly well had to be. During his 43 years, he worked in various unlikely roles to support his overriding concern for Preservation, supporting, only incidentally, himself. He would've cringed on hearing our lieutenant governor's graveside mention of how Tad spent his own inheritance saving houses he then practically gave away to others, homes he never really lived in except to work on them. Tad was briefly a garden designer, specializing in period herbal and knot gardens (before they became a fad, so cutesied up). Then he owned a profitable business which recast old sundials, garden statuary, and obelisks. But daily management was something he mostly left to others. This allowed Tad time to drive his pickup on secondary Carolina roads, seeking vine-covered subjects for "mere salvation," his dachshund always in back, barking at all chickens and most trees. Tad was a sought-after caterer (though that sounds too menial for somebody who came in and cooked for his friends and later sort of permitted them to slip him a little something oblique if princely). His softshells — dipped in lime juice, then battered with crumbled pecans and sautéed — were truly not to be missed. He acted as a paint contractor and period consultant for Tryon Palace and other such sites. But never Historic Williamsburg, a bête noire he never tired of "dishing." Tad didn't consider their scholarship serious and called them "the Walt Dig-nys." Forever strong in his likes and dislikes, our Tad. He did a lot of things quietly well. Tad always assumed that everybody else could, too. Well, everybody else can't, actually. But young Mr. Worth never ceded his amateur standing; Jefferson remained his god. The 18th-century's farmer-statesman-gourmand-classicist-architect was Tad's long-range ideal, and therefore his daily yardstick and reality. And though half the world still genuflects to Jefferson's undoubted genius, Tad was something that Mr. Jefferson never ever thought to try to be: I mean that our plumpish, rosy Theodore Worth stayed, to the end, a very very funny person. And even Tad admitted, "Marse Jefferson was, if not all things, then most. But nobody ever did accuse him of being exactly a laugh riot."

It is important to stay realistic about one's mentors.

Can you hear me trying?

I saw Tad sit down and play brilliant backgammon and then lose on purpose, if that was required. Say there was a resistant elder citizen, some old gal very unlikely to hand over a group of "important" farm-building dependencies; say an incoming mall was already waving bushel baskets of cash at her for that same tract. And here was Tad "throwing" a backgammon game for preservation. "There are many ways to win"—he grew quite snippish when I teased him about this later. I've also seen Tad go right up onto the fourth story of a slate roof just after rain, and only say, "Whoo, I gots them Hitchcock Vertigos" after he'd spied whatever mountain goats go up that high to see, and then (like a kitten I once owned) he needed aid and ladders in getting down, almost needed smelling salts. From the ground, a martini was often held aloft and sloshed around for inspiration.

And none of us shall ever forget watching Tad veer into action at Zoning Board meetings statewide. I went to school on how he managed those.

The local boards would know only that some outsider had requested an extra session. Like all of us, the poor things were already "meetinged" to death. Their arms were crossed, their shoes already tapping, their watches exposed for easy consulting. In Tad would sweep, a bit chunky and therefore somewhat more trustworthy. He wore his one dark conservative suit, and was looking fairly neat for a change. No paint on the pair of brown wing tips he called his "M.B.A. drag." For once he left his pesky dog in the truck. I'd begged him to.

Since his family was an old one ("old and rotten," he liked to quote William Carlos Williams), he had a sense of other towns and who their leading families were. He'd always arrive at the town hall a bit early. There, he could mill around out front and chat up farmers about crop allotments and outlawed pesticides, he could talk to housewives about the mahimahi being sold at Piggly Wiggly since March and how rare you dared to serve it, and he was not above mentioning his other vice: *All My Children*. Tad once told me after an especially successful meeting (in which he saved the 1873 Conger-Halsey Academy for Girls outside Rocky Mount), "I swear, Mary Ellen, keeping up with a good soap, it's the next best thing to being a Mason."

Meeting was called to order; first thing, he'd get up and say his usual grinning "Hi," then tell a joke about some boy hick getting the better of a society woman trying to cheat him out of his sainted mother's pie-safe at a flea market over in Swan Quarter. His accent was one kind of icebreaker, the seeming irreverence another.

Tad would then begin his slide presentation about some local building these folks had been driving past their whole lives, one they'd assumed to be merest shack and eyesore, one held up mostly by its own Virginia creeper and poison ivy old enough to grow berries big as scuppernong grapes. Tad Worth's talks never lasted more than 22 minutes. I checked. Others, watches readied, forgot to. He congratulated locals on the important period piece they'd all helped keep standing till this very hour. He presented stories about who'd built it and why; he specialized in the early builders' faults, erotic peccadilloes and hobbies and, always a plus, the deaths of any of their young children. Not a dry eye in the house. Right up to the wainscoting ledge of the shameless, young Squire Worth oftimes went. He used to quote his beloved Jane Austen, "One does not love a place less for having suffered in it." He told what church the homebuilders had attended, and which of that sanctuary's rose windows they'd donated in 1814, and by the end, our Mr. Worth had mentioned the family name—legitimately mentioned—of most people present, including the security guards.

Tad never scheduled anything after. He knew that if his pitch to save a structure worked he'd be instantly invited to one, if not three homes of the competitive local hostesses. (Here in society North Carolina at least, each town is going to have either two or three "leader art patrons." There's never only one.) Many's the night we arrived back home in Hillsborough after 2 a.m. Tad understood how this was all part of it, making himself available (to each jealous hostess in turn, if need be).

I don't know when he caught the missionary fervor about old houses. He'd grown up in one that had been lost. Maybe that set him on his course. Or maybe during college, at Charlottesville? I once asked him why he matriculated there. "For the real estate?" He laughed. I'm not sure if such long local midnight parties bored him as they sometimes did me. (I shall hold my own tongue here.) But if so, Tad certainly never showed it. He never condescended; he had his loves and his strong dislikes but he did not fail to look all kinds of people in the eye. "Never met a stranger." We now claim 110 city chapters in this state, and each represents dozens of not-that-riveting 2 a.m.'s, much Triscuit-eating by our Tad. Two-thirty and he still sat there, overanimating some creweled wing chair, discussing the recent tuition increase at Ravenscroft School and the best way to make your new garden statuary look ancient: pour a half a gallon of buttermilk on it and watch the setting in of what Tad called "the blue-chip greenies."

You will remember that young Mr. Worth was accompanied most everywhere by his brown low-stomached dachshund bitch, Circa. He said he called her that because, whenever you thought of her, she was "always Around Then." She was the bad dog you often find near your most accommodating people. (It seems they let their dogs take it out in trade.) Some people complained Tad Worth's zeal for saving broken houses was overshadowed by one dog he never housebroke.

I recall how the construction fellows at Sandover, the hired workers (not we volunteers), always got a kick out of Circa, her carrying on in that intelligent if indolent manner. But, you see, they heard her name as "Circus." And Tad was much too gentlemanly—meaning too smart, kind, or efficient—to try explaining the joke ("No, boys, 'Circa,' you recall, is an art-historical term," etc.) "Tadbud, you got her name right," one fellow called from the gable roof, " 'At dog's a pure-tee circus." Just then she was running around the big house, and Tad, that quick, pointed as she wheezed around the corner a third time, said, "Yeah, Bobby Ray. A three-ring circus." Roofers, laughing, shook their heads. I saw again how good Tad was at taking others' mistakes, period mistakes, class mistakes, even our failures of nerve or character, and setting some period pediment atop them. A true Jeffersonian. He did that during this particular widow woman's Chapter Eleven of life; walked in, "Knock knock," and placed a finial or crown upon the head of one old lady wearing an extremely unattractive pistachio-green chenille robe.

Tad himself was also always around, always talkative, and his shirttail forever seemed to be coming out, and he kept threatening to do sit-ups when he someday got around to it, "just as soon as Burleigh Hall is finally secure." He did have faults. If I've already presumed to point out Jefferson's, I don't think Tad would mind my adding a few of his own. I never quite trust eulogies that make out anyone to be angelic. No one utterly is. Such saccharine gush would, to employ one of Tad's own oversalty phrases, "absolutely gag a maggot." (I am trusting his own brand of luridness to call me back from my inherent sentiment about him. Maybe that is a form of immortality—giving one's survivors tools to avert their being overmaudlin in recalling oneself? I don't know.) We all understood this much: Tad could really get his feelings hurt. He could become excessively silly at times, and you couldn't pull him out of it, not even during emergencies. Once people crossed him or played dirty pool to cheat him out of some church he was trying to save, well, Tad never forgot. "They, my dear, are off Mother's" (he sometimes comically referred to himself as "Mother") "list, for good." He either loved you or he really just didn't.

Once you were off "Mother's list," special pleading—be it Presidential,

Papal, or from on high—couldn't reinstate you, oh dear me no. All his own considerable skills (what a diplomat he would have made!) had long since been lined up and pressed toward one end—preserving what was old and handsome and in jeopardy. He'd given everything he owned away to save the beautiful and local.

Plain obstinate selfishness baffled him. (There is, I hate to tell you, a lot of that around just now.) But every time Tad bumped into it, he seemed to find it brand-new. It could be a bore. He literally did not understand greed. "Why wouldn't she give it away rather than see it torn down?" He sometimes made me feel guilty for how the very people I despised behaved!

More than once, in our legal wrangling, we came up against some old person who would literally prefer to see his or her own family homeplace burn; better that than allow one Yankeefied stranger to set foot in it. This Tad puzzled over, as if he had heard wrong. "What?" he asked, and at times seemed to be blaming the messengers. In the face of such meanness, Tad himself grew obstinate and childlike; you saw he didn't really want to know that part of people. How lucky that he saw as little of it as he did.

There are about six Republican families, major landholders in our fine state, tribes he couldn't abide; these were groups (nameless here, please) who could—with one phone call, or a signature—have spared the places he tried daily to preserve. They did not. They let treasure after treasure go. And they assumed nobody knew. Well, listen, if they'd half-guessed the social damage their own stinginess had done them and their climbing grandkids forever, they'd have handed Mr. Worth a stack of blank checks and just run.

As with all people who're obsessed, every turn of conversation led Tad back to the house he was just then trying to spare. He used to joke that perfect happiness would be to save the Shadowlawn Plantation down near Edenton ("my possible all-time fave") and to lose that 15th midriff pound of his, and on the same day. He was always almost going on a diet, but only once he had sampled whatever it was that we were cooking. People did love feeding him. There was never a more appreciative eater of one's work. Our leader claimed that his mother must've been a Jewish Mom switched at birth and uneasily disguised as a bony Episcopalian "who inherited only the garnets." Tad claimed the first word he learned from her was "Eat." And the second two were "Duncan Phyfe." And it is a sad note to admit that, though he did finally gather contributors and grants enough to begin Shadowlawn's "mere salvation," he also lost more pounds than the anticipated 15.

If I'd been told that, at my present age, I would feel fully at ease with computers, I would simply not have believed it. But here I am, facing a blue screen, writing this. I now possess copies of all the disks left in and near Tad's laptop when he died. I scan through documents with a burgler's guilty joy. It is a holy trust. It feels like continuing notes and mail from him. I cannot help — even if out of sequence — saving two things found there.

First, he'd noted George Macdonald's observation, "Home is the only place where you can go out and in. There are places you can go into, and places you can go out of, but the one place, if you do but find it, where you may go out and in both, is home."

In one file, I found the outtakes Tad had deleted from the Elkton Green description with which I opened. Coming on it filled me with such dread. I recalled the day I first understood that something was terribly wrong with Tad's health, he who seemed a sort of Friar Tuck, invincible.

Not two hours after the wedding ceased, newspaper accounts of the day tell how a young man carried his drowned bride one step at a time up onto the porch, moving slowly, bent across her, weeping like a child, moving toward the silenced father of Concord. The same mansion was still glowing golden, set there within spiders' webbing that now ceased seeming whimsical, that now looked only, and ever after, sinister. As if inviting spiders to a wedding had meant, from the start, courting disaster.

Pressing the Midas image forward to its usual end: Tragedy struck as it so often does when any person makes so spendthrift a display as had Caleb Coker. He felt he'd finally achieved his fondest wish, to build a house meant to contain the "wedding of the century." Whenever anything we do drives us to say it is the whatever "Of the Century," perhaps we should back off a bit. Our dearest wishes we must never utter quite aloud. The golden rice tossed, Concord's trousseau had been loaded onto the roof of an enclosed carriage. Said conveyance was swagged of course in white satin ribbons and the gardenias she so loved. The horses were matched and extremely white. The travel to the train station would be but the shortest of jaunts. Not two miles from the spun-gold mansion—at what is still a difficult junc-ture of what's even now a poorly planned twist where U.S. 40 meets U.S. 98 over the still-too-narrow Melius Bridge—the married couple's coach driver, having imbibed many a celebratory rum toddy, mis-judged that hairpin curve. The great weight of 12 steamer trunks strapped atop the vehicle caused it to tilt starboard and then wobble four inches off the Melius Bridge. Just one wheel slipped past its sid-ing. But such was the weight of one father's gifts, Concord's new nov-els, unworn fineries, furs, the silver hairbrushes and mirror, that the whole wagon fell into what, just there, was but a shallow brook. Four white horses naturally followed. Concord had been seated on that side of the vehicle which struck rocks first, and she was either drowned or crushed by the bulk of her unasked-for luxuries. Her young husband survived. Contemporary accounts never fail to sketch—with that day's love of melodrama and stagy tableaux—the inevitable final scene. Caleb Coker was now supervising the exqui-site comedy of his slaves, 20, armed with butterfly nets trying to recapture the rental spiders, themselves long since powdered gold. (You can survive that and even safely eat gold dust in small amounts, as the vulgar 1980s party-food vogue in Japan and Manhattan makes clear.)

Contemporary accounts insist that the bridegroom, himself unscratched during the dreadful mishap, caught a ride on the first vehicle to chance past the broken bridge railing. And while the coun-try crowd yet waded in the river's shallows to fish out silks and the drunken coachman, one black farmer, guiding his mule cart, deposited the groom at the curb of a brilliant home still festive. The orchestra played even better, now that most guests were gone. Up there on Elkton Green's great gallery porch, Caleb Coker was yet visible, continuing to offer and accept champagne toasts, laughing, flipping a gold piece to the slave who'd caught the largest spider fastest. When up the carpet toward Elkton Green, his wet shoes leav-ing traces, came the bridegroom, bearing in his arms the body of Concord.

Imagining the moment when the girl's doting and ecstatic father first caught sight of his only child, dead . . . it remains unimaginable. No, not quite unimaginable . . .

I'm struck again by what a religious nature young Mr. Worth had. I simply mean he wasn't simply anecdotal; he believed in more than experience, far more than mortal brick and mortal mortar and English boxwoods that grow only a half-inch a year, which simply makes your bigger bushes mean more. It all implied a sort of "belief system," as my son who did Divinity School might say.

Maybe this explained why, as an adult, Tad lived in that comfortable but perfectly ordinary little cottage built in the '40s, the 1940s. It was really fairly spare, the way he lived. Tad never acted happier than when he was in one of the properties that he himself, with all his wiles and charms, had saved. But he didn't yet feel quite entitled to occupy one himself. Maybe that's why the older houses were so free in revealing their secrets to him. Safe to 'fess up their former family problems—safe, their offered news, preserved with him. He saved face for real estate, a sort of go-between for occupants living and dead, as I shall demonstrate in a bit.

As I stated, he attended the University of Virginia. He worked each summer as a day-labor gardener on the grounds of Monticello.

Tad claimed that, in the household's former vegetable patch, they were forever tilling up weather gauges or oxidized iron yardsticks, 18th-century glass beakers drilled with holes. Science was a cottage industry there. It reached Tad so clearly and daily that Jefferson's whole enterprise had been an experiment, a tester's waystation. And, in later talks, Tad would mention this vision of Democracy as a series of go-for-broke if scientifically observed risk-takings. Pushed far enough, these make Democracy theological, not just coolly rational. Jefferson's quest to understand some Divine Master-Scheme presupposes one. It assumes some ferocious Palladian blueprint, a golden mean of absolute proportion underwriting all our messy doings and our failed designs. Just such striving and good faith shaped the Federal buildings Tad loved best, their symmetry and modesty, their frontal candor, almost virginal.

Tad Worth's relation to Jefferson became immediate for many of us locals. There is a handsome illustrated volume called *Mr. Jefferson in Motion: A Documentary Biography in His Own Words.* I'm told that the book is still in print; it is by one Jean Garth Randolph. One photo's caption reads: "Contemporary Model wears a favorite red under-waistcoat owned by Jefferson circa 1800–1820. Silk crepe with brown velvet collar, woolen sleeves, and a lining consisting of cut-apart knotted cotton and wool fleece stockings, upper back embroidered 'TJ. Monticello.' " And there, in three-quarters profile, his long auburnish hair tied back with a black grosgrain ribbon in the simplest revolutionary manner, stands Tad. Nineteen if unsmiling, he's still recognizable; but he looks like some overpretty Renaissance page of about 12. Of course, he was shorter than Jefferson's six three or, some claim, four. Still, there is our boy, on record.

"Puttin' on Marse Tom's gear, that's my Tidewater idea of real high cotton." But Tad always refused to look at his own printed image. For a while, that big book was on absolutely everybody's end table.

Tad once confessed to me, while half tipsy, that he had—as an undergrad history major—overstepped traditional respectfulness at Monticello. He'd been helping to catalogue Jefferson's remaining clothes. "I knew that traces of his DNA (not to mention plain ole man-sweat) must still be soaked into one of those outsized white linen nightshirts he most wore when he was around 35, and incidentally writing the Declaration. So, one rainy afternoon, once all the nice docent ladies tripped upstairs for tea, I stayed on. First I sniffed Jefferson's white shirt. Eyes closed, I admitted I could smell mainly only basement—just time. So it was then, Mary Ellen, when I couldn't *scent* him, I decided I'd better *taste* it. Just to make sure. I soon pressed my li'l mouth to the underarm of that fine linen, and before you could say '1776,' I was just suckling like a kitten." He grew oddly bashful, he hushed. And that made me come right out and ask, "What did . . . ?" (I knew how far I'd come when I allowed myself to articulate this. . . . I feared I was about to learn more than someone of my age, upbringing, and conventional beliefs strictly needed to know. But I had asked, hadn't I?)

"What did it . . . he taste like? you were wondering aloud, were you, darlin' M.E.?" Tad actually made me nod then; nothing would do but that I become his Compleat Conspirator! Finally, a sly smile, and Tad's lips smacked, recalling. I saw a dreamy, lit-up carnal Cheshire-cat grin begin as our friend bent nearer my good ear. He whispered, "I'd say . . . the great one's flavor was funky if semi-steely—busy, a bit overly Scottish, but ver' ver' salty. Naturally athletic. All too mortal, all too real. I mean, of course, all too male. But mainly Jefferson tasted . . . mmm . . . preoccupied."

"You don't say," was the little I managed to remark.

Our five senses, I suppose, each practice a different sort of preservation. And I'd just met one novel way of gaining knowledge. My upright, innocent mother had once stated that she hoped her little Mary Ellen might "someday develop a taste for American history."

I had, literally. That Tad. Chewing Jefferson's laundry! Preservationists *are* literal. That's what makes them necessary. That's what lets them know so completely what they know. And once you know those things, ceremony or good manners cannot force you to unlearn them. I just mentioned my mother. She was born during Victoria's reign and a dearer if more orthodox lady you never met. She is long dead, Mother. But it just struck me that, were she to read what you've just done, her only child writing about one man gnawing on another man's article of clothing (most especially if the chewee proved to be Mr. Jefferson), well, Mother would quite simply have a small stroke, Mother would. And if she further understood I planned to let my written account "out of the house," placing it before the eyes of dozens, possibly even a few hundred, perfectly respectable people like yourself, Mother would then haul off and have herself a second, far more massive stroke. It would, in fact, have killed her, this. And yet I am doing it, aren't I? Because I was taught to. Because it feels right. I know what I know—now.

I later told a lifelong friend, a retired federal judge, about Tad's wonderful imagination in suckling the third president's shirt's armpits; and it was only upon seeing the dear gentleman's face go fairly haywire that I understood. Some lucky people keep growing, while others happily sign off early on doing that. I was, at 78, still having my assumptions enlarged. I can thank one young fellow for keeping me perpetually off-guard and, perhaps, occasionally, off-color. (Oh, but my dears, I wasted so much of my life being needlessly embarrassed!)

Tad dropped out of the Architectural School after an argument over period authenticity, and I am sure that he was right in both his scholarship and his assessment of his enemy's flawed character. He never shied away from the concept of a worthy opponent. He was a voluble "Yellow Dog Democrat"—which means that he'd have voted against a Republican even if a yellow dog—meaning some farm-dog of no distinction—were running as the Democrat. His politics lost us certain bigtime funders. "We don't want that kind of money, anyway. They're always expecting you'll let them throw their granddaughter's debut ball in the 18th-century Lutheran church they helped pay to save. I had a woman tell me she could just picture her little Courtney and Courtney's dad doing a waltz on the altar of a sanctified church; this dizzy dame would then have Courtney and her young marshal whisked away in a white carriage with matching white horses. Caterers there even for the horses. They've learned nothing from their lives." We've all heard his favorite toast, inherited from a late great-grandfather, Major A. B. Worth, who fought so gallantly in the War, "Confusion to the Enemy!"

When Tad got a grant from the state of North Carolina, an objection was made by an oldtime far-right-wing walleyed Senator who mentioned Tad by name, in Raleigh's *News and Observer,* as "a gay rights activist leeching taxes from the life's blood of decent normal family people." Tad had this letter framed, a central relic and badge of honor in his crowded fascinating basement "office."

His friend Patrick was, even more than some of us, changed by Tad's strong influence. Pat could calm him down as no one else could; and Pat's unbelievable know-how got us out of many a jam. Patrick Trevor winched our big cars out of many a horrid red-clay ditch. Pat's kindness shored up more than a few sagging roofs. There are contractors only interested in building new structures, and ones who're in love with saving old ones. We are lucky Pat belonged to the latter group. It was through helping Tad save the old Conger-Halsey Academy for Girls outside Rocky Mount that Patrick came to know him first. By the end, they'd become inseparable as foxhole survivors. But it did surprise us when they moved in together. (Pat said it shocked him too!) After Patrick left Carolyn, his wife, the gifted potter, once Pat started living with Tad, those three became models for us. Patrick's wife and Tad managed to remain close friends. I must say it really was sort of unbelievable to somebody of my years and expectations. Carolyn has worked wonders as our major brochure-designer and volunteer bookkeeper. Tad became the loving unofficial godfather to young Taylor, Pat and Carolyn's son. It was Taylor who spoke with such beautiful simplicity at the funeral service last month at All Saints' Episcopal. It was he who played a tearful yet perfect recorder solo that fairly well destroyed some of us. Young Master Taylor proved useful to us all at last Sunday's wrenching service. "Not a dry eye in the apse, hunh, kiddo?" as our Tad might have put it.

Maybe I should say, along with Tad's idol of a generalist, Mr. Jefferson, "If I'd had more time, I'd have written you a shorter letter." Like all of us who knew Tad Worth, I benefited from quite a good teacher. He was forever leaving me scraps of good things he'd come upon. I'd step out for my mail and find these slips of paper clothespinned to our battered box. There was never a signature, only very careful noting of where he'd discovered what. I put them up on our household altar of the present day, the refrigerator door.

I quote just one, the most recent. He must've sent it over via Patrick because Tad was by then too weak for walking, even the short distance from his place to mine. The passage is out of Rilke's *Notebooks of Malte Laurids Brigge* and serves as epigraph to a book of photographs Tad loved, the book showing one beautiful decrepit Georgian house in the Irish countryside.

"It isn't a complete building; it has been broken into pieces inside me; a room there, and then a piece of a hallway that doesn't connect these two rooms, but is preserved as a fragment, by itself. In this way, it is all dispersed inside me—the rooms, the staircases that descend so gracefully and ceremoniously, and other narrow, spiral stairs, where you moved through the darkness as blood moves in the veins. . . . All this is still inside me and will never cease to be there. It is as if the image of this house had fallen into me from an infinite height and shattered upon my ground."

III.

This is the story I've been getting to.

Once, not that many months ago, though it seems about half a decade, Tad urgently summoned our little architecture-discussion group to gather quickly. We had to meet him at Shadowlawn on the coast. This meant a three-and-a-half-hour drive. He called from the pay phone down there, insisting he needed us there and today, and he knew it was very short notice, but that we must arrive by a certain time of evening. To the minute, we must be there.

Well, we're all very busy people—self-defensively so, I sometimes think—but he rarely gave us any direct orders. Tad never actually asked much of anything for himself. He let you offer whatever you felt able to provide the Cause. He had 40 immensely capable but very different major people doing this, which is why our organization has been, I believe, in the end, so successful. Tad Worth didn't just praise the idea of the individual contribution and then get quickly bureaucratic and lord it over us minions from his too-new mahogany desk in some high-rent headquarters. The power was always out there in the community. As our lieutenant governor said at Tad's funeral (in a short but fine address), "Education was behind it all." We'd been schooled by him, our eyes had. (And as Tad said, "Once your eyes know, the heart follows. It's a matter of zoning.") But, oddly, Lt. Gov. Whitt Coventry might have been speaking of Tad's own far-ranging education. His pickup truck was a bookmobile. He read at red lights. Tad taught us by always teaching himself to keep learning. Then we personally applied the lesson.

So we said, "It must be important if he insists that we turn up by six-oh-seven sharp." I do think that was the actual time, 6:07. He was on the drug AZT by then (now proved, as some of us suspected, to do more harm than good). Tad's T-cell count was at its lowest so far. (Though back in those earliest days we didn't know what low meant.)

He'd finally got hold of one of our state's most beautiful of domestic masterpieces. The message he left on my answering machine was just, "Girlfriend? Shadowlawn—home-free!" Tad only got it after years of honest legal chess and much backgammon dishonestly inept.

Having got his hands at last on Shadowlawn, he wanted to spend his own last energies restoring this house of houses. He wanted to live right there on the coast, alone in the big house. It was still an absolute wreck at the time (this was March). I insisted he stay at a motel nearby. I set up an account by phone with them, I made them call me when he didn't turn up for a night. Patrick would spend every weekend down there with him, chipping paint and hauling things. But, like most people, Pat had part-time child custody and a regular day job that kept him inland during the week. We all worried not just about Tad's diminishing health but about his falling in a house that'd never had a phone. But Tad was like that, when he'd finally acquired a property, this one especially. He felt exempt from harm once he was on the grounds, once Tad knew the acreage had finally been saved. There had been vandals swarming all through Shadowlawn for years, and to imagine him in that barn of a place, with its exterior doors too weather-bowed to lock, all alone there on a cot! Circa would be his only guardian, a bit lowslung if snippish. And by then Tad was not so strong as he thought. As he pretended.

It's odd, in thinking back: He was very cautious about getting from historic property to property, an almost recklessly safe driver. Bad at it, but at least aware of that. "Better he shouldn't know he's such a menace on the highway," as our dear friend Mimi Goldberg might say—"The Divine Miss Mimi," as Tad called her. But, once there, on the saved sites, Tad acted fearless. He'd go crawling under houses or clambering straight up on the roof beams, and then somebody had to run get the ladders again to help lead him down. And with a drink, as reward.

I rode to the coast with our hurriedly assembled group in somebody's Volvo wagon. I think it was Mimi's car, because there were several thermoses of libation, as I recall. The Reverend Sapp had brought one of his famous goose pâtés. I confess to feeling scared that Tad had hurt himself, that he'd half-slid into delusions thanks to all the toxic contradictory medicines they had him on. I'd let my husband go to the coast unsupervised, and I vowed none of that would happen again.

Well, we arrived down there quite close to the assigned hour. The place looks extremely presentable now, thanks to Tad's day labor and many volunteer Saturdays by a devoted core "salvation" group down Edenton way. The approach to the plantation house had been slyly planned in 1810. A good idea has simply got better. You follow twin rows of now-enormous magnolias interspersed with apple trees, long since past their bearing years. And when you make the turn, you see the Federal house, a white Greek temple built to some goddess or no, more surprising, like the severe young goddess herself, upright as a dare against the bright-green water of the Albemarle Sound, and you literally gasp. Despite the leaks and years and teenaged pyromaniacs, "It is," Tad would say of the columned place, "like some old lady come into a party, and who can still make a hell of an entrance. Even on two canes."

Still, at the time I am discussing, Shadowlawn's Doric plantation house was as yet a firetrap and a total mess. Only somebody with a certain amount of nerve would attempt to even set foot inside the big house, much less sleep there. Every fourth floorboard was spongy with "blue-chip greenies" and you'd fall right through. Vandals had seen fit to build fires in the middle of 14-inch-planked heart-pine floors. They didn't use the fireplaces. These, weirdly enough, proved perfectly functional when somebody (Tad, I think) finally thought to try them. Day-Glo swastikas disfigured the walls up and down the spiral staircase, whatever of its handturned balusters had not been burned to make the mid-floor bonfires.

Skulls and hate-crime obscenities were painted on the walls, misspelled. These racial cursewords looked pornographic in rooms so graceful and, in many ways, despite their age, as yet so innocent.

It's awful how a beautiful old house, abandoned, draws to itself the worst element, Satanists and Hell's Angels, drifters and the Klan. It becomes a blank screen onto which such riffraff projects the world's wickedest emotions. Saving such a house means calling back the world's best again, to balance out such awful ugliness. I am told that the word "Religion" means to physically literally "bind up again," to repair something pre-existing. And in our modern world, even with so darn much "available for restoration," the rejuvenation of a fallen temple is, quite literally, a mission doubly religious. I know that now.

I remember Tad greeting us from the portico, waving, cutting up, calling "a big Hi Hi Hi!" As we walked nearer, we saw he was smiling and looked absolutely filthy. Tad was happiest dirtiest. He was, I can say, the least claustrophobic person I have ever met in my life, and the cellars and crawlspaces he jumped right into, those make me . . . well, I started to say, make me feel that he's safer, wherever he's got off to. Basement-wise, underground-wise. There. I will stop all that. He would scold me terribly for that. He loved true feeling, but hated sentiment—except in Grand Opera, Mad Ludwig's castles, or in '50s melodramas (Susan Hayward's electric-chair weeper, *I Want To Live!*, was ofttimes quoted).

He stood there filthy, with green mold on one cheek and smiling, looking even thinner than 10 days ago. But absolutely beaming.

"What've you found?" somebody asked. Then Circa came charging us, growling, protecting him. She went for the Reverend Sapp's ankle. He kicked her a pretty good one. Tad had told us that any self-defense must be judged legal around Circa's testiness. I can show you marks on my left ankle that prove how often Liberalism fails.

It was Tad Worth himself, contrary to what he told the papers, who turned up the heavy silver service for 60 buried behind the collapsed well-housing at Pilgrim's Respite, out past Belhaven. It was the sale of those 30-pound silver punch-bowls, shaped like a group of plunging dolphins reined and ridden by putti, that helped us fund most of our restoration of the grounds there. We assumed he'd come across some major booty here, too.

So Tad now crooked his finger at us, led us around toward the back of the Big House. I remember how he idly touched one side of a massive column, he acted like someone taking an inventory of its crackled fluted surface. I knew he did this for support, I knew by now the house was there to keep Tad standing. I remember the way a few of his oldest friends looked at each other, immediately recognizing his greater frailty, but doing so behind him, saving face. This was in early March, I'm sure now, because some of those immense forsythia bushes nearest the Sound were just popping out their first brave yellow. The whole mansion smelled of wood rot, a scent we have all learned to recognize and loathe. (Just as new-cut lumber, especially cypress and cedar, now outranks yours truly's old standby Shalimar as my new all-time favorite scent!) Tad, thinned to looking somewhat perfect if pale, had lost his stalwart outline. He was becoming honeycomb-candlewax, translucent.

He now stationed himself in the crook of Shadowlawn's major chimney. It stands fully three stories tall (three if you count the overseer's parapet). Its outer brick is inset with pale oyster shells that form the founding family's initials a yard high and all vined together with Chippendale high spirits. As usual, Tad wore on his belt a ring clinching three full pounds of keys—old pirate-sized skeleton ones fitted to many of the good 18th-century homes surviving along our Carolina coast. Though the day was chill, Tad leaned there without a sweater in this brick-heated little natural alcove. I think there were two large English boxwoods screening and enclosing half of it, making it seem even more a secret resting place. The sort of place that children find and love and where they hide first. The crenellated chimney's orangish bricks (said to be ballast from an English ship, the *Plentitude*) retained warmth from whatever sun there'd been that day.

"I want us to have a little seminar, my folks. About occupants of historic homes. The people that get left behind . . ." We had already talked at length about which kind of independently wealthy, professional, and very rare young couples are likely to put up with the headaches of dripping roofs, custom-cut joists, and 1790s termite damage, with tourists knocking on their doors and grad students announcing they did a dissertation concerning your stairwell and so must be let in. I believed that by saying "the people that get left behind" Tad meant such potential buyers for Shadowlawn.

"I've held off doing this till you-all got your dear carcasses on down here. Can't start to hint how ver' much I 'preciate you-all's coming so dog-gone fast." Then Tad pulled from the torn back pocket of his spill-art chinos a favorite Smith and Hawken trowel. He kissed its blade, as if for luck. Next, in this little spot of late light filtered and glimmering across the inlet, Tad bent painfully down. It was like watching someone 80, 85. But once on all fours, he starting digging as if he were about eight, and possessed.

Circa soon got into the act, scratchy and snappish. She tried to claw the dirt right alongside his. Defending him, the dog acted jealous for all Tad's attention. I guess each of us wanted that. Come to think of it, so did all "his" houses. They were competitive for Tad's fullest energies, ready to monopolize his talent. And the mansions used opera divas' pet tricks: when Tad spent too much time with one grande dame, the others had breakdowns, sprung leaks, threw material tantrums. Possessive, the great homes. "They're childlike as brilliant singers are," he once told us, "that are pitifully in need of our constant reassurance. You'd think that, the greater the voice, the less hand-holding they'd require. But *au contraire.* Never get enough, these ole gals—coquettes, geniuses."

If we'd been watching anybody but Tad, we might have asked why this fellow had dragged us down here on a weekday afternoon, a three-and-a-half-or-four-hour drive one way, and just to study him scooting around in clay for some stray tulip bulb or minié ball or something. It certainly took him quite a while, hacking down there. It did seem maybe . . . delusional, this digging. Skinny as he'd got, I found it hard to watch him strain. Even his back looked narrower, which made the shoulder blades poke out like starter kits for wings. His dog was going even crazier than usual, poor overbred creature. She behaved as if he were about to uncover some dinosaur egg in the act of hatching. He laughed over at her: "Good Circa. I know, I know. You smell them, right?" I remember watching perspiration darken the back of his blue shirt. Digging this hard had used up about one full week of Tad's waning energy. But we would not have dreamed of saying, "Here, let me." Still, the long wait was almost dentally painful.

About the time that even we, of his faithful inner cadre, were starting to picture the remaining half-full thermos, the Saran Wrapped pâté in Mimi's old wagon, Tad's blade struck something stone or metal. He shouted, "They're right. I knew. They never have lied to me."

We stepped closer, we saw he'd dug a trench about a foot or 18 inches deep, cut right up against the foundation's powdery brick footing. By laboriously leaning on the chimney, Tad finally stood. I worried, I saw that he was light-headed, rising too fast, and him embattled by so many competing primitive drugs. You learn to hate these stopgap "cures" as much as you respectfully despise the gin-clear anti-preservationist disease itself.

From the hole, our Tad lifted a dark tin box with a latch on it, two feet long, filthy it was; he dragged it free of pinkish tree-roots and up into sight. Grinning, he held it off to one side the way my husband displayed the fish he'd caught, as if to use his own body as a yardstick, scale of reference. Once Tad had tugged the thing to better light, he flopped down beside it, panting with transparent pleasure and exhaustion. I remember the look of his long hand touching the tin. How blue-veined and aristocratic his wasting hand looked, stroking the black prize. All of us, no matter how old and creaky we were (chronologically in most of our cases), managed to drop right onto the grass in a rough circle close up around and against him. His hands shook so, prying it open. Somebody finally tried helping, but Tad, uncharacteristic, snapped "No!"—setting Circa off. And we all grew more still, more withdrawn, afraid to even glance at one another. I can't explain the tension. Expectation mixed with social embarrassment. Dread, and something a bit ghoulish, this caffeinated kind of curiosity.

Once opened, the tin casket proved stuffed with what'd been yellow straw, but a very long time back. Then some cloth, homespun, even I could tell that (I, who seem to have no knack for historical fabrics—one of my own sundry blind spots). It was sewn into a cloth valise, joined shut with big childlike stitches, faded red thread. This packet had then been sealed, crusted over, with what appeared to be about 20 candles' worth of wax. The Reverend Sapp, who claimed some archeological experience in the Middle East from his Virginia Episcopal Seminary days, frowned a bit at Tad's utter lack of methodical scientific technique. Tad was ripping into this item like some Christmas present meant only for himself. But that didn't bother me one bit. None of us ever found the objects he did. Hadn't we piled into the car to come and see exactly this, this thingum, whatever it was?

I knew how sick he already was (though he could still hide it cleverly well). I knew how much work he felt he must do down here. (Some of us would later labor alongside him here, at Shadowlawn, as he scraped 90 years of varnish off the carved ivy paneling he'd found under beaverboard upstairs. By then Tad worked while hooked to his IV pole on a rolling tripod. He wore an oxygen tank, clear tubes in his nose. "Lorgnettes for nostrils," Tad called these tubes, with a whimsy that came to seem more and more courageous—more of a buttress, somehow more "architectural"—as we watched him all but evaporate before our eyes. He was doing restoration "against doctors' orders." Somebody'd made a joke of the IV pole by taping cardboard Chippendale claw-and-ball feet onto its tripod castor legs. By then, we understood a thing or two about Tad's glorying enslavement to the work of "binding up again," his will day by day to make this last house perfect.)

But that early evening, with us bunched all around him, as he tore open the shroud cloth, Tad gave off a little howl. It's that I remember best. Every quality we loved in him was in that sound. It was a kid's Cowboy-and-Indian war whoop but contained his knack that managed, in the worst of circumstances, to find something funny and pleasurable waiting. It's the quality that let him proselytize so effectively for our cause; he showed people the pleasure of old houses, the pleasure of letting the places yield up their separate secrets to you. Allowing them to confide in you as you, trusting, dwelt in them. One revealed detail at a time. As your human friends will allow—"Oh, and did I ever mention how, once, here . . . ?" People were soon hooked, they became addicted to old houses. He was actually a sort of marriage broker. And people thanked our Tad Worth here, for hooking them to the place whose lies, pretensions, secrets, whose own looks best matched theirs.

From the box he lifted two joined dolls. One was a dark wooden effigy, almost a totem. It was obviously home-carved, maybe 10 inches long. The other had a porcelain head, a stuffed bodice, two simplified bisque hands attached to cloth-tube arms. Sawdust was sifting from her torso at the narrow waist. She had hair painted in a buttermilky brown and with delft blue eyes, and you didn't need carbon dating to know the thing was 18th-century. Oddly enough, the arms of this porcelain doll were literally wired around the black carved wooden figure. That one's hair was, or had been, knotted rope. If the porcelain doll was obviously English, the gumwood one was African or African-inspired in its angularity. But however stylized, it seemed strangely more human than the costly porcelain one. The dark form's only facial features were two red bone buttons set deep into wood, representing her eyes. This wooden one's arms had also been rope, square-knotted at their ends to signify hands. Both rope arms were trussed around the bodice of the porcelain doll. Embracing, the pair had stayed bound to each other, face to face, further joined by loops of circling wire long since rusted red-brown and staining the yellowed muslin.

Tad held up the clinging two of them, a unit. We considered this fused team from all angles. Circa kept snarling, competitive-sounding, guarding, in the quince. Of course we looked from the effigies back up to Tad's face. Ready to be told what they meant. We were always expecting it from him, and Tad certainly usually gave at least an educated guess. Sometimes his intuitive faking turned out to be truer than the gathered experts' mustiest certainty. His going directly to that silver, buried by the stone wellhousing out back of Pilgrim's Respite, is but one profitable example among dozens, hundreds.

I saw he had done right, to get us here just at dusk. Since all this happened on the westerly facing of the Shadowlawn plantation house, the sun gave off this wintry red but full of gold. The light had moved far higher up the chimneys. Our being so in blue shadow made us feel a little underwater and unreal here, squatting on the ground. The inlet's reflection threw moving highlight lines, wavering across the uncertain faces of our little group. I remember looking hard at Tad and he gave me this open stare that was confused and awed yet pleased at once. I could see his cheekbone's sweeping edge, so suddenly elegant you knew it would be terminal.

I worried he had been feverish down here and without phoning me or telling any of us, sick in that grim little motel he enjoyed "because it looks like the one in *Pscyho*" and had a blue neon star blinking out in front. But before he explained this twin effigy, I guessed he'd first have to say something silly, wry or indirect, the way he did. "I know you've got a toddy or two hidden out in Mimi's car, and I can't believe you've made me get down on my dingy knees and fetch this thang up and that I still have to beg you all for one li'l ole drink." Somebody ran for the thermos, and I mean they ran. Because we were waiting. We sensed it, you see. We already did.

He started crying then. Or laughing. I think it was the only time I'd ever seen Tad Worth actually shaking with emotion—though his eyes were forever tearing up over seemingly small things. He leaned against the Flemish-bond brick chimney, he touched the shell initials of the founders. It was odd to find him, of all people, abruptly speechless.

Usually, talking off the cuff, Tad could populate any front porch's

Windsor chairs, could describe the familiar (if long-dead) occupants right into them. Call it fund-raising via hackle-raising. At some meeting, he'd say, "Imagine it's the notoriously cool summer of 1840, no birdsong, the doomed young consumptive Annabella Cameron's journal noted . . ." and you'd see the most hardhearted of city managers gaze back, eyes narrowed, as if resisting a sudden interior draft, necks stiffening, a bit defiant and even furious, but already cooperating despite themselves.

"Well, what?" I asked him. We were seated scattered all around him and somebody touched his shoulder, and he was smiling but with eyes running water. I had hoped that the disease would spare him possible blindness. I'd read everything on the subject. I knew that—for Tad—Blindness would be just one zoning district shy of Death. The smell, that close to the dirt in March, spoke about our many chances at finally thawing out; and with spring rushing in from the inlet and up from underground, we waited there. We sat in the sad smoky smell of the beautiful crumbling house.

"About 6:07 yesterday," Tad said, "I saw the girls who buried this," he looked from face to trusted face. We glanced at one another. Faux-casual. First it seemed he meant that some local children had dug this box up and then maybe they'd reburied it, maybe he had caught them. But the dirt he'd been hacking at was good packed red clay, weather-baked nearly bricklike on the surface and, it seemed, unbroken for centuries. Reverend Sapp now scurried back with martinis sloshing in a red thermos lid. He had brought one of the leaded crystal tumblers we unregenerate drinkers travel with (a bit ostentatiously) and that we sometimes broke. Rev. Sapp said, "What?" like some kid who hates missing something by going for refreshments and is bitter at seeing how just that has happened. We shook our heads to show we didn't know, not yet.

Tad downed his drink all at once and choked, then laughed at doing so, which helped. He said for the record that he had been stooping, right over there, not four feet off, at the corner of the portico the afternoon before. It had been exactly this time of day, with light reflected from the Sound moving curved lines across the brick, much as it did now. Tad said he had been cleaning out some of the giant honeysuckle that'd claimed the lattice lathing under the broad front porch. There was a clump of mint (for juleps), and he was doing battle with honeysuckle vines in hopes of saving the mint, "which I admit has held its own since 1810 but it's never too late to give a thing a break finally, right?" He said he heard a chiming knock, like some shovel striking the chimney, just three times.

"I was squatting over yonder, there, just there near Circa's quince. —Hush, darling, please do hush, now, girl— and, you know me, as usual, sweating like a pig. And when I wiped my forehead with the back of my hand and looked toward the Sound—and when I took my hand down?— I saw two little girls. They were charming, one black, one white. About 8 to 10 years old. They were holding on to one another, standing there and just facing me, looking me over. They had an expression that seemed to hint as how I was the one out of place, and they—of all the people on the farm—were at least glad to be the first to notice me. I said something like 'Hi,' something witty like 'Hi,' right? At first they only stared at me, each keeping very very still. But extremely there, you know, and conscious and seeming amused that I was such a mess and down on my knees. They both seemed to be wondering what was I doing on their farm. I could see plainly enough that the white girl had light-brown hair chopped off just at the shoulders and was in a sort of gingham dress, checked, brown and red, floor-length, ground-length out here, but it could've been some '6os hippie-child's 'granny dress.' And the black girl—blue-black African black—wore a homespun almost burlappy thing, very simple, with long sleeves and a boatneck, and she had pierced ears with small star-shaped pewter bits—pewter, I was sure of it—pewter stars in her ears. For some reason, that seemed a tip-off, like, you know, 'pewter,' tin mixed with lead, antique, get it? But, no, I was just as dumb as before. They were standing there, arm in arm and not quite smiling but very pleased-looking, very much together, as if about to laugh but scared to hurt my feelings. Behaving as if—how to explain this?—as if there were many other people all over the plantation, working the place, and like they had strolled off into one quiet corner—a favorite place, I felt—for a nice moment alone together and instead had found me. (I sensed how crowded the farm really was, busy and productive but sort of hostile to children; something in their sense of secrecy, the bond between them, suggested that.) And it was only then I noticed they were pointing down, they both were. Toward the same spot. I just hadn't seen that, not at first. Or maybe when they guessed they could trust me they indicated the one spot. I was here by myself, Circa excepted. I mean, the volunteers had left about 4:30, and I was just doing a few last clean-up chores. Needed a quick nap on the cot in the foyer. Then, and only then—and by the way, all this is just taking maybe just, oh, 8 to

12 seconds, this whole loaded glance—very quick, very matter-of-fact—it was only then I noticed the texture of the bricks behind them, and only then, like a dolt, does it occur to me that I can see the goddamn bricks, like THROUGH them, right? Well, here's the really dopey part, I smile at them, as if they live here, as if I'm the slave gardener and I know so, and yet to prove I also have a reason for being here too, right? I go back to the vine I've been yanking on, and I actually lift my gigantic vat of RoundUp I've been spraying at the honeysuckle, like I'm bored, like I'm just going on with my work, and only then, having turned my entire back on them, do I do this incredible Three Stooges eye-popping double take. 'Boing,' hair up—eyes out to here—and of course they're gone.

"You know the phrase 'disappeared into thin air'? Well, that's what I had seen happen. I'd never felt that term meant much—isn't all air thin? Well, air so recently evacuated does, believe me, feel damn 'thin.' Who says air can nevah be too rich or too thin, hunh? But I kept thinking 'thin air,' 'thin,' like snatching at that phrase, because I so wanted to touch them, to hold on to them. Mainly to ask them things. I didn't run to phone anybody, didn't tell a soul. Not at first. Didn't even ring Patrick—I mean nobody. And then, about two o'clock this morning, at the Norman Bates motel, I wake and sit up and say aloud, setting poor Circa to barking, 'They buried something. They were burying something. And I caught them at it and so then, they went ahead and showed me where they'd hidden it.' I was that sure of it, I called you up.

"Now you're all here, and here is this cask, these doll things. I mean, I wanted you to see the progress on the house generally. But I felt I had to have my sanctum-sanctorum nearest-dearests here for this. I figured that if I didn't hit anything, I would stop digging, as if suddenly even more than usually absentminded lately—then I'd maybe stand up and just show you the handpainted horse-and-river French mural paper we're beginning to uncover in the foyer, and then I'd take you all to the Fish House over near Edenton for dinner, but I'd not say nothin' and jes' keep rollin' along. But to find these things, the one a slave toy and the other something porcelain and plainly English import . . . I believe it was a pact between them, the girls, to go ahead and wire their arms around each other, the dolls. Like they knew their friendship couldn't stand whatever tests were coming—a salable slave child and the owner's daughter, or the overseer's—but to plant these here. As a sign, near the house, a sign they loved each other. To show they knew that, and to save it some."

.   .   .

By now the light was mostly gone. Only the tips of the four chimneys held a charged kind of sandpapery red, like the heads of matches. The shadow where we stooped felt privileged but too permanent. It'd got some colder. We could see the scallop boats, their lights blinking way out there, coming home, nets hoisted after the long day's catch. Two bats kept diving near the house. And Tad lifted his effigies, Tad moved to pass these into the hands of the person nearest him, everything—that tin box, the wax-sealed bag, and those odd dolls—still bound together. . . . He handed it to somebody, who instinctively drew back, acting almost comically repulsed. She—actually, it was I, alas—pulled away as if fearing that this thing had come direct and scalding from some infernal oven. Would it burn, or freeze? Maybe it was how quick and saturated the darkness had become. I felt he was placing some image of himself dead into hands not willing to accept that, not yet. (Still not.) I steeled myself . . . hating this squeamish-ness which seemed so unlike me, at least the "me" I could admire even a bit. But then Mimi, God love her, laughed and said, "What is this, hoodoo voodoo? Gi' me it!" and reached past me, grabbed the thing. Out of order. Then we each took hold of his find, all of us, me going right after Mimi. I think it was something about my husband's death, and being so near the water. Made me hesitate, then feel that I had let Tad down. I felt like Saint Peter, denying on the crucial night. It's odd, but we all held on to the dolls, and even the box, and for quite a while. As if greeting them, a cordial welcome, to aboveground. It seemed we'd expected the dolls to melt into the same thin air where the girls had gone. We expected the dolls to melt when they left Tad's hands as he tried to fit them into ours. We knew then, that "thin air" was already welcoming him. But the object(s) remained, solid, like his legacy—like Tad himself till then—so reassur-ingly material. These figures had lasted the way inanimate things get to (lucky for us, as compass points and referents). Lord knows, we don't.

Then our group drove over to Edenton for shrimp and oysters and scal-lops which were excellent and right off the boat, everything's so fresh down there. At dinner, no one really mentioned what he'd dug up. I remember how quiet was the long car ride home without Tad. I begged him to come back home to Hillsborough just for tonight. He'd have none of it, of course. On the long trip back, it wasn't so much that we were spooked . . . though we were, and in some new way. I'd always felt a little scared for him—bodily, I mean. Worried for his fragile bones, a fall, things like that. Now something else took over.

I'd heard him joke about certain young lady ghosts that lived around/inside the stone privy yet standing at an old girls' academy, The Burwell School, right in Hillsborough. "The Haunted Outhouse," Tad called it. I asked him what it felt like, his freely moving around this particular ghost-nest; his knowing that they knew that he was there, observing, enjoying. "Oh, M.E., I'd say like 'walking through a rain of talcum powder too fine to notice but it still gets your hair feeling whitish and you can sort of smell it, dusty humany basementish almost rose-smellin' sorta"; but he grinned as if only teasing. Even so, it stopped me, how certainly (I mean how lightly) he'd said all that.

In the car, I sat shoulder to shoulder with my friends riding west. I recalled his "They never have lied to me."

Well, you need not be Sherlock to deduce as how this means a critical mass of earlier sightings, or promptings, promises. In the car bound home, I think we kept so hushed and a little glum, because we knew—if we hadn't before—who he was. We knew that Tad wouldn't make up such things—he'd never, ever lied to me, or to anybody, except out of white-lie kindness, or during something like losing at backgammon for Preservation's sake. I chastised myself for that three-second delay in taking what he'd handed me first. But, even so, we all suddenly unwillingly knew he was going to die. Soon. Somehow his seeing the occupants of this last great house he'd saved showed us just how soon (four weeks). He'd made us start to see the bricks through him. Come to think of it, we'd always seen the bricks through Tad!

Tad's mission (and I can use that word in good conscience here) was about so much more than just saving certain pretentious properties for a few more generations of socially ambitious Carolinians who could afford to replace octagonal slate roofing tiles that can cost, as we all know, up to $69 per. The houses *whom* he'd saved were suddenly extravagantly giving groundbreaking housewarming gifts back to him. Presents from Presences! Farewells. They meant, "Well done, thou good and faithful servant."

That's just one story about him. But it's the one that came to me. I know there are people in historic preservation who are only interested in the architecture, in the pediments, the lemon-oiled perfectible period detail. I fear I've met a few. I fear I myself have been wedged into more than a few mullioned window seats with Laura Ashley floral prints and

peppermint-stripe piping on the cushions under my increasingly historical whatever (and there till after 2 a.m.). These experts consider the people who actually live (or lived) in these fine places as something like the
furniture—you maybe need them there to make the house seem finished,
but they're incidental to the structure's superior claims. With Tad, the living, the livingness of the place and what went on there and what might go
on there next, that was the definition of his passion, boxwood by old rose,
slate by slate, mantel to passing mantel.

   Then Tad died. At noon, March 31, Patrick left a message on my
machine; he said that during the night, Tad had typed in caps in his computer notebook, HERE GOES. Pat suggested maybe I should get to the
hospital? "It's started," Tad told me in his quiet way. By the time I found
the message and rushed in there, it was almost over, and I held one hand
and Patrick was on the other, as at some birth. He was spared nothing,
Tad, but he presided over it, "inhabited" his dying. Our boy half-hosted it
as he'd done everything else. With one of his final breaths—by then far
past language, which had been a great ally of his—he blew sort of a kiss.
   Patrick Trevor—after contacting Tad's parents (who were, for various
reasons, unable to be with him at the end), Pat, after signing the coroner's
papers, after speaking to doctors and nurses and the many close friends
who'd gathered—bent toward Tad's computer. (It was still glowing in one
corner of the unlit room.) At 1:04 a.m., Patrick withdrew the disk containing Tad's final "Available for Restoration." I had agreed to take over this
newsletter, so Pat handed the disk to me.
   Back home, and right after the funeral, soon as I saw the pages printed
out, I understood that, despite Tad's determination to finish Issue # 14,
despite Tad's victory in staying one room ahead of the dementia, certain
lapses had occurred. Confusions about sequence and details beset him at
the end. Because of a final throat infection, Tad was sometimes unable to
speak ("the worst indignity, damnit"); so he'd commenced typing notes to
Pat and others, using the screen of his Toshiba Notebook. These were
interspersed with hard-sell raves about some condemned home's architectural niceties. The computer's amber screen was often his hospital room's
only night light.
   Tad's notes and personal asides found their way into what, without such
personal interjections, might have been a more official, if less original, text.

With Patrick's permission and after my having misgivings about it, I want to offer a sample of this final document. I do this, being sure that Tad Worth, always able to see beauty latent under surface rust and seeming ruin, would approve.

In the final hospital stay, during his clear early weeks, Tad wrote the portrait of Elkton Green with which this issue started. (Despite his, I thought, irresistible come-on, we lost that great house to the insatiable yellow bulldozers.)

After describing Elkton Green so well, after thinking his portrait had sold the house, if now unable to talk effectively, Tad still tried to interest some new buyer in Shadowlawn, too. He would work on this document during his stray good 10-minute patches. By then the plantation house had been largely restored by Tad and the crew. And I'm glad to say that we have now sold Shadowlawn to Pam and Joseph Wainwright, who know exactly what they have and are willing to do whatever's required to pull it back from the edge. So, Tad, it is saved.

This, the end of his Shadowlawn entry, was the last thing he typed. Of all his final ramblings, it's what I choose to print:

The carriage house retains its frilled facing and a small family chapel, close by the water, still have traces of an ebonized Maltese cross atop its modified cupula. . . . The records show that slave and master worshiped here as one and

Needs further expertise regarding modern plumbing. Still suitable fr. occupancy. Somebody is out there, sure of that . . . needs.

New systems required throughout, oh true . . . By now there are hookups for natural gas heat and air, the evenings expecially, and the sense of others who've been near and can be . . . Mint, mention mint. . . .

About how close to water, mention. Noble approach, mention noble approach, and English boxes. Many, big as Pluto, planet Pluto, not dog. Joke. How the fires could have been set in middle of floors don't know, we found the fireplaces to still draw perfectly perhaps a hundered years since fullest use, birds nests and old squirrels nests went up like tinders but the thrill to run outdoors at night and see smoke coming curling, like a thing relearning to breathe really, most beautiful though feared for stray sparks, must get screens, Pat. . . .

Pat, hi, will leave the machine on . . . rougher today

. . . if miss you, sorry. Must sleep more, The shakes bigtime. Drench-ola. Tell Taylor hi, and to practice. Any word from parents? Pain is bracketed now. One does not love a place less for having suffered in it, right? Rite? How can I sleep when nurses keep comin in waking me & waking me? Their good cheer wears one dow . . . Extensive remodel needed. Priotico nearly complete. Big family could be so happy there, house has many treasure to yeield. Fish from dock. Smoke house sutible guesshouse, aroma mild but pleasant,. can be shown daily, key at store . . . house dedc to comfort, Mint nearby mention drinks . . . The parlor facing south, original glass throws shapes thoughtful human on wall and mofvews . . . tireder, language going, structre goiim ssNcup[e Confusion to the emeynes-Needs work but for immediate occupancy . . . . . . Keep thinking we didn't pay phonebill again. Is it on? A life spent in non-profit okay! Confusion, the enemy. Hi hon, wkae me anyway? What the name the scrolling at corners, supports? Begins w.C. Look up later. My books. Around here somewhere. The right book. Find what type spiders web would best take gold dust? Dr Fscher glmmy. Last rose summer, pure gloss? Miss you, will

Sq ft: 6,8888844 ik rooms, zned for living . . . . . Where is my father and where is my m . . . Aint no sech thang as bluechipgreenies—its all just greenies . . . , Patrick Patrick why you so kind me? !Boy, talk about AVAIL For resoration! loans availbe, save this one pls. . . . Any word yet? Circa exema ok? Somthng nr chimney esp. signs & wondrs W aake me anyway ok? have M.E. correct this, fake it, will make press time, fine, sure. . . . I hear water. There's a bad break, leak, flor below, chk on rushing water damage close;;;I see certai of Its columns, all Ionic! I knew that. So Dry mouth./ Most of this must go but which of these is the bearing wall? Pme jakbaa

777kkkkkkkkkkkkkkkkkkkkkkkk66#33 can restore to suit any new owner. Fix. I know you out there.

I buried something. They dug it up for me.

Am mostly beyond all tired. mst. ctch winx . . . Treated 2x6s^^I"Smokehouse roof leaki. Fix first. Alwys fix roof first, I keep . . . I forget. All keys, hall drwer.

hi
HERE GOES

IV.

I end by remembering a meal we had together. (One thing I must blame him for is how readily he knocked me off my diet. He'd show up with two bags of stray ingredients from Wellspring Market in Chapel Hill, asking, "But whatever shall we DO with all these perishables? As Marse Wilde said, 'Simple pleasures are the last refuge for the complex.' ")

We were seated at my back table, finishing some raw oysters. This was when you could still eat those raw without worrying so. We'd only just acquired Shadowlawn, work had just started. But already, when he got up to fetch something, Tad was forced to reach out for the counter to support himself. Of course, he made it look quite natural, you know. Regal. Like, oh, he was solemnly recalling something.

Tad had been worrying over some legal issue involving right of way, easement to the entrance of the Shadowlawn big house, and he was frustrated and weak, a combination new to him. He said, "I really don't know nothin' 'bout rebirthin' no houses, Mizz Scarlett." He stopped, head dropping and knuckles going white along my counter's ledge. I'd never seen him conventionally depressed before. Then I understood just how enraged he was at all the details, all the work left undone, and with only us amateurs trying to fake it in our way. However earnest, we all lacked his genius for vamping, guessing, making it LOOK right and therefore FEEL right, in that order of zoning.

"I know it must be frustrating," I said, clumsy but well meaning. "And yet, do think of everything you've saved, 56 or '7 masterpieces that were headed only for the wrecking ball. Tad, do remember what-all you have achieved, m'dear." "Well, it's true we've set aside a single-family dwelling or two. But that's such a fraction. Of what's lost, M.E. Plus, I is so tired of keeping house, keeping on keeping on sweeping them flo's. Turns out, I do do windows after all."

"You are a window, honey." I was about to get started. "You are a window in a door." But he stopped me from saying something even more sappy and far too comforting. Too easy, I mean.

Then he pointed out the kitchen window toward his truck. Circa, yappy, was guarding it. I saw all these clothes piled up in the back. "Everything I've never been able to fit into, till today. And I feel some runway turns coming on. Point me toward your nearest changing room, *per favore,* Coco?"

Tad had brought everything he'd ever purchased just in case he ever lost the weight. Today and today precisely, he'd got down to the very size he'd always imagined being (is this too much? He always told me there was no such thing as too much entertaining truth). He carried many armsful into my front parlor. I set up a chair in the foyer, between those big flanking Victorian pier glasses, 15 feet of beveled mirrors admiring mostly each other. I built a fire in either adjoining parlor, I put on a stack of Bix and Billie and turned them way up. I even let poor Circa in, despite the half-idolatrous way I love my rugs. Needless to say, we treated ourselves to a few stiff drinks. Then he came out in one ensemble after another. First it was very funny, then it got unbearable, finally so sad it turned hilarious. He was no stranger to overdoing, as he'd told me that first day.

Tad wore every outfit, in high dudgeon with that comic-brave business he did so much during the last four years (a little *Dark Victory* in there, as he admitted). Tad staged the privatest of fashion shows for me. All the clean good clothes he'd never once squeezed into. "I've kept these in a separate closet forever called 'Someday My Prints Will Come, in Handy. . . .' " He lugged even more from his green Ford pickup. Heaped were all horizontal stripes, the pleated pants and tartan plaids. Circa was almost comically underfoot, yapping, entering into the spirit, running up to the mirror, considering herself, playing tag with her own reflection. She seemed weirdly smart today and almost charming.

Tad had visibly become exactly the splendid-looking person we'd all always seen, the one that Tad himself had never quite believed was under there. Perfect finally, and startled by it, Tad kept changing outfits; he was soon looping up and down my staircase, cutting through my good steep rooms in this house he'd saved, doing dips and turns, and by the end, and after several more than our usual drier-than-the-Sahara martinis, we were both laughing and crying at once. Soon I was putting on every tweed over-coat left over from my George, and all the houseguests' forgotten raingear and whatever clothes my missing children yet stashed upstairs. Hysterical, we were. Ah, but it was wonderful.

It felt like a perfect weekend house-party, but it lasted only six hours. Just the two of us, taking all the parts. We were playing the way hard-disciplined schoolkids will when given, by accident, the run of the big house. It was a time as fine as ones I recalled from the mid to late '30s. For me, the very pinnacle of fun. House parties at Nags Head just before the second war with all my girlfriends from Saint Catherine's and many of the freckled, courteous, lovesick boys whose planes would soon have to get shot down.

As he finally walked past me, exhausted and practically croupy from the serious laughs we'd had and how it tested his failing lungs, I noticed something. Tad was by then wearing only a wool vest and Bermuda shorts; he was barefoot. I saw how thin his legs had got. How brown, how beautiful they were at that scale. If his frontal padding always made him seem a Victorian edifice with furbelows and curly notches and overgenerous ornamentation, that joyful bulk had now changed. He was reverting, in period at least. He'd slid back down from a too-prosperous 1870, to severer, civic 1840, back to strict, pure, personal 1810. Today, Tad was exactly 1810!

I saw, being a beneficiary of his own architectural-discussion group, that Tad had shrunk down to exactly his own favorite moment in American domestic design. His former happy corpulence had, in ending, finally achieved what he'd once called "the chaste, Greek proportions of the Federal." Tad had always explained to us: The Federal period was the last moment when, believing Mankind (at least of the American sort) to be perfectible, Architecture proved that possible. Proved that perfection, too, can be a self-fulfilling prophecy.

I just wanted to say something nice to him, is all. But, stupidly, I chose to talk about his weight, which also meant of course how much he'd lost. I said, "Your legs . . ." and stopped, just hating myself, you know.

"Why? Are they finally fairly 'good'? Think so, M.E.? Well, then, back kick, shuffle ball-change. All they needed was one serious pencil-sharpener apiece. Quit while you're ahead, hmmm? I seem to have gotten everything I wanted, for the wrong reasons. *Too Much Too Soon.* But, can you imagine me one day actually walking up onto the portico at Shadowlawn, when most of it is done, and me feeling great for one whole week, with a northwest breeze and no mosquitoes and just to be up on that porch, and me wearing khaki Bermudas with hardly any paint on them, and upright at last on legs this thin? Ooh, all I need is a couple more bronzer sticks and another NEH grant, gir'friend. Can I grate some extra horseradish for your ersters, honey? I'm right here at it. I am up."

"Your legs are Federal now."

At last, I managed to say it.

He glanced down, studied them, and looked right back at me. "My

God, they are. *Quelle* achievement!" Then oh how he smiled at me. It was almost worth it, just for that one smile.

I cannot explain the look of happiness Tad gave me then. I cannot explain how I go on seeing all the bricks through him. Can't start to tell you the joy he yet gives me, day by day, room to room.

If—(here, I am going to go ahead and do this)—if, as we are promised, "In my Father's house are many mansions . . ." then there is a little justice, after all.

He's occupied.

He's One, Too

For Edmund White,
and for Patrick Merla

In Falls, North Carolina, in 1957, we had just one way of "coming out."

It was called getting caught.

Every few years, cops nabbed another unlikely guy, someone admired and married—a civic fellow, not bad-looking. He often coached a Pee Wee League swim team. Again we learned that the Local Man Least Likely to Like Boys did! In our town of twenty-two hundred, this resulted in confusion unto nausea.

Our *Herald Traveler* was usually sedate ("Recent Church Goings-On of Fun and Note"). It now encrusted the front page with months of gory innuendo. Circulation beefed right up.

And into jail they chucked the hearty, beautiful Dan R——, my boyhood idol.

It took me weeks to learn why they'd removed him as completely as a carpet stain. I was nine and prone to hero worship. I suffered a slight stammer. I lunged at outdoor activities; accidents happened—often to bystanders. Archery from my tree house discouraged neighbors' backyard cookouts. I felt that 1957 *required* its boys to enjoy a major sport.

Soon as Dan got grabbed, my parents halted newspaper home delivery. I pedaled my Schwinn uphill to the public library. I spotted a stack of local papers set—unusual—on a shelf above kiddies' reach. I dragged over three *Who's Who*s, one stool from Circulation. Then I hid in shadows, safe among 1921's unasked-for *National Geographic*s. I read about the public fall of my secret friend.

(I once hooked Dan R——. Showing off my fly-casting, I snagged his furry forearm. Even bleeding, the guy never blamed me. He joked: I should think of him as my first "big one," the lead "rainbow" in a long, good, lifetime's catch. —I did.)

My index finger now traced the nine weeks and sixty column inches of Dan's descent. I read of his capture, for deeds I'd considered doing, with him. I felt exactly as sick as excited.

This would become a familiar flashpoint for me and my kind—everything we want is everything most others find the most disgusting.

What's daylight to us? that's sewage to them.

Your hope, their shame. I was, at nine, confused. I am now forty-eight.

. . .

Authorities never arrested our town's obvious ones. Maybe in being flagrant, those boys knew best how to hide. The vice squad failed to book Falls's supple florist; comically self-informed—he defined everything as "buttery," "heavenly," "icky," or "Velveeta." Cops spared our insinuating, gifted organist; didn't Melvin play for the Baptists at ten, the Methodists at eleven? Also left unjailed, Falls's admired if overweight mama's-boy librarian.

These ones, born "out," went genially overlooked thanks to good behavior. They hailed from decent families; they told welcome if unrepeatable jokes to generations of mayors' wives. They were clever from surviving. And—if their humor was weekend-excessive—their lives stayed weekday-useful to Falls, North Carolina. The Boys accepted who they'd been assigned to be.

True, they might flaunt their sexuality's effervescent side effects, but they had the sense to do the sex deed (if do it they must, and you guessed they probably must) well out of state. Sure, they got teased, and daily. Did they even hear the rednecks' sidewalk chorus—"Sister Man," "Miss Sump Pump," "Nellie Belle," "Velveeta"? Yes. But otherwise no one bothered these vamping mutant versions of Falls's "good old boys."

"The Boys are inseparable," ran one tired local joke, "except with a crowbar."

An artistic aunt of mine spoke fondly of these three best pals; she bought the floral arrangements of one, marveled at the Sunday Wurlitzer crescendi of another, and—from a third—received (under the counter) steamy best-sellers concerning tobacco-growing, oversexed hillbillies.

"Judging The Boys against our town's gray businessmen, why, there's just no contest, is there? It'd be like comparing, oh, a cuckoo clock, say, with some wall-mounted round thing, just any ole modernish GE school clock. You can get the time from both, but the cuckoo one'll give you real *fun* every fifteen minutes. Never scared of a little drama. Whereas the other is just putting in his time . . . just *up* there."

The married fellows that our cops caught were simply trying to outwit their molten (uncontainable) secret. Failing that, many hoped just to outlive it. Couldn't you slowly lose the central urge toward men, the way your waistline painlessly eventually dispersed?

Your wife, your kids sat inches away; and who would know that, while this service-station attendant shot white foam across your car window, as this punk (whose cap read "Fill 'Er Up, Mister?") toyed with your long floppy windshield wiper, who'd ever need know that you studied such drenching—not to catch a smudge on green glass—but to observe, through it, the beautiful brown ligaments in a perfect, working, young, male, arm.

Desperation for actual sex with living men led some of our brightest locals (ones with law degrees, ones passionate for clever Civil War battle strategy) direct into the crudest traps.

And the very nanosecond queer news got out, these guys fell forever.

II.   A Man's Man

I so admired Dan R——. He golfed with Dad. They often partied. He must've sold insurance or real estate (I never saw Dan actually working).

Father's friends arrived at our house, en route to golf. Our home stood in sight of the club's first hole. Foursomes gathered on our porch, drank there, paced, awaiting today's tardy partner.

Their beloved hostess was Mother, Falls's best-informed young wife. She remembered the nuances of each man's favorite drink ("Exactly three extra baby onions, please").

"Don't know how you keep so many standing liquor orders in that lovely head, Helen," guys flirted with a woman whose IQ was 159.

Hooray! Here came Dan's sporty Plymouth wagon, "cream" and electric-blue (white interior). Seeing me, he always honked, *shave and a haircut*. His sound piled into our drive, activating everything. Riding in Dan's car, young lawyers, young doctors, joshing. Behind them, leather golf bags of saddle-shoe two-tones. Bags, lumpy as boys' marble sacks grown huge, chucked atop each other like some shoulder-padded orgy— dumb, male, goodwill at rut.

Dan never swore, he rarely broke the speed limit. This husband and father and soon-to-be-caught queer served as deacon for that new brick Methodist church—the one near U.S. 43? beyond the carpet discount hut? yeah, that one.

Jocular, adored, and nearly too handsome, Dan was saved by not quite knowing it. That let you stare, let you draw maybe four inches closer than you'd risk with some dude aware of his exact market value. Dan, so visible to others, seemed half blinded by his own inviting innocence.

People rubbed shoulders with him—"for good luck," they told themselves (if they noticed doing it at all). I noticed their shoulders touching his. At nine, I wanted mine there.

Hidden in my tree house above his parked wagon—I gazed down upon this man. My admiration felt almost patriotic: it weakened me, but for reasons idealistic.

The floor of my crow's nest was one closet door, sacrificed in recent expansion; my father had nailed it up a sugar maple at roughly lighthouse height. Just one closet's width held me aloft. It gave a good if sneaky overview, but offered no real living space. Suspended by rope, I kept a net sack full of ice-cold Cokes. A three-legged stool dangled. I pulled things closetward only when needed.

Today, Dan, seeing one stray line, fished a dollar bill from his wallet. Grinning, he tied it on, jerked three pulls. I knew to tug his green up into mine. I saluted over the ledge and, alone, sniffed dampish folding money. Its ink smelled more black than green. The smell hinted at wadded white bread, billfold's rawhide and, not Jockey shorts but Dan's second-day-wear boxers, possibly plaid. Eyes closed, I inhaled mainly Dan, worth hundreds.

Friendly below me, he stood no more than five foot six. And yet, like certain compact guys, he appeared a giant, shrunk—someone monumental rendered wittily portable, more concentratedly male for that. He was the most perfectly made, if shortest, of my father's crowd. These men were immodest ex-soldiers of a won war. They acted as pleased with themselves as with their unearned trust funds.

Dad's group called itself the Six Footers Club. Dan needed six more inches to qualify. These six inches caused lurid jokes I never tired of overhearing.

Men! So simple in beasty anxiousness about their size relative to other guys' vitals' sizes. "Is it large enough?" cannot be called the subtlest question in the world, but it sure remains a biggie.

. . .

Dan, the Six Footers' mascot and pony beauty, again got teased about his runtiness and profile. A tree house was good for such eavesdropping. I knew that—between guy-drink two and guy-drink three—the smut would start. I waited.

Country-Club North Carolina: most days after 5 p.m. from 1949 to 1969 meant bottoms up, three good stiff ones downed in an hour and a half. (Not sissy white wine, either. The hard stuff.)

Men watched our driveway for the last of today's foursome. He'd soon roar up after closing some deal or suturing shut the victims of Falls's latest teen car wreck. Our house had a horseshoe of parking lot, plus hammocks and the open bar.

Mom, perfectly dressed, with a Master's degree, hovered, warmly impersonal. Indoors, two black, uniformed maids did her heavy lifting. Dad's friends lounged and goofed right under my treetop.

After jawing through money news, after gossiping about sewage-bond issues, after the mind-numbing hit parade of their last game's best shots, "So Dan surprises us, choosing his three iron . . . ," they finally got dirty on me.

Stripped to shorts, my eyes half shut, breathing Dan's dollar, nose to nose with George Washington, I'd been ready.

They mentioned certain looser secretaries—those days always named Donna—and who Donna'd "done" now, sometimes three in a hotel room at one time. Smut hushed when Mom reappeared wearing a Dior flared skirt, carrying the silver tray that—some summers—seemed jewelry fused direct to her hand's red nails. As she swept indoors, trash restarted mid-syllable.

I never tire of hearing deep-voiced, long-legged guys bray through the six key words in human reproduction. Holy Man-tra!

What did a youngster hear, those corny days of sexed-up '57? Often simple dick jokes of the kind that little boys my age enjoyed. "Hey, Dean," remarked our youngest bank president, ever, "summer sure has bleached your hair. Or you been dipping into one of Jeanie's Clairol bottles? So tell us, big-time Lawyer Man, is it true blonds have more come?"

Tree-high, I kept still.

"I'm not answerin' that directly, sir. But you can state your question direct into my Bone-o-Phone, Phil. Put Mouth Against Tip of Receiver and Inhale Hard . . . right *here.*" Many yuks. Above them, half stiff in my seersucker shorts (shorts whose very fabric's name gave me a minor-major boner), I listened in a trance of premonition, dread, desire.

At anything off-color, Dan grew shy and pebble-kicking. The Six Footers admired him as "too straight an arrow." When he literally blushed, they seemed not unexcited, watching somebody so handsome redden, laugh, then hide his face behind two palms while bowing forward.

Quiet, he reigned at their group's dead center. If any Packard or golf cart broke, Dan was first under its hood. The joke ran: he could fix an engine without getting any oil on him. Dan wore his snug, pressed clothes like some proud, poor boy—quietly defending his one good school outfit.

People always included young Mr. R——, though his family wasn't *from* Falls. He was token Elsewhere. Dan seemed more mysterious and attractive, being uninitiated. Locals took him aside to explain the genealogy behind a recent land deal—some webbing of tribal traits and 1790 betrayals so complex, you could see he hadn't a clue. It didn't matter. Around here, nobody new ever truly *knew.* Two hundred and fifty years were involved; strangers could never catch up with that many genes and so much ownership.

Dan R—— (no last name, please, though it's thirty-nine years later) showed one immodesty. He had a charming, actorish way of planting knuckled fists onto his hips. He had this lovely way of letting his well-made head fall back as he laughed. He laughed often and—if the things he said were the things that, at church, on fairways, they all said then— Dan said them in so ripened a baritone, and with such banal complete conviction, it made him seem even more a man.

Originality has never been required for admission to a country club. Originality would soon lose this guy his membership.

My dad was himself a chopper and clown on the links. His own ambitions for his game made him far less good at it. Dan R—— played golf to relax. Golf worked my father's every nerve. "That darn Dan," Pop shook his head. "Guy consistently shoots in the low seventies." My father watched the younger man's natural swing; Dad's groans sounded close to lust, not the simpler vice of envy.

"I swear, Dan. I keep telling the pro—person can't *learn* it. Guy either gots it or he don't, and—Dan?—you're loaded with factory options, damnit. Maybe bottle it? For us mortals, pal? Sell me a six-pack at cost, what say?"

"Well, thanks, Richard. I do really usually try hard, I do. And sometimes, I admit, I'll get m'balls to set down at least *near* where I wanted 'em."

Be careful what you wish for, Dan R——.

If this were fiction and not the blunt, hyperpictorial, and unlikely truth, I would assign "the Dan character" some personal peculiarities. These would separate him from his leggy, same-ish junior partners' crowd. Maybe I'd make him a bit accident-prone? or give him some slight endearing limp, a major stammer. Fact is, he was too able-bodied.

He was plain and good, and as visible everywhere as Wonder Bread was then. "Builds Young Bodies Twelve Ways." (I felt built by every vitamin Dan's company and little gifts provided me.)

From my tree house, through fieldglasses, I stared down on a Dan foreshortened. His beer-loving pals had already begun the tragic waist-high unraveling that gets most guys. From my perch, they looked like stacks of pebbles, largest on the bottom and the smallest, pinkest, right on top. Dan's build still reversed this.

From overhead, his brown locks and foursquare shoulders eclipsed narrow hips. Just shoe tips showed. I'd memorized the hair cocooning his ridged forearms. Back when I put my fishhook in poor Dan, I touched arm fuzz growing haywire, all directions. Hair sprouted every color, blond, brunette, and Lucy-red—mixed, like the pelt of our brindled boxer dog.

I'd never seen Dan shower at the club; I didn't dare, but liked know-ing *I could've.* I feared he would be burred across with many-colored patches. The taut chest and high butt—speckled, furred thanks to helpless handicapping manliness. Strange, that his perfection almost made you pity him.

From my closet perch, through binoculars, I now bird-watched a friendly compartmented bulge in the front of young Dan's ironed chinos. From direct overhead, you could see its smiling sickle curve. He always "dressed" his due right, like some driver signal's courteous extended arm.

"What you seein' from up there, John Jay Audubon?" Hands on his hips like a goalie, daring you to score, Dan stared right up into my suction-attention.

"You . . . look"—I felt caught—"close."

"Excellent glasses, hunh, buddy? German, I bet. One thing's sure, those Krauts flat-out know their optics."

No other friend of my father's took any time with me. Passing, guys might rub my blondish hair but always the wrong darn way. Puppylike, I growled. They never noticed.

Dan did, laughing. "You're too much, little buddy."

III.   Wanted Dead or Alive

Then Dan was not. Not in Papa's golfing party. Nowhere near our home, the couples swarming for Friday-night bridge, arriving as solemnly intent as if planning new Normandy beach landings. Something'd happened.

I, a watchful boychild, with the man-sized interest in him, retreated to my tree house, soon overheard tag ends of stifled driveway conversations. "Never in a million years'd guess . . . him . . . one . . . those."

My favorite had descended from such visibility. That same year he'd headed our Community Chest charity drive. Dan was often shown in the paper, grinning beside a giant plywood thermometer. The hand of his arm—muffed as in downy Shredded Wheat—touched painted mercury. Mercury shot up as cash poured in. He smiled a hopeful grin one-sided; he rolled his eyes to urge our town toward generosity—a salesman's readiness to look however foolish for a sale.

I myself gave forty-seven cents.

Though the same picture appeared week after week, I still scanned it for small message differences.

.   .   .

Now, no photographs, no word. Missing in Action, one electric-blue Plymouth (its pale interior startling as a white sock around the calf of some dark, older boy). My parents having purged our house of any tell-tale *Herald Traveler,* I grew so jumpy/bold from missing Dan, I blurted during dinner, "Wwwwwhat ever happened to . . . ?" (I didn't even need to finish—they'd been waiting.)

Mother stiffened from Casual to Regal. Using her linen napkin, she blotted her mouth, then—napkin stretched between her fists—studied it as if my question had made the cloth go beautifully bloodstained.

Dad cleared his throat, public speaking, "Someday, I'll explain, son. Once I figure it out more myself. There are certain men, often not the ones you'd expect . . . Dan went and tried something that . . . Dan's left us, basically. Nobody understands it. Pass the turnips, son, and take more or you'll never make the Six Footers Club. Mighty good turnips tonight, Helen, crispier. Son, I know how much you, all of us, feel so attached to, but . . . Fact is—son?—around our town?—what Dan tried?—it's the one thing a man cannot come *back* from. . . ."

This passed for clarification. I simply nodded, swallowing it whole. I would need to bike to the library. I understood I was not meant to know . . . how bad, it was, whatever Dan had chanced. . . . Did Everyone's Great Shame come from his having attempted it, or his longing for something Dan really truly wanted but never even nailed?

He ceased being. He stopped being, as Mom put it (her joke, not mine) "The Heartthrob of our Community Chest."

Monopoly had one card we most dreaded: GO TO JAIL. The worst part, you could only sit, could just admire the others' hopping happily forward, snatching up your better hotels. Eventually, your fellow players quit even addressing you; you could watch them from up close forever, but could not get OUT.

IV.   Book Me Passage on The Fellow Ship

When Mom complained about the hours Dad squandered getting even worse at golf, he reminded her: the happiest times of his whole life had been spent at war, with other loud good boys in mobs and squadrons. "Helen, I need my weekly fellow ship time." The Fellow Ship. Guys spoke of it often, as being golden. As something craved nearly as much as women were, by all real men. Me too. I heard about a local high-school athlete winning "a full Fellow Ship to Duke" and envied him his crowd on board, the jolly boyish upriver voyage clear to that steepled campus.

At age six, I made The Fellow Ship a pirate craft, longer than wide, a carved dragon's head snarling at its rapier tip, a barge almost too point-edly male ever to float on nebulous female water.

At nine, I pictured a torch-bearing Viking boat, its rowers shirtless doctors and lawyers, its cargo monogrammed leather golf bags, its destination the Links of America, but its true goal: grab-assing, the dirty guesses about who that slutty little Donna wouldn't "do" dry. At the prow, hands on hips, lit unevenly by violent orange torchlight, shirtless yet bandoliered with those leather thongs Kirk Douglas wore in *The Vikings*—Dan, Captain of The Fellow Ship of choice. His deep voice called, "Stroke, fellows. Stroke it good, pals o' mine. Pull hard, because The Fellow Ship is for us *baad* boys only. Pull hard, good men, because you *can*."

I imagined my tree-house closet was a Fellow Ship franchise. Or at least its outrigger offspring, The Boy Raft. Sometimes, among maple leaves, I took off my seersucker shorts. Because I could. Who'd know (robins excepted)? I let the breeze be my buddy, my coxswain.

There was a new verb, used mainly in churches then. Mother found it vulgar. "To fellowship." For me, that latent active verb sounded like a pillage itinerary, some oarlock means of transport, and my own future port in Paradise.

PROMINENT EXEC ARRESTED
FOR APPROACHING YOUTH, 15
(AT PENNEY'S TOILET)

Dateline: Raleigh—A 33-year-old Falls resident, recent chair of our town's most successful Community Chest drive and a four-time winner of the Broken Arrow Country Club's Amateur Golf Tourney, was apprehended on morals charges Saturday while in Raleigh doing family business.

The week before, having already been elected Rotarian Young Man of the Year for 1955, Dan R—— was named it for '57, too. The suspect's wife has taught third grade here for six years. Within one hour of arriving at Big Elk Mall, Raleigh, Dan R—— was handcuffed and already on his way to prison. Arrest came swiftly for the beloved local church and business leader.

Executive Officer with J & L Realty/Insurance of this city, Dan R——, of 211 Elm Avenue of Falls, was caught in the Men's Room of Raleigh's new J. C. Penney Department Store. According to authorities, he was apprehended while "making sexual-type suggestion-advances" to and "having sustained manual contact with" a 15-year-old boy "at the urinals of the new Penney's restroom facility, 2:32 p.m., Saturday."

The father of the boy propositioned chanced to occupy a booth in that same bathroom. He was planning to take a faulty camera to the repair shop there in Big Elk Mall. The father also happened to be an off-duty detective (still carrying his service revolver).

The resultant photographs are, according to a reliable source who asked not to be identified, "conclusive and pretty damning." No sooner had flashbulbs cooled than the boy's father himself made a dramatic arrest. The suspect was then marched in handcuffs the full length of Raleigh's newest luxury shopping facility. Photos are now in the hands of capital police, said Raleigh Sheriff's Department spokesman Red Furman. He would indicate only that young Mr. R—— was being held for "Corrupting a Minor," "Soliciting," and "Indecent Exposure." Other charges are being considered. A printed statement on this case ended, "The snapshots prove past any shade of doubt—*some touching was definitely involved.*"

Mrs. Dan R—— would make no statement when reached by telephone at home after not answering their door all day.

But Reverend Elmo "Mo" Haines, of New Hope Road Methodist, pastor to the once-popular young couple, went on record. His single comment ran, "This is just not the Dan I know. Dan rates among the finest young gents I have fellowshiped with or ministered to, ever. I am sure there is an explanation. I don't yet know what it's going to be. We do just pray for the R—— family, and for Dan especially. Despite this being such a true and total shocker, we remember that, in the end, all things work together for the Glory of God."

The hearing is slated for Thursday at noon.

V.   Stakeout: Crime Scene Pix

There was once a brand-new J. C. Penney store. It dignified an early shopping mall in glamorous Raleigh. It was built prior to four-lane highways. Achieving the state capital meant a tough three-hour drive from manicured and clubby little Falls.

While Dan's children made fast work of their Jumbo-Tub popcorn in the dark mall theatre (then known as just Cinema Twins, not yet today's extravaganza of bad choices), the R—— kids' dapper father—with time to kill—purchased golf balls (used and new, old for practice, new for real for-keeps games).

Finding he'd secured himself two whole hours by his lonesome (unusual back home), maybe Dan checked out the mall's haltered adolescent girls. They drifted to and fro across the vast space, always tacking at obliques in bright attracting "schools" of three to five. Not unlike the pet store's neon tetras glorifying aquarium windows of that shop exotically stinky.

It is our rarest luxury, sufficient time alone. How often we forget, it is a "hall pass" we so crave. Solitude becomes especially precious to a father of three this overtaxed and hectic with blood drives, land closings, putter practice, sidewalk edging, car-pooling kids from dressage to clarinet lessons. Today, atypically wifeless (her asthma acted up each August), now briefly unhooked from children, Dan must have felt like some once-clunky appliance suddenly retooled to be, the miracle of 1957, "A Portable."

Alone at last, free of wall sockets, maybe he probably got so doggone horny. Maybe it crunched his lower body like his wife's worst cramps coming on all at once, doubling her over. Was it a nausea of displaced attraction? What made Dan feel this strengthening weakness for some action *now*?

If the female genitalia can be considered (in certain magical functions) an inward-looking device requiring plug-in, the male ones remain perversely, indeed sinisterly, portable—extruded, independent, air-able, always primed for the latent test drive.

They'll get a guy—unchaperoned—into all kinds of freelance trouble, quick, even at a fluorescent mall. What to do with a healthy set of portables, at 2:30 p.m., at Big Elk Browse 'n' Buy, before the baby-sitting Disney animation ends?

Maybe surely Dan endured the driven sexual thoughts of a young man—in so tumid an August—just at the peak of his need to implant. Maybe these two hours among attractive strangers helped Dan admit to a more unsettling itch. It was an itch you couldn't even name, much less sate, slake, or properly dig at in reputation-conscious yard-work Falls.

Itches can go unscratched only so long. Watch.

VI.   He Grows Up, Anyway

Soon as I got older, I got out.

It's 1970 and I have just bought a batch of spring flowers. Not a single dollar-bunch, but three I've artfully merged. That's a notable percentage of my weekly food money. I now take night courses at Harvard. I sell art reproductions at the Coop. I am studying painting and have allowed myself to be in love. With a. Man.

He's ten years older, four inches shorter, Japanese American, also a painter, a fellow Gemini. It seems ordained. A Columbia grad, he once published a prose poem in the *Saturday Review*. It concerned the first winter snowfall in a gray city—imagistic if not controversial.

All this impresses me, but what matters most, his kindness, his deft watercolor hands, the sense of shelter his basement apartment provides. It is full of cloisonné and mirrors and screens—gold-leafed cranes flying. Our sex depends on adolescent friction and it smells of Johnson & Johnson baby products, both clear and pink ones. His laughter contains all the lucid giddiness hidden in puns, unguents, and champagne. A buzz available anytime I can get him giggling, which is most anytime.

I've rearranged this bouquet, rewound it in green tissue paper. Then I bind it all with one argyle shoestring tied in a bow, looking jaunty, semi-butch. I wear brown suede bucks and my good old blue-and-white seersucker suit. I'm riding Boston's Lechmere subway line out toward Brookline. I'm hand-delivering flowers to the first man I can say I truly love.

I am a boy, and I am a healthy boy, twenty-two, and I do not look the way unimaginative people believe a queer one must dress or sit.

I have shoulders now, and a real jaw, and can appear somewhat lifeguard-worthy. I have grown up to be a complete and manly man, I could be Dan R——'s own son. His Beloved First Mate on The Fellow Ship. A member of the Six Footers Club, I sometimes manage the look of old money, though I myself lack any.

Today is April and our subway car has climbed free of its tiled tunnel and now spills along the center of the street. The driver has (illegally, with glee) opened all the doors to let spring breezes in.

Seated across from me, three white-haired pretty ladies are mid-conversation, visiting, well-kept. They look like girls who sat down to play bridge one day in 1920 and, after many laughs and a legion of rubbers, rose with difficulty, shocked to stand up old. But—even so, all during aging by accident—they've basically had a lovely game. Even their dresses—chosen at separate homes—show complimentary pastels. You feel their lives' essential agreement. Now I see they are smiling back here at me.

I have been deep in my own young man's vernal sexual and romantic thoughts, I've been staring down at jonquils and one ratty peony, busy sniffing French lilacs. I'm gazing so hard at three dollars' worth of flowers, rapt with such inhaling joy, it must look as if I'm going to drop my pants and—here and now—fuck these blossoms good.

Wondering what the ladies want, I grin back, mild. I love my grandmother and the artistic aunt who once compared our pathetic swishy hometown Boys (so unlike strapping *moi*) to pert "fun" cuckoo clocks. If possible, I plan to like these Boston ladies—beaming, placid, entitled.

Nudged by the others, one powdered one nearest me leans off her seat's rattan, points to blooms, and smiles, "For your girlfriend."

She does not ask, but tells.

I know I am only required to nod. Even a shrug, a grin, will do quite nicely, thanks. The one thing they'd like more? Overt baritone confessing. "Yes, ma'am—fer my Melanie. We're to wed come June, ma'am. She teaches third grade and she's as good as she is beautiful. She's taken such super care of my mother, who's an invalid with one shriveled leg but a great disposition, and Ma already loves Mellie like a daughter. Melanie put herself through school by making the best darn marmalade, ever. Think she'll like these posies?"

I understand what these nice ladies want.

I am being asked to reinforce the natural order, their own middle-class romance. I imagine how they see me, a boy charming, young, and tender as the flowers he's paid dearly for. They note my pressed suit, but cannot smell its aura of Niagara spray starch. I washed this seersucker thing in Woolite, dried it on towels spread across my tenement's tar roof, then ironed it myself, unable to afford both dry cleaning and nosegay.

"For my boyfriend."

I say it louder than I even planned. The tram driver checks his rearview mirror. Ladies' faces shift. I haven't spoken "boyfriend" to hurt them, to teach them, or to scold them.

I just want some of my complexity known (since they asked). There are stemmed and petaled layers of complexity, involving the weird unexplainable innocence of all this, of simply He and Me and Us in the World. Is pleasure such a threat? Is a little privacy too much to ask? It all seems, to me, as innocent as the phrase "for my boyfriend."

Itself, a bouquet.

The ladies look hard at one another, then some glum muttering. Their leader checks back, describing, debating. An argument's in progress. Do I fuckin' *need* this? Why do I keep *doing* this to myself? Which means, of course, Why does the world keep doing this to me and my kind? Dan, among us. How much pain can be inflicted for one species of involuntary joy?

Then something happens. It again proves how complicated, the world. Shoulder to shoulder, they're all smiling back at me, anyhow; their leader lady nods.

They have—through knowing each other so deeply, through a basic lack of experience with anyone "out," through some abiding belief that every good-looking boy on earth is really created for one equally fine gal—decided that "boyfriend" can't possibly mean *that.*

They opt for thinking I don't quite know how my statement might be misread—by other minds, far dirtier than theirs. They decide male friendship is nice but not so important as actual love. They choose to feel I am too fresh-looking and ethical-seeming. I'm visibly from far too good a Caucasian family (I could almost be a son of theirs). And so they're going to go ahead and enjoy all this—me, the flowers, seersucker, spring. They are going to pretend I didn't really say that. I didn't really mean that I was . . . one.

Despite them, thanks to my mission, Brookline's street-center tram line smells improbably today of woods abloom, citric-scented wildflowers in late April. Despite Boston's Athenas' indicating what I'm *not* to do, the town still feels whimsical, this Northern spot I came to to come out in. Its central lake in its emerald park has boats shaped like giant swans. Even here, Wagnerians hold sway.

So I get away with it again. I am not arrested. And when I rise to leave, my honey-colored hair ruffled by breeze, as I pull the cord, and hold my floral tribute, bridal before me, the ladies wave. Their leader mutters fondly, automatic, as if speaking nonsense syllables to some grandchild, "Toodles. Enjoy."

I never marry.

VII.   Walk Your Own Stiff Plank, Sir

It is 2:28 p.m., August 7, 1957, in a pastel department store, and it's about to happen because Dan has got to pee.

Through Hi-Fi Stereo, past Glassware and Rec Room Needs, he wanders into the men's room at our state's flagship J. C. Penney store.

I admit, out in the open: I wish I'd been there then. I wish I could have saved him from the high price of desire fueled by decades' sickening secrecy: the erectile trend is further crazed by the late-summer heat of Carolina. Barring my helping Dan out or my feeling Dan up, I guess I wish I coulda just watched. . . .

People later praised the two-way mirror. Some Falls gossips swore that's how cops caught Dan, and on movie film. Others claimed that this unlikely toilet had become a secret breeding place for capital-area inverts. (If, of course, they *could* breed.)

My own belated adult guess is that: A restless Dan chanced into the absolute right bathroom on the absolute worst day.

If only he hadn't already seen *Snow White* four times. If only it hadn't been 1957, when you could freely park your kids in any movie house.

There were many reasons Falls condemned their ever-popular Dan R—— overnight. The following is one:

Dan's children came out of the cinema, blinking, scared after seeing the witch's poisoned apple eaten. They felt spooked by so spiky a green villainess. (Always, in fables and life and the Disney movies, Evil's more photogenic than any sappy virgin dumb enough to bite an apple so obviously laced with chemo. An apple this good-looking dares you *not* to eat it. So you really shouldn't.)

Dan's kids, perhaps with buttons of popcorn strayed into their fine silver-blond hair, were first surprised then shocked, next hurt—not finding Dad.

"He said meet right *here,* right? And at four. I'm sure."

Imagine them staring at the mall's terrazzo flooring—still influenced by the movie's wishfulness. Just because they wanted it, couldn't their dad break through this paving, hands on hips, head tipped back, and, rising, laughing?

The kids felt mainly ready for the long nap home in the back of their Plymouth wagon still new-smelling, somehow male-smelling. Cross, then bored and—when an hour'd passed—irked with a first hiccup of completest fear, the youngsters finally sent their oldest brother on a mission. "Go and scout out that dern dad of ours, Dan Junior. The car's still parked, so he's here, okay. Hope he's not sick or somethin'. But, naw, Dad's never sick."

If, in Falls, these kids had been stood up, some other parents—friends of Dan and Julie (his wife)—would have spied the familiar pretty R—— features. They would have noted his kids' worry. They'd have noted how children of such different ages—usually quite eager to appear not *with* each other—clung together now. But, see, this mall stood in faraway cosmopolitan Raleigh, and life was harsher there and faster and so crowded. And no one knew them.

Only later—during the mall's lockup around 10:30 p.m., only then did a black security guard find three children sleeping, roughly spoonfashion, behind one huge imported palm tree. Like kids from some Grimm tale, lost in the enchanted woods, they'd stolen back among the decorative plantings nearest where Dad said to meet this afternoon at exactly four. Six and a half hours later, discovered tucked behind the fountain—back by its transformer where the rushing water's clear recycling tubes were coiled and snuffling like their mother's asthma—three kids waked. They felt sure Dad had found them. Smiling, they turned.

But, no, uh-oh, it was a worried Negro guard, chancing half a smile. And the kids understood they were all in so much trouble. They'd spent their last coins on further Milk Duds. They didn't know how to phone Mom collect long-distance. And if they had, they might be getting Dad into real hot water. See, without even understanding why, they already knew to be ashamed.

The R—— kids attended Methodist Sunday school; bruise-colored consciences were forming. Starter cultures of the ethical and, when need be, the self-punishing. At home, everything usually worked on schedule; so—when it didn't—somebody got blamed.

The mall guard seemed to be half-eating his foot-long walkie-talkie. People were being called, the lost kids' father's full name uttered. Then Dan's children heard a minor stir. The walkie-talkie picked up one downtown cop: "Oh, him? Yeah, we've got him. Guy's already been printed, guy's been booked. Good riddance to bad rubbish, hunh?"

"Booked, what fo'?" the kind guard asked. Then Dan's kids, eyes large, hands laced around each other's necks and shoulders—they all knew first, knew first what their father really was.

The rest of it interests me because I am one, too.
Like Dan, who was locally noticeable and then became hypervisible en

route to being totally unseen, I am trying once again to make myself more opaquely and superstitiously visible an invert. I am trying, through this story.

I am fairly smart and a decent actor, and I've had sex with women without soliciting immediate reviews, or expecting ladies' awe at my versatility; and I can pass. I know that.

If I'd married, and stayed put in Falls: I would now teach art history at a local junior college. I'd have a smart if no-longer-slender wife named Alice, and the one son, Kyle, five—a prodigy-brat-joy.

I didn't. So I don't.

Still, I think of what authorities did to Mr. Dan, who slipped that once, then slipped into the searing spotlight before falling so utterly out of view. And—incidentally—out of the life of a kid who liked to look at him, loved just being near him.

When Dan took his own lucky kids to visit Shiloh Battlefield, he brought me back a greenish musket ball. It looked old as Rome. It tasted of salt. I still have it.

Recently, a famous men's magazine asked for some of my fiction. I told the editor I planned mailing him a good new story about a gay sailor, one stuck on a ship off Vietnam. The editor whistled. "Oh boy. I hoped you'd be professional. You planning to rub our noses in it, hunh?"

I wanted to tell him, "I bet if I were Toni Morrison and you phoned to ask me for a story, and I sent you one about my fellow black people, you sure wouldn't use the term 'rubbing our noses in it,' I betcha." Rubbing our noses in it? Isn't that how you train a puppy who keeps shitting in your house? You jam his little nose in his brown illegal leavings. That'll eventually cure him. Besides, your getting to punish him legally (for his own good and the Oriental rugs') will certainly make you feel better, before cleaning up his mess again.

They sure rubbed Dan's nose mighty hard, they broke it, rubbing it in.

Did I say so to the gentleman editor? No. I never even sent that story out, to anybody. He'd already jinxed it, see?

Still, I forgive myself. You learn to. You go crazy otherwise. But know what? It's so damn tiring. I'm no natural hero. I just want to do my work, eat okay, have a place to live, and get laid once every month. —Okay, twice a year.

I pretend I don't mind outing myself daily. (There's one huge reason not to be a black person in the U.S.A.: you've got to talk about that all the time, if only out of enlightened self-defense.)

I claim I don't mind the risk of getting marginalized. I keep putting my hands on my hips, like some Errol Flynn pirate, acting proud to be so wild and so well paid for it. I throw my head back and laugh to prove I just don't care who knows. I care.

I pretend it doesn't cost me every single bloody time I remake the point, every time I bust again toward full prison-break Out. But In keeps sealing over, the hymen grows right back so damn quick. And once you are Out in the Open once more, old threats feel fresh and jagged. Loud sounds make you jump. If you have, in your day, checked out a few boys' butts, you'd best watch your back full-time.

It's not enough to have healthy, Six Footers Club self-esteem; you'd best be Superman, and just to break even. You cannot marry your true love. Your idea of daylight is their idea of sewage. Make love, risk jail. You're starting over absolutely every day. You'd best know why you bother. Assuming nothing, it can sure take major traction. You need psychic four-wheel drive, for life.

Q: To whom shall you, the cuckoo clock's pet cuckoo, explain your calorie-requiring Self-Outings every fifteen minutes?

A: Explain it to Yourself. You will become, in the end, the world's hardest party to convince. You'll soon sound like your own conservative, protective, loving wife. Her familiar voice will grow unbrave, quick to tell you, "For God's sake, let the others protest. Relax for once, Little Ms. Firebrand. Stay home tonight. Stay *in.*"

Some days I feel like a 185-pound shrimp, peeled and left at noon on a huge white plate in some Courthouse Square downtown—drifting car fumes, gawkers, pigeons pecking. Too nakedly glistening. And, since nobody's ever seen one this size, they ignore it. "If it's been left out here in this heat, bound to've gone bad by now, anyway. Don't look at it."

At least I haven't made Dan's endgame mistake. I am still free to make others, better ones, slipups more mine. At least I'm not the married man with three kids waiting. At least the first time I tried something, I did not get nabbed, exposed and fined, imprisoned. Instead, up front, I say I am one (the principle of inoculation—a little of it, taken on purpose, cures you, if you survive).

I emerged from hiding a decade after 1957. And I get to remain free. If only under my own recognizance.

Dan, caught in public, at a Raleigh urinal, had not been wise as The Boys. These buddies survived Falls only because they took their unusual appetites elsewhere. The good ship Fellow Ship sailed The Boys across state lines. And if they'd docked in Raleigh to seek adventures around mere malls, these experts at hiding would have known the safety code for bathroom pickups.

You go into a booth, you don't risk public detection as poor Dan did, standing out in the open. You take your classic position on the pot, then tap your foot, setting up a signal that shoes to either side of yours can acknowledge or ignore. By the time you peek under the partition—or through a burrowed portal called, in terminology both profane and sacred, the Glory Hole (no Fellow Ship should be without one, above decks)—you have received a Morse-code marriage proposal, tap-dance prenups from the soles next door. Everybody's implicated, notes on scrolls of toilet paper passed. "What you into doing?" has given total strangers more upfront candid sexual info than most wedding couples know about each other. Physical description, list of fave sex acts, signed, sealed—prior to first touch, a veritable contract. If society makes your lust illegal, you might as well become efficient at subverting those laws. Men! What won't they do to get some? And guys seeking guys are spared all female indirection, all the ladies' emotional subtlety, decency, and marriage-mill formality: guys'll just stick it through the hole, and get "done" in the time it's taken you to read this page. It's honest, if illegal.

The Boys judged Raleigh a bit too close to home. No telling which Falls preacher or city manager you might run into. And besides, the men you snared at Penney's would be suburban, too married, far too penitent for The Boys' intended caliber of fellowshiping.

No, weekends they traveled direct to the Ships of Many Fellows, also known as the Atlantic Fleet.

They leaned coastward—eventful weekends at run-down tolerant Norfolk hotels nobly named: The Monticello. In formerly grand Deco lobbies, reconnoitering with other small-town escapee florists named Hiram, Buford, and Earle—*"avec une 'e,' please, Mary"*—they drank treacherous Windex-colored drinks titled after ports far more exotic than Norfolk.

Then The Boys, feeling Out, wandered Water Street; two aircraft carriers, six thousand young salts, were in.

A little drunk, The Boys talked inherited Spode.

A lot drunk, they trawled the sailor bars and—come morning— phoned each other's hotel rooms to brag in inches.

How, at age nine, could I announce to the world, that I preferred, I think, fellow sailors on The Feller Ship? My tendencies and character were probably visible to anyone with eyes. The Boys surely guessed about me long before I did. (Just, as I later learned, they "spotted" the unlikely Dan before Dan probably knew.) They taught me lore about their jobs. They acted kind, familiar, courtly; but they never "told me" about myself in a rude way, never took advantage of a ready, wistful kid, as many Republicans will tell you they *all* do—correction, *we* all do.

Coming out to my parents was literally tougher than going on record in *People* magazine. Telling them was like saying I had some news: I'd been arrested at J. C. Penney's pee trough, and why? Because, the other good news was . . . They dared me to tell them. Short of clamping a hand over my mouth as I formed the syllable, they did everything to actively prevent me. They knew all along, of course. But maybe they remembered the dreadful fate of our friend, ridden out of town for reaching toward an apple too perfect, too easily achieved, too good not to be pure poison. The very sleeping potion makes the fruit's red shine so.

They kept asking which girls I was dating most, how impending an engagement, howbout the promise of grandchildren, when? Which likely family names for that first boy?

These were people who'd dropped a suddenly depraved young Dan. Is it any wonder I feared blurting? As they feared hearing? I told them gently at first: "I'm married to my work." "Don't expect me to go out with the daughter of your next-door neighbor, that plump but pretty-in-the-face personality girl you keep mentioning, the art teacher at the public school. I am not erotically interested in women, period."

That seemed sufficient. I didn't want to be a guy who'd brutalize his parents in the guise of coming clean.

VIII.   Tell It to the Judge

What went on at the urinal of the brand-new J. C. Penney's at that early mall still holds me. It holds me in part because I remember how beautiful Dan's forearms were as he pressed both his fists, knuckles downward, onto the farthest points of his fine hipbones.

The arms were wound in every color including—near the right wrist—a sprinkling of first silver. I recall the way his dark eyebrows sent a translucent chevron (ambassadorial) to negotiate those black wooly dashes into staying perpendicular above so very Roman a nose. How blue Dan's jaw was where he shaved so often, how it looked like tempered steel—a dented icebreaker chin, its metal neatly folded (oh to rub my nose in *that*).

.   .   .

Oh to wander back in time. I'd shinny down my tree-house rope, and—with me magically advanced in age to become a guy, say, thirty, with Dan still thirty-three—maybe we'd adjourn to the shower room of the club, no, to his family's Plymouth wagon, but parked on midnight Lovers' Lane, his daughter's stuffed dog toy wedged under the front seat. And I would interview Dan, and maybe, later, touch him. "There, there, pal. They can't hurt you now. We're safe out here. Safe 'cause this we're in is a fantasy of mine. It's the one place they can't go, can they? Except for your being the first of my several beloved married men. Oh well . . . nothing's perfect, not even our escapism." And I would ask Dan when he first knew he was, one.

I would ask him how—before his regionally publicized Raleigh arrest—he'd managed it, living locally with all that competent wildness crammed so far, far down in him. At one Adjustors' Convention in Houston, did he try some room-service hanky-pank with a red-suited winky bellhop, a Tex-Mex kid as interested in the tips as the kicks? Had Dan thought about doing it with another man every minute of his life, or only quarter-hourly, male-male sex rearing its circumstantial head like that comic, startling, makework clockwork cuckoo bird?

Did he, as with so many before him, coach a swim team of teenage boys and make the occasional spot check of the shower rooms, but not so often as to be conspicuous, and always with a clipboard in his hand, always faking some set-faced chore as he swung into the showers, gruffly barking,

"Anybody seen Smitty? Got to get Smitty's darn parents' signatures or we're not going to have a bus for our away games. You seen Smitty, Butch? No? Well, dry the heck off, and quit popping towels at guys, down there, savvy, bud? Cover yourself, look at you, grab-assing buck-naked dripping-wet. Grow the heck up, m'pal, okay? Umkay."

How openly did the young boy, in snug blue jeans, entice an itchy, married Dan, who led the Community Chest so well and made the red part of the plywood thermometer go redder, faster than any other fund-driver, ever? How did my hero fall prey to some pimply if pretty boy? And did authorities insist the boy's policeman father fill some monthly quota of morals charges? Or was this simply off-duty sport, done on spec, for the glory?

Dan's court-appointed lawyer would place most blame upon Dan's tempters. On both the young son and his hidden father, readying the camera. What overcame Dan, as his own children sat intrigued by seven small men in love with one brunette wearing an outfit made via cookie cutters, each dwarf named for his own comic vices/shortcomings? (Mightn't there have been a little "sensitive" one called, not Sneezy, but . . . Velvety?)

Shall we blame that blazing August's having twenty-four non-raining days? Or was it Dan's depressed asthmatic wife? Was it Julie's unwillingness to "let him" lately, given Dan's solemn rigor at it every Friday—and this bad recent humidity? What drove young Dan to eye, then sidle nearer, and finally touch the secret, if offered, velvety parts of a younger and seemingly more innocent fellow male, fifteen?

All this they discussed at the hearing. It was reprinted in our local *Herald Traveler,* barely euphemized. I sat in the silent library's shady stacks, backed against the *Geographics'* egg-yolk yellow and egg-white white. I sat reading some and crying some and reading more, in painful little sips, and not understanding how—between the lines—I understood all this so well.

They showed Dan's picture, once the trial started. It was early, a locally made portrait taken just after he arrived in town, so hopeful (the top studio of Falls's two), the file photo they'd used for all his awards as Young Man of the . . . whatever. All the drives, and that big banquet he'd meant to end world Muscular Dystrophy. A well-intentioned guy, not yet thirty-four, smiling in his white, overlaundered shirt and with such teeth, and the starchy, believing whites of the overlaundered (unsuspecting) eyes.

IX.   This Town's Not Big Enough for Both of Me

Six weeks after Dan's arrest, three weeks through his jail term, his wife still lived in Falls. She prepacked, ready to depart, while hiding as well as you could in a town this small. No further church attendance. She had groceries delivered to her back door till her husband—released from his imprisonment ("Unnatural Acts," "Liberties Taken with a Minor," "Indecent Exposure")—could travel wherever they'd picked to settle next. He would get a new job—if without too many letters of rec.

Till Dan sent for the loved ones, his kids were kept indoors. When Julie R—— dodged into some store, seeking milk, she wore a kerchief and dark wing glasses. Most people avoided her. A few confident veteran clerks did speak (if only about the weather), and later they sought brownie points for having treated her as a regular human being. "After all, she's not the one's been going on all fours in J. C. Penney's boys' rooms. See the bags under her eyes, even behind those glasses? To find that out about the father of your sons—poor thing, crushed-looking . . ."

Dan served a seven-week sentence. Though he'd golfed with every white-shoe firm lawyer in eastern North Carolina, not one stepped forward to help. And he—shamed—simply accepted the court-appointed choice, a kid from Ohio fresh out of a so-so school and nothing special.

We never saw Dan again.

I, I never saw. Him.

(When in airports, grown, waiting for the rental-car line to dwindle, I'll still thumb through local phone books, checking under R——. No luck to date. What would I say to him? Is he still with his wife? Or maybe splitting the rent with some younger man? Alone? Alive?)

My dad played eighteen holes a week with him for six years, but that was neither mentioned nor admitted. Dan, once considered indispensable, seemed—overnight—not just dead but unmissed, except in certain tree houses.

I would aim my bike toward the R—— home, its staked FOR SALE tilted, cockeyed, out front. Sudden weeds everywhere. A split-level brick rancher with mature evergreen plantings, it looked like most other homes on the block; it was a Duke of Clarence. Myself a little pedant, I knew the model-home names of every suburb in biking distance. Musket ball in my pocket for luck, I stayed seated on my bike, stopped before Dan's unsold home. I regretted having snubbed his three skinny kids at the club pool.

Every car approaching from behind made the bristles of my crew cut stand on end, tentacles predicting him. I was sure he'd keep an implied appointment with his "little buddy," as he'd called me. But the sun set. It got cold. Dan never arrived.

One month later, I expected I would miss him less, not more. But it was more. So, with a certainty peculiar to the insane, I biked direct to a hanging "colonial" sign: J & L REALTY/INSURANCE—REACHING OUT TO THE COMMUNITY.

Wearing shorts, barefoot, I approached a gargoyle secretary powdered in hopes of looking younger. She did not. She gaped at my question, rose, stood wedged half behind a frosted door. "Boy, no shoes, asking ways to find Dan R——. Seems upset. Thin, well spoken . . . nervous."

The lady tipped back, smiled, disappeared again. "Maybe around ten years old?"

"Oh, dear God. Now they're coming in here to *us*. Where will it end? Payments is where."

A man veered out, his hand extended, the smile enforced as a laminated name tag. "Can I be of help? What do you need with him, son?"

"Nobody knows where Dan went. I miss him."

The secretary stepped one high heel back, but the executive tipped forward, considered touching me, then thought so much better of it, his right shoulder spasmed. "We have no address. Even if I wanted to trace him, which I don't, I couldn't. Who are your parents? Have you told them any of this? Because you're going to need help with it. More help than we can give you here, son. This is a workplace." The big phone rang and the two adults practically giggled, both lurching toward one black receiver. She beat him to it.

"Who is your father?" he asked. "Tell us who your people are."

I turned so slow, I padded out, bare soles smacking on cold lino, soles gingerly across hot pavement. Then I pedaled off so quick, swallowing all the air, eyes burning. I knew then. I could not afford to find him.

X. Hard Evidence

The boy Dan "touched" was the attractive youngest son of the heavy-set arresting officer. It later came out: This lieutenant tended to place his fifteen-year-old on nonschool days at better-known public urinals. This ploy rarely worked, since the intended victims enjoyed a communal word-of-mouth expert as their not-unprideful oral sex. Raleigh queers were long since on to *that* little trick and morsel. They did acknowledge as how the cop's kid looked a bit like James Dean, and—why lie?—he was extremely well hung for a boy who'd only shaved the once, for Easter service. They nicknamed this troubled, smoldering boy the James Dean Decoy, Bait Meat, and, best perhaps, The Trojan Hose. They knew to run from the sight of him (only some jerky married out-of-towner—hiding from his own kind and their helpful information—would've gone *near* that infamous young beauty holding his infamous older-looking beauty).

The Lieutenant encouraged his son, once stationed at busier urinals around our state's capital, to unhasp his all and, having unzipped, to, what?

I find imagining this father-to-son pep talk a very tough assignment. It may be the hardest thing to know. Eros: a magician's implement bent on disappearing everything put in it.

I understand Desire better than the Desire to kill Desire with a Desire of superior force, superior because fatal. To use your kid as other fellows' ship direct into prison. To me this seems as Martian as I might appear to some cop willing to dangle his boy as fishing bait—literally, dangle. "Son, just maybe think of, oh, say, Marilyn Monroe. Then, nature being nature, what happens'll happen, and don't mind letting the old one near you see your whatever . . . peek, whatever. . . . Not to be scared, either. 'Cause Dad's right back here. You just get the evildoer started and, by God, Dad and the long arm of the law'll do the rest."

I have myself experienced joyous moments in public restrooms, commingling and looking at, and more. Some moralists would say that Dan should not have touched a boy that age, even if the kid seduced him. Some readers will not have got this far because I seem to be pulling for the wrong side.

It is a medical fact:
You can kill a starving man by feeding him too fast.

As I write this, trying to reconstruct the start of Dan's arrest, I'm still turned on somewhat. The impending tragedy adds wallop to a humid scene in this large men's facility—four sinks, six stalls, eight urinals, all down the carpeted hall past Customer Services and Handy Layaway.

Perhaps this bathroom became so popular because its unoiled entry-way door squeaked—because the foyer entrance is obscured from the urinals and booths—because this gives its friskier patrons two seconds' warning. (That's of no use, naturally, if a secret photographer is lurking behind the only closed door of stall number five.)

I know all this because, at eleven, I insisted we go see a movie at this very Raleigh mall. Soon as my parents left me alone to watch Fred Mac-Murray and some irrelevant flying sheepdog, I slipped out, rushing straight to Penney's.

I found the sign still saying CUSTOMER SERVICES, HANDY LAYAWAY. I felt sad on discovering the crime scene abandoned. I paced off everyone's deeds. My already adult dick out, I was crying some, feeling now nauseous, now aroused, titillated at acting it all out, at letting my part take all the parts.

Dad is about to *leap and photograph.* At home he has two years' of complete incriminating snapshots, stuck into a store-bought album that came stamped with the gilded words "Our Best Memories . . ." When he's feeling discouraged about his other work on the force, some nights late, he'll get them out and peruse the terrified faces depicted and feel . . . achievement? a quickening? The father knows that, when lurching forth, he must look only at the culprit. This'll give Junior time to hide whatever just made the malefactor (on first seeing it) jump so, made him grow so immediately culpable when, invited to reach out, he does so, *flashbulb.*

Booth's metal door is kicked wide open. First bulb fires off, blinding in a mirror four sinks long, and another one is caught . . . red-handed, red-whatevered. The yelled legalities, barked sounds so loud on tile, and silver handcuffs flashing out. They're soon cinched onto a fellow whose dick is yet quite free. The culprit's dick is yet left sticking out, it's unable to change gears that fast, belonging to a human beast, if a decent Rotarian one. Hairy wrists are bound in metal bands, but the sturdy papa hard-on is yet poking forth so far that even the cop, a fellow male after all, lets the pederast try and wedge it all back in, before the officer pulls his perp through the bustle of our leading Penney's store, past MEETING YOUR KITCHEN AND BATHROOM NEEDS, UP TO 40% OFF, EVERYTHING MUST GO, where shoppers will be perplexed enough to see a handsome young man—head nodding shamefaced forward—bound in cuffs, and really shouldn't have to deal with such a boner on him, too.

It's tough forcing yourself back into your britches while wearing the cuffs that've already cut reddened slices into downy wrists. Best to either deal with your zipper or your handcuffs, but both at once is pretty much a killer.

XI.   The Fellow Ship Docked Below Fourteenth Street

Somehow, I've lived, grown, flourished, and fled Falls, by many, many states and jobs and beaux, and somehow, it's 1990: The newest of my escape-hatch tree houses is called Greenwich Village.

We speak of a lovely Saturday night in spring, and I'm carrying sixty dollars' worth of rubrum lilies, careful that their red-black pollen not stain my pristine clothes.

I am bound for a party whose parchment invitation insists overartfully, "Come as you would be, and as you are, but, if possible, tonight, in white, dear."

So, feeling good after a day of writing fiction that spawned four actual living, kicking sentences, I am gussied up in white bucks, white ducks, a pale tie, an off-white shirt—and I'm feeling nautical but nice when I hear a passing hot rod yell one word that I, in a naval mood, believe to be *"Farragut!"*

I get hit full-face. Two Jersey-flung paper cups, one full of warm beer, the other all cold Orange Crush, and I am soaked.

I hear laughing as they roar off. I'm left here gasping, doubled over.

The shock of it has knocked the wind clear out of me, but nothing worse. I set the flowers on a stoop. Take stock. There's a small cut on my forehead. Could one piece of flying ice have managed that?

"Everything's fine. No harm done," I tell myself. But I am so stained and sogged. I smell like someone else's four-day binge. I look down at the lightning bolt of orange sogged from my chest to the once-white crotch. I realize that even if I dash back home to change I have nothing white left to wear.

One block north, I dodge into an alley. These lilies are trembling so, like still-living things. I hide against the hoodlums' coming back for me. I know, through friends beaten or worse, that these New Jersey boys—if they got off a "good one"—tend to circle the block and swerve on back for further fun. I imagine fists next time, or hammers. This season, they favor hammers—the gay-bashing fashion accessory of choice. Innocence, my own, makes me wonder how they ever *knew* I *was* one. Duuhh! (Probably, I overdid. All the Wildean lilies, right?)

Caught, I'm moved to explain to them: I don't usually walk around all in white like Mark Twain, who claimed to be straight. Shamed, I consider just skipping the party. Maybe I'll go late, when a spotless entrance will matter less. I pull out the sogged invitation, double-checking the address.

We'd thrown White Parties all year. "Come As You Are" ones had recently been done to death. I now reread tonight's prissy, funny, self-defensive "theme":

> COME AS YOU WOULD BE, AND AS YOU ARE,
> BUT, IF POSSIBLE, TONIGHT,
> IN WHITE, DEAR.
> R.S.V.P.

And, vowing to tell every-fuckin'-body how I got so orange and wet and why I smell of Hoboken brewery, I soon make myself into something of a party hit. Our specialty: a brand of bravery as flashy as some new perfume's name. Cheap yet necessary, it's the comic art that only other survivors will all recognize. I am become a tale of woe transcended—I am my own only sole excuse. I am the opposite of apology. Maybe I courted grief by being too far "out"? But I don't seek to become a nose-rubbing-in Target, believe me.

I have not been tortured fully. I am in good health, and have had hun-

dreds of lovers, and I've never been arrested, yet. My heart's been broken, but that's pretty normal, right? I am not sick, nor do I think of
myself as "sick." My parents still ask for credit, having somehow hero-
ically accepted my "life-style choice." They still remember my birthday.
But they swear I've rubbed their noses in it.

*Mother took me aside one year after Dan was driven from town, when
she saw me still gloomy and jumpy about the speed and injustice of his
going, and—trying to help, I'm sure—she said, "There's something we
never told you about Dan, when you were younger and all?" I felt scared,
seizing her white wrist, begging for news. "He was not exactly smart, Dan.
He had other qualities that made up for it, and sweet as the day is . . . but
not like your father or our doctor-lawyers, he was sort of always along
because of his charm and the way he looked and his . . . not reTARded, just
not all that swift really, and . . ." She saw my face and added, "I'm not sure
why I'm telling you this. Maybe trying to make it easier for you to . . ." And
I knew, in that absolute way we, so hooked genetically, knew each other,
that Mom was about to say "get over him," but stopped. See, that sounded
too much like a boy-girl romance. "Maybe I'm trying to make it easier for
you to forget him, son." It was the wrong thing to have said. This close
against my face, she saw that.*

XII.   The Captain Hook

I once literally hooked literally all of him. It proved to be a fad. This
was the year those others caught, then vanished him.

He had station-wagoned over to pick up Dad for further golf: *shave
and a haircut.* Dad, fighting his latest financial reversal, was late. Those
guys never tired of golf. Maybe their dick jokes helped? I owned a new
green Spaulding fly-casting rod. I'd been practicing alone a lot.

I felt I was getting pretty darn accurate. I could place my weighted silver hook just about where I wanted it. (Be careful what you aim for.)

Dan discovered me tossing line at a chalked blue ring on the side of
our white garage. Waiting for my father, Dan had come wandering seeking me. On our white-frilled porch, his golf buddies audibly milled,
swilling vodka, massacring baby onions.

"Why not cast her my way, pardner? You're gettin' good at it, I see

that plain. Here, maybe try and put 'er about here?" Dan had spied a red
plastic ring. It was the chew toy for Tuffie, our boxer. Dan lifted it free of
a boxwood bush, then held red out, an exact right angle to his body. His
jaw so square and blue, his face so blankly direct, he looked earnest as
some model in a Red Cross diagram for Boating Safety. I felt weakened
by appreciation, patriotic.

Dan squinted in April sunlight. With his face screwed up, you saw
how he must've looked as a boy, winsome if underfinanced, rawer. He
was not like me. He'd been born poor. Part of his sexiness came from
some lasting smell of that. I once believed that dogs were the daddies,
cats were the moms. I once thought women were rich and men born
poor. Go figure.

Today Dan wore fresh-pressed chinos, deck shoes, a plaid short-sleeve
shirt. He smiled across sixty feet. Distance reduced him to trout size. But
his hundred-watt attraction remained a lure, immense. I readied my aim.
I took a bowlegged stance. It was my own approximation of the Male. I
posed, tough, fifty-six whole pounds.

Dan's pals played raucous Twenty-One on our side porch, they gossiped hard (some young country boy who worked at Aetna had got
engaged to Donna!). Big drinks' ice cubes clinked. I readied my rod,
checked all my interior devices. It was a day of birdsong, temperature in
the seventies, a day both gold and blue.

Studying Dan's pale inner arm held direct off his torso, I so wanted to
touch him. "Here she comes, Dan. On your mark . . ."

I aimed. I recall the thumb release of line. "Go!" The reel sang its precise ratcheting, pure play-out. April!

(Later, during sex, I'd recall this giddying suspension. A man feels his
release "go off," you feel the aim-out pleasure unspiral into air, your reel
line is moving, about to mainline joy throughout your groin, then flooding every cell of you. You know it's literally coming, *you* are. You know
that nothing on the earth—not even a jealous macho God—can stop it
now, your gusher, eureka!

The Fellow Ship fullsteamahead!)

My silver line lifts a C shape of rolling light, midair. Settling. Then I
feel the snap of my hook find something hard/good—a surface firm yet
yielding—springy, live, worthwhile. There's much game "play" in it.

And, even as I realize I've hit, not the red ring, but one pale human wrist (not the left, holding a target, but Dan's other one), some excitement, some malice unaccountable, makes me jerk it anyway. Gotcha, mother-fucker!

Snagging the arm of a man who's always been only kind to me is a response so male, so savage, automatic—it scares me sick. The Sports Gene! *"Owwweesh!"* Dan howls. (Might this not be Dan's exact sexual-release cry?)

My rod drops to grass. I speed toward my prize. Even in pain, even after studying the wound I've caused, Dan is easing down. He's kneeling on our lawn. Readying himself, because, at my level, *he* plans to comfort *me*!

I follow line to him. Filament burns a hole in the center of my chubby fist. He's before me, guessing how upset I'll be. The guy prepares a grin. He means, even in his shock, to protect me from embarrassment.

On his knees, Dan is just about my own height fully standing. This close, his head appears enormous as a puppet's, its handsomeness gone jagged as Sherlock Holmes's hat and pipe and shoebill nose. He receives my running weight with a little grunt. He shields me from seeing his bleeding arm. Cardplayers have heard Dan's holler. Two lean off the porch. "It's nothing," Dan's baritone calls, warming my neck and ear. The one good arm cradles me against him. It pulls me closer to my target, home direct between a squatting hero's opened knees.

Tuffie's chewed red plastic ring is now suspended—bull's-eye—just above my friend's clumped crotch. Other men are toasting us with bour-bon, laughing, calling all their usual usuals.

(In polite Falls, you never ever say what's gone previously unsaid. If something has not yet been spoken, it probably never needed saying. So: "Caught you a big one, hunh, kiddo? Six inches shy of a six-footer, best just throw him back, what say?")

Trying to keep our dealings private, Dan smiles at me, apologizing for those clods. His fibrous arm flips over, accidentally showing me white skin, powder-blue marbled veining, and one long spittle of opaque red leaving the silver beak of my own hook. That surgical hook puckers a two-inch sample of someone's bacon-fat flesh. "Noo," I cry. The barbed beak looks too big ever to cut quite out of him.

We're bound together for good, flies tied. I nuzzle, sobbing, "Didn't mean to, not to *you*, Dan. . . ."

I feel half faint, daylight overdoing it and drenching me, accusatory. I'm pitched even deeper in a pliant vise between Dan's open sinew thighs.

Mother, seeing my latest tangled mess from her kitchen window, will soon come running. As ever, perfectly supplied, she'll hold a silver tray supporting Merthiolate, pedicure scissors, cotton balls plumped fast and hostessy into a silver salt-dish (Grandmother Halsey's, 1870 or so). Plus Dan's favorite drink—a light Cutty and water. (I heard "Cutty *Shark*," I liked knowing that its label showed The Fellow Ship.)

Dreading others' seeing us, hating how pain alone permits our union, I cry "Really sorry" into splayed legs. They remain wide open. I've run right into their V-shaped shelter. I wedge now farther between.

I am sobbing, he holds me fast. I am getting to touch good fur on the one arm I failed to hook. I find that, in his suffering, Dan doesn't much notice how I hold him. And so, sick with boldness, I tip against the inner fabric of his much-washed pants.

Mid-thigh, I read the Braille outline of sexual parts, his. They're presented plain, canine in guilelessness, grapelike in gentle plentiful cascade. The very symbol of abundance, Mr. Dan's portables nearby.

Birds, disturbed by his wounded cry, go again all song. I hear Mother clanking in the kitchen, assembling emergency gear. And me? I'm just crazed enough by guilt and proximity. Using bloodshed as my excuse, I find nerve enough to cup my open right hand lightly—light as light itself—against them, against all his. Just overtop, no pressure. I simply do it, crying as distraction.

First Dan only holds my shoulders, staring at my freckles. Then my pleasure—stirred, overambitious—leads me to tighten my clamp on him, his. My reach exceeds my grasp. I see his face change, slow.

(Meanwhile, back at the crotch, my subtle squirrelish fingers register: my Dan today wears no underdrawers, unusual in Falls in '57. My palm can tell: unlike Dad and me, my Dan here is not circumcised [born poor].)

I see concern fold the brow of a squatting man who clutches a child, holding, unexpectedly, that dude's own central credentials. No "Ooops." No, "Errr, would ya please let 'em aloose now, son?"

Instead: Dan himself glances down between Dan's own mighty legs. Definitely checking on a little scoop-shaped paw now curved against his right-dressed member. Beneath my grasp, it feels as spongy as a round loaf of sandwich-sized Wonder.

He still half-pretends not to notice. No one near the house can see what's going on. Dan, metal-blue jaw, gives me one sleepy, dubious half-smile. In it, amused recognition, some pity maybe, much fellow-feeling, sadness, a father's patience for one kid's guileless curiosity. Oh, The Fellow Ship.

He makes no move at all to close his legs or shift my hand. But—being Protestant—I know to remove my hand, for him. Enough. For now.

The moment I let loose, he laughs about my hooking him. "No sweat, buddy. Hurts about like a mosquito bite, tops. Just shows how many you're gonna land ahead. You got some touch on you, know that? You just did what they say do, in the books: 'Concentrate, then "spot" your trout, then flick 'n' hook.' "

Oh God, here comes Mother wobbling on high heels and carrying that clanky glinting tray. "I hurt him," I apologize, partly bragging. Mom hostesses me aside. Soon I've inchwormed up into my tree house. I am coughing with sobs, staring down at my gentle, bloodied trophy.

Mother, like some comic waiter, keeps the silver tray level at all costs. Kneeling, ministering, she offers Dan his Cutty first.

(Carolina, 1957, The Golden Age of Silver Trays.)

I yell down, "I didn't know it hurt. To fish. Hurt the *fish,* Dan."

"Mustn't blame yourself, pal. You've got the sporting touch. . . . You'll land hundreds more ahead, and 'rainbows' too. Glad to be the first in line—a great long mess o' keepers. Your only problem is, your aim's too good. Every man should have such trouble. Definitely no more crying, umkay, m'buddy-ro? Promise your Dan?"

"I pwwo-mise, . . . D-D-Dan."

How could you not love such a fellowshiper? Had my big buddy just talked to me in code? Did he even deeply mind or notice as I—leisurely, entranced—felt his dick's noble heft? And did Dan allow me or prevent me or invite me? Who'd *had* whom?

Even today, when I hear the phrase "child molester," I think, not of One Grown-Up Who Molests Children, but of some kid who diddles unsuspecting innocent adults, grown-ups who glaze over immediately, going child-passive.

I'm told that the victim-adults—wracked with equal parts guilt and interest—sometimes never get over it.

Dan? I count on that.

Inside your right wrist, even with the lights out, can you still touch a little scratchy signature of scarring?

XIII.   Over and Out

I "came out" in whatever room was left, after Dan—whatever space remained to stand up in. That zone proved no larger than one store's men's room, one stall of it, a tree house, one closet door laid horizontal, opening downward, only onto spine-cracking gravity.

Me? Born guilty as any Calvinist sinner (guilty prior to even getting it up once, much less forcing myself on another male). I struggled past the threat of local arrest. I didn't even feel safe in Norfolk. I needed four to six state borders between me and Home before I tried anything. It was way out of town, up north in Boston, before I dared unzip for any reason beyond legal peeing (and even after that, I scrubbed these paws but good). I'd been well trained in pain—pleasure was a night course I would have to teach myself. (Not to brag, but I found I had a certain latent talent for it.)

Alone with my first, I had to know for sure that the person who seemed to want me to reveal my lower body to him was not just doing this to please his dad, one alcoholic copper father, waiting, with a reel-to-reel recorder underneath this very bed.

Dan R—— failed to become what authorities intended—a reason for me to stultify erotic life. Sure proof of why to keep it forever sealed up in your pants. Instead, my Dan—who let a worried nine-year-old boy lightly touch his crotch "for luck"—became a reason *not* to hesitate sexually, ever. Dan's real crime wasn't the one they creamed him for. His true sin was earlier postponement (all the joy a man so splendid, skilled, and energetic might've given other men).

Fear led to his lurching, damning recklessness. He is my hard-on polar north. Hands on hips, he's innocent even of his own scary magnetic looks, the teeth too white, the face too decent not to have a lot of patsy in it—given a world as mean as ours.

Sometimes . . . I believe my artistic aunt was all too correct. Those days, you know what I feel like?

I am a mechanical cuckoo. Lots of laughs. I got built, a charming

Tirolean timepiece that I myself did not design. A clock is both my castle and my cage; I guess you could say I have the penthouse.

But I'm really just the mechanism's star-quality *Hello, Dolly* doodad. My loud, mandatory appearance announces each hour's timely high points. I never do get over my stage fright. Every quarter-hour of human history, I brace, required again to act cocky and jaunty and artistic, decorative. And yet, what's weird, I feel completely unprepared, each time. I am both star and target.

I get popped out anyway, my nose rubbed in the blinding light, I'm terrified even during my most cheerful chirping.

Otherwise, rocked back on the governing coil, my beak tip rests against two round shut swinging doors, I feel most grateful for usual darkness. They named this whole clock for my carefree two-note song.

But, truth is, I am usually "in." My tree-house closet is shut. Then I don't have to think of how I look, or which latent assassin is waiting out there this go-round. I prefer not thinking of it much each day. But, four times hourly, I'm totally and publicly "out," outed. It feels self-conscious and short-lived as someone sticking his own tongue out. You can't ever really say much that way, can you?

Even when you hear me sing, *tweet-twitty-twit,* even when you set your watch by me (and do, by all means, 'cause I'm so reliable), even as you smile over your shoulder on hearing my musical comedy again, even when I seem all charm, pure velvety buttery goodwill—truth is, I'm not singing.

It's a shaped scream.

Thanks to Dan, I can't afford ever to comfortably abstain. Not—with a two-hour layover between trains in Milan, and after meeting somebody kind and at least half attractive, someone whispery and nodding, with a borrowed apartment just a three-minute walk from this terminal, some guy so visibly willing—not to let time go, not to let this pleasure pass. I remember Dan. I go with him.

I expect eventual arrest. I am never fully safe in this, my country. Times, I seem to live scot-free, I'm healthy, I'm allowed against all odds to exist in my own way, and to write this toward you, fellow innocent. If I were not gay, I would be supporting Alice and Kyle and meeting at this moment with the Search Committee at the college—afterward, stopping by a busy but dangerous rest area on the interstate—and I would not have written this, and therefore, for whatever it's worth, you would not be reading it.

XIV.   Last

Coming out I managed. *Staying out* is hard.

A day in the life?

I came out at 7 a.m. today—I did so just by tucking one cream-colored silk hanky in my blazer pocket. To me, it didn't look fey, it just looked right, manly, necessary. By three this afternoon, I was having a late lunch with two co-workers. Who told a gay-bashing "Hear about the pitbull with AIDS?" joke, one I really might've/should've protested. The lunch had been so heavy, and I'm getting over a hellacious summer cold, and I just couldn't find the energy to make a scene, to force the point again, to act so nunnishly doctrinaire. Didn't want to make another dreary plea for tolerance, yet again, Killjoy.

Walking back to work alone, I saw a truly great-looking boy. And—before I quite censored myself properly—I'd tossed an appreciative stare at this blond, aproned clerk. He stood spraying down the eggplants displayed before our corner greengrocer. And he offered me some visual encouragement—top lip curling back, a toughening of his flippant stance—but then, three seconds later, reverse, he flipped me the finger and muttered, "You fuckin' *wish*."

I crossed the street, my face neutral, spirits silenced. I now felt sure he'd holler an insult (the actual name of what I am). I felt sure he'd aim his rubber hose at me. The Trojan Hose. At the very least, he'd ruin my best suede shoes.

See, friend, I came out at 7 a.m. today. And, at around 2:48 p.m., I went back in.

Tentative, I re-emerged around 3:43, until that aproned blond flipped me the bird and threatened me at 3:44, till he drove me to tiptoe boldly back in yet again where many men have gone before. By 5:10, feeling stronger, I risked it again . . . but then . . .

In the dream I am still nine. Not "out," but up my tree house. There's been a lynching or some act of piracy in Falls. It's late, just before dawn.

Our neighborhood echoes with men shouting, "Not in here. He over there? Found yet?" Manhunt.

I'm huddled, flannel pajamas, on my closet door. When I notice torch-light, I discover you, Dan, tied to the tree above me.

In the filmic way of dreams, a voice announces, "Women look finest in candlelight. Men are best seen by torch."

Torches smoke all around us up here, the maple leaves sizzle. Somebody has bound you fast. Your chest is glazed as a Viking ham, drenched in salt spray or blood or honey. Varnish shows ribs' every perfect fold, the bulk and hollow. But there are hooks in you. Lures with wet feathers, savage broken lines from years ago. Your hands are tied behind you around the tree's main trunk. I fight to release you. Your eyes are aimed up, sainted, lost. My fingers prove too small. The knots seem permanent, grown barky as the tree.

Far below, voices keep mapping the search for you. You wear only a white towel around your waist. As I stare past it, toward your face, I see that something immense bulks up underneath the terry cloth. I say, "Dad, are you okay, can I help here?" but I mean "Dan." I give you many chances to object as, slow, I touch your thighs. Finally, with you in such pain and beauty, I don't await invitation. I tell myself that what I do is just First Aid, I reach under your towel, unfasten it.

Lit by orange light in my tree, I understand that they have hurt you. Where I expected your manhood waiting, springy, perfectly cheerfully complete, they've slid a giant fishhook. It has been stuck all the way between your legs and I see its barbed tip gleaming in the flame. It's perfectly down-curved. I see how cleverly it's made, so it will go right through but never get back out.

And, looking up at you, I touch the hook they've hooked you with, so cruelly, Dan. Depriving you of such a right. Kneeling in a state of worship, sobbing, kinship, lust, I find it's warm under my palm. Now, finally unshy, I kiss your thighs and crane up nearer it. I am your fellow fellow. I place my mouth to it. I find the taste is ketchup, metal, Milk Duds, bitter money, milk, and salt and sugar mixed.

. . . The taste is equal pleasure, equal pain. I wake. The first thing I know is: I am no longer nine. You're still gone. They caught you out.

Dan, are you alive? Might you really read this? If so, please, please drop me a line care of the publisher. I'm older. I've learned what to do—

for pleasure, after pain. I've got questions. About that kid, the cop's yellow-haired son, how good did he look? How much did he do to draw you those few urinals closer (into camera range)? I think I know a lot about you. But it's just based on those first nine years, when you honked at me. And paid attention. And sent bills on strings up my tree. Did you suspect I was one, too? Did you know that you were? Was I funny then, or somewhat sweet? Or even pretty, in my longing looks both up and down? Listen to me, this old, still fishing for compliments! Jailbait. I just want to check in.

You didn't seem to mind a fellow's drawing close against you, even as you bled. His little mitt nested on worn pants just above your crank. Your grin was relaxed, secure, if fairly tired. (Did you already guess what it would cost us?) Still Ideal Captain of My Fellow Ship, my first "rainbow," "big one," at times I feel so sound and lucky. I myself never got caught, never did get sick. My very occupation is to tell the truth—as much as will still sell.

I feel I owe you everything, Dan. Times, it seems they did my damage all to You.

I bet you're still in the world. Your youngest kid finished college— what?—twenty years ago. You are barely seventy. That, increasingly, is not so old. I'm forty-eight already. The hair on your arms must be mostly silver now, not unattractive. I sense you ended up in Arizona, maybe Colorado, somewhere dry out there.

Are you still her husband? Or by now splitting house payments with another guy? But, no, I picture you as living alone. I picture a blue car, your climbing into it, driving to some modest restaurant, heading home, stretching, putting hands on hips, going back inside.

Despite my therapy and the wish to think well of myself, I am still a subdivision of desire. And here I choose to end it.

I am the horny guilty husband, noticing one sullen blond boy slouched at the urinal three down; I move his way, beckoned by his head wave, the one slow wink, and something that he shows me.

I am the blond boy, aware of my poisonous beauty, ready for Dad to pop out of that green stall with a black camera in lieu of his pink face.

For now, I'm mostly a youngster enjoying the weight of my blood-stocked dick. I am feeling the full power of being male, which means, in an odd way, being fatal for others.

And, alas, I am also, alas, the tortured ex-Marine cop, forty pounds over his Parris Island weight, a major smoker, rifle collector, registered Republican, with fifteen long years till retirement, a disappointed man who—having built rabbit-catching boxes as a boy—finds entrapment lots more fun than giving speeding tickets. He is also a guy whose own sexual fantasies let him display his son (nearly as pretty as he once was). He does it in order to catch the vermin he sees swarming everywhere, the shameless weirdos who'll be the death of this Great Land, the queers that he knows want, most obsessively of all, *him*.

Sure, he might have drinking probs and the so-so marriage and no further prospect of promotion anywhere near even as*si*stant chief, but at least he's not that far gone. He is the detective about to detect. Sick behavior like . . .

Mine. Like Dan's. And I keep silent, in a stall already unlatched for kicking open at lethal speed. I unpocket the necessary flashbulb I'm about to insert into its reflector socket. I hear whispering. Good boy, my son is waving the perpetrator closer. I prepare the flashbulb. The glass sphere's metal tip I dampen with my tongue. I am ready, now, I breathe, I kick toward desire illegal. The blast in a tile space this small sounds like a cannon going off. I holler "FRee-eeze!" at heat. As I capture, for eternity, the Older Me just as I touch the healthy prong of Me Young. And, armed with pictures of me molesting myself, I am going to have to turn me in. Otherwise, admit it—I'd be less than a whole man.

Hey, Dan? Missed you.
Find me, sir.

Saint Monster

In Loving Memory—
Mac Dancy (1888?–1979)
and
Ardelia Smith (1930–1966)

1. OLD TESTAMENT

Expulsion

I. Genesis

"The Expulsion to the Garden"

And the Lord God called unto Adam, and said unto him, Where art thou? And he said, I heard thy Voice in the garden, and I was afraid, because I was naked. . . .

Genesis 3:9–10

Dad screams I mustn't see them at it but I race across our backyard toward the darkened house. Under me, short legs are stunted flippers spinning. My old tricycle on its side, I hop. Lagging, Daddy bellows, "Come back, son. Leave them be. Don't go in and look. Let sleeping dogs. She loves us anyways. . . ."

Three lawns behind, he waves the white sling of his newly broken arm. He's a smoker and is stumbling and keeps hacking, the old sweetie. Daddy begs me not to catch the two of them at it, at some deed. But I clamp palms over my ears, I must not obey Dad, I am only doing this for him.

Our rear screen door is latched. I make such a fist. Knuckles break through rusted wire, a fry of brown powder. I jump then chin myself on the door's crossbar. Reaching in, I unhook everything.

"Don't looook," Dad's voice smears. But I am through our kitchen and clear into the shadowed living room. I've run five paces past already seeing them, joined. My elbows out, I slide to a car-brake-screeching halt.

. . .

My mother, so pale and beautiful, is so beneath him. The couch's many printed roses look cactus-sized, thirstier, as smothered as my Mom. The man's back is tanned and stretches longer than three of me. His bare bottom is vanilla, rocking like Mom's foot-treadle Singer. But somehow into Mom, a derrick over/into over/into her. Her fists hold hair behind his ears, hair gold as coins of my play money. White summer pants bunch around his ankle planted on our rug.

Though he twists and sees this woman's eight-year-old standing right beside the couch, the man's lower back sneaks continually on, letting Momma have it, blam, there, blam, there. Letting her have what? I'd like to know.

I cannot figure how I understand what I am partly seeing. I simply know he's giving Mom a major one of those. Pinned under such thudding, her knees have risen not that far from Mom's own ears. She now turns slow, notices me whole here, screams, "Can't beee!"

"What say, pal?" Doc's tone comes casual. Bugs Bunny. He talks right over at me. He's naked so happily. Dead level with my frown, he crunches one dry wink my way. "Wha's up?"

My chest quaking, I point to him, "Bad bad baaad man!"

Then, for reasons past anything merely sayable, I jump onto a fellow facedown in Mom.

I have mounted him like that bucking dime-horse downtown. I am riding the long spine of the veterinarian, who seems someway out of, then too IN my mom. Out of, in. Out in. In in. Innie.

"Baby," she speaks through him to me, "your weight's too much, it's hurting me."

"My weight? MY dern weight?!"

These fists of mine are really slamming hard the back of a man so accustomed to being caught, that he is finishing. He is going to. I feel a tally mounting in him and now sledding quite unstoppable downhill.

I understand this payoff without knowing what it means or where it goes or how it feels to them. I'll just keep trying stopping him. I cling around his tree-ringed neck. I yank his yellow hair way back, I scratch under one braced arm. A dark sliding voice says, "Bite that ear, you're dead, you little mongrel bastard. . . ." I am kicking his bare butt so. "Go away from off my Mom, Mister. Go on off from us, get . . . off of her, you . . . HURT-ER!"

His whole back seizes. He does undo. In Mom. And, riding him myself, I feel those rhythms spill. I ride his surge. It plays out like some shark taking the whole hook to the blackest corner of our ocean floor. Cold. I am now staring past a strong man's leather shoulder, I can look direct into my mother's hollering mouth.

One time at school? I saw a dog? do what this one's doing to my Momma? but to another, lower shorter yellower dog? And, they got snagged? So the principal had to turn a garden hose on them and everybody laughed except our prissy teacher screaming for "Absolute Silence!" Could a big dog do it to a little cat? Could a . . . ? I am look-ing right in at my mother's silver dental spots, her wide mouth screaming, "No! There's not a way this's possibly hap-ning. Don't let it see him, Doc." He collapses, then I do. She too then. Down go Mom's knees, drawbridge, tickling my either arm.

Next, from this place on the man's mattress of a back, over the kitchen's reflecting linoleum, through the blue gauze of our torn screen door, out in April's gold-green light, I spy my Daddy, my ugly, decent Christian father. "Toadface," "Liverlips," "Dick beak," neigh-bors call his grade of homely. This, of the kindest person who ever probably breathed.

He tiptoes nearer our house. Then—too good a man to maybe live real long—Dad backs off toward fencing. His face looks opened like a tin can split end-wise by some ax.

I yell toward the one who pays to feed a lady that'd let some horse doctor ride her. "Don't see this, Dad! Go on home away from it. They're just talkin. I found nothing, okay, Dad? But just stay out the house a minute more, umkay? Cause we're in here getting things nice. For you."

Then I understand: Where is more home base for Dad than Mom? For Dad, I'm pretty much the Home.

.   .   .

Through screen door, I watch Pop's busted arm flap out to keep him standing. The broken one, all white, is plastered fat. He half-falls anyway, supported by our neighbors' chain-link fence. Dad keeps beating the back of his head against that metal upright. Fencing shakes, tense steel mesh ringing, two hands cup beside the mouth. It keeps calling my name. He knows I have already seen everything our town's been saying. Everything Dad has never let himself quite know. At last I understand what "do it" means. My own mom nicely showed me first.

Dad waits, bent out there, still struggling to light a Camel with his one unbroken hand. Needing it that bad, using fence to steady the latest match shaking out, he can't even smoke. It's then my dad starts hollering straight up, "Why'd my baby have to catch them? You were gonna save him, remember? Ain't I been being good enough? Why us, God?"

The rest is mainly blackness. First I feel the naked man beneath me turn. By now, I am so weak I've stretched across him like some soup-noodle starfish. I have pounded his whole back with all of my five points, head included. But I've stopped nothing. The stranger scoots over, spills me, stands. With the strong impersonal hands of a Large-Animal Vet, Doc easily palms me off into the other room.

He takes me from the sight of Mother's half-remembered breasts. Each one a white clown-face, its snout a red-gold maple drawer-pull. Below, one browny-yellow yarn pompom; her two middle fingers hide dead-center. "Son, why?" Her voice so flat. "Why today?"

Mom's worst hurter totes me to a room not mine. He lays me with real care facedown across my folks' chenille. I look over at his naked front. There is a confusion of amounts. Do doctors catch contagions off large beasts? Did being too near bulls make him go big? He's saying, "Ever hear of knockin, kid?"

And louder, to her still moaning on our couch, "You went and whelped yourself a biter, Grace. Hate the biters. Don't worry, I'll be back. But for now I'm outta here. I can take a friggin hint." After he's hopped around the other room to pull his pants up over it, I hear him kiss her then dodge free. His huge Pontiac leaves us in a fuss of gravel, it squalls off, shortwave antennas whipping.

Silver-blue fumes settle.

Such silence clamps down.

Finally, for city blocks, there are just two noises—one bird singing its routine song, as if trying to cover for a grown man's backyard sobbing. And Dad. Who sounds like something almost-monster perfectly newborn. There's coughing in it. It's somewhat a cow, a hurt one.

Sheeps go, "Baaaa."

Cows go, "Moooooo."

Birds'll mostly "Tweet" on you.

But my Poppa, the salesman, the joke man, the joke, the giver-away of God's free word, the ugliest white man alive in Falls, is out there now alone, face-first into our fencepost.

Poppas they must often go, "Noooo." Mine sure does.

I find a waiting darkness black as Bible. I walk between its cast-iron covers; they clank jail-shut behind me.

When I wake, it's breakfast, everybody acting like nothing ever happened. "Want toast?" But I see the screen door torn open down its center like lightning permanently let in. Some kids have little brothers or sisters that live with them. I have a li'l lightning bolt I invited in this house forever. I brought the world home. All of us must now live so unzipped into drying public sunlight.

I know I saw what I did not understand but will, ahead. I've saved each second, every shift of it. I know I slowed it once. But now things feel way worse. Thanks to me, things have only broken open even more. I guess from my parents' faces that what I stopped one time, it has not ended.

And when, passing butter, she looks disgusted right my way, when he stares tender, checking how things are with me, I receive a four-ton load of all I am too young to know yet.

I see that I have ended them.

In trying to save my Dad from Mom, I have already killed them both.

II. Exodus

"Our Motel Bible Route"

And I appeared unto Abraham, unto Isaac. . . . And I have . . . estab-lished my covenant . . . to give them . . . Canaan, the land of their pil-grimage, wherein they were strangers. . . . And I will take you to me for a people, and I will be to you a God. . . . And I will bring you in unto the land.

Exodus 6:3–8

Owners of second-rank motels need time-consuming hobbies. Your last customer's car leaves. You go in and change the nasty sheets. Nothing else will happen this whole afternoon. So far into country-side, everything is lazy but the flies. If you've ever felt one itch toward suicide, hot hours in a cinder-block lobby will clambake all such urges to your surface.

Why not take up jigsaw puzzles? Learning to make mosaic coasters might be nice. "VACANCY"? Well, accept Jesus as your personal Saviour. Then, especially at your time of worst despair around 3:16 p.m., reread your Bible. John 3:16. Unique ideas and handicrafts do help time pass. Start such projects. Pronto.

My father, a believer and a cuckold, belonged to the club that places Bibles in transients' rooms worldwide. Sundays, Dad delivered. And so, so did I. As his only kid and son, as someone Mother preferred not to see during leisure afternoons spent with mysterious headaches that kept her sick in the bed each Sabbath, I became Dad's "Bible Special's B-52 copilot."

My father sold flashy shirts and haberdashery novelties along a three-state route. This made motels Clyde's weeknight home. His name was Clyde Melvin Delman, Sr. He wore two different kinds of cufflinks he called "m' demonstrators." Dad, exactly as gentle as ugly, could make any chore go adventure for a boy. He let me reset the odometer, clocking exact distances between oncoming Guernsey cows. Clyde let me keep my best arrowheads in the glove box, just in case. I "drove" on his lap. I was salaried thirty cents per Sabbath. Dad encouraged me to spend it all on nonessentials.

We considered his brand-new 1954 Packard 165 HP Clipper Sedan our Third Musketeer. Father, Son, and Holy Coach. A really good car is a Godly benefit. Thirty cubic feet of usable trunk more than housed our weekly Bibles. Still in my possession, the hardbound *Owner's Manual*. It remains an epic poem to that age, and to Clyde's own sweet 8-cylinder faith:

> *Few homes are as tastefully and lavishly furnished, few private clubs so richly appointed as our colorful Packard interiors for 1954. Faultless tailoring . . . an almost unlimited selection of supple textured fabrics (from our new Nylon matelasse to traditional flannel broadcloth) . . . the gleam of chrome . . . the hush of sound-proofed bodies . . . all contribute to a feeling of luxury matched by no other car on the road.*

For one of the last times in American public relations, all this was absolutely true. And my father was the kindest man alive.

Dad's plainness seemed to release others toward cautionary pity then noisier good times. His funeral would prove Standing Room Only, almost as many black people as white. The chapel soon grew monkey-house loud with adult (Caucasian) sobs. "Never in my career . . . ," our town mortician told me later.

But turns out it's a mixed blessing, sainthood. Goodness can make your daddy be too public, gullible. I spent a lot of my time guarding him, guarding for him—and with an overzealousness at which I have already somewhat hinted.

No one but this guy's loving son can tell you simply enough: Clyde M. Delman, Sr., was truly nothing to look at. Some fellows' ugliness renders them Untouchables, clock- and conversation-stoppers. Not

Clyde's. I still marvel how his rubber face seemed to limber up others, unleashing first their pity then their fondest wit. In the English language, no single noun describes this effect. German offers a near miss. There should really be a word!

At the PTA open house, Dad's curdled buttermilky features, his "rust" houndstooth jacket, the racehorse tie-clasp with real chain bridles, made even my antique third-grade teacher ("Absolute Silence!") smile then flirt. I sat amazed. With powdery half-vampish glamour, one broken-down flapper suddenly opened laterally, like some drying newborn moth. She batted lashes, touched one side of her calamined neck, she grinned four pointy yellowed teeth Dad's way.

No one ever wanted Clyde M. Delman, Sr., to leave the room. (Except maybe Mom.) Me least of all.

Poor Dad's separate features began life as factory thirds, then really botched the arrangement! Eyes set this close threatened to become unanimous, cycloptic. Forehead low, skin more "manila" than pink, ears attached like opened armoire doors, wide-wale nostrils on too short a nose nubbed above a mouth like some gift-shop nutcracker's. It was the facial equivalent of scrambled eggs.

People divorce each other for "mental cruelty." And my mother could've made her court case with four simple mug shots—sides, the head's front, its gourdy back. For "cruel and unusual ugliness," Grace Delman might have received major alimony. Instead she seemed to have settled for a platinum veterinarian every Sunday.

Mom had a way of making nothing much seem fun. At least nothing she ever planned showing us. Carnivals were loud and "cheap." Christmas just meant further work. "Hanging doodads up can be nice, but taking them down just kills me. The sadness of their going back in dusty boxes for another year." Then came a sigh the size of a soup bowl.

My overeducated mother was a thin, stark woman with ideal breasts and a big undirected intelligence that seemed, like her chest, fastened to her by mistake. Snobbish, sickly, "intellectual," she lived at the uneasy mercy of a rustic, watchful little town.

Maybe if she'd gone to church? If only Grace volunteered to read aloud for chain-smoking bomb-blinded soldier boys out at the VA. What if she'd kept our yard way nicer? Could anything have made Mom popular? She had no womenfriends: always a terrible sign. Nobody came near her, nobody but Dad and me, and maybe one more.

Newly married, she'd read every book in the town's public library, even electrical-engineering texts; then Grace Meadows Delman began to buy new novels by mail order, at retail. Soon this expense nearly outstripped our family's meal budget. Three novels a day, Mom speedread without much training and very little retention. She claimed she read to escape—but I noticed: it didn't make returning any happier.

Her costly book-habit seemed to keep my dad a traveling salesman. In this, I now see, there might have been a plan. Mother's unhappiness was "catching," like the flu. So was her desire.

Mom's sexual indifference to my father drove him half-insane. Come sundown, the itchingness grew palpable in a tract house small as ours. His longing for her soon drove me crazy. Clyde cringed with needing her; he would be smoking midnight Camels, patrolling one room; I'd rest wide awake, wearing blue footed pajamas, uneasily erect in another; and we'd both listen to her, their bedroom door half open, Yes? No?

She'd be pacing in her sea-green nightie, mumbling names of people she probably knew only out of books, "Ramona told Gregor told Buck told Philip IV told Mona . . ." Sometimes she'd half-hum place names: "In Casablanca, Verona, Boca Raton, or Antibes. In Seattle, maybe Glasgow, then, of course, in old Bombay." You know, she never mentioned North Carolina? Not a single town along Dad's Bible route and mine. —Finally, the bedroom door creaked shut. Uh-oh, a "no" answer. Dad scuffed outdoors to his beautiful Packard. He sat for hours in the dark, just the red tip of a cigarette to mark him there.

Clyde joshed about his own appearance; poor guy had little choice. Standing six feet one prevented hiding all that much of it. Nervous people laughed when he walked into the room—with or without his mismatched cufflinks, orange bow tie, and forty free Bibles. I once heard a lady desk clerk (who created Last Supper "scenes" from numberless glued seeds) call Clyde—to his face—the Human Basset Hound.

"You mind, Clyde? Your face makes people happy but in reverse, like. Probably just glad it ain't them. People swear you're so plain you're almost cute. You mind much?"

Shy, he shrugged, "Heck, Verna, that's a step up. Most folks say I'm so ugly, I'm just real ugly. . . . Yeah, when the Lord was passing out looks, I thought He said 'books' and asked for somethin' funny." She folded double, laughing as if this were new to her.

Only once did Mother join us on our motel jaunt. She took a wry and girlish interest. I saw the legendary charm. Her family had been rich, at least compared with us. As a child, she'd owned a pony all her own named Lucky. Given Dad's unmentioned dirt-poor history, he considered her folks regular Rockefeller runners-up. The Sunday she came along, Dad was so glad for Mom's company he nearly wrecked us, staring her way too much. If Clyde looked at her long, irrational grins—actual tears—would form.

Mom pronounced our pals—the hobbyist innkeepers—"stitches." After riding a hundred miles, she decided they were "basically pretty eccentric." By next morning, our friends had sunk to "loner nut cases."

Mother's migraine blinders deserved a Sunday-school-perfect attendance pin. We lived in "Falls, pop. 2100, bird sanct." Low-grade rumors circulated—about how Mom spent those ailing Sunday afternoons as we toted God's word from Manteo to Mount Mitchell (North Carolina). Someday I planned to prove to Dad such gossip was untrue.

2.

Once we'd endured church service, after Pop placed cool white terry-cloth to her forehead, soon as he shut their bedroom's Venetian blinds as tight as gills, we regained permission to leave her.

We emptied Clyde's black Clipper of its spring-tension chromium crossbar; this supported half a store's worth of sharkskin suits, irides-cent shirts. Into our front-hall closet we loaded outfits that no self-respecting church-affiliated Christian of any race would wear. These threads were intended for handsome disintegrating men with gam-bling probs. The designer had laid odds that four colors on one shirt would snag the snake-eyes bookmaking interest of some railroad-hotel Romeo who preferred to always work the angles.

Soon as our Old and New Testaments (printed in one handy twin-pak) got spirited into the trunk of a highly waxed Bible-colored Packard, off we set.

Three miles into countryside, we began feeling relieved to be alone together and merely male. Dad and I were admittedly far simpler for that. Whatever Owner's Manual had awarded each of us a stick shift seemed the Good Book, too. I'd sometimes say, "Man, I wouldn't be a girl, not for a million buckaroos." As if all women were my mopey sexy young mother. And, of course, to me, at six, they were.

Dad and I hit the far-flung motor courts of either Carolina. En route, we fought to overcome Mom's higher-grade intelligence. We left it beneath a washcloth in their dark room; we'd abandoned her to the bedspread's white chenille that cut Braille messages into Mom's pretty pinkish neck. And once we sped six miles from town, Pop and I commenced to simplify and strip ourselves. Her moods always left upon our skins a sweetish smell; her sighs were clinging Persian cat hair you must shuck off all your darkest things. Each trip meant our efficient male jailbreak from her impossible female need to escape.

We soon grew wild with plain male speed. "Into the aiiiir, Junior Birdmen, Into the air upside dow-wnn," we sang dumb songs I've not heard since.

We couldn't really carry a tune, either of us. But that just made us louder and more male. Equally loud if hopelessly monotone, miles from her, we began to forgive each other.

Before front desks of many a motel, we did our Laurel-and-Hardy routines. I'd puff out my rosy cheeks, fluteplaying the air before my chest to mime Ollie's fussed-with necktie. Clyde, a beanpole with huge hands and that bungled masklike head, became my immense overqualified Stan. He'd tug upward at his topknot of coarse hair; he'd give off dim Stanley's weepy little pipings. And clerks dropped, laughing, literally dropped, behind their plywood check-in desks.

I now understand, the simple sight of us must've caused more merriment than our conscientious acting skills. —We never knew, until the end, just how we looked together.

Clyde took public pride in my blond blue-eyed memory. He encouraged me to quote aloud the titles of all the books of the Bible. These Incan-sounding tin-can syllables meant nothing to me. Doing them ever faster seemed any smart boy's logical goal. Driving, Clyde would time my "GenesisExodusLeviticusNumb . . ." I, drowsy, counting cows, sat crackling holy syllables. Dad checked his Bulova, "Second best. But that doggone Ezekiel tripped you again. Break it down, four units. It's 'Easy-ki-el.' Now, think, son."

My coach inhaled another unfiltered Camel. He kept his car window open, a huge hand fanning. Dad admitted knowing: every costly "weed" took an entire bowl of rice out of the mouth of some little Korean girl orphan.

"Name one," I said. "—Besides, which orphan would WANT a whole bowl of rice shoved in her li'l mouth!"

Well, this cracked Clyde up so he had to pull over. He chuckled unto coughing then, pointing at his chest, snaffled even at that. Dad retold my quip at each of that day's far-flung motels. I was forced to rattle through the Bible books ever faster as uninterested eye-rolling adults scanned their lobby's sunburst clocks.

3.

Desk clerks at Pecan Grove and Satellite Sputnik Lodge Acres became our all-time favorites.

Our pet client was the plump aforementioned seed-art woman (Pecan Grove Sleepytime Auto Cabins, "Serving the Weary Traveler and the Weekly Boarder with Unequal Courtesy Since 1939, New Canaan, N.C.").

She made amazing Biblical-topic mosaics from pet-shop and seed-store grains. Verna lovingly called them her "scenes." Exploiting the job's abundant free time, she'd already served up twelve door-sized Last Suppers, formed of mostly oats and millet. (Trillions of innocent seeds had been introduced to Elmer's Glue then crucified onto Verna's pine planks.)

Pecan Grove's cement-block lobby looked positively bumpy with earlier seedy references to Christ's Passion. John the Beloved's hair shone, so much glinty barley. Ours was the Golden Age of Hobbies and Shellac. This deep-voiced lady manager, wearing smocks stitched from the giant floral prints of couches, battled a drinking problem that pounced her between projects. "It helps, do I stay busy," she spoke the homemade way many country people did then.

Verna sometimes phoned our house midweek. She complained, even to Mother, about the record number of Bibles being swiped from good ole Pecan Grove Sleepytime. "My type clients I'm gettin me here lately, they are true lowlifes, lower. If this place's sheets could talk prior to Oxydol, they usually do! The Godless is winnin, honey. Tell your men to bring Bible replacements P.D.Q."

But even I, at six, guessed: Verna hid the Testaments herself. She was that needy. And her new canary-seed Resurrection had to be seen to be believed.

Even after the two-hour drive, Dad did not disappoint: "Museums. I swear, Verna, museums'd fight to get their mitts on these o' yers." Between visits, the tibbling lady forgot she'd shown me her lifetime's art. Though I felt put-upon, one glance from my Christian father showed me where true duty was. I again followed a heavy artist, fumey with gin. I exclaimed from scene to gritty scene, I asked which grains formed apostle halos (morning glory). I asked, wasn't that Last Supper's broken bread maybe . . . ? "Wheat," she winked, nodding at her leisure-time pun. "Smart cub you got you here, Clyde."

"We think so. Takes after his mother's side in that," he touched my silvery-blond bangs. I let him. My mom, Dad's wife, was back home, maybe busy being unfaithful to Dad. His marital "we" always galled— since it left out me.

Clyde marveled at the skill of "Miss Last Supper," shook his head with genuine wonder. I forever wished I had been born more like him. —I've since tried daily faking it. For my students. For my own kids now. But from Clyde, it flowed, most natural. Perhaps because of what I'd had to see at eight, I myself am not so kind.

Before distant service stations, with our family on holiday, Dad would chat up the gas-pumpers. He learned all sort of things. Mother sat examining her nails. Head tilting back, she let her eyes go in and out of focus to make red polish look less chipped. "What does our poor Clyde hope to gain from those colored boys?" she asked her hand. "Look at him, Meadows, forever backslapping. He'll never even see them again. Your daddy running for mayor, is he?"

Till he spoke, you could miss his character's many beauties. Dad's baritone ran ripe as black olives, it soon spread river-delta-wide. Clyde owned a hymn, no, a hymnal of a speaking voice. He hadn't been a Christian many years. He often mentioned how recently the bright light of conversion had sun-cured Evil's syrup-dark recesses.

Back home, first grade was new to me and just okay. Mother, alone on her good days, could be lazy-acting but all right. My three friends were pretty much fun, especially when we played down by the ditch. But nothing matched those Packard Bible Sundays with my dad so briefly home.

Our assigned motels bore such longing names: The Whispering Pines Deep Sleep Cabins, Perfect Starlite Lodge, Moonstone Lake Court Retreat 'n' Cocktails.

They had about them some of the yearning exuded by my father, the half-worldly Christian business gent. They were based in fact but soaked in longing. Motel names combined a New World love of scenery with some mortal nostalgia for the silence we all hail from, the peace we hope to find in nightly, then final rest—

Whispering
Deep
Sleep
Perfect
Starlite
Retreat

—all blinking in the period's hissing neon tubes—blue or pink—set high above a black silhouetted cornfield's orange sunset.

. . .

I am now forty-nine years old. (I don't know how or why but am.) I also find myself a linguist, a college dean, and the father of two teenaged girls. It's mostly for them—I've decided, on the windy cliff called Fifty—to set all this down.

Till lately, I've never really thought my life particularly notable. Maybe curious. Funky? Certifiably! But now I see: Modesty itself might be an act of lingering suppression. From Dad, I overlearned the will to disappear. That deathblow—finding Mother pinned under a massive fellow not my Clyde—convinced me: All my boyhood up till then had been quite bland and regular. It wasn't, though. Because Clyde wasn't.

Clyde Melvin Delman, Sr., had a way of giving others almost too much credit. But, afraid you'd prove him wrong, a person grew toward such kindness. You unwittingly became Clyde's own best dying hope for you. I'd been named Clyde junior but Mom—when asked to sign the birth certificate—just couldn't abide having "Melvin" attached to a child of her own; so she scratched it out, substituting her maiden name, a prettier M-word: "Meadows."

Now recalling our Bible-delivery Sundays, I can say that, apart from lovemaking and research, at no task have I ever been happier. You felt you were doing good. You were getting to have fun on purpose. You left her behind and didn't need to know what went on. Seeing that could wait. Could wait till two years later and what I call The Worst of All Possible Sundays. That day evicted us from our simple lives and routes. It became our family's nonrefundable one-way Exodus from Genesis.

By forcing Clyde to see what he knew too well but forever allowed himself to doubt, I would doom my mother to the public role of Whore; I would fox my father out of his own life. I would lose my place in mine.

Except, of course, in this. I mean: in holy memory.

I sit here on a Saturday in my college office stacked with almost-brilliant freshmen applications. Vines have overcome my single leaded window. The electric wall-clock above the door seems to lurch every two minutes with a little snap like baby teeth breaking.

Given this building's stillness, I feel sealed voluntarily into some cave of choice. No one knows I'm here. Recalling 1954, I forget the concept of tenure, of divorce. I feel far too young to have a kid myself. Much less adolescent ones with figures, interracial boyfriends, politics already. I picture Clyde's ungainly features, grinning, unaware of anything but his son. I become eight, then six, and soon transparent. His.

III. Leviticus

"Seen Pictured Here in Happier Times . . ."

Thou shalt not wholly reap the corners of thy field. . . . Neither shalt thou gather every grape of thy vineyard; thou shalt leave them for the poor and stranger: I am the LORD your God.

Leviticus 19:9–10

And now, before the sight of those two naked grown-ups doing that and little me hopping on board and the lethal harm it worked in all of us, we get to talk 1954–1960. Good deal!

We're back before motel chains took over. Chains, indeed. Bible delivery to "automotive camps" (as some of our older clients still called themselves) now seems the ideal chore for recalling that honey of an American moment.

It was a time of plain good luck, possessed of a simplicity only half dumb. With the world war so freshly won, most everybody made money. That marked it as a great decade to be their child. Treats abounded. Yards were big. The beagles were named Snoops, and our block's many yellow cockers, Blondie. Our clubhouses, the large crates white appliances had come in.

Kids love tasks like delivering newspapers. Kids enjoy repetitive jobs and the voltage of giving adults something that they truly need. Add the quantum power of Bibles and you quadruple that pleasure. Our Sunday mission seemed a mixture of a-tisket-a-tasket, hide-and-seek, getting gold stars on your best school assignment. Plus feeding the multitudes from one ambitious Packard trunk, enough sardines and Wonder Bread for all.

But I was still my mother's son, and those early motels exercised on me the profoundest erotic pull. Puritanism wants us to believe: a male's sex desire begins the day he shaves and gets his driver's license. Ha. Being Grace Delman's boy, I was born erect. And now that I'm more than middle-aged, only scholarship and romantic love have provided blunting detours around that doggedly upstanding feature! During board meetings, awards ceremonies, even funerals, my thoughts still tend to take a filthy turn. And not toward the healthy sort of married lovemaking promoted by manuals that advertise at the rear of liberal journals. No. Smut. The sexual comics that boys then showed other boys. Popeye and Olive Oyl and Bluto locked in nasty three-ways.

Trying for self-improvement, I carried more than two thousand Bibles into love nests. Each tourist cabin held itself off separate from others. Every detail of a real home—gutters, chimney, shutters, siding, shingled pie-crust roof—had been lavished on such clubhouses for adults. Cottage windowboxes spilled white petunias epileptically elaborate. Flanking each door, two metal yard-chairs, backs tulip-shaded and painted either red or green. Inside, those portions of the room not varnished or linoleumed stayed mainly Bed. Boat-sized mattresses dented with the signatures of industrial-strength double occupancy. Two all-work adults drove out this way. They rented a hidden bed to serve as—what?—some silly form of trampoline? To help them in their playing . . . with each other?

I would find out. Bible-toting, I tracked such knowledge with a glum detectiveness. Boy, would I ever find out!

Jaw set with my holy mission, arms flapjacked with God's grim threats and uncollectible promises, I got issued the passkey. One size fit the slit of every single cabin. Like X-ray vision or God Himself, I imagined barging into rooms I had been warned contained "honeymooners, late checkouts, kiddo." (Wink.) As I scattered those ineffective poultices and wet blankets, God's Laws, I sniffed scents my dirty innocent little mind then simply titled "Clues."

Of course, I had to earn my passkey. Dad and I were forced to stand at more front desks, inspecting further clerkly handicrafts. Along with cheerful "Miss Last Supper," our second-best blue-ribbon obsessive was a retired Marine colonel. He grew begonias.

His plants were huge overtended things that seemed—in being this adored—by now conscious as cats and as smug. Set on the steps of a ladder painted white so as to perfectly display them, these specimens invited light to swarm among their leaves' embedded red and purple flecks. They looked like chunky angels considering going off some high-dive. That was their coach's plan; we now faced Parris Island for begonias.

Colonel was proprietor of Satellite Sputnik Lodge Acres. Colonel spoke of his plants with the stern pride peculiar to drill instructors. The Colonel resembled a leader whose men have just won the battalion colors, some proud guy being interviewed by *Stars and Stripes*.

"Now, he"—the crew-cut old salt pointed to one plant especially translucent, serrated, chevroned. "He kept trying to be a slow bloomer. But we got him with the program. Rationed him one pinch of fertilizer per month. And just being so near the other fellows seemed to give him first the idea then the needed get-go, and, well, you can see. With him this healthy, there's been pretty much no retreating. . . ."

Our host now studied his spit-shined shoes—knowing some compliment was due him. And Clyde Melvin Delman, Sr., was a compliment in a handpainted hula-girl tie. My dad, as optimistic as funny-looking, shook his head. "Museums. I tell you, Colonel, whole greenhouse-type museums should be phoned about what you've got going here. . . . It's too much to believe, even for in Nature. . . ."

The owner did glance up, a longing shyness. To see just how handsome his boys looked in stair-step formation. "Well . . . with the recent humidity, their stem tone HAS firmed to advantage. . . ."

My father encouraged everybody: hobbyists, Bible-readers, counterfeit Ollie Hardys, kids, adulterers.

2.

It being 1954—our being working-class North Carolina Baptists—school days, ball games, bachelor parties, annual physicals, all commenced with prayer.

This embarrassed me, a secret pagan, a college-professor agnostic (if still in bud formation). Other restaurant patrons saw fit to praise Jesus via short silent pre-salad nods; I considered this tony, stylish, "European." Dad proved noisier.

Clyde felt so glad for even half a grilled-cheese sandwich, he shuddered, closed his eyes, took both my hands in his (salt and pepper shepherded within our grasp). As his molten orange cheese cooled white, Clyde spoke a most unquiet sermonette. "Dedicate the goodness of this food into a strength sufficient, Oh Lord, to bring, Lord, others to Thee. And make of us, Your wicked servants, a worthy . . ."

Starving, I sensed others wishing he'd just shut up and eat. Glad only for the fiction of shutting my eyes, I vowed I'd never—once free of Falls and Clyde—ever pray aloud. Certainly not during daylight. And never within earshot of your classier people sampling T-bones. Amen.

I didn't much mind Clyde's benedictions while we traveled. But once we were home in Falls, my little friends from school might see. I peeked around as Clyde's voice shamed ten tables into whispering, as my nice hot mushroom soup most prayerfully congealed.

During long rides, Dad never spoke of being a boy. True, he recalled the intricate ankle-level lore of marble-shooting. He still knew how to find my next slingshot's perfect green forked hickory. But Clyde had no childhood keepsakes; he owned not one photo of his family.

Mom's vanity table stood clogged with half-used pots of cold cream amid ancestors in browning silver frames. Good-looking men sniffed past the shop signs of their huge mustaches. The women appeared embarrassed to be so chesty with the buttoned-up predictions of my mom's own dreamy strong points. But about Dad's folks, I could fit all known facts into a single folded hankie: his only sister never visited us, sent no Christmas cards, but worked high up in Washington, D.C.'s city government. Their late father, a brakeman on the Atlantic Coastline Railroad, had moved about as often as his trains did. The mom died young of drinking tainted pond water, diphtheria. When Clyde was a kid of twelve or so, his dad transferred north; the boy chose to stay forever with an unofficial stepmom, "Aunt Sutie," someone he still considered his truest family.

Though she lived just across the Virginia line, Sutie had never once come calling. I always pictured her as that virtuous side-facing lady carved (oval) into every cameo. She must look like the aunt of Oz's Dorothy, some stern yet decent stay-at-home. A loving, pasty, aproned lady, this Sutie would know her Bible and make exceptional biscuits. She'd tried to prevent Clyde from becoming a wanderer like his dad. But Sutie never quite saved her skinny boy from a drummer's route, the cyclone's upward suction.

Though I pleaded for news of Dad when he'd been my size, most of his stories began with "my coming to Christ at thirty-three, same age as Jesus when He died. Got in just under the wire."

No man more childlike ever kept quieter about his youth.

3.

Pop being on the road during the week, I begged Mom to take me to our county fair. "It'll cheer you up, the rides and all. Plus, they have every kind of chicken possible. They show them in one room. When the man ones crow, it echoes great. You'll see." Mom surprised me; she sulked off, brought back her cardigan and purse. "Will this be warm enough, you think?" Grace Delman asked her son, Meadows, age six and a half.

At the Twin-County Agricultural "Expo," Mom ate hot dogs before she rode even one thrill-ride. She wouldn't let me do that. And, boy, it sure did make her sick. She had to be helped off the Ferris wheel. Wedged in beside me, after warning me against even thinking of try-ing their cotton candy, she got so terribly ill, and in more directions—onto more screaming lower local people—than she could ever quite "live down." The gallant man who helped her from our "gondola" carried a doctor's bag. He was blond and tall and hospital-looking, metallic as some big new galvanized country mailbox.

At first it seemed they had just met. Later, I guessed otherwise. Even I, staring up at how he stared down on her, even with Mom shivery and gone matte-gray as shrimp not boiled yet, even I understood that he had scented her. From the ground, looking up toward this rare smell's source, he'd sniffed my mom on high.

The odor of some half-hurt fully horny animal, hers had registered from two hundred yards: the scent was her great backlog of soured intelligence; too many retail novels consumed too fast (all scenery skipped), then never reconsidered.

The man offered his pocket hankie to a lady (needing that far less herself than did those heads now screaming at her from suddenly the top of our abandoned Ferris wheel). The man must've guessed how Mom's smartness might be transferred downhill, to another, lower currency. I saw the glazed way he studied her legs as she wiped her mouth on a lifted skirt hem while she struggled up ungainly from our rocking seat. I watched the drudge's way she let him look. "Here, madam. Trick is, to lean against me more here. I'm a site biggern you." She did, lean. I followed. I was in first grade but guessed precisely what was happening. Even then, I hated him because I loved my dad, and actually loved her. My father was as marvelously homely as the fair's non-prize-winning ducks, whose heads were all red wattles. The stranger seemed a huge white-yellow thorny rooster; this side's amber eye kept burning so mean it looked half baked, half dead. I knew this guy was going to "get" my mom. I just didn't yet know what "get" meant.

4.

Our national Bible Club was founded in Wisconsin in the 1880s. Two traveling salesmen, married guys, wall-climbing-lonely on the road, chanced to eat at separate tables in one boardinghouse. They noticed each other praying public thanks—despite the meager fare. Upstairs later in one man's room, sin did not happen; no, a Bible appeared from the other fellow's sample case. Such sweet communion then spread man-to-man, both now on knees beside one bed. Couldn't hotel rooms become the cells of a chain seminary? If one legible Bible dwelt in each.

. . .

Stamping sanctity into the bedside drawers, I came to feed secretly upon three decades' sexy misdemeanors done here. A year and a half before I saw Sin plain, I sensed it got performed daily/nightly close by, with management playing dumb for reasonable rates.

Few will have bothered to recall: the word "Motel" tried coupling the noun "hotel" with the verb "to motor." Only in America.

I still love motels. Still find them insanely erotic, as my ex-wife will attest, poor thing. Hotels, being classier, with thicker walls, nonsqueaker beds and much more frequent paint jobs, feel far less alluring.

My ex always begged me to drive into the center of any vacation town where the multi-storied hotel stood. Bellboys would park your car. Tennis coaches were available at 4 a.m. if you'd pay the premium rate. But to me, such spas still feel about as sexy as university hospitals.

I yet prefer some outskirt's crumbling pink stucco "single," the same framed litho of *Hiawatha in Canoe* twice, a little smudge of lipstick so low down in the showerstall, but why? Picture it. Even newly seven, I already sorta could.

Duty took Dad and me to a then-minor state's more obscure swampy outposts (exurban Beargrass, Gilead Dam, Leaksville-Spray). Tourists didn't exactly flock to such places. So—why this many motor camps?

I guessed these ranked as our age's favored sex-act hideouts. I now sing those small mazelike complexes where, after sleep, the most frequent activity was local Adultery. Adultery was practiced with Sleep serving only as the paper-thin bologna wedged between two mattressy whitebread slices of that sweet other.

(And I, scholastical in temperament, criminal of soul, no taller than the keyhole, stood right there scouting for it!)

The War was newly ended, returned GIs still had lots of "When I get home, no woman'll be safe. . . ." Certain zestful women, abandoned four years to men either too old or too young, also apparently felt overly primed.

In many a lobby I pushed unoiled postcard racks in circles. Cards were bright-colored, rank with ass puns, images of ladies holding cats while speaking of the care and feeding of their pussies. Snappy, eh? Even ignorant, I knew to laugh. Hard. Too hard. Others soon knew. How little. I knew.

Signs of lovers' struggles and payoffs abounded for a nosy boychild hunting "Clues" with an open-season passkey and seven random Bibles to disperse. My freckled nose wriggled, involuntary. The very air held sex's recent argumentative double-occupancy musks. In the many far-flung registers that I, pedantic, perused—the same well-traveled guests had stayed: "Smith, John, Mr. and Mrs, one night only, early chk out, extra twls."

I found a policeman's handcuffs still manacled to an old iron bedstead. I found major blood on sheets—blood not, my father patiently (mildly) explained, always from murder. What from, then? "Well, people cut themselves shaving," Dad stayed vague as I, Nancy Drew, felt let down, having dragged him over to see. "But . . . shave, in bed?" "It's a long story." "I've got time." "Not yet, you don't."

The very knotty-pine walls seemed unevenly if permanently darkened thanks to fugitive smudges from transient acts. I poked through postcoital cigarette litter, found half the white butts lipsticked a lavish sickening edible red. (Oh, I was born into the Periclean Age of the Unapologetic Bedside Cigarette.) As I circulated, sent into the world to give my mom some bang-up privacy, as I placed black books in abandoned rooms as yet "unmade," I gathered proof of the very lust these Bibles sought to "make up" like so many hourly-rental rumpled beds.

Written over one bathroom mirror in lipstick before maid-service purging, "D. R. Eames made me get in his car. Has gun. Phone Momma at 512——." And a long greasy stripe bespeaking violent (sexual?) interruption.

I saw huge oil handprints on the walls above torn pink chenille. I saw varnished evidence of various makeshift lubricants like Vitalis hair oil, Wild Root Cream Oil. For those too young to recall all this, I will tell you straight, I am not making any of it up. The world, in being simpler then—as frontal as a puppet stage—was even more overtly weird than it is now. It just didn't know it yet. That made things even sweetly stranger. The world was too naïve to quite yet hide its sticky poking-out dorky facts.

Any child of seven might guess what had just happened in this room. And, if not prevented by someone supervisory, if not checked by God's own barricading Word, that child might push to see still more. And it might end very badly.

A father and his son deliver free Sunday Bibles. What could be more innocent? But I already knew it was a world where a man on the ground could refall in love with a pretty woman vomiting over the protesting heads of every Ferris-wheel rider below her.

Connections got made. It was not exactly e-mail, but it worked.

5.

I plundered motel trash cans. I checked under beds. I hoped to trap still more that was "off-color." If my father had only guessed, the poor man might've kept me home. Well, no, not that, at least not Sundays . . .

"Off-color" is what we called it then. That meant "too colorful," like those liverish postcard pastels.

Here is some of what I saw. I saw it because, in the days before central air, there had to be a screened back door left open for ventilation. Otherwise, you could not survive these charming Tirolean johnny-houses.

Because such lodges got stuck way out in countryside that was still actually farmed then, the privacy of tobacco fields often stretched behind the place; so, if you looked in through a back door, it was like my boyhood fantasy of being Superman with X-ray vision, no wall opaque enough to keep your eager-beagle-cocker-eagle-boner vision out:

My 1955 Police Blotter

• I spied one old guy with white white whiskers kissing a very little girl, and his hand, as if it didn't know what it might find there, wandered under—"Intsy Bintsy Spider Climbed Up the Water Spout"—her short pleated skirt, and, boy, but did her eyes ever get huge! When he looked out and saw me, his face puffed to jug size from being shocked and then grew real mean, and I knew to run. I sat in the Packard and waited for Pop and finally honked and he came out and we drove off. In silence.

• I saw a woman who'd filled her whole room with caged birds unloaded from her station wagon; I first noticed all the seed crunchy outside her door, a trail from the wagon. The cockatoos were very white but touched with the tints of shells and she sat in the middle of their cages, a small safe space, birds pulled into a circle that she seemed to feel would keep her secure. Their squawking came idle, shrill and comforting, and she sat there, writing a letter, laughing to herself as she jotted something that she liked a lot, and she kept gently muttering, surrounded by those white smooth birds who appeared to know and guard her so completely.

• I saw a young red-haired man with his shirt off, counting more money than I'd ever viewed in any place so noninstitutional. Greenery of the rectangular kind covered not just the bed entire; it bricked all cabin window ledges; cash paved three-quarters of the lino floor. The kid sat rocked back in a creaky desk-chair, counting hundred-dollar bills aloud, but in that human, half-swallowed way people perform routine chores while all alone, "Nine thou fifty-nine, sixty, sixty-one . . ." He noticed me and jumped.

Because his little cabin was built on an incline, because the back door of the place swung open onto nothing but cotton growing, only my blond forelock showed. I just waited there, and he seemed relieved to find how young I was. I wore my damp bathing suit ("Motel Guests Swim at Own Risk") and my black oxford shoes and nothing else.

("Howdy," my father had taught me to say outside any city limits. "Hi" or "Hello, ma'am or sir," in town.)

"Howdy."

"Yeah, right. I lost count now. You nosy or what?"

"Sure do got you a whole lot of money in 'ere, hunh, mister?"

"Yeah. Found it, found more'n I could carry. You think this is good, you should of seen what I left."

"Where? Where'd you even find that much?"

"In a bank, dummy."

"And they let you have it?"

" 'Let'? I planned it so's they'd pretty much have to. Trouble is, one man can only carry so much."

"Should of taken somebody else with you. Hunh?"

"Got a real mastermind here. Regular Wiseguy. You tell anybody you seen me or one dollar of this, you're fishbait. Savvy?" I nodded, wondering what fishbait was. He sensed confusion. "See that scummy pond yonder? You'll be deep under it, in certain fishes' bellies."

"Oh. —What you going to buy? With it?"

"I'm not going to buy, brat. Me, I'm going to live. First time in my life, I'm planning and see how it feels to lay back and just wake up every day and mainly concentrate on how to Live. Rich people don't worry over what to 'buy,' they just . . . have. And me now, so do I. I ain't doing nothin, I'm just being. Being me, but on a more regular and wilder-type basis. Listen at me, blabbing to a farm kid that's some water-headed idiot. Your head's way too big, they ever tell you that?"

"Is not, either." I touched it to make sure it had not suddenly grown.

Then he cursed me for having forced him to lose count. Next the young man came and stood in the doorway three feet above me and unzipped his brown rayon pants and pulled out his sad tube of uncut rusty pecker and starting peeing onto high weeds near me, then nearer, nearest, till I danced clear. "You tell, you're food for minnows in that pond yonder. —I use to be dumb, like you."

But when I rode with Dad, the world looked way more honest. It could seem as Christian as the farms we passed were ordered, newly mowed. Their fences were painted white because that's how it had been done since Colonial days, though white must be harder to keep fresh. Clyde Melvin Delman, Sr., drove slow and well and taught me road courtesy. How to shine your brights when a car passing you has pulled in safe. One sedan coming at us midday blinked its lights on and off. "What's that mean, Dad?" "Traffic cop ahead, buddy. Guy just saved me getting another blamed ticket. And not only did I not know the fellow that flashed me, he had Ohio tags. Who says the Civil War helped nobody with nothin? And lookee, will you? what's waitin behind that Coppertone billboard? Ohio was right, there's a Coppertone copper. Fooled him, hunh? And thanks to that Yankee stranger. —Now, aren't people grand basically?"

"Yeah. Some. What you said. Hope so, Dad."

I didn't tell him what I'd seen while dealing out God's Laws. I tried protecting Clyde from guessing what I knew: (1) That people were doing "it" almost constantly, even way out in the country. (2) That I didn't yet quite know what "it" was. (3) That he was considered the worst-looking wide-mouthed man in Falls, where I had overheard two sensible adults call him Almost Monster.

6.

Once, bored at a service station while Clyde stood around joshing with the help, I noticed his wallet on the car seat. I'd soon displayed across our dashboard all his gas credit cards and business notes (as if playing solitaire). I felt a last bump thickening the billfold's center, and from its secret compartment I coaxed one creased ancient-looking envelope. It contained a single four-leaf clover now aged clear brown as glass. Across its wrapping, shaky handwriting, in amber-red ink, spelled:

> Found this good luck by our creek.
> Go in God love, You His boy and you Sutie's too!
> XXX
> You Good both in and out! "Bow down to no man."
> X,
> Me.

When Clyde slid behind the wheel, praising that attendant's raunchy nun joke, I sat holding up the cloverleaf. I saw Dad fight a flinch. I admitted I should've asked permission. But, having apologized, I still waited for some background.

"Son," he was soon driving us in circles, talking it all out. He spoke as if his explanation had been long prepared. It came forth in swags, uneasy units. It got recited like some essay memorized off a second cousin's job application.

"You notice I don't often brag on my mom and dad. With them, ain't all that much to tell. They moved enough to where, we couldn't call much of anyplace home. Some rental houses will give tenants their first month free? And that's just how long my daddy'd often-times stay. Mom died young, drinking from a tin dipper at farm pond, bad water. Got to where finally, in a railroad town, I found one person. No true kin, she just helped out with our cooking and cleaning, minding Sis and me for cash at first. One fine neighbor. Big church-goer. This old lady soon let me live right with her. Doggone lucky, that. My dad could roll on then without transferring me. I'd already changed schools, be over thirty times, son. Never did get used to it. Hated always being 'new.' Made me feel old early. That's when I started memorizing a thousand icebreaker jokes, to keep from getting my eyes blacked the first day. More than once, I'd walk home from what little schooling I could cadge, and my dad was packed and leav-ing town. Kind of rough on a boy ten or twelve. Sometimes he'd write me a note, other times not. Hey, soon enough, a bright boy gets the big idea, you know? Does Dad really want the person?

"Oh, but by then your Clyde felt extra hungry to take aholdt most anywheres. That old woman was all the good luck I ever found. Only neighbor that'd feed me regular, ask me in, talk with me about any darn thing. So I let my dad just go his way. Good riddance, basically. He took along my sister, who was smart and prettier and so got them into certain places. Made a better class of friend. Me, I couldn't, with this kisser hung on me. I got a face is neither fish nor fowl. I told you before, my godmom's name's 'Aunt Sutie.' That's it basically.

"—Buddy? She knows all about you. She's still alive but oldern hell. I guess it's time you heard more tell of her. Back when Sutie grew up, she had it mighty rough. She got by, eating dandelion greens, selling scrap metal, living by her wits. Was quite the beauty in her day, folks said. But she pure saved my life when I was just up past your age. Meadows, she forever tried getting me to read the Good Book. But I was way too wild then. Bad to drink, a terrible skirt-chaser. Nasty black-hearted little boy, I was. Sometimes, son, while we're putting out the Word in our motels, I feel like it's for her. Like now I'm giving other folks a chance . . . I grew up way too transient, son. The only thing not like that was God's permanent Word and one good woman.

"—Now, there. You've found my history's best thing. Here, handle her four leaves more by their stem, son. Let me slip Sutie's luck back in here safe."

7.

Because my mother had read Falls's every library book, because she'd grown restless, she maybe slept with the handsome veterinarian, and because, early in her marriage, she found she so needed that vet, Dad had started to deliver Bibles to give her a full day alone with her gentleman friend and without me; but because the vet's radio-dispatched sedan was like no other and people in our neighborhood were observant about when any hubby's car departed and the other sporty fellow's arrived, rumors had long since brewed into hardened facts. Tales about me, too. Facts that I myself did not quite know yet. This led me to discover Mother under him, but that would not have to happen for a year. It pleases me instead to recall a time right before. The best time.

No one local understood why my somewhat educated, not-bad-looking mother, who hailed from the fancypants Meadows family of Castalia, ever married a raw-faced shirt-hawking gladhander like Clyde Delman. Times, the one who understood it least seemed Mom herself.

"Your father is the kindest man alive, isn't he? To be perhaps a shade too frank, son, I loved another first. Dear me, yes. Best-looking boy in Nash plus Edgecombe Counties. Others said so first. He was an ace pilot, shot down the third week of the war, my Zachary. Burned alive. They claimed they heard the screams. I'd gone and got myself into a certain situation, false alarm, as it turned out. But just then your sweet dad turned up, bringing flowers and his cute, terrible jokes, holding doors for me and my mother. I don't know," she said flat-voiced, as if planning to fully test that kindness. "I'd been in demand. Probably too much so. Then all those pretty boys went overseas. The crucial ones got killed. My mother was impossible company. She blamed me for being too kind toward lonely soldiers shipped off to die on a beach somewhere. Clyde had flat feet, stayed Stateside. He just worshiped me. I liked his company. He held down two jobs and Mother admired that. You know how he always cheers everybody up. He was so there. I don't know."

Weeknights in our quiet kitchen, with Pop out on the road earning us money, Mom would wander up behind the chair where I sat hunched over homework. I was a proud and literal kid. I worked hard, and Mother encouraged that and—as a person who read a lot herself—she marveled at my memory. "You read to remember, which is good," she said. "Funny, I can feel myself lose a fact the second I've caught hold of it. But for the time I do have it, nice. Sometimes I think my one true talent is forgetting." She sounded almost playful in this boast. "But go on working, honey. . . ." And she'd sit right there and look at me. Some nights it bothered me; mostly I ignored her. "Don't mind me, baby," she sighed. And slouched forward, looking child-sized, bosomy, and lost.

She was like some other women I remember from those days—one whose triumph seemed always looking as tired as possible; even at her loveliest and most dressed up, Gracie Meadows Delman left the third button down unfastened, half intentional in her sexy forgetting. Men's eyes all went to her small grooming errors, guessing how much could be made of a courteous late-evening rebuttoning. "Here, let me help, I got good hands, little missy. . . ." Her natural smell was sweet as fruit. And like fruit, Gracie's scent implied a sensual contest between perfect ripeness and some threatened galloping decay.

Mom was usually one day away from meaning to finally wash her hair. With the rings under her eyes and her don't-mind-me sighing, she seemed so at odds with Pop's cast-iron hopefulness, the energy of naughty jokes he told customers, then instantly regretted.

Stared at now, I stopped doing my Geography, "an isthmus is a body of land that . . ." Again she said, "I love your father so much. He's no Zachary. But could there be a dearer soul on earth? It's just . . . Say I'm weak, pippin. It's just I am so very weak." I had no idea what she meant.

If I'd understood then, I might have shaken her, told her that few fellows on earth love anyone with the force, almost the geography, Clyde brought to loving her. I could have told her how certain ladies at the desks of rural motels wore cologne when Stan and Ollie, the Bible Boys, turned up, and how much kindness Clyde's own kindness inspired out there in the bed-renting world.

Instead I looked at her and said, "It's okay. He loves you back. He says so all the doggone time." "You're an old sweetie pie, you know that?," she drew her sweater around her as if a breeze had happened just for her.

Then Mom sighed, "But I'm keeping you from your . . . what is it?" and she twisted my notebook's blue lines her way, "An isthmus is . . ." But I hid it with my hand. She gave me a look that let me know she knew I loved him more than I loved her. She let me see she'd always make me choose. She wanted me to understand she knew I cared too much for him. Because she cared too little. I was that lesson, every-time she looked at me.

Mom couldn't resist—in her forgetting and her weakness—blaming me for not loving her enough to somehow stop her. And I was seven! I vowed to find a way to make her remember, to keep her strong as she intended. Mother now rose, chanting some showtune, "As Juliet said in her Romeo's ear, why not face the facts, m'dear"; she scuffed off to the back screen door, stood looking out at the neighbors' new anchor fence. "They should have asked us plainer and brought over a drawing first. It's way too high."

Like some zoo animal, she studied fencing till it was time to cook us two some food that usually came out stewed as flavorless—on the white white platter—as one of her side-street sighs. Dinner always turned out the very same greeny-brown shade of weakness.

8.

Our fellow Caucasian Bible-givers met for power-prayer breakfasts at a greasy spoon that grandly called itself The American Bar and Grill.

In Falls, there was a black chapter of our club. We never held joint meetings. From 1954–56, Dad was Regional Bible Distribution

Officer. When the Negro chapter fell short of Testaments, some-body'd phone our home. I, prideful of my motel detective skills, believed I could tell a colored voice from a white one. To Dad, I'd mime the race of a black caller by pointing to my face. Dad closed his eyes, half peeved by such officiousness, acting just a little disappointed in me.

Black men could not come to our neighborhood's front doors. Not even to collect God's Word. So Dad and I would drive over and make "the drop" at his favorite downtown Shell station.

Clyde would park around back, behind stacked pyramids of canned motor oil, off near the bathrooms. These were still marked "White" and "Colored." He once allowed me to run quick into "Colored" just to check. It looked right much like "White" except for lacking toilet paper and a door on the single stall.

Up would drive some silver Studebaker or blue Rambler. Out would climb a dark gent in his hastily tied tie. Nodding to Clyde and me, opening his car's trunk, he acted so polite he seemed half scared. He might be the town's pomaded black mortician or the handsome school principal with his pencil-thin mustache and comically perfect intercom "e-noun-ciation." Clyde always acted courtly, unhurried, bringing recent weather into it, calling his fellow club member "Mr. Washington," even "Brother Washington."

These men held their prayer breakfasts downhill at Hattie's Chick-n-Chitlin Hut—a pink stucco bunker with a lifesized wrought-iron palm tree bolted to its front. Hattie's had a glamorous nightclub look somewhat undercut by the unhappy smell of chitlins always boiling out back.

Delivering black Bibles to black members, I recall, we would stand off to one side of Falls's busiest gas station, our voices lowered as if transacting some drug deal. The men finally whispered a word of prayer over the box of transferred Scripture, as if assuring each other and God that some essential black-white translation was now com-plete. Impressive, these hushed grave prayers. Riding home uphill, I kept quiet, awed by all the codes I sensed I couldn't crack yet.

Though our town was then 60 percent "colored," this majority attended separate schools. It patronized obscure motels even sadder than the ones we served. I remember asking Dad why our white-guy club couldn't meet with its like-minded black branch.

Clyde gave me such a weary look. Finally he said, "Young as you are, you're right to see as that's unfair. Surely ain't Godly, Meadows. But that's how they always handle it, with tongs, herebouts." To me this seemed no sort of answer.

The American Grill's chef wore a white biscuit-shaped hat and did our eggs perfectly; he was one of the few black men who ever said much to me. "That blond hair of yours get any goldener, I'm gone be spending a curl of it down at the Bank. Still like your eggs 'over easy,' Young Capn'?" My folks were too poor to hire black domestic helpers, cruelly inexpensive as they were then. Since Falls is a hill town, since the best breezes happen way up top, "Baby Africa" (also called "The Bottom") rested far down the incline from even our street. And we lived three blocks below Middle Street. School friends' mothers simply asked me, "Is your parents' home above Middle?" You need not be a genius to guess their meaning.

In memory, our favorite waitress seems some great New York character-actress living in Falls incognito, doing five decades' research to become an equally great waitress someday on the Northern stage. All goodwill and hard-edged linens, she unlocked her grill just past dawn each Tuesday for what she called "my believers."

This hummingbird of a lady darted among bull-sized businessmen hunched in prayer; she poured coffee with her own eyes closed. A frequent mascot guest, I sat wide-eyed, envious of her aim. I was impressed by grown men, egg yolk already on some chins, still puffy from sleep, but already nattily dressed, en route, through worship, to work—and all by 6:45 a.m.! Their eyes closed, their coffee "bottomless," they praised the Creator of the Universe for giving them such intense business opportunities here lately on the local level.

All stories in our group "literature" concerned motel occupants about to commit suicide, about to sin with a bottle or a stepdaughter, about to rob someplace. But at the very last minute, their eyes fall upon a Bible opened by happenstance to the passage that halts desire, that makes their sexual organs lose steam and then to dive, that shows them how the lilies of the field do fine without robbing places, see?

And it changes their lives forever. Amen. My dad and other shut-eyed men thanked God for letting His Book-suppliers thrive so unexpectedly.

Our eldest member owned one of those stores that fits you with trusses and false limbs and the portable toilets taken into the homes of people so sick they know to rent. This cheerful merchant had, over years enough, become a doctor. That title first appeared on his business card in the twenties, and when no one pistol-whipped him for it, the pedigree got painted ever larger in red above his shop's door.

The business's front window became a shrine to all the bad things God inflicts upon a single human form. In this display, Doc kept (and it might be there still) one doll-sized female mannequin.

Poor thing stood just two feet tall but was forced to wear braces, canes, jaw braces, crutches, eyepatches, neck holsters. It was always the same pink, sun-faded woman, alone of her size and race. She proved almost curatively well known. By now she even had a name, Blanche. People who'd just rented some portable johnnyseat and a pair of child crutches could pause outside, look in at poor ole patched-up Blanche, then shake their heads and limp off feeling semi-lucky.

I peeked around this muttering table, studying Dad and others. Dark eyes closed, my father humbly mentioned some recent vest and cufflink orders, bright spots along his route. Thank God for commissions. "Amen" came the response. Our handsome class-ring salesman announced that a new high school was slotted to open over in Bertie County, and he just wanted to give the Lord full credit for that and for higher education generally. Then "Dr." Johnson had the questionable taste to cite a recent fourteen car pile-up out near Puttputt Miniature Golf on U.S. 301, and he wanted to mention it had been his pleasure to help, Heavenly Father, rectify, Heavenly Father, the broken bodies of, dear Lord, no less than twelve of the locals so mangled, Heavenly Healer Father. Amen.

Our genius waitress, whose name I have, alas, forgotten—two syllables; Inez? no, Ivy?—called each man by a different endearment. My daddy was "Cufflink," owing to his wearing two different models ("Lucky Shamrock" alongside "Scottie Dog"). I was "Little Bit." Our fellow members huddled nearer, prayed louder. Soon, above the table, there rose a fervid humidity, musty-sweet, the plaid, male form of that, almost a prayerful tent of mist over these burly men, hands covering their eyes.

Dad's pals seemed amazed at their brief prosperity. Suspecting their own lack of business talent, they gave God full credit. And they continued scattering Bibles: seed money.

9.

Once the motel chains got a chokehold on our kindly, tacky citadels of free enterprise—where any ex-farmer with roofs and sheets enough could call himself Innkeeper—some last wild chance at American escape was lost forever.

No state inspector could ever find such spots today. To check into a chain motel, you now need a provable address, two forms of ID, and please leave the license number of your car to prevent its being towed by 3 a.m.

But in those days, anybody on legs and holding five to seven one-dollar bills could become John and Mary Doe, or John and John, or Mary with Mary. No questions asked. These retreats made possible a kind of perfect starlite rest unavailable at home. Motels could shelter your six-week nervous breakdown. Motels permitted suicide. Motels meant side-road second chances.

And I entered my profession while riding toward such tourist huts. One autumn Sunday, Clyde asked would I please read aloud to him as usual? My geography textbook, the glove compartment's white Bible—the kind given to all graduating nursing students—our Packard *Owner's Manual*, didn't much matter. He even encouraged me to do *Practical Math for Modern Boys and Girls* aloud, "Carry the one makes nine. . . ."

Dad, a smile half sleepy, loved hearing my boy voice test anything. That lulling hopeful singsong. Dad heard less my subject, more my promise—an intelligence he wonderfully overrated and therefore helped create.

It was my last autumn with him. The brown countryside we drove through, car windows open, offered a stringent, peppery smell peculiar to peanut fields in late October. I paged through the *Owner's Manual.* Clyde always liked to see me handle the glove box's Bible. Never one to be bored long, I soon found ways to make even God's familiar scolding Word engaging.

First I reread Dad his own favorite, Psalm 100. "A goodie." Clyde shook his head. "One sure bet." Since the open Bible in my lap rested atop our Packard's *Manual,* I soon mixed lines from each. A testament to my trust of Clyde, some fundamental faith in him: I sensed he wouldn't scold me for apparent sacrilege. He would know it was just play, and that play is always free and holy.

It may seem ludicrous, such an absentminded make-work amusement coming to constitute the start of my career in literary criticism, translation. But our Bible-delivery trips took so long. There was nothing on the radio except used-car commercials, Patti Page and Johnny Ray, or some hoarse crazy preaching.

In 1955, we had to entertain each other aloud a lot. In this way, I was called to my task. —How right that the word "vocation" derives from *vocare,* "to call." A joy to be called to your profession. To your own calling.

Secure in a wild good faith I would never feel toward anybody else till I myself had kids, I veered with silly ease from Testament to *Manual* and back:

> *Make a joyful noise unto the Lord, all ye lands. Drive the roads with gladness. Through the gates of the great Packard Proving Grounds constantly pass test cars embodying new ideas. Come before his presence with singing (designs of unparalleled sleekness). Within these 560-acres are facilities for an endless variety of tests devised by*

*Packard engineers to improve each new Idea. Know ye that the Lord
he is God: climbing power checked on grades to 35%. It is he that
hath made us, and not we ourselves; we are his people, and the steep
of his pastures. One such test is Trial by Water! Time after time the
Packard ran directly through our highly pressured water bath. Enter
into his gates with thanksgiving, and into his courts with praise; be
thankful unto Him, and bless his name. Results: not the slightest
hint of dampened ignition (or even dampened driver spirit!). For the
Lord is good: Ignition is unexcelled. Scale tall hills without a thought
of overheating. His mercy is everlasting. In fact, we may vary your
springs' strength with the addition of extra equipment to assure your
comfort on roads of whatever condition everywhere. Expect horsepower fitted to your driving needs alone. And his truth endureth to all
generations.*

"Got to hand it to you," Dad laughed. I slowly understood I already
spoke at least two languages, probably more. I turned to Clyde,
bemused behind his millionth Camel. I asked if, while I read, he'd
always known which lingo I was in. Dad nodded. I asked how he'd
guessed.

"Words, sounds of the words, I reckon. Those two books're doing
mighty different things, now ain't they, cub? Seems like one is trying
and make us think a car is next to Godliness. Which it ain't, not even
a Packard good as our Third Musketeer here. The other is so sure of
God's power, that power just rolls all over it like some song off the
radio. Why, it's a pure-tee poem. I just never get tired of it, do you?"

I wagged my head No. "Dad? In Bibledays, Jesus didn't talk English,
did he?"

"Not at first," Clyde said.

Even then, I loved him for this stab toward scholarship. And for his
coarse-as-a-sunflower hopefulness. Perplexed but willing to risk it,
Dad added: they had mainly spoke their own desert-type pidgin back
then. Hebrew maybe? And there was another word. "They taught us it
at Men's Bible Study, but looks like I forgot, as usual."

I reopened the Good Book fast. A sudden sense of mission steadied
me. My father and I sat discussing God's Masterpiece. (Clyde said it'd

outsold *Gone With the Wind*. Plus they'd made even more movies from it than out of *Tarzan*!)

It seemed to me: no one had ever before thought to speak of this work in such a serious way; this was all extremely important. We sat examining the Book for reasons larger than our own, in the service of others far stupider than us. So I pressed my stubby finger to the title page and read:

"Translated out of the Original Tongues and with the Former Translations diligently compared and revised.

COMMONLY KNOWN AS THE AUTHORIZED
(KING JAMES) VERSION."

My father explained: King James had been the jobber-middleman. He'd paid guys to improve those dusty texts from olden times. But Clyde admitted: even if Jesus had not started as an English-speaker, "by now—around me, at least—my Saviour's mighty fluent." And grinned. I smiled back. I had no idea what he meant.

But a new secret unaccountably cheered me: I vowed to someday learn exactly how the earthly Jesus sounded; I'd find precisely which tongue He'd spoken.

I would then teach my Clyde to greet his Master in Jesus' own sandy-sandal local dialect. I pictured training Dad to lightly say, first thing in Paradise, "I belong to you, Lord, sir."

(And somehow I knew events would conspire to make possible just this joyous passing-on of knowledge. I did not yet know at what great costs.)

Something stirred me—switching from a boastful how-to auto brochure to that laudatory poem in honor of God's test-ground presence. I now counted words, gauged their lengths; I compared the archaic beaten-metallic sounds of Psalms with those phrases forged of mere modern aluminum. Did extra vowels make a word sound prettily older? I determined which phrases made for a poem's ring, which meant clunky, if useful, only ordinary speech.

When I looked back up, the sun had set. I'd sat bunched over my texts for three counties. Dad appeared both pleased and agitated. He acted as he did when Mom was being both most cold and most flirtatious. Clyde had silently witnessed an hour of absolute concentration—my fingertip at skim, jabbing, comparing, circling back. Perhaps he guessed I had the makings of a natural student, even a scholar. And I was just seven.

"What?," I snapped in the accusatory way kids must—to keep from being swallowed whole by their best-loved same-sex parent.

"Meadows, see, this is why I keep my in-surance paid up. It's cause of this I'm settin' cash aside each and ever' week for your going off to a college, son. If you only knew . . ." Dad couldn't finish; he substituted the lighting of another cigarette.

My elder daughter is in her last year of oboe at Juilliard. How good a player is Deirdre? She's been mentioned as a leading contender for that upcoming fourth-woodwind chair in the New York Philharmonic itself. If I may brag. Bethany and I rarely had to force Deirdre to practice. Even as a child of five, even when she simply played scales, I swear we could hear what kind of day she'd had at preschool!

Our baby, Sara, is a scholar with a wild streak and one world-class mind. She's in her first year at NYU and has already published a paper. It concerns Tissot's illustrations of the Bible. When Sara was ten or so, we found a mildewy copy in a junkshop near Burlington. Her essay offers reasons why the leading nineteenth-century painter of leisured Parisian society (circuses, cafés, yachting parties) should suddenly devote his later years engraving Job, the Plagues, and all Christ's sufferings. Sara's paper offers a child's trusting freshness alongside some sage old woman's hardscrabble wisdom. Despite her conversation's crabgrass "likes," Sara writes with logic and grace. In her, I see my mother's rose complexion and sensual literacy, I hear my unlikely father's own crazed reverence for Scripture.

—If I seem to boast about my girls (note: I haven't even mentioned their beauty), it's a habit I learned from my Booster of a dad. And I'm not ashamed of it.

Here in my office on a Saturday, here at the beautiful fulcrum of my middle years, I seek to save all this for my own children. (And if, once I'm done, this account feels too unseemly for girls my daughters' ages, I can always stick it in a vault with some restrictions. I'll insist it can't be read before, say, they are also forty-nine!)

10.

I might list the most obvious reason for my mom's infidelity with the whitey-blond local vet, father of nine. He was a looker whose mother had named him after a dashing silent-film star named Richard Dix. Doctor was a man known literally and smuttily as Doc Dick Dix. It's hard to talk so much about my own father's peculiar looks, and yet that's necessary. Clyde was not just the plainest guy in a town sporting a host of singular nonbeauties. His face was . . . well, I just thought of Blanche, that pink plaster lady fading—trussed—in her downtown storefront. The poor gal stood rigged with the repairs for every trip and puncture flesh is heir to. Clyde's face was like that in how accident-prone yet half comical it remained. Unmendable but optimistic. A face as assertively sad as it was undeniably true. Its rejuvenating power over others could not quite be explained. Though I've spent my lifetime trying.

The in-joke of it rearranged cafés. Such impractical fleshiness demanded double takes. A mouth so large gave Clyde's smile a totem pole's quorum potency. His stiff hair tended to clump like horse mane, like Lincoln's hair in those last pictures. His amber eyes hopped with extra highlights' mischief. Sometimes when he bragged about his sinful youth, I almost believed him. And wished I'd known him then. Before God reduced Clyde Melvin Delman to being simply mine and almost middle-class.

It is still tough, discussing his physical peculiarity. It nearly feels like I am making fun of him. I truly intend the opposite.

But even when you'd loved him your whole seven years, Dad remained "actively ugly," as my daughters and their young friends said till recently.

After outbreaks of our bad if bold singing, after my quoted Bible verses rendered at machine-gun speed, we sometimes drove in silence. The hush of sadness was accepted because shared.

I love recalling Dad's hands on the gray wheel of his Clipper, each knuckle distinct, cut square and separate as a dice. Pop seemed made mostly of bone. His Adam's apple was something like an affliction—a notched jitterbuggy thing, half the size of my domed school lunchbox. When he told motel craftspersons, "Museums should be phoned," I'd see them check out Dad's right-angled neck, his sleeve guards, the lime-green bow tie measled with—what were those?—pink Xed riding crops or something like crisscrossed stalks of celery.

Pop wore as much of his clothing inventory as having one body allowed. At Christmas, his bow tie was made of felt holly leaves, its central knot was stitched red berries. Thanks to a hidden battery, the bow actually lit. My father, unaware of his neck's knobbly ugliness—favored bib-wide painted neckties showing dynamic palm trees, airbrushed native girls. These only drew more attention to how the Adam's apple—when he spoke—did elevator antics, bobbling from level to level with no exact pattern you could detect.

Before finding Christ, he'd been accustomed to greeting his far-flung customers with one icebreaking smutty joke. Folks still said, "Here's that heathen Clyde toting all those clean new shirts and the one ole filthy story, which'll you get out first today? Don't ever repeat that one about the Brownie Scouts, their fudge sale, and the Jergen's Lotion dispenser. It made me physically sick last month. Sick. Rox-anne, come out of that stockroom. Clyde's back. And looks like he's going to spill another nasty one, ready or not. Right, Clydio, ole sport? We're braced."

Over those years we spent delivering God's Word, three of our favorite motels burned. "All that smoking in bed," Dad tossed his latest Camel out the window. A few miles later, he'd grumble then light a new weed while hollering, "Don't stare. Cancer sticks. Eating into your college education. Since morning, I've smoked half a Freshman textbook. I know, I know."

Our Sunday treks had one main rule: we needed nice long visits. We could not return to Falls before mother's "headache" was completely cured. That meant retelling many jokes, keeping two rural counties between us and Mom till sunset.

IV. Numbers

"Excursion"

And the LORD *spake unto Moses, saying, Speak unto the children of Israel, and say unto them, When ye be come into the land of your habitations, which I give unto you, and will make an offering by fire unto the* LORD, *a burnt offering, or a sacrifice in performing a vow . . . in your solemn feasts, to make a sweet savour unto the* LORD. . . .*

Numbers 15:1–3

The Sabbath before my eighth birthday, we made the next-to-last turn toward our favorite motel, saw brown smoke messing up the blue of western sky. We heard a fire truck's scream; its red mass and silver lines overtook us, then three other trucks shot past. "Dad, I'm scared it's you-know-whose." But he was already slumped in prayer.

I'd rarely seen him do so while driving. He mostly muttered, eyes closed, at church or while receiving refill coffee from . . . that waitress with the two-syllable name I keep trying to trap myself into recalling.

Our Packard parked at the roadside, our motor still running, Dad's long fingers closed on my soft hand, "You first, son." I stammered aloud my own embarrassed brand of instant wishing.

"—Uh, Lord? Yeah, well, I know you're gonna let us find Miss Last Supper's Pecan Grove and her place still standing, right? Okay. Cause that ole gal, she sure tries to honor You every whichaway. Good. Amen then, Lord."

We turned the corner. Pecan Grove was all but gone. (Is it awful for a seven-year-old to admit he sort of likes seeing stuff burn?)

Air to the horizon hung with black paper lanterns, freelance ash. Through our windshield, at once soot-dark, I stared open-mouthed. Our home-away-from-home was now just so much silt, wooden shutters still aflame. This appeared a Biblical retaliation on a zone too richly Bibled! As walls burned, you could look right into many rooms. Odd to see blackened towel racks, four toilet bowls all smoked like hams. The bathmat beside one shower became, as I watched, an orderly foot-warming oval of sour blue fire.

One forlorn guest—wearing pajamas previously white—told us the lady owner had been saved. But Miss Last Supper's main unit, her office gallery, all her art, was now just so much charcoal. Having jumped from our car, Dad and I ran to an ambulance as men were closing its rear doors on our hard-drinking Bible-hider. Smudged as for some blackface role, she saw us; then Verna really started sobbing, holding out to us her skilled but empty hands.

"My 'scenes,' my 'scenes'!," she pointed toward piled ash. It made me almost scream aloud myself. The pain of the sound in that. All those seeds and hours. The tweezers! All that faith.

Police couldn't make out what she meant. So Pop interpreted as usual. Wheat? John the Beloved glued to doors? Clyde couldn't seem to make them understand.

Even as medics shut her in back for good, Miss Last Supper waved. Crying, she acted glad to have seen us. She faked smiling through tinted ambulance glass: at least two major admirers understood the scope of her artistic loss. Poor Verna saw we truly felt the scale of that. Twelve eight-foot Last Suppers, countless Resurrections gone—for good. Plus all of Dad's Bibles I'd hand-placed.

But, sad as the loss of Pecan Grove, now we had a newer problem. How to pass the extra hours usually spent dawdling here, the hours Clyde joked and gossiped as I restocked Verna's rooms, chapter and verse. One thing for sure: we could not go home.

He drove very slowly to a truck stop outside Norlina. This town, I never tired of telling Clyde, had been named for the opening and closing of the words "North Carolina."

"No kiddin? You sure do got you a way with language. Makes certain mounta sense, I guess." Poor guy said this almost weekly.

After his prayer of thanks for them, Dad tended a coffee and a cigarette, I nursed my huge grape soda. We sat looking at the greasy clock above the counter. We both guessed why we'd been banished from Falls till dusk. We neither could admit it.

"How'd you like to visit more of my home turf? Couple people up here I still know. My high-school bandleader might like meeting a towheaded Bible scholar your age. What say, copilot? My ole stomping ground's not but bout forty minutes north, cross the Virginia line."

"Good deal, sir, let's go." I hated remembering Verna's "scenes." I dreaded asking Clyde why God would burn such an unofficial Temple to Mainly Him. I felt grateful for any task that'd spare our finding Mom before her veterinary migraine left the house.

2.

Clyde's whitewalled Packard soon pulled into a run-down little mill village—train tracks divided its downtown. We shot along the only street of tidy homes. One place's porch stood loaded with music stands, pig-iron lyres meant to hold scores open. Dad fussed with his tie, then knocked at the door. No one answered. "Must be away at some all-state band contest. Seem to remember they're this time of year."

Clyde now sat parked before the house, looking at me, looking past me.

"You're real close to eight, ain't you?" "Yessir." "You love your Clyde here, don't you?" "Yessir." "Could I ever disappoint you, if I kept lovin you back?" "Nosir." He seemed to make a decision.

"I know somebody," he said and off we started.

Our Third Musketeer soon swerved, bumped downward, gave up all paved two-lane roads.

Twelve or fifteen miles we drove along farm paths barely wide enough to accommodate a mule cart. It'd rained all week. Wet tree limbs lashed the windshield as I laughed; Dad smiled only at my pleasure. Ditches flanked this muddy path, and among their jungle of reeds, a thousand red-winged blackbirds swung and sang a rusty one-hinged song.

I could tell from how he anticipated every obscure branching turn, Clyde knew exactly where we were. We passed two ruined timber mills; we passed three boarded-up general stores—stripped even of signage—proving that some new highway had siphoned life off elsewhere. Dad drove so slow over a loud bridge in terrible repair. He stared down across one little, nothing creek. Clyde braked; we rolled still before a tiny metal-roofed shack. It hid in the blue shade of three immense enclosing pin oaks.

To cover rotted porch flooring, to clamp shut side-wall wind-holes, the shanty had been cobbled across with hacked-apart tin advertisements. Some placards looked ancient with stalagmite rust; others shone new as their bubbled stenciled paint. Product pictures had been quartered then rejoined any old way: from half a big red rose, one cartoon mule ear poked.

Being an orderly little boy with an academic career dead ahead, I now identified all the home's unintentional sponsors: three snuffs, a brake fluid, one chewing gum, Dr. Pepper, two corrosive surefire laxatives. These ads looked hammered house-shaped with a crazy-quilt haphazardness as if by someone blind. The shack was falsely colorful as a witch's toxic gingerbreadhouse. And yet, the place felt homey, safe as our pantry corner's brightest box of oatmeal.

"Just call her 'Aunt Sutie,' " Clyde said, stretching.

I blinked up at him. "Your mom's not real big on having my ole friends come callin. So you and me won't bother Mom with today's li'l side trip—now, will we, Junior Birdman?"

"No, sir."

I remember buffing the tops of my small oxfords onto the back of each creased pant leg. We'd been driving nearly half an hour through the woods in a whorl of dust. Ours had seemed a hidden, second set of roads. No rural mailbox dignified these miles. Here was a zone where no motel existed; no bedside table for a Bible to help humanize.

I slowly saw how one rocking chair, tucked far under the dark low-hanging eave, was really a stooped woman in that rocker. Her spine looked little broader than her chair back's upright laths.

Clyde reached out for me. He signaled I should come stand beside him. Midyard, we fell into a pose as for a picture. Only then did Dad call up dark steps, "Who-hoo? It's your sight for sore eyes."

"Whoot?," one owly sound swung forth. "Whoot at? It ain't, not my answered prayer? Can't be no Clydie Melvin mine. Unh-unh."

"No other. Brung my boy to pay you court like, Sutie Mae Fancy. You primed for company? You decent?"

"Naw. Why should I start now?" It was an answer, a delivery, even I laughed at. Dad smiled my way as if saying, "See?" Up five steps, we approached a brightened toothless face. I found that she was very old and very very black. I had not expected this, her to be a . . . had not expected this.

Clyde guided me, himself grinning with a sickening half-pride. He kept winking at me. When I saw water squeeze from this side's eye, he pointed to that wet. I read how she must be blind or nearly.

"Sutie, you'll remember my little un here, m' Clyde Junior. You've not seen him since he was way too small to know you. Ain't often we ride back up this far, the both of us together."

I wanted to tell her about the motel fire. About our poor Verna. But I thought better of it. Aunt Sutie's ivory-palmed hands shot forward. I stepped under them as beneath a running shower the exact right temperature. As Clyde watched with a disturbed blubbering bashfulness, she felt me up.

"He smooth," the old woman remarked, her neck stiff, blank eyes gazing past me. "He a right good size for seven, right stout." She tested my bicep as if I were some market pullet. Helplessly male, I made a muscle for her fingers' leaf-dry tickling. "Whoo. My. All man." Laughing so close, she bared a blue-black toothless gum. I found it marbled with strange reds and grays, like the lips of a neighbor's chow dog. This both scared and attracted me. It made me feel wider open, then far worse.

I was surprised that Sutie should know my age; I felt far more shocked when her hand reached right between my legs and gave my teapot one serious tweak and waggle. Ticklish, I hopped aside, to Clyde's delight. "He young yet," she seemed to be remarking on my size. "Give him time," Clyde said, "the acorn never falls all that far from Poppa Log." And they hooted over this. Vain, I held on to my wounded silence.

Her bone hands kept straightening my collar. Which didn't need straightening. She never offered us a seat or a drink. I asked if I could use her bathroom. (Her groping me like that had made me somehow burn to pee.) "It out back," she croaked. I knew she kept a privy. The choice of "holding it in" or fighting backhouse wasps and scorpions left me little choice. I just stood here. That seemed to make her somewhat mad.

Newswise, she told Clyde next to nothing—excessive wet weather, his sister's office promotion up one whole paygrade in D.C. government. Sutie passed us stray facts battered in the flaky owllike lurches of her sound. This voice had aged all glassy, then past glass and more toward dust. The sides of certain vowels now sounded mossed. And yet, beneath the failing tone, you heard a saucy starter-confidence, some beauty long since missing from her droopy raisin-colored skin. She was, all over, the color of a third-degree Caucasian bruise. Yellow-purple, suedey royal brown, the shades of a healing if terrible blow to someone's face or head. Still messing with my collar, she stiffened like some startled woodland creature; she seemed to feel my doubt and scrutiny and to abruptly hate it.

"You still round here, boy? Too good to use a outhouse?" Sutie sounded pissed. I answered no, I'd changed my mind. Her hands released my white wing collar. But fingers found my either shoulder and, with no warning, jerked up me against her so hard my big head snapped. Auntie was suddenly shaking me so. Before her, I danced spastic. New front teeth twice chopped my lower lip. "Bu . . . what?" I called loud, begging her to stop. I pressed a finger to my lip. Still clamped within her grip, I saw blood there. Clyde looked stricken but kept absolutely still. He leaned back against a porch rail, proving he had no control here.

Aunt's dark and sightless face, so near, asked my scared upturned one, "Is you in any way worth it, whiteyhead?"

How could the young Whiteyhead wisely answer? Worth what? I didn't understand her sudden shift. I didn't understand my father's silence. He offered to let her hurt me if she chose. I felt myself a sacrifice and hated Clyde for not preparing me. I glared at him. He only turned away. Silence seemed my single choice. I rode that out. I sampled now the flavor of my own mouth's blood. It seemed the very sunny, salted taste of blondness draining down my throat.

"I said," she pushed at me, " 'You worth it?' You half as good as him?" She swung her head in almost Clyde's direction.

"As my dad, you mean?"

Her eyeball's fronts had cataracted to the beaten glimmer of raw steel. Odd, but such metallic discs seemed to let daylight fall even deeper into her. I guessed that Dad had come to feed me to this witch. But his dopey look still begged for my indulgence. Clyde acted half intrigued to see whatever'd have to grab me next. For a second, I felt sure: she could strangle me and Dad would simply stand there, mumbling, "Now now, Sutie. Now now."

She reached out for me again; I backed off so quick I almost stepped off the porch. Her hands clawing, swiping, seeking me, Sutie spoke now in a voice far lower than most men's. "You been being as kind of a boy as you daddy here done been? Cause ain't ever been a boy was sweeter younger than my Clyde. You halfknow whatall you costin him? You know who you got?"

"I do. I bet he was. —No, ma'am, I'm not near as nice as him. Hardly nobody is, though. But—Miz Sutie?—I reckon I'd sure like to be."

(I half-noted I'd just let my straight-A grammar slip—as some new and saving eloquence for her.)

The old woman, sovereign here, did nod. My remark seemed to help appease her. Clyde waited to one side, tearful, kidlike suddenly, so spindly and weak-looking. I didn't understand a bit of this. But, somehow, feeling simpler, I told Aunt Sutie in my loudest voice: Clyde was the tiptop thing in my life, and I said about how people lit up when Dad came into a room, how they called others out of the back as if paying them some real favor, which it was. I told Sutie the number of dozens of Bibles we weekly sowed across our entire sinful Bible-swiping region.

.   .   .

"Praise Jesus, leastways for that. —Now," she still sounded serious if a bit less mad, "Clyde ain't lost his looks, have he?"

That only made me gulp. I stared his way.

How could I win here? Dad, recovering from this talk's strange violent turn, offered me his usual conspirator's wink.

"No, ma'am," I said. "Well. At least his looks haven't gotten one bit worse." I tried for traveling-salesman diplomacy. And wound up sounding just like him, of course. My wisecrack folded Clyde double, so glad for any change of tone. "He's a caution, ain't he?," Dad pointed my way, though she was blind. But I could see I'd hurt Aunt Sutie's feelings. Her neck lengthened straight up, its hanging swags all flattened. Her voice assumed some ancient haughty force: "My Clyde he got he daddy's eyes."

We didn't stay more than twelve minutes. And it'd taken us forever to thread our way along that cowpath through high reeds. We'd driven past those lonely, deep pine woods, their floors so covered with needle straw, no underbrush could grow. It was like peeking into giant empty chambers—warehoused secrets—far back in.

While Clyde and Sutie said goodbye, I explored her shadowy front room. The whole house had only one. Her bedroom was the living room or vice versa. Sutie's bedstead rose up huge, old-fashioned, all darkly carved with invented birds and garlands. On a cracker barrel nearby, three framed four-leaf clovers, some Bible-verse plaques, and her family pictures. (I sneaked over, amazed to be studying a school photo of Clyde at what seemed my age. Grinning pitiably wide, missing three front teeth, his face was already mishapen like a lima bean, the Mr. Potato Head features gouged in any old way. Beside him, a very pretty paley black girl; she wore satin graduation robes. And behind this, a big formal studio photo of one white boychild, framed in overfancy silver. He was wearing the sailor suit I felt was very sissy and had always hated; it was me.)

"Come give us a las' kiss," she called my way. "I don't care who you are, Sutie sure do miss getting regular sugar." She leaned forward, forgetting she'd just snatched and hurt me. She angled out now into daylight—a face like some old turtle's as it flexes frontward from its Stone Age shell.

I took one extra breath then bent toward her. I kissed the smoothest skin my mouth had ever touched. Such skin must contain more lanolin than any white lady's. Compared to her, my mom was all-over made of sandpaper. My mouth stayed there two/three beats longer than planned. And, suspended, I seemed to enter a crackling zone of thought or electricity around this blind gourd-sized skull. It was the strangest thing, as if her head were some radio transmitter tuned to a station where static was about to clarify toward being steady band-music, but not quite yet.

"Sutie, they still delivering such stuff as I send?," Clyde already stood behind me, squinting in her brilliant muddy yard. "They bringing you your food right steady?"

She waved us off, "I ain't ever done less work and et more biscuits. Sutie'd feel bad if she could half-remember to." Then she gave us a sucked-in laugh, fond and half familiar. "Now don't you boys be strangers," Auntie called last thing.

Leaving, still tasting the healthful iron of my own blood, I turned. She sat rocking, her hand lifted with goodbye. And I—helpless not to— soon waved back through our car's rear window. Her patched shanty gleamed bright as any bottle cap.

"She can't see you, baby," he said, kind. "I know," I told him, feeling strangely as happy as I was confused. My hand still flap-flapped toward the porch. "But knowing her," I said, "she can probably feel it. She's mad at me, Dad. I don't know why. I never did one thing to her. But I tried not to let her be just mad. I think, down deep, Sutie still likes me some." I said this, simple. Overreaching myself only partly to please him. But Dad grew quite strict-looking. He seemed angry with some feeling I could only guess at.

"You're mine," he said in a new hard tone. "She loves you cause she's mine and you're mine, too. —Mighty small club, hunh?"

He spoke again only when we reached the first mended asphalt road, where white-owned property began.

"Anybody present like a three-scoop Dairy Queen special?"

We arrived home even later than usual.

We never mentioned our side trip to Mom, much less to each other. Not ever once again.

We are getting to the Sunday when I killed him. If I seem to drag my feet to slow that some, forgive me. I was such a trusting little bastard. I just didn't know. You can maybe see it coming. But I? was eight. And couldn't stand to know the truth quite yet.

3.

Well, I'm finally grown; in the waistline, perhaps a tad overgrown. I'm semi-solvent—decent medical-dental plan—and am a fairly good listener. At least a conscientious one. But, maybe because of those Sabbaths spent among chatty desk-clerk hobbyists, I do still feel this morbid terror of bores. Of being cornered by the underoccupied in one of the world's remote banished corners where its biggest bores most naturally lurk. Of course, I listen hard to my daughters and to my students. I try for them. So young, they're still too fresh to yet be boring. "Dull" takes practice.

I'd hoped, by now, to have become the kind of guy that some dish-washer repairman might naturally confess to: his single hidden mis-deed, say, as a newly divorced and suddenly lovesick Boy Scout leader. My late father was just such a self-employed confessor-priest. To per-fect strangers, Clyde conceded details of his own pre-Christian career at sinning. And that put people at their ease; that lubricated their own worse crimes, then here came amazing sins flying at him, us.

People could see how gentle Clyde was now he'd been saved. He seemed to live daily relieved of some ordeal survived; there's the champagnelike buzz a person feels on walking unscratched from an otherwise shredding car wreck. Folks believed Clyde's tales of early bourbon binges (since bourbon bottles are notoriously "easy," going to the highest bidder).

But when Dad mentioned sins involving "certain ladies of loose virtue," people grew more still. You sensed they figured, where love was concerned, major money must've changed hands. They'd start to doubt his prodigal boasts, my father's face was that much a novelty item. I felt lucky not to take after him, except—I hoped—in spirit. Like lots of persons born-again, Dad's best fun involved admitting to the starter decadence. Maybe he forgave my mom her public infidelity because he himself had erred (he claimed) so often in his first, more restless life? Being newly eight and having sinned far less myself, I felt less willing to ignore Mom's misdeeds.

Dad would gladly drive 190 miles one way on his sole day off to replace a Bible that some clown had packed by accident.

Unlike me, Clyde M. Delman, Sr., never held such Bible-robbers' crimes against them. I—homework done, arms crossed, tipped back against our Packard's broadcloth seat, marveling how bad most motel patrons must be. Imagine carrying off God's Word, and both darn Testaments!

"No," Dad would tell me. "Pal-o-mine, live and let. . . . See, to do its wonder-working best, the Good Book's gotta be in the sinner's hands. Has to be out circulatin, agitatin. So—fergive a little. 'It is He that hath made us, and not we ourselves.' —Remember, son: A stolen Bible is a noticed Bible."

I'd spy Doc Dick Dix speeding around town in his glinting white Pontiac; it was a cabin cruiser of a car, back seat piled with the hideously large hypodermics of a doctor to livestock. Dix's back seat featured black rubber plungers used in the insemination of prize heifers; there were half-gallon cans of things called Bag Balm and Dr. Beemers' E-Z-On Castration Salve. His vehicle was rigged for powerful shortwave and had two fishing-pole-sized antennas whipping silver angles off its back.

Doc Dix's old nurse (the young ones, manhandled, quit) radio-dispatched him all over Person County. She voiced him toward troubled cows or barren horses in a territory roughly the size of my dad's Scripture one.

Doc Richard Dix preferred any woman to every man. He dismissed all other males as malformed jokes, failed attempts at becoming him. And a good number of ladies agreed. Falls celebrated its hundredth anniversary and most local fellows grew beards. Patriotic women sewed long dresses and there was a huge parade. Doc Dix turned up downtown to mock our earnest spectacle. All year, he'd remained clean-shaven and in slick modern dress. Others jokingly resented it. Doc Dix and his enormous brood were seated all along his white car's hood and roof.

Fourteen fluffy-faced men, pulled behind a tractor, formed a tableau depicting the solemn signing of Falls's Charter. "Hey, Doc?," one whiskered fellow hollered from the float. "Where's your beard?"

Dix's answer is still quoted: "Bitch, I'm sittin on it."

No sane fellow would allow his unchaperoned wife to take the family pet to Doc Dick Dix's office alone. There were many postcard-funny stories of how Blondie, the female cocker spaniel, lay anes-thetized on Doc's brushed-steel chrome operating table. Mid-spaying, she was all pink, split end to end, while Dix chased her upset lady owner round and round his table, baying, "You know you want it. I see you're wet and open as Blondie. Admit you're in heat and need it right this second. Say the word, gal. Doc'll slip you nature's most calming of all shots."

Then it was not called "sexual harassment." It was just "being fresh." Like the motor-court lobby postcards, people mostly joked about such open-season sex. Doc's chasing worked often enough to make the aerobic outlay worthwhile. His procedures kept certain agreeable wives quiet. Kept their animals often seeming sick.

Dix's own long-suffering wife spent most of her time having babies and the rest turning a blind eye. Her legs were wrapped like Maypoles in flesh-colored swaddling to help ease her terrible varicose veins. She'd come from a family of doctors (people doctors). Her dowry helped pay for Dix's vet school and the semi-mansion where they lived. It had separate dormitories for the five girls, four boys. They all looked towheaded as their big blond randy dad. Sundays, though we owned no pets—thanks to my headachy mother's allergies—Doc Dick Dix apparently made house calls. By then though, Clyde and little Meadows Delman, spreaders of God's Word, were miles, motels, and hobbies away.

Still, en route to righteousness, I pictured our small home. I imag-ined Doc Dick Dix's showy Pontiac pulled up, hogging the whole drive, where one elegant black Packard belonged. At school, a few kids had made recent scary comments. The Dix clan was blessed with fine-spun white-gold hair, cheeks that burned pink all winter, and eyes of the deepest purple-blue. So, coincidentally, was I.

Once, I got a crush on a nice girl in my class who happened to be Doc Dix's daughter Berta. Our ancient third-grade teacher seemed to know something I didn't. She actively discouraged my interest. She changed our seats. Teacher even put us in different reading groups, though Berta seemed almost as smart as me.

Though I am technically listed as a "junior," Mom's early insistence made me, fussily, C. Meadows Delman. (Grace's folks were the family-proud Meadowses.) "One Clyde Melvin per household is quite a sufficiency, thanks," my mother said. Dad just laughed.

4.

Now I wish I'd kept his Packard Clipper De Luxe Sedan. "Eight cylinders in line, treated aluminum alloy, 14 mm. spark plugs. Oil Capacity: 7 quarts. 165 horsepower." I can just picture my two daughters out for a joyride in it, wearing dark glasses and windblown headscarves, laughing while waving. When he died on the road—in a motel—Mother had his car towed home, then sold it to the Shell station's owner.

Dad's spiffy Packard—a ship's-wheel Clipper insignia set on both dash and trunk—was rigged with gizmo comfort items, every available car-lover's convenience. Racks to hold your Kleenex tissues (though a single dusty box of those lasted my entire childhood).

There was a tire-pressure gauge tied with a black tassel like a diploma and it would—if held up to the light—show you one very blond lady whose red dress drained away like thermometer mercury to reveal her pink skin, her two red nipples so heavy-handedly retouched, they seemed an affliction to be pitied, and possibly needing to be somehow (I could now faintly imagine) helped with. "Don't look at that, son," he told me every Sunday I looked. "Got to throw that out. Been meaning to. It's left from when I was a wild drunk always panting after the ladies. Looking like I do, even the ladies o' Spain in red kinda resisted." "Oh," I said. There were separate maps of Canada and Mexico and the forty-eight states I would pore over just in case we two took off like wild geese, because we could. There was a plywood implement, enameled gray and looking made in special-ed shop class, for holding six of your beer cans; though Dad no longer drank anything wilder than an ice-cold Nu-Grape. Which left his flat lips as noticeably purple as two matching holiday novelty items. And of course there was the Bible, one known to us club members as "a Nurses' White."

The word "fundamentalist" has lately fallen into much disfavor. That's partly due to sleazy TV ministers who would've loved Dad's three-tone clothes while lacking his character's simplicity. Those guys all started squealing on one another—and from that there's no return. But in 1956, being a fundamentalist could still mean something as honorable as all good fences' being painted white since George Washington, something that just felt right, at least for my Clyde M. Delman, Sr.

In those days, you could believe more readily in a good God. In '56, as I rode around the state delivering God's Word with Pop, "fundamental" seemed a beautiful and basic word. Like "barn" or "tree" or "Ike."

In a voice as red-clay rolling as that landscape, Dad retold me how he had been "saved" by accident. Rendered downward from the overly complex and selfish to pure-as-well-water fundamental:

Drunk, aged thirty-three, jilted by a girl on their first date (she left the dance with somebody better-looking, as everybody present was), Dad'd swerved to avoid a cow but hit a tree instead. Way out along some nighttime country lane, he found his front left tire flattened. No spare. So Dad, staggering, that looped, was soon rolling one bad tire to the nearest station, right hand already filthy rubber-black. He first heard music then chanced upon a lit-up late-night tent revival in progress.

Thinking he might find a ride to the closest garage, my young father hand-rolled his whole tire through the tent's rear flap. He let his flat rest in sawdust, he noticed the organ and piano plus a general sense of roiling spiritual commotion that at first seemed merely sexual. Clyde saw the pale bare waving arms of girls sixteen. Cries from grown men came up like private zoo noises: "Oh, urh, unh, take me unk, Chrast."

And—six minutes later—listening, recognizing, reeling from three words—"sin," "sick," "soul"—Clyde said he felt change turn in him like some deadbolt lock unlatching. (Sutie'd told him he would know when.) Dad said that—flat on his back in a matter of minutes—he saw all sorts of novelties swim before his eyes during that spell spent in sawdust smelling of black rubber; his entire sin-sogged life pulled-pranced before him. Clyde said he knew now: Sin was not some minor rule you broke. No, Sin was everything that cut you off from other people. Meanwhile, alongside him, real ladies were literally wholly-rolling in the aisles, their summer wash-dresses wet from sudden between-legs feelings and the specific trance of a distant yet close-in God.

The tent's boy preacher was hollering just how corrupt he himself had recently been being in mo- and ho-tels (especially the ho-ones) all across our newly expensive South.

The dashing young preacher swore he'd sure acted real real bad, via pills, booze, and do-anything B-girls, sometimes four at a time. (Four women, not just four pills.) The more ladies he admitted waking up with ("wives of friends and, Jesus can forgive anything, the wife of my older brother, the war hero, Christ forgive me what I did to her in front of those young girls, what I did to/with/and/on my sister-in-law and what the other teen Jezebels forced her to perform on them during, oh, do pray for me"), the more the kid conceded, the more his congregation loved him for confessing, the more cash spilled his way, and the more his donors agreed—despite all his vices' excesses—the boy had not lost one inch of his fine looks.

Dad slumped beside his deflated tire at the back of a defrocked former circus tent. Dad stretched out guilty on the ground, dust to dust, flat to flat. He liked to say his life had spun before his eyeballs as he wallowed there in circusy sawdust. He said he saw what they claim a drowner glimpses. "Your life flashes before you—highlights, like. Scenes. Whole perfect Christmas-card-colored pictures. Your Hit Parade of the good times and bad. But spelled in pops, like a set of news-camera lightbulbs going off . . ."

Clyde swore as how his conversion moment registered like this: till that moment, he'd always breathed through his mouth, and afterward he discovered what the person's nostrils were drilled there for.

. . .

Eight myself, I always pictured a short series of fairly sad events. They'd be lighted like the diorama gallery of some local-history museum—lit too much from directly overhead. I pictured Clyde's lean parents changing towns real often. I saw the helper, blue-black "Aunt" Sutie, staying put and taking him in. Museums should be phoned. To show successfully his sin-soaked life: Clyde as a train brakeman's only son, his dropping out of high school to live with Aunt Sutie in her tin can of a hut, the revelation of haberdashery, the pleasure of finding he'd been fated by God for fatherhood.

Listening to his born-again account emerge again, I shoehorned Dad into every picture he described, making each one go more glamorous and movie-ish.

But I sometimes found to my horror, that the man I'd cast in Clyde's part soon quit looking Clyde-like. Homely Melvin Delman kept swelling into some beefcake film star of the day, a Jeffrey Hunter or Rock Hudson, who, by scene three, somehow turned around and had the head, then hair, then face of Dr. Dick Dix. I canceled that, but Dad's own cheering grin kept switching back to Dix's self-satisfied smirk. Even in fantasy, Clyde's kisser would simply not equate on the silver screen. Not in the pipe-and-jacket role of "Dad."

Clyde, at the wheel, smiled now and admitted, soon as he had taken Christ aboard as skipper of his Clipper—now that he was married to a woman he adored and had a car this good and a white-headed child as pretty as Clyde himself was not—life felt A-okay. Amen. "Great," I said. We drove.

I'm pleased he kept his sense of humor, even in his reborn state. That made the saved condition feel a bit more possible to his Bible copilot but secret doubter. It did seem sad—a religion that made things so safe for Mom's two-timing us once every week. Headed home, I studied Dad's worried profile.

Taking care never to arrive back early, honking fair warning as we pulled up our own drive, Clyde handed Mom roadside-stand zinnias wound in soggy Virginia newspapers. I presented her with sticks shaped like anything other than a stick. Dad hovered over her bed saying, "Feeling some better, beauty?"

"Oh, much . . . Day and night, you have no idea. . . . World of difference. And how, pray, were our looney-toon motel-owners making their Ferris wheels out of pea pods and Popsicle sticks, hmm?"

At school, a bully hinted how his own dad said I was not my dad's, my own dad's, but I'd been brought by a stork, brought in a horse doctor's bag, and how "stork" was one word for what'd poked me into life. I clobbered this kid—my blow inexpert but effective thanks only to surprise. When he rose up and came at me, I asked him (with a simplicity that seems to prove, even from here, I was Clyde's genetic heir), "How could YOU stand to hear that your own daddy was a fake one and had lied to you and that the only really bad man in town was your real dad, hunh?" He'd already blacked my right eye. But my question had the power to stop a bully whose knee I had just skinned if by pure accident.

The question had been fundamental, so it worked.

V: Deuteronomy

"Saddest of Possible Sundays"

If there arise a matter too hard for thee in judgment, between blood and blood, between plea and plea, and between stroke and stroke, being matters of controversy within thy gates: then shalt thou arise, and get thee up into the place which the LORD thy God shall choose.

Deuteronomy 17:8

The Worst of Any Sabbath hid beneath routine: I woke to my usual stubborn if negligible morning erection, to our innocent April sun, to her usual headache.

We had so many Good Books to scatter, Dad let me skip both church and Sunday school. Hooray! We ate our standard lunch but early—baked chicken or corned-beef-and-cabbage. Mom always served Ocean Spray cranberry sauce to simulate its being an occasion.

Clyde and I purged his Packard of that season's pink-and-gray masculine finery, the martini-glass and dice-motif accessories. We counted our Bible-list inventory into cardboard boxes. These had been created to hold canned pineapple and Tide detergent and still smelled sweet or eye-burningly clean. Then off we set. We left her before noon that Sunday I would understand then lose him.

I was freshly eight, quite proud of that, still squinting through the purpled eye. I "rode shotgun." Bearing down upon our Clipper's blue leatherette *Owner's Manual,* I tried writing a story for third-grade English, the accelerated reading circle.

"Is it going to be a funny story, son?" "Probably bout as funny as I can make it." "That's a good thing to be. Funny keeps them glad to see you coming back," and Clyde added with a moment's strange bitterness, "Some of them."

But quickly recovered: "Your mother is a wonderful woman. Grace remembers everything she reads." Even she admitted this was just not true; she said so often. I looked over at Dad.

2.

It can hurt you, loving somebody that others you love keep punishing. This was April 15, 1956, near as I can tell. (I used to know a simple formula to determine which day of the week any date in history fell upon; but at my present age, I swear I think I've cleanly forgotten it!)

I do recall forsythias' bursting out their yellow exclamation marks, upsetting the bell curves of otherwise modest farmyards. I recall how even the oldest trees looked younger—wearing an April green that is the truest green of all because it is the color of first trying.

Our car trunk was stacked with books enough to overcome a higher-than-usual number of sadnesses and thefts. Packing Bibles, I'd decided that they smelled of hot black rubber. But maybe I confused the vehicle with its merchandise, the Spare with the Saved.

Dad sang us well past Falls and out into brown baritone country: " 'I was sinking, deep in sin, far from the peaceful shore. Very stained and soiled within, sinkin to rise no more. Then the Master of the Deep heard my despairing cries, from the water lifted me, now safe am I.' Join me on the chorus and feel better, Meadows? . . . 'O love lifted me, when nothing else could help, love lift-ed me.' —Boy, but that shore hits the spot."

Rubbery good news as black yet promising as rubber smells. I sat picturing Christ as a circling buoyant lifesaving inner tube, just in time, His bobbing by.

Then Pop stated again, as he did on certain Sundays, "Your mother's a mighty excellent woman." I grunted, bored of hearing this. My eye and forehead throbbed, especially if I turned my head his way too fast. Neither of my parents, pressing ice to me, had dared ask why I fought. I tried not remembering what the bully said to me before I hit him and he hit me worse and I then tried talking sense. He sangsong loud at me, "My dad says you're just one more trick out of Doc Dick Dix's big ole dick, is what Pappy called you."

It's not a phrase you're likely to forget. Not when you're the little mongrel-bastard they say it of.

Now I slid over. Across the flannel car-seat toward him. Lately I had chanced this less and less. But today I laid my head into Dad's lap. Looking up at him from below could be better than our trip to the Norfolk Aquarium. Upside down, Clyde's face became all flaps and bones and yesterday's Nu-Grape traces. From here, even his good-natured singing of hymns sounded wonderfully upside down, almost okay. Dad was that splendid and rarest of "novelty items"—a good man. Maybe they're the ones most destined to be disappointed by this meanish Bible-swiping world?

He soon let me "drive." "Got to earn your keep, chauffeur boy." Below his loose one-handed grip, my fists tightened on the wheel. His sharp leg bones contained then forgave my weight, some stream-lined ashwood sled I slid along on. Usually I resented his huge feet working my pedals. Today I felt content to let Dad do all that down there.

. . .

With so many Testaments to give away, we'd left town by eleven. Our first stop proved disappointingly close to Falls. Pop visited a desk clerk proud of his two card tables' jigsaw puzzles: mostly Niagara Falls and the Grand Canyon, either coming or going, and of absolutely no interest to me.

So I explored behind the Whispering Pines Deep Sleep Cabins. I had a feeling I would find some major cluelike event. Today's agitation came partly from the hurt eye, partly from my fear of Monday's far-worse schoolyard charges, names I could neither explain nor ever quite deny. I dreaded our teacher's panic every time I said four nice words toward Berta Dix, or when I'd once handed her a small red dime-store valentine.

Most of what I knew was this: I, Clyde M. Delman, Jr., did not want to be anybody else or anybody else's son.

I would find a way to prove and stay it, this, his.

Behind the cabins proper, I came upon an older couple. They were kneeling in high grass beside something. It rested on a pillowcase. I drew nearer. One small spotted brown-and-white terrier. Its front legs stretched out, its dried black lips drew back. (The pillow slip spelled WHISP. PINES ETC, maybe to cut down on embroidery's expense.)

"Uh-oh. Look, a boy," the old woman nudged her stooped husband.

"It's okay, Shirley. Sonny, come see what all's gone wrong here. You have quite the shiner. Bet the other guy looks way worse. But come see what a mess we've got, and still so far to Florida. Wouldn't have had it happen away from home like this, not for any amount, but who's in control? Do they ask us? No, sir, they do not so much as check, just do it. Then you got to deal with the results. Smartest dog ever. And now here she is, finished. Trixie knew thirty tricks."

"More," his wife added, but deferred by lowering her voice.

"More, sure, maybe more. Our daughter give us Trix. Our girl's a gym teacher in Toledo."

"Physical-education supervisor for the whole Twelfth District," the wife corrected.

"Like he cares about Betty Jean's title! . . . Son, we'd best bury her here. The heat's getting so bad we're not likely to take Trix in the car, not for long. My wife wants we should try fitting her in our drink cooler. —But if we do leave Trixie, and if we was to make a grave marker, will you, as the son of the place, keep your eye on her? Cut back the weeds and just, you know, KNOW she's here? Because that'd sure make us feel it's not so far to Florida. It'd be like Shirl and me had left our Trix with somebody. For instance, I would say, 'Trixie, would you rather be a dead dog or Vice-President Nixon?' and she'd keel right over, legs up, and I mean she'd stay. Got many a chuckle on that one in our travels, 'm I right, Momma?"

The woman nodded, wiping eyes on the backs of speckled hands, "Nowhere we stop will it be the same now, ever. She went first. Trix was like our . . . ambassador."

"Got a shovel, son?" I saw they'd been trying to dig a hole. Digging with two motel water-glasses, one already broken. I found my dad absorbing war stories from the puzzle-loving clerk. "Any shovels?"

"Toolshed. Open. Beside 108."

I found the large room full of washing machines and a huge dryer. Tools lined one wall. There was a calendar showing this woman with naked bosoms, sitting on a desk and saying, "I'm ready for Dictation, Mr. Wembley!" (Definite Clue.)

Once we got Trixie buried, I gathered two good sticks and some rusted wire. We set a cross upright in the newly turned red dirt. I found a pile of nice white rocks and placed these in a big "T" (for "Trixie") crisscrossing the whole grave. Finally, I helped the old lady get to her feet. Then, in croaks, she was crying, counting on fingers:

" 'Sit up.' 'Lay down.' 'Beg.' 'Dead dog.' 'Beg pretty.' 'Walk on hind legs.' 'Shake.' 'Jump rope.' 'Heel.' 'Fetch.' 'Would you rather be Nixon?' . . . 'Stay,' " she backed away from crossed sticks. She half-ran to an overpacked car, yelling, " 'Stay,' Trixie, 'stay.' . . ."

The old man thanked me. He apologized for his wife. He told me how much it meant to them that Trixie would be with somebody. He walked off slow. He shook his head. "Seems like nothing is . . . Seems like about the time you get . . . and then . . . and before long it's . . . and then where really ARE you . . . ?"

I heard my dad honk the car horn. His usual "shave and a haircut, two bits." I waited till the couple's Dodge sedan pulled off. I replaced the shovel beside an almost naked calendar secretary. Then I trotted to his Packard. I wanted to tell Dad: Guess what? I just helped an old, old couple bury their old dog, one that knew so many tricks its name was Trixie, in praise.

But I found I stayed quiet as we drove.

I kept picturing the crossed sticks and pretty white rocks behind Whispering Pines etc. We'd buried Trixie in the pillowcase. I had told those people that my dad could spare it. Somehow I had posed as the motel owner's son. I had let them believe this. It was one of my first adult acts (deceptions). That started off this strange Sunday. I told them I would keep Trixie's grave looking nice. Could be, I'd bring flowers. I said things'd be okay, seeing how smart the dog was and everything. From now on I would stay in charge of her. Goodbye.

I was getting to adulthood fast, if adulthood means breaking minor stingy laws for major kindly reasons.

But instead of saying any of this out, I turned to Dad and, without knowing I would, announced, "Mom is a wonderful woman." It scared me. This was the first time in my life I recall opening my mouth and speaking the total opposite of what I meant. Just jumped out. Greek. But Clyde smiled, he hiccupped on sadness, part pleasure, then drove along in silence for six whole minutes.

I felt that Pop had needed something good today. Just as the Florida couple needed to believe that Trixie's grave would have a fine young guard nearby. Someone who would bring Trix blue hydrangeas as big around as schoolhouse globes, plus maybe Queen Anne's lace stuck in a red coffee-can. Odd, though I knew my dad did not own the motel, I'd half bought into my own well-intended lie and promise.

In our Packard's trunk, we'd stacked replacement Bibles for our distant begonia drill-instructor. Thieves had made quite a dent in his inventory. I looked forward to the fuss Colonel always made and to the joys of my passkey's opening everything. We were bound due east, like on any other day. We faced the three-hour trek one way toward our Colonel Begonia. Now I believe that helping the couple with Trixie's burial had made me feel too capable. I vowed, the way kids do, that this would be a day of solving all problems.

3.

So I set aside my homework plus the *Owner's Manual.* My story could not become as funny as Dad had seemed to hope. I felt worried. My wit failed to help me much today. I kept touching my own swollen sooted eye, kept convincing myself it'd probably given me a concussion, worse. Funny meant weak. Jokes seemed small and false and I was growing up, I told myself. The solemnity of an only child, an intelligent eight-year-old, platinum-blond and male with his first black eye. The self-importance of all men is really one of God's great triumphs and perversities!

Most days at school I now got shoved and cornered, got told I could not be Clyde Delman's own blood son. But how could a loving boy believe this? I must be. His. His if anything. Boys told me that my dad was not my dad but that my mom sure was a floozie. I felt I could remember the county fair when Mom first met Doc Dix. But, slow, it came to me, they could have staged that. Even though I'd asked her to go, Mom might have slipped into the bedroom when she fetched her sweater, she could have phoned. She might have arranged to meet him at the Ferris wheel, and since he was late, off tending a blue-ribbon horse, maybe she stayed on there, going around and round till the sickness. I knew I didn't look a bit like my poor sallow father slumped over there smoking, driving in his usual mild silence. Even set in neutral gear, especially in neutral, such a genial kindness coasted with our Clyde. Here was a man who had, against all odds, learned to entertain himself, then others. He radiated some earned interior attraction, a secret vaudeville of power everybody felt.

The physical difference between us was so obvious, people on our Bible route never mentioned it. But I could see them, scouting back and forth, amazed at how little the barley-sugar Ollie looked like his tall dark frizzled Stan.

Once the Colonel said, "Our young recruit must have a very very bea-*uuu*-tiful blond young mother, is all." Someone else, studying the fineness of my features, asked Dad if he'd been plain as a child. "Dern straight! Takes years. You can't get this ugly all at once!"

I still longed to meet his sister. Had he been the family runt? Even as a kid was he the butt of jokes around his house? Had Nursemaid Sutie been his only friend?

I looked fairer if more frail than Clyde. True, our minds worked in different ways, but that's what made Dad's trusting presence such a sunny pleasure to my cooler and more watchful nature. (Only later would I see my childhood fascination with sex as latent proof of who my driven, shameless parents truly were.) But then the idea of being genetically beholden to the rooster man I'd first met at the fair, it felt beyond me. It saddened me till my whole white-boy weight felt like one blacked eye throbbing all over. What pained me most: how such rumors cut me off from Clyde.

Still unaware of them, he drove slowly toward Edenton, toward begonias and the far-flung favorite of our territory's unburned motor courts. It seemed that silence was our only enemy today.

"Dad?" "Yes, son." "I was wondering." "What about? Shoot. Is it something about out of the Bible? Because if you want me to go over that part again—background of 'For God so loved the world that he gave his only begotten son . . .'—I will. I'll tell you the little I do know on that score, a not-educated man like me:

"Seems like God made this earth all up, then He got just one thing really perfect, His Only Boy. And then God hauled off, let Him be killed by worthless fellows like me. And just so's God could save the killers . . . Well, that kind of sacrifice, it's way past anything we're ever gonna understand. Still, it's important to try. But the exchange of good for bad and back again is mighty doggone complicated I can tell you."

"Not that. It's something I don't know how to ask about yet, but need to."

"Welp, we got nothing but time, pal." And Dad hummed a few bars of something part hymn, half Tin Pan Alley.

The week before, I had made a big experiment. I told nobody. I'd walked up to the columned "colonial" manse of the Dix family. As my excuse, I held a book. I'd prepared a homework question for Berta about our world-geography quiz. I wanted to see what the other Dixes would make of me. Would they know—nine further blond-headed children with my same rosy skin, my very size and eye color?

I knocked too hard. A black maid in pink uniform finally unlatched the door. She stood looking toward the height of an adult, and when her head fell down my way, she appeared shocked and made her mouth move sideways then go click-cluck, "Who you looking, little lost bird?"

"Berta."

"What bidness you got with any Berta, chip off the block?"

"Jography."

Just then someone stepped up behind her, asking who it was, and the door flew open, almost hitting me. Mrs. Dix, legs bandaged and appearing fairly well used up, took one look at me then leaned against the doorjamb. It was how she stared at me, with that black woman lingering—mumbly confidential—right over her shoulder like trying to comfort but seeming to enjoy the latest twist of a whole new mess here.

Suddenly, lower even than me, past the white door's enameled edge, three blond faces that were my face when young, shot around wood and brass; they peered out at their own sober face grown sadly older. That did it.

"Tell Berta . . . somebody came by about tonight's hard homework. I'll just get the isthmus-delta notes from somebody lives closer."

"Who you?" the maid asked. But I turned away, walked fast. I had not spoken gentle Clyde Delman, Sr.'s name. What if I someway got HIM in trouble?

Near passing farmhouses, the blooms of fruit trees were just opening. Some still showed how, in bud, each blossom had been pink; but once unlocked all shone the same translucent white.

Dad and I now headed lazy to the last and easiest of today's stops. We had forever, time, nothing but. He'd said so. He slumped dreamy in his thoughts about a Son-sacrificing God, one I did not credit, having never seen. I'd lately grouchily wondered why our church's trademark wasn't something prettier and more hopeful. Like, say, a rose? What does it tell you when your Club's mascot (and whole meaning) is one skinny nude dead carpenter still pincushioned with bullies' nails?

I now pointed to my own blacked eye so fast and hard I nearly jabbed my finger in the cornea; I hurt it half on purpose. That way I wouldn't fail or stop.

"See this big ole shiner, Dad?"

"Is that your question you were working up to?" He laughed. A wonderful spiraling kind of sucked-in chortle my Clyde had. (If I could redo one thing I've risked in life, I'd retract my next request and all it took out with it. I might have made him notice those frothy white blooms or three distant mules or some pond-fishing red-haired farm kids. I could have made my sharp yellow pencil press deeper into the spongy lined pad, bearing down upon our *Owner's Manual;* I might've written out several of Clyde's own jokes, then read them aloud to him. The generous guy would have given me full credit and slapped his knee with joy, and literally not known those jokes were his. But I did not do this. So . . .)

"Daddy? I got this eye on a argument. Boys rag me more and more. It's got to where I hate school, playground especially. I always say no. But there's way more of them. Dad, you know Doc Dix?"

I heard the massive Adam's apple snag. There came a pause one-eighth of a mile long. "Sure, he's right prominent in town."

"Teddy, Ralph, and Walter Early. Some other older boys, sixth-graders? They said I was, that he might could be . . . Is. They say Doc Dix is my . . . REAL ONE."

I had just called Clyde Melvin Delman, Sr., my sole reality, unreal. Even today, I must re-explain to myself how often I'd been punched. I felt so tattered by the daily denying. I simply meant to beg my dad for some assurance.

"Talk, idle talk," he mumbled, head shaken sideways.

Then, alone, so loud he scared me as our car lurched, my father started singing, "Into the aiiiir, Junnnior . . . upside down . . . keep your noses off the ground!" And he was doing it very hearty but I could see his chest grow tense, bucking as if trying to close down over one huge latent cough.

With trying to sing, he meant to stop me. But I would not give way. Why not? Was it my mother's crueler genes? Why was I demanding both Dad's promise and denial?

Then I said, "What if you and me are not really . . . ?"

I did not make much sense. I was in most ways working blind. Pressing toward some fact literally unimaginable. It meant taking away the only earthly thing that I felt sure of standing on. What else in this life was I—except Clyde M. Delman, Sr.'s junior? Where else geography? Homework? Home?

Still driving, Clyde now turned and looked at me. I can say it was the first full moment of my adult life: he greeted me as a naked man greets another bare grown man in Hell's own locker room, no secrets possible now. First time ever, I saw what others meant when they called him Almost Monster. Now Dad's face was so unsmiling, inert. His eyes lacked a light forever present there before—some dancy will to see the best in me. And I knew now, oh yeah, he truly was ugly. Ugly as the big boys claimed. I felt ashamed of suddenly so much. I had tricked Clyde into letting me see him complete. Because I had stunned his love for me completely shut for just one second. It seemed like some protective current that had wrapped the two of us forever, stopped. And no Utility Company on earth could ever "resume service" fast enough. All interior clocks would need resetting. Everything must be renegotiated now, invented as if for the first time. And I was only eight.

I am still trying to forgive myself. To know where I found the foolish courage to blurt all that aloud. Blame trust. Blame how tougher boys just taunted me at school. I hated fights. Even more than being hit, the hitting back sickened me. That in itself seemed proof that I was this man's here. I believed that Dad could now hand me some one fact unassailable—a sentence that'd stop the bullies, proof to end such local savagery, which must always be a mistake, right?

. . .

Across my father's face—and head and throat and upper chest—I saw a scalding pain born. That sudden. Two forehead veins bucked forth. He tried appearing in control, but I heard Dad's breathing now rush out through his mouth. He no longer appeared jaunty; he seemed stripped of all the hope of comedy. He'd lost even the lingo of Salvation.

A guy, some odd arbitrary fish-mouthed atheist guy, sat looking at me. But he also seemed shrunken down to boyhood, backed raw into a corner. I now rode alongside another kid, too visible, somebody the worst boys love to torment daily. —"Fish Face," I remembered now. As in a radio echo-chamber, I regathered all the taunts Clyde had ever endured, now and at my age and younger. As his whole life had flashed before his own eyes the moment Jesus penetrated his heart, Clyde Delman's diorama of nicknames entered my life just as he was leaving it.

"Fish Face." "Scrambled-Egg Lips." "Dick Snout." "Dufus." "Nigger-nose." "Bottom Feeder." "Almost Monster."

He slowed our car, he parked beside the road, he lit a cigarette. He smoked a quarter of it. It went nowhere in one sad sucking rush. He sat staring forward at two fallow fields. He said finally, "Welp, what can I say? Of course you're mine. —You know you're what I love best in this whole dern world. Y'do know that, don't you, son?"

I nodded.

I could see how it was going to be with him, how decent he was, even when trapped, how good Clyde was fundamentally. Accused of rearing some worthless other man's child, never once did Dad ask for gratitude. He claimed me absolutely, but never did he brag that he was more to me than just the one who loved me best. Again I nodded. Sick feeling. Wondering if I dared slide over now and touch him. I found I was afraid to chance that yet.

"When I say 'son,' " his dark words cut through smoke, "I feel like every tiny bit or piece of me just knows you're mine. Is all. Son. Even diaper changes—why, I'd almost welcome those. Your mom was usually off reading. You'd seem so much more comfortable after. And so I would . . . feel better. Understand? Look, a couple idiots in Falls say things. —Don't you feel like you're my boy?"

I wagged my head yes. "Am," said I. "Just asked. They . . . I only . . ."

"Buddy? Ain't I been *good* enough for you?"

"You're the best thing. It's not that. . . ."

"You must know, son, I'd give my life for you. And it's not just something I say to be saying a thing. You should understand how . . . much I've . . . already . . . who all I had to . . ." And here his head bobbed more my way. He made his mouth open wide like some bird dog yawning. Dad resisted showing how bad I'd made him feel. Even so, he let me guess how much I had already taken from him.

—Maybe the belief in something is the thing? The main part of it.

Dad now rested one bone-thin arm along the top of our seat. He had turned almost totally toward me.

"Son, come sit in your real poppa's lap. We got us some time to burn here. Even with the Colonel being so far off, we're still running mighty early, us Birdmen in the air upside down. Really upside down today, huh, champ?" So fast then, I climbed over and he took me up onto his legs, he closed his stringy arms around me. And pressed me hard, almost too hard, against him, as if, now he knew what I'd guessed, I must soon be taken from him. He acted like our touch must be forever after rationed.

It had been bad enough when we were only looking at each other, but soon as I curled up and became a full weight wedged between his painted Hawaiian tie and our steering wheel, my father said, "Uh-oh. Fine mess we've gotten us into this . . ." And in a low snort, like making fun of himself, " 'Fraid this un's been a long time comin, boy," and cried. He cried over me. Literally.

My bare arms soon shone wet. Clyde bent his chest, shoulders, forehead over and across me. For a roof. He made a roof that rained. This was a rehearsal for his later howling so our town came running to its windows, but out here in the country, arriving as this sound did from anywhere I'd known, it surprised me even more.

He rocked with it till our Packard's springs responded. And during, Dad held on to me as if crowds were gathering outside our car to drag him to some tree and hang him while I screamed to get him back.

During, he tried to comfort me. The noises I heard should have told me who he was, all he'd hid from me and others, and what that daily cost him. But I just clung to his bone shoulders, and we both cried so; it was almost calming how full-out we cried. Not like God-fearing men, brave and tromping around in the male countryside. No, we almost sang. Young girls enduring their first cramping pain. Simple together, pressed low beneath it, we nearly yodeled with the hurt's first smart knifing.

I found I now knew more than I'd imagined. Just as our bad singing, Clyde's and mine, usually blended, making it seem, not skillful, but full of forgivable spirit, so did our emotions and spillage now mix. I further dampened the front of a white shirt Dad's crying had already wet. How translucent it became, one oval air bubble trapped under there and backed by his olive skin.

I felt some rage kindling now, anger over the level of harm done him, not only by Mother and myself and her fancyman, but by everyone who'd ever yelled mean things at Dad from passing cars. I hated every dope who'd ever laughed about a homeliness I now found narcotically endearing. Dad had guarded me all my life, with his life. And so would I ever after do that for him. This, I vowed. Finally I leaned back and the car horn accidentally blared and that, at least, let us laugh.

"Fine pair we make," he wiped my eyes with a hanky featuring two Scottie dogs wearing plaid neck-bows and facing one another. "Yeah," he shook his head. "A fine mess us Bible B-52 Birdmen has gotten ourselves into this time, Ollie! So—dry off your sweet ole snoot, you. What say you to a Dairy Queen special dipped in chocolate and rolled in nuts big . . . as my demonstrators here, hmm, copilot?"

"Yes, sir, Dad!"

I saw we were done talking. Done, I felt, forever. He smiled but it was now a fixed, ceramic item, mail-ordered. The new grin seemed ill-fitting as some stranger's cut-rate dentures shoved in hard. This was, I slowly understood, no more than Clyde's weekday-salesman smile. He'd never before turned loose on me anything so slack and standard. This was not the usual trembling jokey sweetness reserved for me alone. Clyde had always taken such joy in every little thing I did—did well, or badly, it didn't matter. I had never seen him so upset. His trying not to show it only made me love him more.

"Here, you ole weed-fiend," I plucked cigarettes from his shirt pocket. I pounded the pack's top against our dashboard the way us kids knew to do from watching adults and all their ads. One white one slid forth, attractive. Even his Camels wanted to cheer our funny man Clyde here. He laughed because, in trying to light it, his hands shook so. I had to fire the thing up for him. Took me four strikes before I got it truly lit ("not in your mouth, handhold it," he ordered). Then I set the cigarette, proud, against his twitching lower lip. His eyes were wet, the lashes bunched. His pale-brown eyes looked, I told myself, almost handsome up this close. I made my own eyes go a little out of focus as a help. And when I touched his face, it felt softer than any woman's.

I wanted to consider him beautiful in some of the ways a lady might be. Kneeling beside him, inches from his face, I could hear cigarette paper crackle with flame as he inhaled. Toward him I felt a sad, almost hypnotized gentleness. I kissed, one last time, my father's cheek.

"Dad is a Dad is Dad is," I said, simple as some three-year-old and not my usual grave first-reading-circle self. "And I is me am I. My dad here is the man Clyde Senior and I am really mostly his junior Clyde, and right straight through me, too, sir."

"Dern tootin." But his voice came thin. "That's the spirit. More like it," but his voice came thin.

Then Dad turned the ignition and we started fast toward our last "drop" today. Smoking hard as if for the very first time, he drove quick, using just one hand. I sensed now that, when by himself, when not poking along with me and singing about God, Clyde usually traveled far faster.

He'd got many speeding tickets in several states and had to hire good local lawyers to help keep his license and our livelihood. Dad maneuvered now with just one floppy wrist. Fingers of his right hand dangled far beyond the wheel. The cigarette was palmed within his left. He kept squinting through blue smoke, kept looking overly concerned or, no, concentratedly aimless. Clyde's face was set at seeming neutral but its color had failed, grayer, even ashy. I could not yet know what all my question had released in him, the fishhook wickedness of a kid's innocent asking.

"Sometimes, son," he said a few miles in, "you wonder if the thing you love most is half enough to somewhat make things up to you." He smoked and drove. "You want something to come along and punch you in the shoulder and say, This makes stuff worthwhile." He picked a piece of tobacco off his tongue. "But until that happens, you pretty much have to just bump along, just try and figure out what matters, if anything. —I do try. That I know. I do get tired, like everybody. And I'd be a liar if I didn't tell you straight, pardner—there's a lot of humiliation connected with it."

We whizzed so quick past white farmhouses, checkered laundry draped sodden on the lines, denim and weekday colors absorbing this bright Sunday. (I knew that truly righteous households did not leave clothes out drying on the Sabbath. Christian kids could not play rummy, could not attend moving-picture shows. Mainly you just sat there with your Bible in your lap and thought your private sexual thoughts and waited for God's day to end.)

At this speed, our Packard, motorcycle-black and snaggled all across with chrome, seemed a different car. Not the stodgy high-mid-price family sedan, not our usual pilgrim Kleenex box. It suddenly felt like something dangerously smooth, and not unwild. I noticed how some people, clumped on a porch, stared after us. One shirtless young man in the front yard stood waxing a new red wrecker-truck as pretty as some toy. I felt proud of the farmers' attention till I understood we earned it by racing so.

I'd never seen my dad drive this fast. He now acted floppier, some beautiful slow-growing vine just ripped down off its lifelong trellis. Over there he slouched, dead-eyed, lax, hands huge, his face an unfilled order form, almost carefree, aiming us at high speeds. He used just the underside of his right wrist. Only the buckle of Dad's plaid watchband rested on the wheel. "He's lost interest," I thought. His lower lip hung open. He now seemed to be breathing only through his mouth.

We passed a red barn spilling golden straw out its upper holes. We passed a low stone wall. Just ahead, one yellow diamond sign showed a black deer's outline leaping right to left.

Hoping to slow Dad, to maybe reinvolve him in our life, I planned to tell him, for a joke: Wasn't that the silliest thing—ever?—how some guy at a desk in Raleigh figured he could say right where a deer might cross the darn road way out here? A riot, hunh, Dad? Dad?

That same second there spun before our windshield moving right to left midair three pinkish shapes like hurled doormats carpet-sized. They funneled toward specifics and into being creatures and looked to me like tall odd dogs with bottle racks for heads. The point of one such pronged unit now turned our way. The beast had bristles on its muzzle, a wet black nose, and this became all of one live deer veering right at us and going ninety. It got closer fast but in the slowest way that all of this can happen.

I had time to know. It was going to hit us. And we, it. Time to think. That we were sitting as still as bowling pins who've got whole animals swimming down the alley at them. I saw two others, white-tailed, lift into the air around our car then back-move over it. But the big one, his red-blue tongue out, his longlashed eyes all damp, let his front hoof poke our windshield, as if in the politest water-temperature test. And our whole green male view went female blue with spiderwebbing then to bits then clear. All in total silence. Over the fender, other animals, back-tumbling, became a good clown act. Their speed was as great going north, as our speed grew even faster headed south and gathering them all against and over and then under us.

Dad's right hand, still holding the cigarette, shot out, raised itself above my face. His huge hand stretched wide like a pointed star—it accepted the full spray of glass that otherwise, I knew, would now be taking my blue eyes. Dad received all sharpness; he did so—glad as any catcher's mitt absorbing all it was designed to snag. But (no hands) the car meantime went just where it pleased. Dad stared hard my way, yelling "rightson?" (which I knew was the end of "Are you all right, son?"), and as three bumps each bigger heaved us left so hard, this is what I can't describe. Even as I'll try again. This was it, and I, age eight: About to go over with our car, Dad gave me one possibly final

look, a look that—in the strange current of time's slowing, of adrenaline's emergency-brake favor to us—let me see a new man. I saw my
father as some stranger might. And while I braced for impact—as I
stared at him all softened up and wounded by my accusation, only
now, for the first time in my life, did I understand:

my father was a Negro.

Not "a full-blooded Negro," as we said then. But I knew—clear
from my scalp to my scrotum—that, somewhere in his recent history,
some one member of his family, had been. . . . Then I guessed "Aunt
Sutie" was his mother, his father some white man submitted to or
only half chosen. The railroad brakeman? I now saw in Pop their
strange joined moment of forced entry or impossible romance. And
Dad's stiff hair, his skin's high goldy undercolor meant something
else forever. "There's a lot of humiliation connected with it" now
offered me far more. I knew why no townsfolk ever believed I could be
Clyde's. All this rushed forward, unscrolled itself at a child's own
fumbling stubborn pace.

But, last thing, in the bright flash as our Packard found air and literally left the road, I wondered, why oh why had I just used against
him the word "REAL"—used it like a club? Not my REAL father. He'd
been born to be a perfect dad! And, in every way but maybe one,
he was.

Right then, with a sound like a house-sized nail being pulled out of
a world-sized board, our car refound wet earth and curved so hard
into its ditchward roll.

I was knocked out, or else kept my eyes closed through a white part
then the blue part then a moister final black. But after a spell lasting
one minute or half a day, eyes somehow freely opened. Funny, all the
sound of it came last. Like one full season's delayed memories: shots
and rattles, the shatterings of some short eventful war played back to
you full-blast.

After: some birds went right on singing, "tweettweeter." Seemed a
good sign. I tried to move, but felt my father's weight pressed flat all

over me. He had rung down like a stage curtain. You never know how big a loved one is till you try accepting his deadweight. I shook him and for the first time ever called him aloud "Clyde," not "Dad." But I think this mainly came from fellow-feeling, with our being now in such a scrape.

The mammoth Packard tilted on its side, tires spinning. Our missing windshield now opened only onto smeared mud, sudden plant life. Beyond a dark fringe of Dad's hair, I could just see clear sky straight up and through the driver's window. I tried crawling toward that, first depending on the handhold of the rearview mirror, then stepping over and breaking, with the noise of some huge egg busting, his plywood drink-caddy. But I scrambled out. Once I made it up to light, I looked down. It was like staring straight back into a well. My father rested at its bottom; he seemed dead asleep or dead, balled up down there indifferent.

I checked back along the road, surveying carcasses, two on tarmac, one half opened in a ditch. Past that, small people, those farmers, came running, big bigger still. They had been sitting on the porch and milling in the yard and had seen us and now they'd trotted a good half-mile. They must have heard. We must have just been pretty loud.

I leapt the five feet down from Clyde's window. Then I ran back toward them jostling my way, me screaming, "Howdy. Please, quick, my dad's hurt. Howdy, hurt in there . . ." I was pointing as they swerved around me, their shoes hard on pavement, a beautiful manly motion directing all of them.

I saw one slither through our car's open window and soon start trying lifting my dad out. Clyde looked dead. Even at his liveliest, with the big knobby hands and large head, he could act slack, some demonstrator puppet man. He now appeared looser still. Like he had given up on everything, or been abandoned by it. Hard to explain how changed he seemed from earlier, and not just from being knocked clean out. Maybe it was my guessing aloud I was another man's. Maybe it was Dad's even suspecting that I knew his race and history.

They slapped him, one fellow cupped a handful of water from a ditch and threw it at Clyde's face, and they were working his head from side to side. I waited behind them, winded, as he finally opened one eye.

"He drunk, son?" the oldest farmer asked, no judgment. "No, sir. He is born-again," and then it seemed to me Clyde really had been. After seeing him pulled out of the driver's window like from the wrong side of something black's body. The oldest farmer pointed: "For a man, sure is wearing a lot of jewry."

"Sells it for a living, sir," I said.

"Well . . . that's all right, then. . . ."

Clyde stared at me as at some short adult stranger.

"Stand out where he can see somebody he knows," the farmer said, then shifted Clyde's shoulders forward just a bit too rough. "Know this youngun? Recognize this here boy? You got him some kind of upset, but you're all right. Know your own boy here?"

Then, hurt at being called "upset" by people unknown to us, I understood I had been crying without noticing—like it was just a more serious way of breathing. I drew close to Dad, I did my Ollie, puffing my pink cheeks, fooling with the phantom tie, aiming a slow-burn eye-roll: I offered him my all-time funniest expression. And I saw Clyde start to smile his best crazed hopeful grin. It always made a kind of pocket dawn—the way it opened, breaking horizon-to-horizon across the most unlikely pleasing face. But, soon as he smiled, I saw him remember. I saw him know I knew I might not be his.

Then he fell back into the big hands of the men propping him forward, he let out one pinched cry straight up. It knocked me aside with shame for what I'd done—asking, insisting. Clyde's groan scared the fellows holding him.

"Could be it's his neck," one said, professional. "Don't nobody shout out like that unless he's got something's bad broke." Come to find out, it was his arm. "He's favoring the right one," the farmer spoke of Clyde as of livestock. "Look at him guard it, like. 'At one's busted, sure."

It was the day we never got to Edenton to see the Colonel and his Marine Corps of begonias. It was the Worst of All Sundays because I had not played dumb, I had overtrusted.

.   .   .

I had thought adults could solve things, and that I would help them do that. I had thought a life was some advanced math problem you could just answer and then be done considering. I didn't know that the last person who knows how to solve a given problem is usually the person whose life created it. I understood nothing. But I already guessed I'd made a huge mistake, and that I'd only just begun to see its sad results play out.

And yet (I tried to help myself through this) wasn't my mistake what'd finally introduced me to my dad? I surely now possessed his past's single hugest secret. For that, at least, I felt half grateful and even partway proud. I wished we could be driven fast to Sutie's house. We'd recover there, the three of us eating biscuits on her shady porch, us steadily visiting, me asking everything at last.

All I knew: I'd far rather be Clyde's—if that meant "black" or Packard or maple syrup—than "white" in the cold snide way of Doc Dick Dix. I'd do anything to remain Clyde Delman's boy. Whoever Clyde was, whatever-colored a Clyde he'd likely to stay, I would be right there alongside.

Could you choose? You can choose.

Standing here with farmers acting nice to me and asking did I want a drink of water or some sweet-potato pie still hot back at their house, I guessed I must become way stronger. Would these men be acting so kindly if they knew my dad's real race and maybe mine?

I would have to try and correct everything for my father now. What had I really glimpsed about his past and color? Was it even true? And of me, too? Didn't knowing you might not be white itself revoke your front-row pass? So willingly I gave mine up!

I must now struggle far harder for Dad, I must take over some. Clyde wouldn't need to know I'd guessed about his and my's being black and all. I'd hide from him how I must defend forever the man who'd defended and "changed" me from birth on. Clyde I would protect, as he had said that he would die for me.

I felt my whole life reorganize itself, around the sudden single goal of keeping Clyde my real true dad. I had never asked to be born "White and Blond and Blue." He never begged for "Black and Blue and Brown and White." But he'd sure signed on for me. And he sure had me now, forever.

My one wish: To shield him. To beat the others back. But, standing here, I suddenly felt so old. Older than Clyde. I was now his beholden if maybe unbegotten son. Weak-kneed, huge-headed, I waited here by the side the road feeling older than our world.

See, I had just become my race plus his—and, I can tell you, that combo is work.

4.

Since the farmer's shirtless son owned the new red wrecker, he said he'd tow our car to Falls, just for the price of his gas plus one in-town meal for him and his folks, okay? Just so's they'd have something to do of a till-recently slow Sunday. (Now I see this was their country way of not making us feel overgrateful.)

The red truck soon got our muddied car free of its ditch, back right side up. The tires were okay. So the farmers climbed in; they'd ride in our handsome towed Packard. It was strange to look through the wrecking truck's rear window and see them, proud, windblown, fiddling with dashboard knobs, playing like they were city folks and us. The youngest boy worked a steering wheel that had no say-so.

Dad held one arm, cradling it like a baby. He pressed hard and silent against the tow truck's passenger door. They pulled a spare quilt up around him. Times we would hit a big bump, he'd half-groan. I heard his head knock the rolled-up window, him barely noticing. I felt worried, and I piled against his yellow quilt, maybe hurting him.

Though the farmers were being very good to us, their strong ruddy son, our driver, couldn't help criticize Dad's speed. And on a secondary road and with plenty of warning signs.

"City people don't know how many head of deer we got back in these woods. Why, won't but just last summer—Jenny's brother's son?—he seen him a bear, not ten miles from the highway back in Pike's Woods. A good-sized one, too. Black. And just a-padding along like it owned the woods, which it pertwell used to, I reckon. It didn't know there was so many head of US out here!"

And he gave off a grim and snuffly country kind of laugh. But Dad and me didn't bother to respond. "Funny" was not being much help to us here lately.

Riding, silent, I became a pop quiz of listed questions: When had my mother learned of Dad's true racial mix? Had she ever really known? Did she only sense it? Was her fling with Dix a revenge on Clyde's homeliness or his race or both? Did Falls allow her weekly blond betrayal because it half-suspected? Did all those colored service-station attendants guess Clyde's history at once? What other codes had been forever lost on me? And how fast could I make up these lapses to "Almost Monster"? Such a name for so kind a man, so true a dad.

Clyde had asked, "Buddy? Ain't I been *good* enough for you?" Ouch. Helping him, I wanted to hurt somebody else now. Proof.

The farmers said they'd leave us at Falls General Hospital. Then they'd pull his car to the Shell station that Clyde liked. As we finally entered Falls, we passed my school, our church, our American Grill. We drew near the house and—though it was one block over—I saw, through moving trees, one white Pontiac still gleaming there.

I tipped against Dad's yellow quilt. It smelled of lye soap and sun from being dried on a line. I still recall the scent as fully Dad's. Seeing how Dix was yet visiting Mom, I felt an even higher level of guarding was due this fine man I'd come in with. Clyde pretended not to glance that way, but I knew how every pore on that side of his body became a form of eyestrain.

I felt shaky, as if something great would be expected of me soon. I found myself ready. Ready to do whatever to protect him. I felt that our driver had been hard on Dad about his speeding. The boy didn't know how good Clyde was, or how many Bibles were in his trunk. I now blamed Mom for everything.

If she had not done that thing with the Animal Doc and got me in her instead of letting me be my true dad's, everyone could see I looked like him. And even though I might have got a face catfishy, like father like son, folks would never doubt that I was his. That was the problem—not who or what color Clyde had been all along, but how quick I could become that with him.

If I had not said the thing straight out and made Dad cry then smoke then rush, if it weren't for those crazy deers from nowhere, everything'd still be perfect. I could not abide my part in hurting him. Instead I blamed her for all of it, and vowed she would never get to harm him ever again. But I was just making Mom become the only bad part of the world. That just came from my feeling guilty and being so young.

Now his arm was broken, more help from me was needed. I would be like the Adult. Just as I had vowed to check on that dead dog Trixie day and night. Just like the Ohio man who'd blinked his lights to tell us where the cop hid, I would now take charge of signals. I would straighten everything out and get us past this habit of everybody hurting everybody all around them. Then Mom, Clyde, and me, we could start over clean. I simply had to clear the route. I would be the train's cowcatcher, sweeping bodies off our silver tracks ahead.

Parked before the hospital, farmers helped husk the quilt off Dad. With his one working paw, Clyde gave them too much dinner money then offered handshakes to everyone, including the women; and I saw they appreciated this and that he knew the country way. Then I whispered and he bent down and nodded and I scrambled up into the towed car for its keys. I hurried to the trunk and brought out one black Bible for every helper-person present. I saw how this impressed them, it proved that we were not just careless city speeders, but sober citizens, important and God-prepared. I liked having come up with this and felt it showed I was thinking clear for everybody now.

Receiving God's Word, the farmers grew stern-faced but pleased, very ceremonial, the way country people are, especially in town. They said their "Thank ye kindly"s as much to me as Clyde.

Then Dad and I walked right into Emergency. He was known on sight from where he distributed the Nurses' Whites at their little graduations and visited the sick so regular.

A blue-black man in a starch-white uniform introduced himself to me and laughed to see Dad. "Well will you look what the cat drug in, what bit you, Clyd-i-o?" My father told, but the short way. How his arm got broke. How we'd got to hurrying. How this here's what usually comes of that.

Rory said, "Knowing you, you probably already heard the one about the Nun, the Sheep Dog, and the Preacher's Wife—or did you tell me it, knowing you?" But when he touched Dad's arm, Rory stopped joking. Dad said would I consider waiting out in the lobby, please. Rory turned my way and was very nice: "We got us many a funnybook out there under the fish tank. You like funnybooks, *Green Lantern?* Cause my kids do. —But wait one, you're right banged up too, look at this eye. And little cuts all over him. But this shiner's half ripe, older then the others."

5.

It was after they set his arm and did paperwork and swabbed me off and got most of the big glass out of his hand and released him. They said they would drive him home. No problem, not in an ambulance with red lights going, maybe just in Rory's car, though home was only seven blocks off. But Clyde said no, he was in no hurry, beautiful day like this—are you kidding?—we would hike it easy. Air'd be good for us. We had never made it to our last Bible stop at Colonel Begonia's out past Edenton. I knew Clyde didn't want to get us home one minute early.

So, with my small pliant hand holding Dad's one good sinewy one, with him protecting the bad arm, we set out. He moved old. I squinted up at him, thinking I had never seen anybody age so quick. I blamed the wreck, and not his guessing all that I knew now.

I wish I could quote directly what we said, hiking toward whatever seemed necessary next, one fate awaiting us all. Something had changed in Dad's spry step and sassier ways. Suddenly his jewelry hung on him like so many separate responsibilities. I told Clyde I would look out for him now, from here on in, now that he had a broken bone and all. He must have heard some new pity in my voice. He must have felt I had ideas about him, ideas even past the father question.

We'd always understood each other. We just guessed certain things. But I didn't know, at that age, what was appropriate, what not. If I felt a thing, I showed it. (Except about me, Aunt Sutie and him all being possibly partially mainly colored. That, I saved to work on later.)

He despised being pitied. Mom treated him with a sour sighing regret for being the one who hurt him most often and not seeming able to stop. People in town acted kind toward him, knowing about his wife and maybe guessing a bit about the rest. But at times, the way they welcomed him, it must have felt like Christians leaving out table scraps for a beloved local dog just gone three-legged. Maybe Clyde never knew if they laughed at his jokes out of joy or mercy. Even his clients on the road—who'd never heard about his home life—found him mainly a character, not serious, something of a case.

Why did he attract and galvanize everyone he met? Because his features offered daylight such a public secret. Maybe that's what stirred up around Clyde the constant curious commotion, some strange continuing release of joy. People remarked his being so ugly, but its effect was almost that of beauty: some of Clyde's features seemed bad white ones, others were unfortunate black ones, but these joined in a new tragic-happy mix that left you feeling half allured without your quite asking to know why.

Had that made him always joke so? Had this kept him distracting us with his flashy novelties? Clyde was forever canceling—through what now seemed a painful minstrelsy—all outside evidence that one fresh glance of him gave you.

Only at far motels in the middle of fields, those places where he was a stranger but a kind one, only when he turned up with the little show-off towheaded Bible boy, only way out there on our Sundays could he feel good and solid and safe. He was a Big Man solely when he gave God's Word away for free, with me along as proof of who he truly partly was.

And now he knew I knew I might not be his. Except by choice, I mean, but not assigned. Not his from the beginning but something that is left in the nest by another bird and so must be brought up, or else shoved out. He had brought me up by hand. And now, walking, both my hands clasped his one free mitt. I pulled hard, as if to really truly help the man get home safe.

But the nearer we drew to our white rental house—edges of it just coming visible if still small ahead—the more reasons Clyde found to stop and admire an azalea bush. He dawdled before that new lamp-post with street numbers worked right into its wrought iron: "Probably costs somebody a pretty penny."

He kept staring up at neighbors' picture windows, like hoping people might duck out toward the Joke Man, the Funny Suspenders Man, to talk with him so he could stall. Dad couldn't admit to me how, even after all the delays from busting up his fine car and getting his arm broke then set, we'd still missed that last motel's six-hour round-trip. And another man might linger yet in our house, with all this free time to enjoy her. Clyde knew what maybe waited. I did not, not quite, not yet. But I saw Dad had begun to sweat. With our being back in Falls, with us both on foot, he could not invent much of anywhere else to go.

Considering it was Sunday, everybody seemed napping or indoors, and so we simply walked undistracted, walked a little closer. Red tulips bloomed in tight rings around trees in certain yards. One sparrow and one jay were splashing at a lady's salt-white birdbath. The sun was moving to its setting slot.

The more tired he sounded, the more whipped Clyde looked, the more he blotted his forehead with the good arm's sleeve, the slower he dragged. The longer he lingered, sitting on someone's curb, the angrier and surer did his junior grow.

"Why don't you just bust in and stop her, Dad?"

I'd moved around before him. I hardly knew what all I wanted ended. But my directness, coming on again, seemed to hurt him even more. He held the one free hand over his face but still peeked out through fingers' openings.

Terrible to hear his child confide all this, as some grown man might—to a buddy after many drinks in a dark bar—something the town had urged him to say out plain, something he'd long meant to blurt and damn the consequence.

I pressed ahead, a bossy, confused little boy: "Dad? We've just got to run in there right now and make her show she loves you! Is all."

It was a logical plan. So logical, only a kid would conceive or trust it. I now stood waiting in the Sunday street for my father to join me in acknowledging this sudden good idea. A Bible mission right into our own house!

"Son, son. It's not like that," he slowed then stopped. "People do what they do. You decide if you can live with it. But to want to undo everything that's ever happened to you, it's like wishing you were dead. One thing leads to another and before long, to send away any of it means you expect nothing else. . . . After all, she gave me you. You should have seen you at the hospital—all six pounds four ounces. Pink as anything and bawling loud enough to wake the dead. —Haven't we had ourselves one fine time, though?"

And I realized that he was talking of the past. Already it had become Over, and I was barely eight. It was this, I think, this split in time, that really made me act.

There is the mystery of being male. There is the need to get the seed out of your body to the exact deep spot, and to do that well. Or at least to think you did. You are always being judged by Physics. The long male adventure stories tell how certain men can hunt and plan exactly, can trap any game. The invigoration of How To Aim and Accomplish. All that hit me with such a bath of adrenaline, I became, right there, almost pubescent. In the next few months, my body subtly changed—an unexpected scent like some brass doorknob's, a sudden gloomy stringiness, my new front beaverish teeth growing positively ridged.

I'm certain I got pushed toward adulthood by the toxicity, certain visual shocks, of this one lethal Sabbath.

I would, for him, now break all rules. I had just become the Passkey. "They will never hurt you ever again, Dad." I announced this to a sweating man wearing his new arm-sling, a man seated on the curb of a bright abandoned Sunday side street. In a sudden all-white neighborhood.

Even when Clyde saw me scamper off backwards from him, even when he saw me tease him with my half-smile—some dog waiting safely far outside the range of its master's first toss in fetch—even after I'd begun backing homeward at a clip part run, half hop, the poor guy could not move.

Dad just shook his head from side to side. He did not believe I would or could do it. I think this came from his denying the thing so long. Mom's other love might have been going on way down in the earth, in some deep missile-defense silo way out west, a shadowed bunker known only to those generals with codes and maps. That anyone could simply trot toward it like this in plain daylight while laughing part of a crazy little-kid's cackle, that any boy might run right into a Sunday house and freely see them at it—this went beyond his five senses' faith, past Clyde's own best religious reach.

But he soon guessed. Where I was going. With me dancing from foot to foot, suddenly madly nimble after hours in a car then a tow truck, I was too aware of my arriving power. I kept chuckling, as playful, fundamental and powerful as any righteous wicked full-grown man. Dad shook his head No, once. Dad saw what I now planned to try for him. He saw that I, this fast, this young, might now run with the pride of speed, with the state of becoming someone so perfectly stupidly male.

(How beautiful at running that shirtless young farmer who had sprinted past me, how I'd longed for a chance to exert myself with that much length and grandeur. And now, here, already, my main manly chance!)

Dad appeared so slowed, so weakened by this day and by the weighty doubled life he'd been assigned. He'd even forgotten to light another cigarette. Dad had already grown too old to stop me. He saw what I was going to do. He slowly stood, uneasy. He raised his arm in its new-made motel-bed gauze. First he tried running my way hard. The taps on his pointy shoes snapped the asphalt. Head down, Clyde heaved himself along the street, giving off little by-product moans. But you need full wind, both arms, to go your fullest speed. Soon the man could only scream as I shot a hundred yards ahead of him, as I skittered lithe across strangers' backyards, as I pirouetted down alleys, turned showy angles past hollyhocked garages, did banking shots along one hedge, me drunk within my potent swerves.

Two short blocks still left till there, I danced backwards, gloating just "Hehehe." I ignored a grieved man bellowing behind me, his sound already bringing neighbors to most windows, a siren's civil-defense alert. Dad's *"God, noooooooooooooooooooooooooooooooooooooooooooooo oooooooooooooooooooooooooooooooooooooooooooooooooooooooooooooooooooooooo ooooooooooooooooooooooooooooooooooooooooooooooooo, son!"*

6.

The morning after, she asked if I wanted toast. I nodded that I guessed I did. So she slid white bread into the silver slot. It click-clicked, turning brown, till she laid it on my plate. He sat at his regular spot. I at my usual. And she would pause at her worn place nearest the stove. She held a spatula in one hand. And the frying pan in another. And wore her pink Sunday best and rouge, though it was Monday. She seemed to feel her only hope was cooking well. And looking great. And acting overbusy. We two men sat. She stood three feet away. It was a meal eaten all in silence.

Out our torn back door, a view still split, a bolt that let the day through screening like some huge man's zipper opened irresponsibly. Not even with the finest wire could you ever stitch it shut quite right.

I saw our back-door neighbors wander out to their parked car, and—through their prison-high anchor fence—talking, nodding toward our house in lowered voices. The woman shook her head but her husband laughed and said just loud enough for ears as young as mine to catch, "Serves him right, ask me," and I knew they were talking about it.

First I guessed they hated Dix as I did, but then the "him" came to seem maybe Clyde, or even me. But probably Clyde.

Now it was out in the open. And I'd done it. I had only tried to help. Now everything felt worse. Felt even way more sad. We no longer had our small blind ceremonies to protect us. What a luxury, to hide from others all that you don't know yet. (A privilege I forever forfeited at eight.)

That gray morning, a Monday, Dad would head off selling as usual. The Shell station had just started staying open Sundays. They knew his car on sight. They liked him the way people did. So they had, without even being asked, worked just on Clyde's black Packard, knocking out worst dents and even finding a new windshield to wedge in.

Hearing Dad awake and stirring on tiptoe, I rose early. Silent, nodding at him, still in my pajamas, I helped him move his sale clothes from our front-hall closet to his de-Bibled Clipper. Having two good arms myself, I set the silver spring-pressure rod back into place. I lined its black rubber tips into their usual dents in gray flannel broadcloth.

We kept very quiet. We had done these simple tasks hundreds of times before. But today I'd waked so sore I couldn't move at first; snags and angles of pain seemed to remind me of something. Only these four decades later do I understand it reminded me of old age waiting. Old age with its outsized morning-after aches, its sly subtractions and nasty taxes on our simplest deeds.

I dressed for school in Monday's white shirt, starched half hurtful. I gathered my books and a science project that needed baking soda and salt. All were rubber-banded in a shoebox. I was ready to set off, though I had not written the assigned story, funny or no. I found Dad still sitting out front in his car, smoking. I thought he'd already slipped away, silent. Had he slept out there? I knew he would be late for his first stop at the best (and only) clothing store in Efland. Dad was usually prompt, long gone before I got my breakfast. Today it seemed he could not be in the house with her. It seemed he couldn't go far from it without me.

I didn't say goodbye to her but slid free of the front door, carrying my school things. Mom took her place at our bathroom window—irked and stationary—right there watching us.

Through the rolled-down glass of his banged-up car door, Dad said, "Here he is," as if we'd had an appointment.

My father climbed forth, stomped out his Camel. I walked to him. (My mother's head, a sweet smooth taffy-colored blob in the frilled window, looked out and down at us.) Surprising, Dad pulled me hard against his front, my cheek was almost cut by the fancy arrowhead-shaped belt buckle. He held me there for the longest time. His right arm was in the cast and sling but it tented out to make room for my head. The sling soon rested overtop me like some lean-to's roof. Then the arm lowered slowly, fitted cozy as a cap across my head. It seemed a big clean gauze wing. It pressed me flat against him, dry and hot. He still smelled of the sun-cured quilt. I could hear, literally hear, the emotion churning in his gut just beneath my ear.

"What's your name, sonny boy? You Clyde M. Delman, Jr.?"

"Yessir."

"Well, how bout bothering to say it out loud? Would you speak it once to where your ole peckerwood dad can hear? And make it sound like it might could one day mean something."

"I Am Your Boy Clyde M. Delman Jun-i-or! Sir! And I can put a 'Melvin' where the 'Meadows' is, to make me even *more* yours, sir." Then I repeated his full name but juniored, my head hidden beneath his hurt arm. I squeezed him so. I pressed my swollen eye against his ribs for whatever pain or healing, for whatever I could get from him.

"More like it," his baritone came beautiful and deep. It buzzed certain small bones in my head. It made the tip of my nose tickle. I ducked out from under the snug awning. I looked up at his dear rubbery face.

He said, "Sure does have a good sound to it. You remember who named you, son. Work hard at that geography. Psalm and Packard, think of all the languages you know already. Why, there's no tellin. . . . You can't even guess yet how smart you're going to have to keep on getting. Open season. It's got no limit to it. Your being so smart is one of my main pleasures up ahead. 'Professor C. M. Delman' has almost a rhyme to it, now don't it? Wouldn't surprise me a bit. Someday this mess'll make more sense to you. It's got a lot of parts to it. I saw something I loved. I walked up to it. And by the time I guessed I should go back, I couldn't give up what I'd found. —But you, now, you stay good till Friday, heah? Colonel Begonia's waiting. —But, son?—listen, being your dad, it's been the best darn job I ever had."

Then Clyde crawled into his car and backed out.

I stood here watching. I was still only half awake, bruises just commencing to fully smart. Squinting in raw light, I felt so left behind. I felt sick, weakened, an albino, blinky. I just watched him go.

In my toybox in the house? I had a tin car? And the man driver was made of the same metal as the car and that's how Clyde looked backing away from me.

I walked again into our house, holding my books and shoebox and all. We lived close enough to school that I heard the first bell sound, then the late bell. She never told me to go. She just kept sitting at the kitchen table in her best pink suit, face distorted between two supporting fists. One room away, I heard Mom's whispered chanting start, "Madrid, Rangoon, St. Paul . . ." We lived like that for seven days, eternity, her pacing one room, me doing that identical duty in another, and us at least drawing comfort from the sound of each

other's feet on wood or on linoleum. For something to do, I alphabet-
ized her books stacked everywhere, the hundreds of popular novels,
their covers all wrought-iron balconies, silhouetted motorcars, cres-
cent moons. She sent me out for our few groceries but I always hurried right back, as if my leaving Dad's house was disloyal, even
dangerous to his health. We had to hope. We had to hope him
through the hardest part. We knew it would be tougher for him far off
out there alone on the road in motels run by strangers, without even
the sound of another person's sighs and scratching, without at least
some fond adjacent restlessness.

Waiting, I thought I understood more. It seemed to me now that,
even if those deers had not flown at us out of nowhere, Clyde was
already planning to just wreck the car himself. He'd driven using only
his inner wrist; mere watchband. Dad seemed addled as someone
drugged. Maybe he'd decided that, in a world this unfair, if a man part
black could not succeed at convincing a part-white kid like me that he
might be my own loving father, then he'd do us both a favor. He
would just crash the Packard, kill us two. I never blamed him for lying
about his race, or mine. I couldn't fault him for letting me live eight
whole years believing both of us were white. What had he missed most
about being that other color? I recalled Sutie's shaking me: "Is you in
any way worth it, whiteyhead?" I knew the answer. "No." I told
myself I even sort of understood why Clyde would kill us both. Out of
mercy.

—It's a lot, to imagine that at eight.

Dad usually checked in on Thursday night, telling Mom when on
Friday he would show, but all that day he didn't phone. In the shoebox, my science ingredients stayed sealed. The school never called.
Those few times our phone rang, we jumped as if tortured and ran to
it and literally watched it ring until she grabbed it. Always it was a special onetime offer to try and get us to subscribe to the local paper. She
hung up on everybody not him. Just put the receiver down, and shook
her head at me, no. Resumed her post.

Monday, I begged her to ring his home office in Newport News.
They said he was out on the job okay and selling no worse than regular and he had talked to his bossman that same morning. This gave us

something anyway. The old secretary there said Mom was not to fret so. This lady had grown excellent at turning back (in her clove-smelling auntish voice) just such worried calls from other wives left briefly, then long-term. But we sat and worried anyway. I joined Mom in it, and would drag into the front room, toward that floral couch where I had seen it all. Heaving myself down, I'd lean against her as she lolled, head back, beneath an overly colorful afghan. Sniffing it, I recalled the yellowy quilt pressed all up around him, and how it'd smelled of straw and Clyde and health and country sun, and not, as did her coverlet, of unwashed human hair, interior space, and worse—sweetish natural desire, the killing hopes.

Somehow, I'd brought into the house his *Packard's Owner's Manual.* I'd been using it as a writing tablet for the false starts of my assigned story. It had a blue-simulated leather cover, like one meant to hold some pricey school diploma. A crest was embossed there. I now carried it from room to room; now I memorized its car-care facts like catechism. "If I commit just four more pages to memory . . ." By then, all we did was eat soup twice a day and stare out separate windows at opposite ends of a five-room rental unit. This was the year before televisions up and down our block would ruin the dignifying solitude of people poor as us. No radio on. Just two folks guarding an outpost, silent as Roman duty-soldiers placed a goodly distance from each other before slots of some dull crumbling desert fort. Waiting. But for what? The enemy. Any unusual movement.

Monday night she kept striding to and fro, and in her mopey airless way, crossing and uncrossing arms over her beautiful hopeful breasts, putting on different shades of cardigans and taking them off and folding them up, and sometimes standing looking out at the lighted end of our drive, its twin grooves where Clyde usually parked and Turtle Waxed his beautiful machine.

The whole left side of my body now showed many bruises rising to the surface, blue-black shadow-spots as big across as lilypads. "Damn Dalmatian boy"—I, naked, faced our bathroom mirror.

If you can get your eye blacked in a fistfight, couldn't some War fierce enough black a boy's whole body? I wanted that. To be the color of a tire, the ace of spades, used motor oil. To just get all my changing over with. I felt I'd earned that. Puberty, pigmentation, execution, bring it on. The sadder I grew—the sorer my neck and shoulder crooked, like missing each other, drawing painfully closer.

I asked Mom if I could borrow three sheets of her excellent blue notepaper. I didn't tell her why. She brought me the whole box, tossed it down, never asked. I would now write my new secret friend, Aunt Sutie. I considered apologizing, explaining, saying I finally understood her being somewhat cross with me. I'd ask why Clyde had never told me anything, much less everything. Had I made him ashamed of his true past? Or had the world? Had he left off taking care of her so he could come tend me? And how might I now help correct that, hunh? I'd request from her my own real history: meaning hers and mine and how they joined without my ever having known or noticed. I'd say I'd never understood I had so much of it: a past so colorful. Using my fingers, I sat at the kitchen table counting years; I guessed her parents had been slaves. Maybe she'd been born one, too, then got freed as a baby. I formally requested Sutie's life's every fact, however hard. Nothing on earth interested me more: how black was my dad, how white his mom, and where'd all that leave me?

But, I mainly begged, would she please join me? In, yes, prayer—praying actual prayers—out loud if need be, for our Clyde. Public prayer had embarrassed me till now I lacked him. In cafés, I'd mostly wished to just look classy, and not be the kid accompanying a mumbling head-wagging Clyde. But prayer now seemed one way of talking to my dad. I felt ashamed of having ever been ashamed of a man so generous. I had been "white," uneasy near emotions of more colors than my own. "White" is not a color. It's the total loss of those.

I explained to Sutie, our beloved one was off somewhere in such bad trouble. I felt this, every second. His sacrifice for li'l Whiteyhead here had put our Clyde in all this terrible trouble. He just needed to keep interested. Either in me, or in Sutie. If possible both. But whoever of whichever race caught his interest next, in the end it'd be good for both and all of us. Sutie and me, we were members of the small exclusive club that loved him.

It helped to write her. I took my time. My penmanship, if slow, looked nearly good as my schoolbook on penmanship. Clyde once proudly told our favorite waitress I was "definitely real project-oriented." So be it. I covered both sides of six borrowed pages. I used

permanent blue-black, refilling the marbleized Parker fountain pen
Dad himself had given me for Christmas.

I ignored Mom's peevish sexy sickroom sighs one doorway down. I
put my whole heart into writing my new colored grandmother. "Hello
there!," my letter began. I felt this'd be the first of a hundred such bulletin petitions to our Sutie. It must be perfect in grammar and the
feelings I admitted to. I could not offend her by accident. Six pages
double-sided took me twelve whole hours of cuticle-biting, frequent
starings into space. I committed each wish, each idea in civics-class
calligraphy. At last, I reread it, almost believed it, licked it shut. Venturing some guesswork, offering an eight-year-old's stumbling phi-
losophy of race and God, it was about the hardest thing I'd done. The
hardest, at least, since seeing him drive away without me.

I asked Mom for a stamp, please; she told me where she kept them
rolled. Gluing it on, pressing its serrations, I slowly understood Sutie
was blind. But others would surely read this aloud to Granny. Once
the stamp was at a perfect right angle, I uncapped my pen to write the
name of her town, her road. And found I knew neither. I almost
turned to Mom for those, then remembered—Clyde had sworn me to
secrecy. Mom knew even less than I. When Dad returned, I'd ask him
first thing: Did this old lady live in Virginia? North Carolina? I'd seen
no rural mailbox along her boggy path.

"Aunt Sutie . . ." what? Not, "Delman." That must be Dad's white
father's last name. But what was his mother's?

I felt that I could save Clyde, by coming to know my Sutie all at
once. But I was eight. Eight years away from driving, I slowly understood I could probably never find her on my own.

Could I ever tell her how sorry I'd become without quite noticing
I probably should've been all along? Alone on foot, I would someday hunt her magic cabin. I would even use her outhouse (and
for Number 2!). But even if I rediscovered that bottle cap of a hut,
wouldn't she resist my begging for her news, her pain? For news of her
son who'd hauled off and adopted someone else's worthless pallid little boy? Why would a man choose the parching hardship of seeming
white over the riper fact of being born black? Was the setup that
completely rigged? I had only questions. Even my dad—the strongest
simple declarative statement in my life—was minute by minute
becoming one.

7.

Nine p.m. Monday night, I sat doing my math at our couch's far end (assignments I gave myself. Nobody from school had called to ask or punish. It shocked me how casual they took my also going-missing). A knock on the door and we both leapt inches into air. I came down half on the chair as Mom ran at the front door so hard, she bumped right into it, then swung back, opening it wide, her arms already lifted toward him.

There stood Rory from the hospital, a brown car-coat pulled over his whites. "You Mrs. Delman?" He saw me here at the kitchen table and smiled and waved, called, "Hiya, Funnybooks," though I had never touched the stack of limp comics under their rancid bubbling aquarium.

He asked could he speak to Mother outside for a second? What he said was low but I at least heard her statements in the dark (she always forgot to turn on our porchlight for company): "Forty-three years old. Where? Anybody with him? How soon? You will? Oh thank you, yes, we'll wait. No next of kin past us. You are kind. But tell me, 'natural'? You're sure 'natural'?"

I set down my yellow pencil. I studied her back, still posed in the front doorway. Very slow now she closed our door. Mom leaned one shoulder against it while turning—smiling, but so broadly her gums showed. It was like the fluoride treatment at school. We were ordered to smear pink medicine across our teeth but told never to swallow or let lipskin touch gums. So we just stood there like that, till the time passed, too afraid not to go ahead and look ugly awhile. You had to just stand there and let it do its work on you.

Since I'd seen her naked, I now always saw my mother naked. The many sweaters and skirts she kept slipping into since, these only made her look more anemic and more white, more beautiful to me and more debauched.

She now settled beside me on the very couch where all that happened. She reached for my forearm, like a kind big sister in some warm fakey family movie from the forties. "Honey? Is about our sweet Clyde, son. It's bad, honey."

She said a motel had phoned the local funeral home who then called the hospital where he was known and Rory had generously walked over to tell. They said it was either a heart attack or an aneurysm, in a motor court called the Restée Arms just this side of the Virginia line up near Norlina. He was considered young for the heart explanation, but he had not taken too much care of himself, had he? He sure smoked. He certainly worked too hard. Whatever leisure-time he earned he gave to those damn Bibles. One doctor said it could have been some brain clot knocked free by the shock—of the car wreck, of the bone break, the all of it together—a freak thing, a strange instance, but it happens. Their report would later say about his death, "Motel room was found secured. No signs of a struggle."

I knew that was not true.

I sat here. As usual, she stared at me. But now, I slowly saw, my lovely mother already fairly well hated the sight of me. She felt that, by busting in on her under that white man, I had done Clyde in, had ended her. I'd also hurt her love for the one she maybe considered my "real" father. The Worst of All Sundays, she had turned my way and seen me right there staring at them doing it.

Some people might be curious to know exactly how their moment of conception looked.

That privilege—I can promise you—is highly overrated.

VI: Revelation

"And I Saw the Dead . . ."

And I saw the dead, small and great, stand before God; and the books were opened: and another book was opened, which is the book of life: and the dead were judged out of those things which were written in the books, according to their works. . . . And whosoever was not found written in the book of life was cast into the lake of fire.

Revelation 20:12–15

. . .

Soon Mother learned that Clyde had been quite well insured. It was somehow like him. Three life policies nearly paid for left face-up in his overly colorful sock drawer. With that money she would send me off to military school. Five days after the funeral. Looking back, I guess I asked for that, so eager to depart a house where I had seen too much.

Falls was now several thousand faces—white and black—all aimed my way. (Every drugstore I entered hiccupped around a hush.) Eyes-blue, eyes-brown begged this eight-year-old please to describe certain recent interrupted sex, two nude attractive people nabbed wriggling at it.

Oh, I was a prodigy Detective, okay. Sex-crib motels had whetted my snooping skills. The Hardy Boys as Only Child. Breadcrumb by breadcrumb, I'd followed all those tourist-cabin Clues straight back to It. I'd thrown aside cigarette-burned chenille and yelled to all of Falls, "Here, people. Here's your problem, thumping away right here!"

Falls hoped to squeeze from me what I have told already. But only to you. And just at the start of this, and that one time. "Janine!" The American Grill's genius waitress was a fine old gal named Janine.

I showed you what happened, just as I still picture it, despite myself, certain nights, before I try and sleep.

If you need, you can turn back to the start. You can reread that part once I'm done. Eventually, I will be. Maybe I should wedge that discovery scene right in here again? But no. If you like, flip to pages 165 through 170—then swerve on back and we'll meet here. If, by then, you can still abide the sight of me, that nosy, interfering, little mixed-up well-tossed racial salad.

—Why did I *do* all that? I've had most of my lifetime to wonder.

Waiting around for his funeral, I stripped before our bathroom mirror. Poking darkest bruises, my fingertips' pressure briefly lightened dark-gray spots. They turned my usual Anglo-Irish butterscotch. I felt relieved and then ashamed of my relief. I remembered answering the phone and guessing the race of all Dad's callers. I'd pointed to my face only when someone sounded black. Naked in this tiny bathroom, I pictured Clyde's disappointed glance my way. I must apologize when he got home. He'd instantly forgive me. Then I remembered, as if first learning, my own dad: dead.

My arrowheads stayed coffined in the glove box of a Packard recently sold out of state. I wished for those, for the nudie tire gauge, for anything everything Clyde's.

I carried Sutie's stamped unaddressed letter all over town. In order to wedge it into my child-sized shirt pocket, I bowed its blue envelope. On Main, I scouted each black face I passed, to learn at once such features' types and blue-brown beauties.

I noted how white eyes, set in a black face—if bloodshot—looked almost yellow by contrast. Contrast seemed all. I became an ornithologist specializing in starlings and blackbirds. I had so much to notice now! I imagined I might run into Sutie, blind but pulled along our crowded sidewalk by the noble seeing-eye Rin Tin Tin. Aunt Sutie's blindness seemed appropriate now, even merciful. Like me, she would never see Clyde M. Delman, Sr., again. Unlike me, she would not expect it.

At eight, you're too alive to quite believe Death is more than some pal's brief coerced afternoon nap. "I'll just wait for him right here till he's back up. Send him out then, okay, ma'am?"

Mom continued to indulge her favorite flavor of mistake: the extremely public kind. Having smudged on makeup, having slid into her good pink Sunday suit, she lived in those full-time.

Seeking public sympathy, Grace might've continued moping. She could've gone on being basically pretty if fairly unkempt. What if she'd fainted, out of grief, downtown on market day? But nothing, of course, could now redeem Gracie Meadows Delman in the eyes of Falls. Everybody knew what she'd allowed her hubby and child to find her doing. And in the living room of their very home. Mid-afternoon. With the sun out. On the Sabbath!

People now blamed themselves for not taking poor Clyde aside sooner. They should've snitched before the showdown that likely killed him. His endless scream toward God then me, it already echoed in local legend. For once, gossip did not exaggerate a deed's capacity to terrify.

Silly rumors seeped into my hearing: how Mother had been slowly poisoning Clyde, successive thermoses of arsenic-laced "café au lait" sent out on the road with him. Everyone agreed—"as sure as if she'd point-blank shot him"—Grace had caused the heart attack. She'd provided Clyde a spectacle literally unendurable. The one that yet replays itself for my insomnia's private benefit:

I see the exact pattern of upholstery fabric under her (pink roses basketball-sized repeated against a livid apple-green). I yet live hammocked, sandwiched, in the vision of my mom and her lover joined. That image long ago became my sleeptime's neutral starting-point, a geometric TV test pattern. The image of them linked, it underwrites and color-tests my stubborn wakefulness.

Some chess master might recognize his incoming insomnia the moment that he pictures an idealized board. It's all set up and ready for play. "Here we go again!" The first imagined move, the opening gambit's complexity, predicts for him tonight's game ending at 2 or 5 a.m.

In just that way, wide awake before dawn, I reconfront a locked if rusty rear screen door. I've brought to bed my adulthood's spindly towering plates of lists, usual chores left stacked half done. I then try, systematic, working my way through pending resolutions: which ex-student's letter of rec. is nearly overdue? Dare I mail my elder daughter's oboe coach another little note of thanks and some new Cimarosa CD? Abed, face-up, I practice office triage.

And just as Sleep works its way up near the top of my "Must Do"s, a child fist jams through back-door screening; again I hear the mildest frying sound: corrupted wire yields to a punch so solid; I chin myself on the door's crossbar; its fumbled latch comes too easily undone; I must once more run right in on them. Sliding past my intended stop, too soon I climb aboard. "Baby," she cries up at me, "your weight's too much, it's hurting me."

"My weight? *My* dern weight?!"

If only Mom had dressed in black that week before Clyde's funeral. Maybe if Grace had sprained an ankle, then wrapped it up as Doc Dix's wife daily Maypoled hers. —Or what if the young widow actually stayed home and comforted her eight-year-old? Neat idea, her building community support for us. But no. Claiming a need to "talk with the other adults who'd known Clyde best," Grace started going off in cars. With certain handpicked friends. Of my late dad's. I could not help notice. That these pals. Were mainly. Male.

Dix himself never came calling. But other well-wishers sure did. And Clyde's funeral—needing time to get my traveling salesman's body home—wouldn't happen till next Tuesday.

The first to arrive, to honk once, then sit nervous out front: the dashing class-ring salesman from our Bible Club. He always combed his hair the way a soda jerk constructs that first free sundae for his girlfriend. I knew this man had bratty active kids and one mousy wife. In his class ring of a car, the pink Imperial, he looked guilty, highly groomed, and overmarried. Mom waved back at me, trotting toward his vehicle. She teetered across damp lawn atop very high heels, leaving behind divot clues. She endured these tall shoes with the sportingness of some high-school quarterback in his one-time-only Halloween costume as: A Lady. I saw four neighbor women, arms crossed, watching, glancing at each other, watching.

Clyde's send-off would be tomorrow afternoon. He and his Bible buddies had apparently planned it. But planned it when?

Once the ring-seller's tail fins slid away, I chose to walk around our town alone. I wore a blue windbreaker. I checked the bathroom mirror like some President's son preparing for his father's televised funeral cortege.

When I, counting the last of my chauffeur-salary pocket change, stepped into the dime store, my face caused double takes. So I decided to wander downhill, where Falls's many black people lived. Nobody'd know me there. I could have the pleasure of being near such folks and their consoling busyness; but I'd go blessedly unrecognized, unpitied.

A strange haze hung over The Bottom's chinaberry trees, its rusted tin roofs. Clyde had told me how—lacking good drainage and decent window screens—black people burned rags to discourage huge mosquitoes. My head now drooping forward, Sutie's undeliverable letter crackling the jacket fabric over my heart, I trudged along. I hurried as with some urgent errand. In Black Town, I felt alive and yet invisible.

But I soon found myself observed. From many crowded porches. Generations slumped on discarded upholstered furniture. (White people's old couches went into storage behind the house; black people's seemed transposed, half proud, onto front porches.) Old folks and infants—abandoned during work hours—babysat each other. My courtly little nods brought me not one greeting. Instead, my platinum presence released darker older people into showing just how tired they were.

Some folks rolled their eyes; they turned aside, yawned irritated snorts. And I slowly saw they knew exactly who I was. I guessed they'd known—all along—who my Clyde had truly been. They understood everything he'd given up for little Whiteyhead me. They had already heard about his death. And, like Sutie, seemed to blame me. But why?

He hadn't even gone into his grave. And yet I—eight—was already down here looking for an entrance! I sought some back door left unfastened, half welcoming. I'd hiked downhill in search of company, music, vowel tones, maybe one warm drink.

The day before Dad's funeral, I had faith some circulation system hid in Baby Africa, the quick and secret life of Falls! The choicest currents in our hill town all seemed to beat and lurk today inside those hovels' smoky parlors.

But as Negro-owned dogs barked just at me, as blackfolks refused to return my eye-to-eye, I knew finally to stumble silent back uphill. In Colored Town, I seemed viewed, not as the joy of Clyde's life, but as some pale leech who'd used him up. Someone who'd lured him half uphill—away from Dad's real duties, his true kin. Not one black citizen smiled my way or asked me in. —Without Clyde, I would never know these folks. Without him, maybe I would never want to!

I returned to an address and destiny that felt far more coldly random. I opened the door of our rental house. I saw, nailed beside our porch mailbox, a new white wreath of fresh carnations. I leaned nearer. At least I could sniff flowers' cleanly reassuring scent. Receiving none, I touched blossoms. Dad's proved celluloid. Maybe leased? Part of a package deal? Some kit provided by your friendly white-man undertaker.

Fake flowers: that most Caucasian of Caucasian inventions.

2.

Clyde's funeral overenlivened Falls's Second Baptist True Gospel Tabernacle. Pews of our "church home" were absolutely jammed. More folks stood up in back. Crowds made the tongue-and-groove balcony ominously creak.

Dad's ceremony had the tension of a sports event, the macabre citizenly charge peculiar to some public hanging.

"Never in my forty years . . . ," our town mortician told me later.

Mother held my right hand tight all during. Maybe Grace felt frightened at the emotion Clyde M. Delman's exit inspired in everyone but her. No, wrong—her, too. I knew that. Since we'd got the news, I heard her being sick night after night in our small echoing bathroom. And yet the sight of mourners come off the night shift in their mill clothes, the very working-classness of Dad's funeral, the way its music rocked—all this seemed to grieve my mom as much as his long blond oak coffin. A vanilla box to hold, I explained to myself, the rarest of white chocolate. What a stupid thought!, but my own just then. I was out of my mind that day. I was a kid, after all. My saliva tasted like canning paraffin. My eyesight fluttered at its outer edges, winglike tugs, little extra jelly tremblings.

The organ prelude sounded soggily overfamiliar. Hymns like a row of windowsill pears left ripening in sun too long ever to eat. Mush, but all lined up most beautifully colored. When the sentimental pipe organ left "Old Rugged Cross" and slid oily into a secular "Danny Boy," Mom groaned loud enough to turn five heads. She hissed my way, "Poor clod. He would, without my help. 'Danny Boy'! We're all in so much trouble, son."

Her brothers had arrived. They were handsome Nordic men as tall as Clyde. They looked so much like twins you knew they weren't. Seeming talcummed with Presbyterian rectitude, their sideburns were cut precisely straight. Professional in new black suits, it seemed they'd come not to console their sis but to serve her a summons.

My lawyer-uncles appeared to disapprove, not only of Clyde's disreputable lonely death in a motel; they also frowned at Mom herself, their pretty little joyride of a baby sister. But as I sat beside this woman so generally despised, I clutched her palm with both my fists, to comfort. I traced my index fingertip along her endless lifeline, down into her deep, deep pocket of a heartline. I wanted to forgive her. Who else on earth could I forgive? And, sure, I hoped for some vice versa. Far more than Mom, I myself had put him in this box.

Clyde's seemed almost a classic Negro funeral. I wondered if others noted this. It worried me in ways that shame me now. If I was ready to admit my dad had been a living black man, then surely having him be just a newly dead one should've felt far easier. Right? Well, no. Really openly emotional, the music wasn't one bit canned; it absolutely swung. It did not know how not to. Both aged lady keyboardists cried; neither woman could quite read her music thanks to running eyes, and so each played by heart. A piano plus an organ and two choirs, Child & Adult. Dad had served as superintendent of the Sunday school here. Everybody loved him. In secret, he'd passed out chewing gum to kids. A saint, he loaned men money and never mentioned repayment, and now he'd died and who would know? Praise God— from Whom all blessings . . .

Clyde's coffin rested open. Mom had asked, would morticians please keep it closed, thanks. But we'd marched in last, the church just mobbed, and there Dad waited face-up. What could we do? Turn tail and run? Rush up and slam it?

I will spare myself and you the description of how much "Northern European" makeup, how much cake-icing-pink sludge, they'd spackled over that dear jalopy of a face. It was beyond Lon Chaney monster-movie, how white they'd tried to paint him, dead.

Dad had somehow urged his fellow Bible-givers to handcraft his burial. Maybe he hoped to spare my mom the chore. She would've sprung for Psalm 100 and "Jesu, Joy of Man's Desiring," period. No "graveside service," no nothing. Everybody go home.

Mom's lifelong stab at "class" got trounced without these rough men even knowing. Her brothers being present made it all the more embarrassing. Grace's tribe had been a longtime dynasty of big-jawed, self-satisfied county-seat attorneys. In Castalia, North Carolina, to be "a Meadows" offered large exemptions, ones Mom had maybe traded on, then flaunted from the start.

For one thing, too many guys spoke. Six, then the class-ring sales-man. Each man stood remembering Clyde aloud and at full blast. Mother's hand tightened over mine at every painful instance of ungrammar. After forty double negatives, my right paw reddened then contracted and soon numbed.

Orations by Clyde's fellow Bible-believers first seemed casual, soon impromptu, next disorganized, then collapsing toward the sloppy, sounding finally deranged. Others' love of him seemed to dawn on them as they described it. The ring salesman now recalled a traffic accident that'd claimed his own beloved eldest child, an adolescent daughter. Mom, panicked, whispered to me, "And what has this to do with the price of tea in China?"

How the cops' 3 a.m. phone call felt. How his poor child looked, expired on the operating table. We all waited for his return to Clyde. We craved that. Soon we tilted forward, cheering the salesman home toward his topic—face-up in the box. Maybe Clyde had offered some consoling Bible verse at 4 a.m.? Or flowers, coffee-to-go? Anything! But no. This speech was not about my dad in any way but one: Clyde's love kept offering others permission. Be yourself, bud. Go for it!

From beyond the grave, "Museums should be phoned." "Not our Clyde," Bible-scatterers addressed a God all the more invisible today.

These businessmen were too upset to make much sense.

And in the end, only that made sense. Finally, I felt my father's presence, forgiving, sleepy, half amused, seated right beside us; Clyde nodding at their every crude confession, at each man's listed grief. From here, I could see one of my actual dead dad's shoe soles, tipped against white satin; a metal tap nailed near its toe "to save on shoe leather, bud." And yet I seemed to also feel him slouched here in the pew beside me. One bony arm proved fully long enough to reach well past me, curl around, and include Mom within Dad's pterodactyl form of a lank angel embrace.

This hug seemed so firm, I remember thinking, "Good, must mean his bone has healed." (Morticians had, for purposes of sparing his best suit, simply snipped the cast right off that mending arm.)

. . .

Soon as Amen ended it, black people and white people I'd never seen, having cried unto coughing, left without addressing Mom. Everybody whispered about her. Strangers openly pointed at us here alone on Clyde's front row. No eulogy mentioned Mother once. All praise sloshed instead toward me, "his little fellow missionary." I felt unconsoled, bitter. I felt a Clyde-like lack of vanity. I felt, in fact, so old.

Black members of Dad's Bible Club sat, for the first time ever, right alongside mourning white members. (By whose order? By some unexpected provision of Dad's will?)

Janine, genius waitress from The American Grill, sent one hundred decrusted sandwiches to our home for whatever reception might happen afterward. White bread, deprived of brown crust, looked nude. Nobody came. Leaving direct from the cemetery, Mom's brothers drove right back to Castalia.

Three hours after the service, Colonel Begonia knocked at our front door. A yellow taxi waited. God knows what it cost him or how he reached us from Edenton, half a state away. He lifted toward Mom one pot, his "best boy" beefsteak begonia.

Colonel said he'd come to deliver it/him personally. Mom didn't understand why, on leaving (carrying five pounds of sandwiches we pressed on him), the old crew-cut gent cried like some unwed mother exiting an orphanage.

"Goodbye," Colonel told the plant comically healthy. "Be a good boy. —Semper fi," he called.

Five days later—his begonia underwatered then oversoaked and already going crispy from its outside in—I boarded the train to military school.

2. NEW TESTAMENT

Return

. . . he appeared unto the eleven as they sat at meat, and upbraided them with their unbelief and hardness of heart, because they believed not . . . that he was risen.

Mark 16:14

When I was thirty, I returned to Falls. One of those class reunions you dread attending. You force yourself and, afterward, can't believe you nearly missed it. Why? Because of stupid vanity over hair loss or your recent job performance, just hating to explain all that.

Since Mom shipped me off to that stern Anglican military academy, I couldn't have named five people from my third-grade class. The Worst Possible Sunday had made of me a nomad like that pitiable jokester, the shirt-selling Clyde M. Delman, Sr.

Odd, in a gym still draped with twisted midnight-blue crepe paper, the very second that my former grammar-school chums stepped up to me, adults now—widened, sobered, overly painted, and sometimes genuinely improved—I somehow spoke their names aloud: "Jennifer," "Walter," "By God, if it's not ole 'Mutt.' " —Like some irregular Latin declension I'd memorized once if perfectly at age eight, these monikers hopped easily free of me. So did deep old fondnesses for them.

My shock at catching Mom under Doc Dix, the added penalty of losing Dad a week and one day later, all that had thrown a shadow Bible-black over each previous local joy. Our old school gym still vaguely smelled of pubescent sweatsocks and radiator-scorching. With its rafters echoing a young young band's startling New Age arrangement of our old "Blue Moon" (itself a revival), I danced. I danced with several different, kind, remembered women.

I held, in turn, the class secretary, our girl math-genius (tragically still no further advanced than chief teller at Falls's major bank). Such "nice girls" had become even decenter women. They admitted having always wanted to tell me how sorry they'd been. About what I'd endured and seen while in third grade. "Whatever you did see," one half-whispered to my neck, still sexily begging for details already twenty-two years old.

Friends swore they'd heard about my recent progress way up north. They claimed to know how hard I'd worked at prep school once shipped away unfairly and in such a hush-hush hurry. "We did wonder, all those years ago, what really happened to you, Meadows. First Reading Circle was never the same after you left. You were always so . . . prepared. We all felt a little scared of you, you know? You kept so quiet but certainly smiled a lot. You seemed drowsy half the time. And we girls all wanted hair your color!"

Nearly nuzzling my slow-dance partners, I admitted how, boarded at a first-rank second-tier military school, I had truly thrown myself at studies. Nothing else to do, I went at Latin and then Greek as if I were some regular kid rabid for sports trivia or car statistics. To these women, dancing warm and ample in my arms, I let myself admit how surprisingly well I was actually doing, considering the early trouble. Still a bachelor, yeah. But I'd just met a beauty, a very witty skinny woman named Bethany. I was already an associate professor in far-off New England. If forced, I mentioned my two—and only—books. (One, that international blockbuster *The Relationship Between the Published and Original Versions of Cicero's Speeches*. My second is *Questions of Authenticity in Seneca's Plays*. And, as of the present writing, the film rights to both remain available!)

This far south, even if my tweeds felt somewhat costumey, they comforted like a flimsy sort of armor, the uniform of choice. I was so aware of being back in Dad's chosen town. I imagined phoning him to meet me for a drink. I guessed how happy my return, my small-time ivory-tower career would've made the Itinerant King of "Swank" Cufflinks.

I had driven south along the superseded U.S. 301; this road once offered the feeder stream to many of our sleeker Bible-clients. Headed toward Falls, I pictured coming upon some old motel; those few rooms that didn't leak would now be rented by the month to squads of Mexican workers. But I might find, in weeds behind the place, a letter "T" still pressed there, fine white quartz crisscrossing Trixie's grave.

I discovered that Janine's American Bar and Grill was now the Hello Deli and Sushi Bar. (Who says there's been no progress in our national culture?) Brave, I now aimed my Hertz car past our old rental home. The property was rendered far more desirable by trees full-grown, fresh yellow paint, and some young couple's new petunia-spilling windowboxes. Beside the drive, a tricycle with a pink seat, new plastic streamers windblown on its handlebars.

During my reunion weekend, I was spared deciding if I should bother visiting my mom. —Veterinarian Dix (no surprise) had chosen not to marry a young widow suddenly too visible, controversial; everybody knew he'd never desert his wife of two decades. Everyone but poor Mom. She waited around for two whole years, that sure he'd change his mind. He did not "call" again. Her little Meadows had fixed that but good! Shunned, even in her favorite hangout, the Falls Public Library, Grace finally moved to Boca Raton. For many subsequent seasons, Mom worked there as "hostess" for an eating place she seemed to assume most everybody civilized must know; her postcards called it "The exclusive 'Thunderbird Supper Club.' " —Right.

The two-star T-bird must've enjoyed a clientele made up exclusively of prosperous, erotically driven, short-lived, lonely widowers. At its entrance find Gracie Delman smiling, fully made up, wearing drop earrings and a long dress, greeting gents fondly, inventing nicknames for pet regulars. (It was a trick I had learned early from Janine. I knew how well it'd worked on me at six. I've since tried it on my sad-sack freshmen.) Mom, in turn, married four of these old fortune-packing seabirds. And she always invited my latest girlfriend and me south to attend her latest surprisingly elaborate nuptials.

Two of her husbands had been named Buck. Then she'd upped and remarried Buck #1. Even for a scholar with a fairly good memory, I found my mother's complete moniker was getting hard to track. At the edge of her most recent engraved wedding invitation, Grace had jotted in the red fountain-pen ink she now affected, "Meadows? I plan wearing white this time. Can you believe it! But Buck #2 insists. Am I crazy, honey? Do you mind much?"

I did not. Nor did I ever attend.

At least she'd improved her situation financially. Look on the bright side: Maybe Grace could now afford sending some little kid through boarding school. Still pissed? Me? I'd once asked her why my trust fund had faltered after that first year of education elsewhere. Why had she forced the boarding school to set me working at age nine? My chore? Twice weekly, all Tuesday and Thursday afternoons, shining huge old silver lacrosse trophies, nut dishes for the Parents' Day she attended once with "a new friend." Mother answered, "Honey, what was I supposed to do, sell jewelry at Woolworth's?"

Well . . . now you mention it . . .

Grace had sunk so far from the foreground of my life: call it a highly successful and worked-at denial. I had not invited her to my college graduation or to my wedding, fearing she'd actually turn up. Wearing red. Grace was now the Christmas bulletin (news about an active couple's latest ballroom-dance trophy; her board sponsorship of a road show reviving some forties musical worthless even then). Finally officially rich, she could FedEx me my birthday card; lately of the comic "You're Really Over the Hill Now" variety. Despite my silence, her memento always arrived exactly on the day itself. My new bride claimed this surely showed some forethought and initiative, didn't it? But, reading Grace's breezy red-inked description of an impulsive Caribbean cruise taken with her latest Texan ("Buck is seventy-three going on twenty years young!"), I again felt the bitter arbitrariness of parentage.

I had one parent. And he, apparently, was not.

Lately—wandering myself so near the privileged vista of Fifty, fretting now as the worrywart father of two—I can only marvel at Grace Meadows Delman, her grief-stricken carelessness in shipping me north five days after Dad's funeral. She is still alive, she is yet sexually active, and (natch) a resident of Florida. I must tell you later: At our curious seaside reunion last year, the woman at least started to explain.

II.

Age eight, arrived by train wearing a brass-buttoned maroon uniform that made me feel like both a chimp and a chest of drawers, I found myself standing at attention on the muddy windblown soccer field. I had been banished here to march in something called the Junior Color Squad. I had no idea what any of this meant. I'm sure I still don't. But, feeling confused while hoisting the snapping flag at a forty-five-degree angle, trying to keep its pine staff upright as my own child-spine never could remain for long, I did accidentally achieve at least one minor-chord form of early immortality. (I guess you could call it my first publication.)

Near the back of last week's Sunday *New York Times Magazine,* beside the Crossword answers, opposite a quaint section devoted to diet camps for the troublingly chubby kids of the persons glazedly svelte, a column is given over to those also-ran boarding schools that still need to advertise. And there you'll find a listing for my make-do alma mater.

The ad's boilerplate photograph—timeless and yet slightly dated in some way now adjudged half classy—shows two uniformed boys. The brunette to the right stands blowing his trumpet. And, beside him, holding a huge flag, heraldic if unfamiliar, another male child squints at you, a blond kid appearing very bullied if noble, mild.

Pitifully pretty, he looks embarrassed at discovering himself far too visible and this overtly Caucasian; the kid stands half lost under a black-billed cap. My worldly daughters look it up every Sunday. They tease me—oh, they're merciless. They call this uniformed child "The Salt Shaker." I guess because he seems the paler half of some matched set. A real little "whiteyhead," he is.

I pretend to whine at all of this; I hide my face behind "Sports" and then go nose-down into the "Book Review." My girls enjoy such fond and weekly ribbing. But sometimes, when they've left the room for a few more gallons of Diet Coke, I'll slowly turn toward the ad. I feel suspense almost—squinting over my now-necessary bifocals.

A few pages earlier, find come-ons for sponsor-seeking outfits that intend to stamp out international hunger. As bait, they offer photos of darling grieved third-world kids. You're being asked to adopt one in exchange for cute snapshots of "yours" shown in his cleanly rags. You can expect your kid's biannual letters written directly to you, and in his own dear crabbed (if now-protein-stoked) handwriting.

I study the picture of my own young somber face. And I now feel willing to send any monthly amount to keep this orphaned kid fed, housed, as far out of uniform and off the gusty lacrosse field as possible. It is in this strange context that—middle-aged, sitting amid the clutter of one daughter's trimming new reeds for her oboe, another's perusing works on Degas sculpture and fan mags showing the latest teen blond actor-sensation—I still marvel at the forlorn beauty (so up for grabs) of one stark parade-field boychild.

Back then, that much a kid, I as yet masterminded the resurrection of my father. Surely we buried the wrong person? A white man who only outwardly resembled my real Dad. Might Clyde not simply Packard through the gates of this pretentious prison camp for delinquent changelings? Couldn't he abduct his child safely back to Falls, return me to civilian clothes, enroll me at a school so near our house that you could always hear the early, then the late bells?

Sundays in particular, at a window seat in the hall of the third floor, staring out the tilting fan-shaped Palladian window just under our roof's central peak, I habitually watched all approaching traffic. I sat waiting for the next waxed black car to activate its blinker, turn in.

III.

> . . . If it were not so, I would have told you.
> I go to prepare a place for you.
>
> John 14:2

The rest is one wing beating, when two wings are required for flight.

The rest becomes my own story, but ghost-written. I had not believed in ghosts. Till Clyde died.

I became, without quite knowing it, a somewhat conservative scholar. My enjoying any career at all still offers me a weekly source of wonderment. It would delight Dad. And yet, compared with certain stellar work in the field, my own can look, even to me, merely "respectable."

I am not, as my daughters now indiscriminately use the term, a "sexy" scholar. All the same, I have published nineteen articles and the two books. Teaching's made a dent in my output; but giving energy away to students isn't something I regret very often. I'm regularly consulted by my peers. I like being a tie-breaker between warring camps. Clyde's son, after all.

My subjects range from Tacitus to the problem of prosaic words in Lucan. Of course, our field's real movers and shakers are those now working on such cutting edge topics as "Gender Theory." Though I'll bet you anything—not one of them has ever come close to seeing his own mother even near her horse-sized weekly veterinarian! Still, these sexual-identity "experts" are the stars presently asked to give the keynote addresses to the American Philological Association Meetings, and I am not. Oh well. —When I'm about to mail some final version of my newest article to a good periodical, I send one copy off to my first boarding-school classics teacher. She still double-checks my facts, my amounts. As Clyde and his fellow givers of the Word phrased it during our prayer breakfasts at Janine's American Bar and Grill, "Blessed." Lord, sir, but I've been blessed.

Approaching fifty, needing to lose fifteen surplus pounds, I confess I find my present age's physical slackening almost a relief: if your hair has gone white, it doesn't much matter whether that hair began as African black, platinum blond, or merest dishwater brown. By now, you've aged beyond your troubling starter beauty. Like some geological Mineral Age—following a newly passed Vegetal one—traces of once-ferns still cling across my roughened rock-facings! I'm glad to be exactly this old. My favorite two ages so far: eight and forty-eight.

Swift said, "No wise man ever wishes to be younger."

Or, I might add, lighter-skinned.

First week at the academy, I got assigned a history theme, "State How White Americans Have Benefited Culturally/Economically from the Enforced Labor of American Negroes." The very topic made me feel singled out, criticized. It also made me marvel afresh at all he'd done for Mom, then me. He'd been our willing wage-slave. But why? In researching my paper, I came across one chapter that exclaimed over how rare armed revolt had been among the slaves. So few had killed their masters and, rarer still, their masters' kids. Somehow "the human element" only seems to work up the ladder, never down.

Fourth year at school, my roommate's father was one of Richard Nixon's presidential-campaign managers. And my buddy, in a phrase I still remember and enjoy, forever called Nixon "Vice President Weasel Breath."

Hoping to defeat and bankrupt said weasel, my roomie gave everyone at school the secret telephone credit-card number for Nixon's headquarters. He passed this code along to dozens of long-distance boys and girls our age at far-flung schools. Before our dorm's busy wall-mounted pay phone, lines soon formed. I made quick use of Nixon's account. Civil disobedience. Plus so darned convenient.

Clyde's posthumous funds paid for my room, board, and notebook paper but little else. I earned my way with silver polish, elbow grease, and a little salesman's charm. But pocket-change, I lacked. So, I further justified my free phone service: the more extravagant Nixon's phone bills grew, the less likely we'd have that in the White House a full four years. "Trixie, would you rather be a dead dog or Vice President Nixon?" So—for Jack Kennedy, really—I dialed directory assistance: Manila.

I requested the private number of a "Meadows Delman." Because I could. I felt half disappointed to find myself unlisted as a Filipino. We had been told that, the day after the election, especially if Nixon won, his phone police would come seeking us lawbreakers; this proved literally true. Only my having used an untraceable dorm pay phone saved me. But while I still had license to chat up anyone on earth, I found the Registrar of Employees for the City Government of Washington, D.C. (I'd always meant to, but couldn't while stuffing a pay phone with uncouth dimes and nickels; I couldn't while still sounding like a child.)

Just tracking down the Registrar took me nine bureaucratic follow-the-dot detective calls. I asked if he would put me in direct touch with a member of my family, please? Emergency. Death-in-the-family-type situation. Female, worker named Delman. She might've married and taken another name. I said we'd been out of touch too long, I said our family sure regretted that. (Was this in any way a lie?) The man explained just the one Delman was listed. First name: Naomi. That somehow felt right. "Clyde and Naomi," yes. I thanked the fellow, effusive while fighting to sound businesslike.

Though I was young, my voice had lately dropped. I now felt drunk with all the master-of-ceremonies power this gave me (if only by phone). I was also proud of my recent report card, pleased with the school's faith in my quiet orphaned poise.

Now, standing at the dorm pay phone, having "cut" Color Guard maneuvers to do this during office hours, glad for midday quiet from a dorm shower room dripping nearby, I imagined myself as some short espionage-youngster. Almost five feet one now, suave yet playful, irreverent if basically straight-A, "Name's Bond, Jim-my Bond." I imagined what pinstriped and paisleyed Sunday clothes Clyde would choose for my costume in this scene seeking him. Clearing my throat to find my voice's most male brown-velvet lowpoint, I dialed Naomi's work number.

I remember wishing I had urinated first. Too late. A woman's voice came right on line. Half husky, her gentle Piedmont accent still held: "Special Consumer Services: Licensing. Miss Delman, may I hep you?"

"Yes, please. I believe you have a brother named Clyde? Your mother is Sutie and lives in a house covered with this whole collage of beautiful signs, I believe?"

(I had once audited Twentieth Century Art Crosscurrents.) There followed the longest sort of pause. I could hear a distant water-cooler conversation; D.C. traffic; one metal file-drawer opened, then slammed.

"Who's this, really? Because I don't have a brother. We all got mothers. But my brother broke her heart. Visited her, made some kind of scene, never did drag back. Mom felt like he kept away over something she did to him or his brat. He quit even sending her the food boxes. It worried her to where she's dead. —Who is this?"

"Miss Naomi? It's the brat. Clyde's son, Meadows Delman. I'm thirteen almost. Aunt Naomi? You're my only kin. I've been looking and lookin. I'm mighty pleased to hear you. I live near you. When would be good for us to get together?"

There came a click. I refused it. I continued the conversation . . . just as I'd run skidding, Roadrunner-like, past the sight of Mom, legs up, beneath that bad man on our couch.

I twisted hard against enameled dorm wall, I pressed as with some wish to sit, recline, be held, burrow direct into the plaster. I told her dial tone: "I attend a school in northern Virginia. I can get into Northwest easy by bus. —Ma'am? Every other Friday they turn us loose. Would you consider maybe letting me buy you a nice lunch somewhere? Aunt Naomi? I already know where Dupont Circle is. We could meet there. The fountain. I have a letter I wrote Sutie. There's so much to tell you. To ask, I mean. See, what's awful . . . Clyde is dead. Gramma Sutie shouldn't blame herself. I'm sorry to call you about this at work and all. But I miss our Clyde to where I dream he's sitting in his car out in my school's annex parking lot. It's the far one, where our faculty with sailboats and campers leave those? And he's there all night looking at his watch. In the dream what's most important is my being tardy, not his being dead. But all I have to do is hike over there barefoot, wearing PJs. He died of a heart attack, we think. Or lungs, the lungs, too. He wasn't but forty-three. So, see, the only reason he stopped visiting his mom, yours, is because—right after I met Sutie?— Clyde got killed on the road. Died, I mean. That simple. Nobody's fault. I'm sorry about our Sutie. Please, ma'am, meet me just the once. We'd like each other. I'll be in the maroon uniform, I'm not that tall yet, okay? Clyde's still the best person ever. Please see me, Aunt Naomi. I need to know things. Our meeting'll go good. Because we're kin. Hello?"

When I think of my late father, I remember that first Bible verse he taught me. It contained the mystery: Father, Son, and Holy Ghost. I felt I understood the first two, having always before my eyes our own examples; but who could comprehend the spare tire of that invisible third party? Our necessary "Ghost"?

John 3:16 was one I never could get my head around, not while he still lived. It's the cornerstone passage Clyde kept trying to re-explain during our many Sunday missions. "For God so loved the world, that He gave his only begotten Son, that whosoever believeth in him should not perish, but have everlasting life."

At eight, I naturally believed this verse must be about me, us. It seemed to imply that true love requires a father's own sacrifice of his son and, in turn, the son's giving up the father, and incidentally each man's surrendering himself to save the other. It largely confused me at age twelve. And I admit, now half a century along, this passage as yet bewilders but still holds me.

Had my father saved my soul, any soul, so he might later gain his own? Or was Clyde Melvin Delman, Sr., just trading in a shanty life near swampland for something ever-so-slightly flashier uptown with pretty easy Gracie Meadows? Did my presence in his life help make things turn unexpectedly rewarding? Or was I why he got stuck?

(I've slowly come to guess, this very uncertainty might've been my dad's best possible legacy to me. Which tribe must be most mine? —Is either? Aren't both?)

Even dead, Clyde's attendance record outranked the living Grace's.

My school roommate snitched a pack of Marlboros during our class outing to a commercial pottery of no interest except its being in hiking distance. Gathered on our room's fire escape at 2 a.m., we would learn to seriously inhale. Three boys slouched out here wearing short pajamas, legs dangling down into the summer night. Cicadas now made such a racket we could talk at normal volume without fearing detection by tonight's duty master. My smooth Manhattan roommate produced his platinum lighter, a Tiffany one filched from his father. He lit up, inhaled with a comical sophistication, sent forking smoke-streams out both his nostrils, smiled glee at us over this effect, then burst into a fit of coughing complicated by his own pitiless laughing at himself.

Others, lighting theirs, faked a certain quirky clubiness as we idled outdoors on this rickety metal balcony. Our mismatching PJs were still covered with images of ball-club pennants, Indian canoes, duck decoys. But, armed with cigarettes and a platinum flame-thrower, we lounged squinting like a cell of worldly undercover agents.

The lighter, cool to the touch, was finally passed my way. I'd had much experience watching Dad puff. I'd fired up at least a few weeds for him. Now, to impress the others, I beat the lighter against one upturned palm (a gesture whose purpose remained obscure but whose authority, learned from Clyde, produced exactly the silent steely-eyed male respect I'd hoped). Having tamped the pack, I flipped out one

weed, cracked our lighter open, and flame . . . but the damned cigarette wouldn't light.

Soon others got involved. "Maybe it's a dud one," my roomie suggested. So, in the manner of "Take a card, any card," I urged my friend
to choose the next. Again I tried igniting it. It might've been made of
marble.

On attempt number three, just as others bent around this (for
boys) intriguing problem, combining as it did physics, pyromania,
and addiction, our fire escape—loaded with so much squirmy boy-
weight—gave one cranking drop. A single wall-mounted bolt jerked
loose and commenced spilling all its mortar's powder. So fast, we
scrambled through that open window!

My best friend would mention it for weeks: something's preventing
me from lighting a regular flammable cig. He said he wanted to try it
all again. Would my weed go out if he lit the thing, then passed it to
me? But, by dawn, that pack was all smoked up. And I had been . . .
prevented.

The morning after, I woke, hands locked behind head, feeling oddly
wonderful. I seemed to be reflecting on a visit Dad had made to
school. I somehow knew, and via some way of knowing tucked far in,
that Clyde's lungs, not just his heart, had fatally failed him. Understanding this (but how?), I found myself gladly volunteering, as in a
promise offered someone eternal, never, ever to smoke. If it'd please
him, dear me, no. And I've always kept my word.

As with a blind boy trusting his painted stick to find the world while
putting it on notice, classical languages somehow led me back to
Clyde. But so slowly. A maze built like a crossword puzzle, it seemed an
unlikely way to find your missing traveling salesman. But Latin then
Greek came to seem some form of string-and-tin-can code we'd
always held in common. Stretched taut, if by a filament, it daily
linked us. After nine months' work, I felt certain barricades lift. After
two full years, partitions dividing Scotch-Irish-English from some
imagined lyrical African-American language gave way. Unlikenesses
between Europe and Africa could be posited, their differences split,
between and among these ancient languages. I don't expect this to
make much logical sense—beyond a child's own faulty absolutist logic.

These languages were generally considered dead. So was my Clyde. And yet . . . Fellow cadets watched my progress with a certain sneering pity. Scrawled across one bathroom partition: "Latin killed the Romans and Now it's killing Us, except that little grind Meadows!" So be it.

"Enter into his courts with singing and know ye that the Lord He is God. It is He who hath made us. . . ." Somewhere Latin squired me gently back into the gong-ringing Old Testament of an imagined Africa, into the sweetness, the cymbal-chime purity, of Clyde's own spot-on company. He still sometimes made me laugh at unjokes I couldn't repeat or even quite recollect. I kept bumping into my father while eavesdropping on the school's black staffers. His weakness for haberdasher curlicues lurked fanning within countryside smells. He winked through certain birdsongs shaped like cufflinks. A born listener now, all eyes, I'd become such a silent child. Without Clyde alive as my sidekick, I found I was really not a funny person at all! Ollie without Stan? Pathetic, fat, certifiable. There's no such thing as half a marriage, is there?

Once, out walking the single Appalachian mountain our school part-owned, I hopped a cool stream, felt watched. And there, conscious in the shallows, one huge black catfish, all mouth and whisker, both knob eyes strenuous, aimed at me. The lips were speckled whitish, birthmarked. It was the mask of Comedy, charcoal-dark, given fins. It appeared aggrieved toward some necessary Wit. I recognized Clyde at once and laughed, pointing. But when (with the short attention span of the dead) he swam away and left me deserted in the air, I felt undone, un-gilled, doubly abandoned.

Only in my second year at school did I finally let myself recall details of our long Sunday jaunts. They respelled themselves in a million little seeds, like Verna's Passion "scenes." I remembered how I'd once asked Clyde whether Jesus spoke English. Dad's unscholarly, endearing, nearly metaphysical answer? "Not at first." *Adorable man!*

That order seemed to apply now, in reverse, to my own linguistic progress. Psalms' syllables with Packard stats, English now shrank to seeming oddly simpler. If it was plain Monopoly, Latin felt like contract bridge. Bid and nuance, you needed to recall your own most recent cunning move. Asked to translate in class, I saw how one full page of English yielded a mere half-page of Latin. This concision, so like the distillation of great poets, seemed as close as I would ever come to being a real artist. I recalled, with surprising fondness, my mother's vanity tabletop, its litter of old family photos and half-full perfume bottles. Once, holding a tiny costly vial of amber under my nose, Grace smiled her full-frontal charm: "Meadows, somehow they fit two whole acres of wildflowers in here!"

I lived busy with reduction and detection, still in pursuit of Dad's gate-opening greeting for his ghosty Redeemer wearing robes. By my third year, I had the Hebrew. I even had its idiomatic Rabbinic form. I now knew the exact pronunciation for teaching Clyde the face-saving greeting his Saviour would best know, most love:

I belong to you, O Lord, sir.

Clyde had been my founder. But by the time I left school my teacher, the Headmaster's young wife, was his cosponsor—I mean my own. And they both might have said of my young mind what Augustus stated about Rome itself:

"I inherited a village of brick. I left it a city of marble."

IV.

I was in Washington to attend a Smithsonian preview. The exhibit offered certain wonderful artifacts from Monticello. Some Jeffersonia from my old school's collection would be shown—his handwritten garden ledger for three seasons' vegetables. My first suave roommate, now a chain-smoking actor, was staying with people he knew. They owned a revamped townhouse in Adams-Morgan and, heading to meet him for the opening, I decided to stroll over early.

Wearing my blue blazer and usual dull-gray slacks, I soon wondered about my safety on this street. I passed rough, then worse-looking beggars, latent cutpurses all asking me for two dollars or more. Three weeks earlier, a young white government worker had left a local Jeep dealership in his red Cherokee. The vehicle was so new, stickers yet gummed its back window. At a stopsign, two armed kids jumped in. The carjacking was discovered only when the owner's body was found burned in a weedy field out past Alexandria. Street names began to sound more happily familiar as I struck a brisker pace toward the house where my pal stayed. I felt followed, edgy.

My memory was not what it'd been (even though I'd then edged only just past forty). I found I had left the written address back at my hotel. No problem. Either 316 or 306. I'd check both. At 316, as I bent to peruse the names beside the buzzers, Event and Sensation overlapped. Like the moment of Dad's Packard's crash when a road sign predicting a deer then offered three of them and let me see my father's racial history in an illuminating bash that adrenaline briefly loaned, today I received this sequence:

(1) The black plastic nametag hand-pressed with rough white lettering announced "Apt 2-B, Naomi S. Delman," as behind me (2) a deep male voice asked, "Delman?" and (3) when I turned to find a young black grocery-delivery boy holding two bags, one sprouting celery stalks, as I honestly barked, "Yes" (already hoping to sneak groceries upstairs toward my aunt), beyond this kid waiting on the steps, I saw—advancing toward me—(4) Clyde. As (5) a handsome old woman moving right along.

She leaned on an oak cane. She squinted up here at me. I fished a fiver from my pocket. I palmed it toward the kid, who thanked me as he all but hurled two bags my way. Leaving, he posed—prepared to hold open the metal gate. Then, seeing how slow the old lady really was, he let it slam, lurched back off to the right.

Her pace gave me time to stare with greedy happiness while planning not to plan too much. Seeing her walking stick, gauging the weight of these bags' canned goods, I just hoped to get upstairs.

2-B. Or not 2-B. At least at last I'd seen her.

She advanced with the labored stalwart posture of some aged Baptist-church deaconess. —From thirty feet, I saw the habit of rectitude, the personal tidiness of a retired chief librarian. She might've been part Cherokee, her hair still dark, yanked back with card-catalogue factuality then filed simply behind her skull, "a place for everything. . . ."

Though Naomi dragged toward this gated yard, though you sensed she'd overspent her energy and gasped a bit, she still showed the hatchet certainty of somebody once considered fairly handsome. I recalled a paley pretty girl shown wearing her white graduation cap beside Sutie's bed. But the old woman I now confronted looked too much like her departed brother to have ever been quite "attractive." Time had turned her far more toward Clyde, his odd lank certainty, the angular dubious knottedness. I could've picked her out of a vast crowd as his kin, mine.

Is anything more intriguing than family resemblance? Especially, of course, one's own? Her mouth was overlarge. She'd started calling my way à la Dewey decimal system. "Delman? Groceries for? Com-ing." I thought, on seeing her up closer, "She looks like Eleanor Roosevelt." So had Clyde! Too broad a mouth, yet kinder for that. Eyes sad, though easily distracted. She resembled Eleanor right down to a club-lady-like jacketed green suit, its skirt overlong.

As Naomi took hold of the stoop's banister, I—slouched up here trying to act "casual"—decided I was overdressed for a delivery boy. So I lifted the celeried bag, hid my striped tie. She called, "They promised me you'd be here later, but no matter today. Slow as I've gotten, though, in future be sure and turn up when they tell me. Understood?" "Yes, ma'am," I sounded (and now felt) so Southern.

"Person can't be waiting around out here in the open anymore." She reached for a handbag. "Not with our young ones gone this mean. How'd they turn so bad so quick, I'd like to know. We'd best take the little elevator, if you can stand to wait. A poky thing, but no pokier than me now." I said I'd walk, meet her up one landing.

"You must be younger than you look." Out came a flick of the edge I had expected. On the stairs, clear of her sight, I shed my tie and, for good measure, half-mussed my hair. I stood waiting as her coffin-sized portholed elevator, lino-lined, cranked to a rattling halt. Much fuss with her purse, then keys. I saw Naomi wore her suit jacket overtop the shoulder bag's strap. She noted my taking this in. "Broke my best girlfriend's hip and got her Social Security and the pocketbook. Either/or, I say. They'd just as soon kill you as look at you round here . . . and I'm talking homeboys."

. . .

She pointed me toward her galley kitchen. Its smell bespoke left-over meatloaf, new playing cards, every kind of Tupperware, one very clean old lady. A large studio, much sunlight, forties furniture. I scanned her many framed photos hoping for familiar faces. Instead, I found groups of G-5 picnickers, Rock Creek outings; official events, good-lookers, pale-skinned "Negro" professionals lined in half-smiling rows, all wearing office clothes even during leisure hours. They seemed tired of being credits to their race twenty-four hours a friggin day. But not a snapshot of Sutie, much less Clyde.

As she unjacketed herself to free the purse and find a tip, I spied above her tan foldout couch (Naomi sleeps here? it's just a studio?), among her diplomas from high school to Howard, beside an ugly beaten-copper 1950s plaque of some long-necked Nubian princess, one certificate frame holding six four-leaf clovers.

How to do this? Ease into it? She, cane first, stumped toward me. I slid my hand inches under hers. Two quarters fell. "Not enough, hunh . . ." She scanned my face.

"No, fine," I said. "Fine, if you'll let me practice on you. Do you believe some people are psychic? Cause, I'm taking a course in that."

"Where, Georgetown? I bet. —'Psychic'? Idn't that just another word for 'nosy'?"

"For instance, Miss Delman, ma'am, I look at you and what I get . . ." Between a thumb and index finger, I press my nose's bridge as if to judge the scale of some incoming migraine. "For you, I get 'a cabin covered in beautiful tin ads, the four-leaf clovers growing all along that creek.' —Now, I mean, why is that?"

Her face revealed nothing except the will to reveal even less. Then, in a deed that made me think so damn much of Clyde, she reached into her purse and handed me thirty extra cents. Exactly my Sunday "chauffeur's" salary.

"May I sit a minute?" Laughing, I sat. "It's been psychic deliveries all day. The weight, it wears on a person." I felt either sick or euphoric, both. Up this close, she looked so like my dad. I gouged my thumbnail into my forefinger to prevent simply reaching out her way.

Cold, she said, "How'd you do that? What else you got up your . . . wherever you keep such bullhockey? Give me my full eighty cent worth now. And where'd your stripedy tie go? And why'd you bribe that boy, make him leave my stuff with you?"

"Shift-change. Mother named Sutie. I see no father, but one loving, complicated sibling. . . ."

By now, with stately effort and a skillful use of cane as fireman's pole, Aunt Naomi had lowered herself into a brown wing chair opposite my couch.

"Oh, I get it. You with the Publishers Clearinghouse, right. Well, it's about time, many *Ebony*s as I've toted up those stairs. —A suit jacket on a bagboy? I don't think so."

We sat awhile. Till I sensed how long she had been knowing. "You Clyde's so-called son, right? The finishing-school brat grown up and already run to seed. Think you're real slick, finally getting in here like this."

"One hundred percent a happy accident. Thanks to the long arm of our Clyde. The man's still got such powers! I was looking for the Mendelsons at 306 or 316. Just happened to read your name, the rest fell into place. I call it fated."

"Call it trespassing." I saw her staring at a black rotary phone twelve long feet across the room. Her hands closed tighter round that latent cudgel, her oak cane. Next door, a TV soap opera gossiped about itself.

"I don't want your purse. Instead, ma'am, I'll let *you* be psychic. Any tips or questions, now we're face to face? I still love your brother more than anybody ever, my wife included. He might've acted unfair, but you should know what he did with all that energy. He saved my soul so many times over. His great joy, ours really, was replacing Bibles stolen from motels."

"Believe I'm gonna to weep here. He sold us way downriver. No sane person's likely to forgive that, sonny."

We just kept looking at each other. I felt avid for the simple feeding sight of her. Naomi Delman's top lip curled up off her very large if well-formed teeth, a smiling snarl too eloquent to ever try outarguing. "Well," I said and stood. "Thank you. You're still an extremely handsome woman, and mighty self-possessed. You sure remind me of your mother. And of him, though he got none of your looks, poor thing."

The way Naomi glowered, I expected her to throw something.

"You got his voice," she said, almost grudging.

"Beg pardon?"

"Maybe you just picked it up, from hearing him first thing of anybody. But the swing of it. That's Clyde okay."

"Thank you," I said. "There's been some confusion," I said. "I always felt," I said, "his. Really his," I said. "And genetically, I mean. Despite my coloring. I still just know I'm literally Clyde's, despite my mother's . . . popularity."

"Yeah, we heard tell she was quite the whore. Soldiers, anybody." Hands on the head of her cane, Naomi sat straighter. I remembered her blind mom snatching me so hard I bit my lip bloody. Miss Delman had already given away more than she'd intended. Her generous mouth now set itself, pursed.

She followed my eyes above her couch. I studied the group of pictures. Beside those ancient four-leaf clovers, a framed needlepoint, signed with her own stitched initials. Its large Legend: JOHN 3:16.

I imagined Sutie drilling this verse into Aunt Naomi. "Clyde's favorite, too," I said, lame. And she at once began, "For Blacks so loved the Whites, they gave up their only begotten souls, that whosoever believeth in Whites shall not perish, but, come Christmas, get a card with maybe a twenty stuck in it."

"It's tougher and deeper than that and you know it. I'm here, you're here. . . . Clyde would be disappointed we had this chance and blew it. —Is being black really so different?"

A stupid question but a question. With her headswing came one guttural groan: "Like Satchmo told the white man wondering what Jazz is, 'If you gots to ask, you'll never know.' Clyde thought it was different sufficient to where he quit his own folks cold, without much fight. Borrowed a truck to take Momma and me to the July Fourth thing in Norlina. Whites hung out on one side the square, and Sutie and our friends the other. There were bands, fireworks. Right off, Clyde gets greeted by the white salesboy from Epstein's Men's Wear. Was the place Clyde hung around staring in their window at all the bright vests and suspenders. That fellow was a real gladhander, owned a Packard he kept parked out front the store. We came from so far into the country, that joker didn't know what was what with us. Soon as he calls Brother's name, Clyde peels right off from nappy us, oh yeah. We could see him off over there, playing the fool for the rich kids. Acting out his jokes, those big hands and that bump head. Bojangles, but the other color. —After bout an hour, Clyde wanders over to buy him some popcorn. The refreshment stand was halfway between, catching sales from both groups, see. Clyde knows he's being watched by his fancy new white friends. So he eats popcorn while facing off from Momma and me. Talking out one side his mouth, he says, 'They got a party, after. They ain't about to ax me twice. Here, gal, you drive Momma home.' And throws me the keys. I was thirteen. That truck had gears to it. Took us two hours' jerking to get half back down the road. Leaving us, he hands me such popcorn as he hadn't eaten. I remember watching my brother walk clean across that square, his back to us, white shirt, red suspenders. Seemed like it took forever. Beside me on the courthouse steps, I could hear Sutie crying. I didn't want to look. —And you thinking I care how you feel now? Oh sure, he'd later send a fifty in some envelope. Food packages—but mostly the kind with bows on top. Nosir, the second that chump-clown figured his race ran more to 'Ugly' than to 'Colored,' why, he just up and ditched us. Drowned-rat nasty-looking as he was, people paid that so much attention, he could someway 'pass.' (I never understood it. To me, he always looked like what he was, but, then, that's family for you.) Sure, he felt bad once he'd give us all the slip. But his fun and those pimp clothes, was them always came first. Had quite an eye for the gals, pitiful. Man never liked to stop laughing long, real knee-slapper. Coming up, I had to borrow my cousin's shoes to walk to school. I got to use 'em two days a week, she had them the other three. Know my nickname at the schoolhouse? 'Tuesday Thursday.' 'Here come Miss Tuesday Thursday Nappy Head.' And I still graduated. He dead, you say? That seem bout right. Don't you ever be comin round me, heah?" She lifted her cane, shook it once, set it down with a knock.

"Well . . ." I stepped toward the door. I half-hoped to be called back. Otherwise, when would I ever see her again? And she looked so much like him, sitting there sad. "You're not going to send me off," I told her. "We'd both regret it. There's too much history. I was brought here to find something out. Or get a kind of blessing from you. Please? It'd mainly be for Clyde."

She looked straight ahead.

"I'll leave a business card. Ma'am? You feel way more mine than my own mother. Don't make me go. I could help you around here. I could help."

"Get on out now, boy. You came hoping to find you're bettern you are. But—son?—you didn't deserve even him. Go back to Hell where you all came from. Any idea what you costs us? You ain't a thing but white."

V.

After my Falls reunion's farewell banquet-dance, I watched a hundred matched-up classmates wander half plotzed to station wagons rigged with child-seats. They all moved, linked romantically arm in arm, maybe feeling, as I did at 2 a.m., about eighteen. Weren't they destined, if ever again, to make love (foreplay and all) tonight?

I found myself alone. On foot, weaving thanks to drink, I was aware of being so richly unaccompanied, an "only-child" feeling like the only white child ever born to a black man, feeling "only," aiming vague toward my downtown hotel (formerly the Bank).

I took my time. Nobody except the Pay-for-Play soft-core "Adult Channel" waited in Room 306. After two blocks, I thought I heard, just half a block behind me, springy footsteps, taps pinging the toes of shoes. —In the manner of noir movies, I kept stopping, a trick . . . to catch . . . the sounds . . . of someone tailing me. I convinced myself— with help from our reunion's generic-brand gin—that the spiffy, almost tap-dance cadence in arrears of me must mean my own departed father's resurrected steps.

Caught up in a drama only partly self-invented, I dodged into the doorway of a defunct pawnshop. Scanning my recent route, I heard three more tentative footfalls slow then, coyly, halt. I saw absolutely no one.

Falls, like most small American towns, has gone all soft and moribund downtown. Everything alive's leached westward toward the malls. Baby Africa, once homemade, unpainted, and organically pleasing as a set of mud daubers' nests, now stands disfigured by low-cost cinder-block housing. Units uninterested in charm, incapable of coziness, as prisons are.

Now, a little drunk, feeling fully blessedly anonymous, I permitted myself the luxury of simply going with this, whatever—this pursuit. A bit of 2 a.m. staggering wouldn't hurt a living soul. And if Clyde did stalk me, my show of willingness would surely draw him closer. That's all I hoped. To lure him. Wouldn't it help if he found his Bible copilot somewhat fallen? Me, all too mortal, fully grown, no longer the priggish teetotaling little boy Clyde had somehow decided to go ahead and love.

In such a heightened state, as I wandered past abandoned storefronts, they looked like 1840. I don't know why—in the eerie orange glow from Falls's new futuristic streetlamps—I noticed one particular window. But, breathless with the footsteps' odd pursuit, a bit achy from tonight's overly athletic rock-and-roll dancing meant to show everyone how hip and spry I'd remained, I pressed one hand against plate glass, steadying myself.

Here, displayed among bits of fallen pink fiberglass wool, still improbably vertical before a scrap of pegboard dropped from some lowered interior roof, one filthy figurine stood.

She yet wore a sling, a truss quite perfectly miniaturized. Wedged under one arm, the tiny oak crutch angled just so. Her neck brace looked squirrel-suitable. This small goddess's temple had crumbled around her. But all the 1950s gear dedicated to keeping "Blanche" standing had somehow left her—these several decades later—miraculously upright. An inspiration still.

Thousands of days of sun had turned her pinky skin to a surface tan, then charbroiled gray, then on toward chalky black-brown. Her hair had once been painted yellow marcelled waves. That tone had whitened toward seeming some old, pallid rubber swimming cap. Her eyes cast upward with a long-suffering mulish patience. Blanche still helplessly presented herself—a devotional figure in this deserted yet monitoring little town.

And I—drunk from four atypical "what the hell" martinis, feeling overwhelmed with years of thwarted postponed sentiment, too aware of being back here and unhappily haunted two blocks from Janine's former American Grill, not sure yet if I were technically a white man or a black one, as unwilling as my dad to surrender either option— now mashed both palms against Blanche's greasy glass. With no kind woman waiting at the hotel, I was somehow going down before her. On my knees, on the sidewalk, I stooped before our poor, dear mascot—mercilessly immortal. No one now strolled Main. Not a car moved. No tricky footsteps sounded now. —This far from the two decent malls, who'd care, who'd notice me?

I knelt, in penance, mock-defeat. And yet, hands joined in some mimed prayer only half comic, I gazed up and in at her. I understood why Falls had given her that name. From the start, Blanche had stood right here in plain view, fading, blanching clear to the shade of tar.

And I let myself, sloshed, hoping unsuccessfully for Dad, practice— if silently—those actual Hebrew words the guy should use to eventually enter Paradise. Might not Clyde, on tiptoe nearby, overhear me? Shouldn't he finally benefit from my education that'd cost him dearly? I mimed his passwords to a platinum doll our holy sun had worshiped for so many bright decades, it had loved her black.

I called through filthy glass, "Forgive us, Blanche."

VI.

. . . no man ever yet hated his own flesh; but nourisheth and cherisheth it, even as the Lord the church.

Ephesians 5:29

For longer than I can believe now, I've taught Latin, Greek, and literature. I'm presently Dean in Charge of Admissions at a fine undergraduate women's college here in New Hampshire. My beautiful, somehow teenaged, daughters now spend more than half their college vacations with my ex-wife and her doctor husband. Preparing for those weeks when my girls turn up, I've rented a farmhouse, one big sunny bedroom for each of them. While my daughters are away at school or are staying at Bethany's upstate, I can at least stroll into their quarters; I can sit on either ruffled four-poster, can look around at their pictures, their makeup, their stray sheet music. During such solitary Sunday afternoons, I feel (at least) the curator of the Small Museum to Deirdre and Sara. It is, incidentally, a Museum to Fatherhood. I feel close to my girls' cultural claptrap, even their stash of female products large enough to stanch the Israeli Ladies Army Corps. Each colorful sock drawer reassures.

Like Clyde, when it came time to marry I fell in love with Beauty. As with him, it did not end happily. But maybe there's been at least some minor class progression? I mean, Clyde Melvin Delman's wife went after a cow doctor, whereas mine proved serially unfaithful with her own highly respected, world-renowned gynecologist. Small steps. Stirrups. Boot straps. Whatever.

Just prior to the divorce, Bethany, Deirdre and Sara, and I were headed south on that single requisite American middle-class trip to Disney World. Walt's first park was called a "Land"; his second, "World"; Christ knows what's next.

I didn't want my daughters someday saying I'd been too much a penny-pinching egghead to have granted them this flashy, trashy experience. (I'm convinced the Disney organization trains schoolkids to perfect this tacit threat.) I checked the map. I found I could probably drive a leased car from Orlando to Boca. I said "Uh-oh" aloud.

My frustrating surprise meeting with Aunt Naomi, the sound of some phantom's two-toned shoes, all these urged me on toward Grace Meadows of the Castalia Meadows clan. To judge from legwork, from my continuing detective fantasies, I struggled harder to find my black kin than to accept the white ones. If I now felt some duty toward my girls, there was also a long-standing embarrassment before my wife of fifteen years. Bethany had never once laid eyes on Grace. I might pretend to be some waif out of Dickens, but my natural mother did still live and breathe, if within arduous driving distance.

I remembered Doc Dix calling me "you little mongrel bastard." True as that'd likely proved, I told my therapist (the seventh) that by shunning Mom I might be avoiding the single living, legitimate (or illegitimate) member of my small, short-lived tribe. In the end, I didn't care to be known as a grievance lister and professional orphan.

Besides, by now, hadn't some statute of limitations passed? Part of me, of course, still hoped Grace would turn up for our Florida meeting very drunk, half dressed, decidedly blowsy. My worst fear was—she wouldn't! I longed to turn, at last, toward my real family, my smart wife and our bright, versatile girls, to say at last, "You see? What kind of person could've done such things, and to her only child?"

.   .   .

I understood how my lunging in on Grace, mid-act, April 15th, 1956, spread-eagle on that rose-patterned couch, an entrance singularly unexpected even after my breaking open the screen door—I knew how that at once reversed her own young life along with mine, and his. I knew I'd razed at least one vestibule of her long lifespan. Still, I could never quite forgive Grace's "dropping me." And at the ripe old age of eight. As an adult, as a teacher, as a parent myself, I still (monthly if not weekly, daily) find her behavior toward me perplexing and quietly, steadily damaging. It's easy to say one should throw all such toxic cargo overboard. But actually doing that is something of a bitch.

Sure, I knew that being sent away to school had probably "been the making of me." Would I otherwise have given myself so wholly to my kids, my serious teaching, my passionate if obscure scholarly pursuits? All this sprang from just such early abandonment. Even my undying tie with Clyde developed during our Sunday banishments, exits that her public love affair forced upon us. I'd been lucky, if not in my biology, then in at least my mentors. . . . So—shouldn't I just go ahead at last and thank Grace Delman for whatever I had—even accidentally—achieved?

My wife forever urged me to phone "poor Grace." At least to reciprocate Mom's most recent birthday gift and Christmas card. "Meadows, she can't be that bad." I gave my cool thin history-major Bethany such a silent tantrum of a look. "I mean," she tried to justify her goading, "she is your mother. No matter who your literal father was. If you ever bothered to carry anybody around for nine months slung directly over your bladder, you'd see how said carrier might expect that parcel to bother phoning her every three to four decades. You're always telling your students how short human history really is. Well, the old crow won't be alive forever. She was probably just a kid then. You lug it all around, Meadows. She didn't directly kill your dad. You're maybe afraid you did. But you'd probably prefer to blame her for another forty years. Here Endeth the Bethany Lesson. But, then, how many times before have you ignored my saying this?"

I gave my wife a single paint-blistering stare. Sullen, it said, "You, the by-product of orthodontia and dressage, you, grown up in total love, cannot know all I lost at eight." I then walked direct into my study. I yanked out the envelope from Grace's last, costly, gilded, tasteless Christmas card. I'd saved it, just in case.

Across the envelope's upper left, a phone number had been jotted in red ink under the words: "New for now." I calculated it'd been six months since Mother mailed this. So which had won? Grace's "new" or her "now"?

After twenty power breaths, I dialed from the kitchen extension so Bethany might overhear. I wanted my darling nearby; she intuitively understood all this; she now decided to make coffee, though lately neither of us could safely drink caffeine after 3 p.m. I felt singularly lonely finally ringing up my mom. I calculated it'd been eighteen years since last I heard her voice.

As I took in extra oxygen before punching a final digit, the scent of fresh-ground coffee somehow helped. Bethany then swung a Jack Daniel's and water before my face, ice clinking. Her rosy hand held it there, ringing like some baby Liberty Bell. (If she had not run off three months later to Oaxaca with her gynecologist after seven secret years of weekly checkups under him, I swear I'd still be with her.)

"Pelican Manor Marina. Larry from Security. What?"

I asked for Grace (had to turn over the envelope to learn the most recent of her married names). Doing so, being this jumpy, I spilled half the needed drink. My wife laughed behind me. Well, Larry said, he didn't usually go and fetch owners, but this once he'd maybe go for Grace, since it was Grace, yeah, he'd drag off and bring her clear back here to the phone, he guessed, but this single time only, understood? And I'd just have to wait and pay the charges, no matter where I was calling from. "And someway, mister, you just sound long distance."

"You have no idea," I told this Larry. But he'd already set down the receiver. I now had time to picture him, then her. I imagined a blond-haired Grace, made up like Kim Novak in the second half of *Vertigo*, down by the seaside selling crab burgers. She'd be wearing some paper cap tipped at a sailorish angle, hawking burgers off a rolling dockside cart. Beneath her striped French patio umbrella, Grace would be flirting with half-nude surfer-boys my daughters' age, and all while Grace tried to ignore the dozen pelicans gathered, barking, unmannerly, expecting handouts. Even among birdlife, word had leaked out: my mom was "easy."

Behind me, Bethany hummed so I'd feel accompanied, filling dead phone airtime. I could plainly hear some Florida AM radio, one of those scary right-wing call-in shows. "Is it just me, Ed, or is the International Communist Jewish Media Banking Cartel gettin stronger every day, Ed? . . ." I was also privileged, during the six endless minutes I waited, to eavesdrop on snatches of three men's listless conversation. They spoke of one mighty big fish, their catching it. Voices cracked, they sounded like old-timers. They debated whether they should have released their monster before the official photographer's boat got to them. Some guy recalled how he'd brought on board one of those disposable yellow cameras, but it'd somehow plopped into his beer cooler and no pictures turned out and, wouldn't you just know, the one time you really truly needed proof to win a goddamn trophy plus get on the six o'clock news!

"What?," it was my wife, now miming interest, face to face across the kitchen counter. I gave her my eye-rolling, exasperated, Ollie Hardy, you-won't-believe-this ask-me-later look. But I did appreciate her concern and hovering. Marriage has its moments; odd, I recall Bethany's hanging around while I awaited Mom as one of our marriage's finest.

"Welcome to the Nuthouse. Grace, Proprietor. Dennis, that you? Because everybody's waiting on deck, still rumless. You fall in or what?" It was a woman's voice but dropped an octave deeper than my own and considerably more porcelain-crackled. (I heard a full-fledged local "character.")

She still sounded perky, oddly girlish, if several steps nearer bass. Had Grace finally taken up smoking? That'd been the only vice she'd missed.

"Dennis? Cat got your tongue? Or the pussy or what?" (I could hear old-timers yuk at this; I pictured Grace's snappy collusive wink.) "And if you bring your usual cut-rate brand, you're not gettin aboard. Meyer's Dark or nothin, Dennie."

"This is actually Meadows." There came a pause. I resisted adding a last name; I resisted restating, out of respect for her time-battered neurons, my actual biological relation to this old whore.

Then I realized, after eighteen years, "Actually Meadows" might sound (especially to someone with the DTs and awaiting her rum) as illogical as "Pelican Manor."

But Grace replied at once: "Well, 'll be damned. An answered prayer for sure. And here I'm talkin m' party talk. You finally followin the sun south, son? —Because, do. Because, *this* Buck has quite a boat."

(Of any sentence in my life's account, the last one, hers, verbatim, is my favorite, I must say. I'll give the old girl that.)

"Grace, I actually was calling about maybe visiting. Given Disney World's location and our girls' ages, and my duty to get them there at least once before college, my family will soon be in your 'neighb.' " I cringed at this locution. Plus, I'd also just said "actually" twice. I feared I sounded like the fussy Northeasterner I had perhaps become. Almost at once, the old woman's voice said, "Great." Then, maybe addressing the gathered fisherfolk so enjoying our phone reunion, she announced, "My long lost son's comin!" Next Grace added what my wife later guessed to be a favorite Cajun French phrase meaning, "Let the good times roll."

Bethany slid a pen before me. I jotted on the Christmas-card envelope. Mother provided surprisingly cogent directions from Orlando. She added how, on "the day of," I'd need to summon her right to this gatehouse. I'd best use the name of Buck's boat. Ordinarily I could phone it direct. But the last trip out, during a sort of party, their cell phone had fallen in, was a long story. But Larry here, see, Larry wouldn't budge from using the boats' names only. He couldn't be bothered with lists of all those owner-occupants.

"Whatever," I told my mother. "I've got my pen poised. What's his boat called? Your boat."

"You'll laugh. Big professor and all like you. Promise you won't laugh, no matter how stupid it's gonna sound to a tweedy Princeton snob like you."

"I didn't go to Princeton. Or have you forgotten? Their silver-

polishing scholarships had all been taken. Look . . ." I grew abruptly
enraged. I stood up from my kitchen stool. Bethany, behind me,
touched my upper back—not knowing what'd happened, and yet
knowing—stroking my neck in the way one cunning, controlled
human will try to soothe some stupid, volatile, and surging larger animal. I mean: here I'd tracked my mother down after years of abandonment, and she wouldn't even tell me . . .

"Okay okay . . . ," she relented. "Sheesh. You never did have all that
hot of a sense of humor, ya know? I seem to remember your timing
also left little something to be desired. But ready to copy? Thing's
named: *More Trouble Than It's Worth II.* —You all right with that?"

And she laughed, hard. She laughed until she coughed the way
Clyde used to, sliding from forgetful mirth to overmindful mortality.
And finding even that funny. I listened to her croupy cackling. I
waited for her breath's ballast to right itself.

I snorted at the name, then asked, "May I be mirthful?"

"Thought you'd never ask," she said. "Been wishing for a little
lightness out of you for absolute ages. Glad to hear some now. Guess
you were just born serious. Never knew where you got that from. . . ."

"Well, if you don't know, maybe a phone directory might come in
handy. . . ." From across the room my wife was giving me the football
time-out signal.

"Whoosh . . . ," Grace said to me and her Florida audience, "fasten
yer life preservers, boys, we're in for a bumpy sail real soon. And, hey,
Meadows, know what? I'm up for it. I don't claim to've been yer aver-
age Apple Pie Mom. But sounds like you turned out okay. Not that I'm
taking much of any credit, mind you. Still . . . Yeah, come on down
with your girls and wife. Oh, I read the papers. I know you have them.
And I'm ready for you. Always have been. It's you weren't ready
for me."

"Yeah, well, I was one of the few in town. . . ."

Why was I blurting these things? It wasn't really like me. My wife
snatched the receiver. "Mrs. Delman? Well, 'Grace' then, thanks.
We're so excited, the girls and I are, about finally meeting you. Too
much time has passed . . . and Meadows is beside himself with antici-
pation. . . . Right, but he's a sweetie underneath. Sometimes way
under. Soon, then . . . Great. Your boy's a good man, a wonderful dad,

if occasionally somewhat temperamental. You've no idea where he gets that, do you?"

As they chatted and chatted then laughed, I had to leave the house.

I told myself, "Look for the silver lining: you now have something worse to dread than Disney World." I loathed the notion of flying south to some Magic Kingdom, paying its inflated monopolistic rates.

By now, my mother's name, if I've kept even the vaguest scholarly track, runs: "Grace Meadows Delman Greer Wrightman Goldblatt Wrightman Koope." She had married, as I said, two Bucks. One twice. I dislike repeating myself. But some things, no matter how often you say them, you still cannot quite register.

In the tradition of little colleges like ours, the yearbook always dedicates its latest volume. Process of elimination, this one they offered me. The page in question shows a large formal portrait and a smaller "casual": me on campus wearing my bagged-out cardigan, pausing beneath our founder's statue, and surrounded by laughing girl students. One has on saddle shoes; and that confused me as to dates. But girls' particular faces soon came back. And of course, I consulted the picture's inevitable clock—how much hair I had at the time. Girls' chuckling over my joke looks wonderfully like wincing. I'd probably offered some play on words of the sort I believe stimulates undergrads into thinking of language as a joyful present-tense game with one long rich history. True, such puns usually yield only slit-eyed groans. But I'll accept it.

I have always taken teaching seriously. I enjoyed such brilliant early sponsorship myself. I still seem able to feel some absolute identification with my own children and those of others. Few tenured professors prefer teaching Freshmen. The administration loves me for this, bullying colleagues with my example. But I just like the young ones.

Students turn up here away from home for the first time, looking exactly as unmoored as tentatively optimistic. They're seeking some stray starter compliment, a single corner's random warmth. I've seen whole generations arrive fox-faced and forlorn, carrying their cardboard boxes stuffed with CDs, T-shirts, huge blooming begonias. Kids look nearly as lonely as I remember feeling on the train to school once my father died. Air chafes around them. They worry that a single incoming zit beside their nose will ruin everything. And you know? One decent adult can really help.

I have taught at this college for—what?—twenty-four years now. I may seem to be boasting here and I don't want to (Clyde would not approve). But maybe you'll see how my quoting from the annual's dedication refers far more to Dad than to me.

Since my first great loss, I have been spared so much. For a life that opened with such violence and grief, with certain terrible sights, mine has proved oddly lucky.

The *Paradigm* citation reads:

We offer this year's book to Professor C. Meadows Delman. A gent and scholar, he has long been famous for his bad puns but good company. Maybe he is best known for his ever-popular "Bible as Literature" class. We call him "Meadows," as he told us all to call him from Day One. There are his intellectual insights and several published books. There are his linguistic gifts and communicated love of letters. But past that he has dedicated his life to a calling even larger.

Yes, he's served as our freshman-studies adviser. He's been our round-the-clock shoulder to cry on. "Meadows" is known for taking upset girls on short car rides all over town for long sensible talks. No hysterics ever seem to scare him off completely. It's almost disappointing, isn't it, girls! Those of us who have imposed on him for help are never left feeling either obliged or even all that exposed. He is always telling us, like Terence, "Homo sum: humani nil a me alienum puto" . . . or, "I am a human, I find nothing human foreign to me." The truth is, Professor C. M. Delman has become for some of us the Ultimate Good Father. And he has offered this to wave on wave of incoming students. Even after many decades, to have "worked with Meadows" still truly means something!

So, Sisters, this sorority firmly binds us all across misty

time. Until we met this particular example, many of us kids of divorce believed "a Good Dad" to be some species like the Unicorn. Without Meadows Delman and his follow-up phone calls, the joke gifts and perfect Latin quotations, we never would have known what a Good Father even looked like!

So thank you, Professor Delman, from almost a quarter century, from all eleven hundred eighty one of your lucky handpicked 'daughters'!

VII.

Confess your faults one to another, and pray one for another, that ye may be healed.

James 5:16

I usually hate those films and books that end by stating where everyone landed up and what everyone became professionally. But here I'm moved to close by assembling such a list myself.

Doc Richard Dix, young to be a victim of prostate cancer, still made erotic trouble even in Intensive Care. They'd assigned him older and ever-plainer female nurses. But, using his last strength, Dix still grabbed their asses. Administrators finally resorted to a tall black orderly, I mean a male one. Dix's reaction to this helper's backside has not been recorded. But I felt nothing, less than that, on hearing news of Dr. Richard Dix's death via his own irradiated, overactive generative organs. The *Falls Herald Traveler* claimed he'd perished "surrounded by his loving family," all nine accredited children, their spouses, and his wife of thirty-one years.

Some anonymous local person with a long memory, my current mailing address (and a fairly mean sense of fun) sent me the full-page hometown obituary. The Hollywood glamour portrait of Dix was marked "File photo. Circa 1955." Bethany, our house's major movie-lover, claimed, for what it's worth, that Dix looked like a mix of Lex Barker, Joel McCrea, and the crazed lip-curling young Richard Widmark. "A major dish," she, the toughest of critics, announced.

Community Leader Fallen, Friend to Falls's Animals, Father, and Beloved "Character" Dead at Fifty-One

That takes care of him.

Now on to my mother. Somehow, the *Paradigm*'s dedication let me see how much I'd really worked to be parental. I'd spent the last forty years repaying Clyde for those first eight with him—with Clyde and his wife.

On the plane ride to Florida, I got a super laugh from *USA Today*. They claimed our most recent census was the first to let citizens choose and graze among seven racial slots: "White," "Black," "Asian or Pacific Islander," "American Indian or Alaska Native," "Multiracial," "Hispanic," "Other." Which'll it be?

It said, "By permitting people to pick from an array of racial identities—the new census presents a matrix of 63 ethnic categories, up from 5 a decade ago. Accordingly, nearly 9,000 Americans indicated belonging to 5 races. And 823 checked all 7 racial boxes."

I found this last both hilarious and wise. So why, with a fairly good mind, was I still hoping for such a simple answer? Either/or. I needed finally to know.

Want a successful family visit? It should not involve sleepovers. Arrive in your own car (assured mobility). You'd better park quite near the house. That way you can scram at the first accusation.

So ran my thoughts. And ran, and ran.

In advance, I forced my wife and girls to promise certain things. Driving from Orlando to Pelican Manor, we worked out ear-tugging signals, exit strategies that'd spring us the second Mom's hurtful topics started to emerge. If need be, we were all prepared to bolt from dockside, before setting one deck shoe aboard *More Trouble Than It's Worth II*.

The overheard AM radio bigotry, the bits of fishing lore—along with Mom's not unslatternly history—had made me expect her marina home would be so many planks laid over some sulfurous-smelling bog. Maybe a peeling houseboat the size of some backyard storage shed—two cinder blocks tied to a yellow nylon rope, its only anchor.

"Does Granny Delman live right on their ship?," our younger daughter asked. Even Sara's phrase "Granny Delman" caused me to wince. I said nothing. But, really, what rights did Grace have to these two appealing girls of mine, of ours? My wife guessed aloud that Mom and Buck must also own a little house somewhere. But we'd been invited to visit their boat first, okay? And "ship" refers to ocean liners; "boats" are what mere mortals own, umkay?

I'd leased a Jaguar, a red one. To show Grace how well I'd done in the world. I know. Pathetic.

I told myself that our daughters would get a kick out of having a sports car; but all the girls noticed was: the trunk sure did seem small, didn't it? (They'd each packed nearly everything they owned. We had an oboe and one music stand. I needed a container ship to get three such well-dressed women to Disney World.) Why should I feel so jumpy today? Why should I half-care about a person who'd sent me off alone on some train, me wearing a monkey uniform and still aged eight?

Our Jaguar pulled alongside the Pelican Manor guardpost kiosk. The facility was manicured, hibiscused. The guardpost had been expensively got up to appear some Nantucket fishing shanty. But its hanging crab-traps and faded designer colors all looked cast fiberglass to me. Though the hut was small as some four-seater outhouse, I saw how overoccupied it was. One guy stood in uniform. I spied various lounge-chaired khaki veterans holding beercans in NFL insulators, and one comely pair of browned oiled female legs. Ignoring my red car and half-opened window, everyone continued rediscussing World War II. Patton—hero or rogue?

I don't like at least one part of me: the part now wondering if the owner of Pelican Manor would actually like this many residents crowded underfoot all day in an official security area. Whenever I feel threatened or insecure, I revert, it seems, to the rule of law. In my childhood, I experienced that one wild lawless afternoon. And look at its results on all of us. So, yeah, I can get cautious. In my field, I'm known as "textual," not "theoretical," never too crazily "speculative." But, hey, at least I haven't devolved into a full-out Republican. Not yet, at least, okay?

I zipped down my window even farther and held out the envelope jotted with Grace's dictation. Since my car rode low, since the old guard (was this the famous "Larry"?) refused to stoop, I had to address him loudly over drinkers and the tanned extended legs. Geezers gaped my way; they hadn't shaved in weeks. I felt somewhat foolish announcing to all, "We're expected. . . . *More Trouble Than It's Worth?*"

"I could say the same for you," one husky voice replied. "Larry . . . meet my son and the beautiful ladies of his life. Hellointhere, Meadows. Red Jag, hmm? High-end rental, hunh? Or'd you steal it off some ride at Disney World?"

I parked the goddamn car. Parallel-parked. Badly, I'm afraid. From their kiosk doorway, the old salts leaned forward, taking note, grizzled heads shaking.

I felt nervous with a rage that left me briefly and atypically voiceless. Of course, my daughters climbed right out and ran right over and just hugged Grace. I watched her making much over them, introducing my kids, showing them off as hers already. Old men ogled. "Now, now." Bethany patted my nearest hand still bunched white around the wheel. "She's an extremely good-looking woman, Meadows. You always made her sound so dowdy mousy. She's certainly got some school–of–Katharine Hepburn cheekbones going there, does she not?"

"Yeah and she's not exactly hiding those legs, is she?"

"Should she be? I'm pleased she didn't go and doll all up for us. This seems her usual getup. It's a compliment, if you could only see that. —Besides, if I had those legs, I wouldn't wear anything."

"Yeah, well, she's tried that, too."

"Get out of the car. I swear, you sound like an eight-year-old."

"There are reasons." I walked to Grace and got it over with, embraced her. She smelled of coconut oil and hot rocks.

She wore her hair pulled straight back into a simple silvery bun. Her lethal tan was set off by a man's white business shirt knotted at the waist over a taut if strangely petrified-looking little tummy. There were muscled bumps my daughters call "a six-pack." How did she get so much exercise? Then I guessed.

Grace's khaki shorts looked well worn, seeming as sunbaked as the oiled legs underneath them. Straw sandals with wedge heels lifted her inches taller than I remembered. They showed her calves to full advantage. Her legs looked thirty-eight years old, and even her face not much past fifty-two. (I was not yet forty-six but appeared to be closing fast on a squirish high-cholesterol sixty. None of it would quite compute. Today's stats seemed a cubist's.)

Though most of the guys crowding the guardhouse stared down at my lovely nubile daughters or at my coolly handsome wife, Larry and two others remained firmly focused on my mother's spunky rounded little backside. Some things never change.

Conversationally, my gracious wife, beneficiary of foreign travel and Miss Porter's training, took up the slack. So did my darling girls, usually fairly quick to laugh. The older woman successfully chatted them up; she stood there, saucy, dark as an Indian princess, ten knuckles on two hips, instructing my daughters, "Here, let me look you two beauties over." The girls comically spun then pretended to be woozy from three makeshift turns. "Damn gorgeous, the both of you," Mom said. Our hostess herself acted irksomely perky. She looked browned too often. Crow's feet bespoke her many seasons fishing while drinking while out somewhere on the ocean yukking it up with a good-times stocks-and-bonds crowd.

This Grace appeared far more direct, funny, and opaque than the girl I recalled. Whatever of her had started as childishly soft as the center of some soft-boiled egg, now looked toughened into an exceptional and pliant leather—the expensive, buttery, Italian kind. You could see she still wielded quite a talent for sass, nerve, the slow-burn romantic leer. You saw how all the oldsters in this hut, shaking their heads over her latest joke, considered her a pistol even now. And I could at least see why. I admitted that and stopped there. But the image of her being drilled by the large animal vet; the face of Clyde screaming a scream that would've stunted the growth of Edvard Munch—all that washed back over me here at noon in the Florida heat. All that history still lifted off Mom's brown body like fumes dancing over fuel.

The words "femme fatale" made odd sense here.

I must've looked stricken. I saw so in Bethany's concerned glance. I was closing on fifty. It was ninety-eight degrees today. And I was busy dealing with this: my mother is among the most attractive women I've ever encountered, still definitely something of a turn-on. No fuckin' fair!

From a shopping bag that Larry dangled her way, Grace now pulled two tourist caps. White ones made for "Sea Captains," they were all polished black bills and cheap gilt braid. They recalled to me my silly boarding-school uniform. Grace'd had my daughters' names stitched across each crown in gold thread (though she'd accidently stuck the "H" back onto our Sara). I guessed my snooty daughters would see at once how touristy "cheap" these were. But no. They modeled the hats and, of course, being beautiful and fourteen and seventeen, looked certifiably delightful. You have to see them to believe them.

Grace now led us past three clanging gates; Larry buzzed each one in turn. Ahead of us, the old girl still moved well, secure atop her straw wedges. I found myself busy not looking at my mother's still-spectacular ass. Other boat-owners now eased down their short gangplanks to greet us. They were prepared with our names and everything. Retired doctors, lean elderly execs sun-cured toward beef jerky. Their creasy pretty second wives wore floral-printed low-necked muumuus and all-too-real overplentiful yellow-gold jewelry.

One guy introduced himself as a former eye-ear-nose from Shaker Heights. "We just think the world of your Gracie. Life and soul of our little fishbowl down here. Don't mind telling you, she's mighty darn proud of you. Always talking up your books. Hinting about your reputation and all. Beautiful daughters you got. One dark, one more a blond, perfect. The older one could be our Gracie at sixteen, hmm? 'Heartbreakers' for sure. Oh, to have another shot at being nineteen. I mean, while knowing what little I know now. This go-round, I'd study less. Oh, I'd get so much tail this time. . . ."

Then he seemed embarrassed: hadn't my children, my mom inspired this fuck-witted flight of his? But I laughed him toward ease. "I'm used to hearing it, believe me," I said, "my whole childhood . . ." and stopped.

I saw he was right at least about the resemblance. It'd taken a stranger to point it out. Our Deirdre, who'd always seemed to me so unique, so full-steam-ahead, and yet quite spiritual, now moved arm in arm with Grace. And I swear to God it was the same saunter, same round perfect arms, same stunning high-riding buttocks, twice. Can a person become seasick on a stationary dock?

I was relieved, then pleased, next confused when *More Trouble Than It's Worth II* proved less "boat," more "ship." A handsome sixty-footer, or maybe eighty? As few do, it earned the term of "yacht." The thing looked all teak and ebony and brightwork, Art Deco. It was perfectly maintained, and its lines must've been conceived during the early or mid-thirties. An ideal "screwball-comedy" set. Apt for Grace.

Buck stood waiting. He looked nervous but only about what we'd think of his boat. Just as I had pictured, he was wearing Abercrombie safari gear. His tunic had enough flap-ammo pockets to start another Zulu War; but underneath, the collar of Buck's favorite ragged orange T-shirt showed, frayed. This spoiled the Great White Hunter effect and forced me not to loathe the man on sight.

A big old yam-colored galoot, Buck thrust one callused hand my way, "Come aboard, son. Bout damn time. Put her there."

It was clear that Grace had told him next to nothing about her sad history with Clyde, with Dix, and me. This alone kept my meeting Buck relatively meaningless and therefore cordial. I hadn't come all this way to talk to him.

Buck's innocence made the rest of our afternoon possible. He grinned through pleated skin so sunned it'd thickened to the surface of an inner tube. His huge and able hands were constantly moving, straightening lines, smoothing tarps. The head—raw, noble, outsized—looked like some battered, lichened bust of Justinian. If not brilliant, Buck was plainly civil and surely durable. Like Clyde, he stood about six one. This made me feel both queasy and at home. Lullingly familiar, to be pivoted, seasick like this—between Buck's sleepy Clyde-like goodwill and Grace's lazy buzz of scintillating flirtation. She was already doing that to Bethany, who kept disloyally giggling about something. Not, I hoped, me. Not quite yet.

Buck said he soon planned to "take us out." But first he rigged my girls with hot-pink life preservers. Not two minutes later, his crew of three arrived. The timing, I must say, was perfect. We were quietly under way in less than four minutes. I could see how well his staff knew *More Trouble*.

Three freckled boys the color of honey-baked hams today wore French sailor shirts. Grace's idea of celebrating? Was this her nautical equivalent of my candied-apple Jag? Having three young strangers in charge made the brisk sail possible and thoughtless. Their presence also kept our talk more general and therefore more bearable. Two crew members must have been a few years older than our girls. Once *More Trouble* slid past the jetty, these kids all freely visited and talked. The prettiness of them, stationed in silhouetted clumps against the brilliant blue-green, gave our day at sea an extra glamour. I felt calmed despite my eighteen years' resolve to force Grace toward some logical conclusion: to explain herself. At last, a full-frontal apology might be nice. For killing Clyde, for permanently shipping me away at eight. One "I'm so, so sorry, son." Was that too much to ask?

I'd hoped our girls might sneer a bit at Grace and her gift of five-dollar caps. But Deirdre and Sara wore those with great pleasure, kept adjusting the brims' angles all day, getting the tilt over one eye ever more fetching. (And our girls took the things home as the prizes of their trips; they later wore them to costume parties, kept the caps up in their rooms at least till college. You never know what flashy haberdasher's knickknacks a kid will take to.)

If Grace acted overfamiliar with our daughters, she stayed slightly formal with my wife, and that, today, seemed wise. Grace flattered Bethany by saying how much *she* looked like "the youngish Katharine Hepburn." The "-ish" made such praise more acceptable. (Grace hadn't overheard that very compliment used on herself.)

"Actually, when we met," I piped in, "I thought Bethany was the image of the young Gene Tierney," I said, "which, in my book, is as good as you get." But my wife, I saw, preferred hearing her calcium compared to Hepburn's, and by a woman herself no stranger to good bones. Mom admitted Tierney had been beautiful, "but waxy. Not a real peach, more a wax one. Better full-face than in profile as I remember."

Bethany seemed as easily wooed by Grace as our two pushover daughters. Decades of hearing about my boyhood abandonment had produced very little chilly reserve among my life's other women.

Gracie impartially cajoled and teased me. She flirted with her crew, her son, her husband. She flirted with seagulls, flirted out at an ocean called Atlantic, flirted overhead with a major necessary star named Sun.

And everything but me winked back.

Buck explained, as the two of us did a little casting off *Trouble*'s fantail, how in '49 he'd come to invent a particular filtering-and-friction-reduction feature now used in all state-of-the-art offshore-oil-drilling bits.

"My first brother-in-law was a patent lawyer. Kid right out of U.T. and real 'hungry.' Just blind luck really, my getting there first," Buck shrugged then cast.

He seemed so at ease with himself in reaching over and matter-of-factly showing me how to snap my reel's release. Our hands touched but he offered none of the usual male cringing. Buck was certainly no beauty. I guessed some might've compared his seamed home-base of a face to that of the late Bogart's, the very late Bogart's.

I could, while squinting into the sun, see new ways he might be Grace's latest try at recouping a Clyde. I felt glad that Mom at least remained loyal to one type! Monogamy takes many forms.

She said they planned to whisk us out for dinner once ashore, before we headed back to Orlando. *More Trouble Than It's Worth II* would ride the waves till just at drinktime. Secretly, I already checked my watch.

While my daughters, Bethany, and Buck eased below decks, settling in the sleek galley kitchen to play cards, as our young crew forty feet aft of us smoked Camels (or could that wafting herbal scent be reefer?), I chose to join my putative mother sunning herself on the foredeck. I knew this private family moment only seemed arrived at accidentally; everyone, the crew included, must be in on it.

Gracie rested slung here in a powder-blue two-piece. She was mostly wearing just white wing sunglasses while inhaling one very white Doral. She'd basted herself all over with several sunscreens or balms or other. She smelled like a coconut just macheted whitely open; she also smelled like overheated rope. There blew off her in gusts a sweet and nameless scent I recognized. At first sniff, I felt some simple infant headlong gratitude; I smelled a girl.

But something clamped down in me like some titillated hanging judge's verdict—"No." I breathed briefly, censored, through my mouth. If she had once smelled like overripe fruit, that'd mellowed. Time had salted that toward, say, braised grilled baby vegetables—a range easier to live with day to day, if also something of a loss.

The bikini showed the body of some rawboned divorced lady park ranger. Strong, but from what? For what?

Still, yeah, admit this, it was still pretty darn "good." As a body, I mean. Is it strange to admit you'd—in a blind taste-test—probably choose to jump your sixty-odd-year-old Mother if invited? And if you didn't know. She was. Your mom.

I flashed on the ancient tale of a young man who—not knowing—marries his own mom and kills his father on the road. Once he understands, he can only blind himself. I turned to stare at her.

This particular matured and glazed Grace seemed related only by marriage to that gloomy pallid novel-reading girl. The girl whose sighs had once contained blank white cartoon thought-balloons, each waiting to be filled by statements, anybody's. I recalled her muttered inventory of people and place names. I imagined I had once heard "Boca" huffed aloud among that wild kid's dreamed and itchy destinations.

Now I hoisted one of the teak deck-chairs and resettled it, angled nearer hers. Surprising to find a young sailor stationed in the wheelhouse, steadily guiding *More Trouble*. He posed beyond domed green glass, just four feet behind Grace's forward-looking chair and out-turned thighs.

I nodded toward the boy as he gave me, through windshield, a mock three-fingered salute. It was then I noticed on the wheelhouse window ledge (the ship's dashboard, as it were) two awful brand-new-looking anchor-shaped import-store brass bookends, orange price-stickers still showing. And wedged between those, one Nurses' White Bible from our old days, flanked by first editions of my own two books. Their only editions, come to think of it!

A felt bookmark had been left at the very back of each. I'd admitted she still looked great; that was hard enough. Now, to find Clyde's gift and my own work on board: it was the only thing so far that had truly moved me. She'd probably guessed how this would throw me way off guard. But maybe that was cynical. I don't know.

"So—Clyde gave you the Bible?"

Behind shades, she nodded, "And the sweet fool signed its front page, 'Because no other Good Book is Good enough for MY little woman!' " Even with our eyes averted, we both laughed. Each of our laughs stretched out and died its own rolling natural death. Two laughs, evolved, complete, but utterly different. Unified only by shared subject.

"And you have my books." Craning around, I kept staring at them. "Which is rare. Hell, *I* hardly have my books."

(The kid at the wheel smirked, seeing me shift again; he seemed to think I was admiring him! What else would he expect of Grace's son?) Overclarifying, I pointed at the volumes then to my chest, and turned my back on him. Next, taking lessons from this woman, I simply faced the sun, soberly as some pagan would—duty-joy: one thing. "Try not to try," some superior, fatherly part of me instructed the callow child. And that boy obeyed him. Briefly.

"You are at sea with Grace," eyes shut, I told myself, "you're drifting with her latest hubby, with your family, with one of Dad's Bibles, with your own two lonely little books and, maybe most of all, with that implied ghost, Captain Clyde himself." I could almost picture him behind me doing some intentionally idiotic Buster Keaton eye-shading pose, staring at the horizon. Or else disguised as a dolphin following *More Trouble,* the one Atlantic dolphin with a lighted Camel in its mouth! The very image almost made me grin, eyelids still closed.

"You must've hired a detective to track down my work," I spoke straight into bouncing sea-glare.

"No," she said. "Amazon dot com. You're listed, right in there with the greats, son. And you know, they rushed us both your books in under seven days? I swear. Felt so damn proud when your name came up onscreen between *Delicious Muffins Anyone Can Bake Fast* and *Delray Beach Oceanfront, Real Estate, a Guide. . . .*"

I gave Grace one side-look. We were on a boat; we had a decorative French-looking crew. My girls below deck could now be heard to exclaim over holding so many face cards. And I lolled here near a beautiful woman (Merle Oberon, Ava Gardner, even a little Lena Horne) whose lower body had somehow fed me to the world.

I pictured her when young, wearing that sea-green nightie, padding barefoot into the kitchen of our small sad home and sticking her head in the fridge, as if always expecting that someone else had just magically restocked it with melons, hams, sliced smoked turkey since last she checked.

"Wasn't that some dive, that rental place we had?" But it was she who spoke these words, and the very second I sat picturing our place.

I felt scared that I was leaking, spooked that Grace should lift so much directly from my thoughts. Maybe mere coincidence, and not some synchronous genetic patterning. "One pitiful little house," I admitted. "Funny, I was just this second thinking of it."

"You know?" she called through smoke. "Buck has all the videos of *The Honeymooners* below deck. And we were watching one the other night—Alice reminds Buck of his second wife, the love of *his* life. And that apartment of theirs, the cheap set Gleason used? It sure made me think of our old Elm Street rental. Ours was even laid out like the Cramdens', wasn't it, son? Same sink, the bedroom door right off the . . ."

"And that awful brass bowl of wax fruit . . . I've wondered at times, Grace, why we couldn't have afforded something just a little better."

I heard her shift then tilt my way, propped on one elbow. "Want the truth? 'Cause Clyde kept saving it all for you. A nickel here, quarter there. Insurance policies. For your college. He was right to, of course. I've read both your books. Read every word except the notes and stuff in back. Of course, I didn't know the Roman speeches and the plays you wrote 'em on. But I can see you're very witty on the page. Sharp as hell. It's real well written. You worked out every single sentence, son, and that sure shows. Plus, you clearly know your shit."

"Thank you . . . Grace." I sat here, staring at the beautiful horizon. Burgundy lines were marbled under water showing an almost milky jade-green. I knew I must now offer her something kind in return. I could half-sense Clyde just behind me, vertical if gangly, swaying Blanche-like in the breeze. It seemed he kept insisting, nodding, trying to get me started, on some belated gentleness, toward her. A kindness that was really all his; and that was most everything I learned from him.

I gazed out on an ocean aqua-blue as swimming-pool paint. The boat now moved through a miles-long hula fringe of golden grasses. I remarked on these growing so far from shore.

"Yeah, they live on plankton, no roots, no dirt, no nothing. We're in the Gulf Stream. Way warmer here. The fishing is incredible this far out. Those purple lines all through the blue? That's miles of coral reef. All alive. Don't the colors absolutely slay you? They do me."

I looked over at her. "For someone who skipped the scenery in every novel she read, you sure have taken to panoramas. I mean, it's great. I'm glad you're showing me." She asked how I'd known she always hopped the novels' scenery. "I saw you. Your finger would speed up. You'd mumble, 'Mountain, mountain. Stream, stream.' You'd hurry toward what you called 'the good parts, the people parts.'" She groaned at the phrase, laughing, "A regular Einstein, hunh? That what you saying?"

"No, you were a real reader, Grace. We had lots more than the Cramdens' fruit bowl. I mean, our little house was packed with books."

"Reader, me? Well, if you call Daphne du Maurier reading!" and cackling once, she took in half a Doral.

"But you were also big on Rose Macauley. There was some Henry Green. And *Brideshead*. I remembered later, I recognized your old covers in used-book stores."

"Well, great. You tell me good things about me. You did take an interest after all. Isn't the temperature out here perfect, Meadows? And hardly any wind. Today it's our Atlantic, buddy. You know, the crew just thinks Buck hung the moon. He's puttin that cute little blond one through aviation-repair school. They're like sons to him. Say, your girls are total knockouts. Sweethearts, too. Not stuck-up in the least. I didn't know what you might've told them. About me. Looks like you spared them the complete blow-by-blow. For that I thank you. I expected I'd have to work way harder on 'em than I have. But I'd be willing to do anything to see you all again. You can't imagine. —Yeah, son, looks like you've done a mighty good job with those kids."

I nodded, fighting forty emotions and one bucket of gorge. I accepted the truth of her praise, knowing it as so. But I waited for whatever else my mom could offer me this late. I just expected further damage, more retraction.

But then Grace added, genuine, "Amazing we're both alive, isn't it? How do you explain it, Meadows, who gets to go on and who not?" I dared not speak. I only aimed my front side half away from her, hers, hoping this high-grade a sunscreen might actually protect me.

"Your Deirdre is a sure-nough beauty. . . ." Grace hung right in there.

"Looks just like you did. Even the old eye-ear-nose guy from Cleveland said so."

"Stan? Quite a character, that Stan. He's told me twenty of the jokes our Clyde loved most. Same timing, everything. A kick to pretend they're new. After all these years, they practically are. —Now, your wife, 'Beth'—no, 'Bethany.' There's definitely no shortcut for 'Bethany,' hunh? She's nice too, but I don't think she's real sure, about being down here with us regular folks and all. Acts like she's a little scared Buck and I are going to pull down our pants and shit on deck."

I had to laugh. I admitted aloud: that certainly did make quite an image, didn't it? I tried assuring Mom, Bethany was really all right. She'd been the major sponsor of my getting back in touch like this.

"Well excellent. She's nice enough, okay. Don't get me wrong. Maybe she still has a bit of ye ole New England permafrost clinging here and there, ya know? Seems great with your girls, though. —But, look, are you two going to make it? I mean, your marriage and all? You sure she's not seeing somebody else, longtime-type thing? I've definitely got a nose for this stuff. She's nice, but I thought you'd have, you know, a potter or somebody. A gal somewhat rounder. Little powerhouse. Probably Bethany's from good stock, though. Her father Harvard? President of the stock exchange or somethin? You mind spreading a little oil across my upper back?"

"Yes. Have you always talked like this? And can you take it as well as dish it out? —So you think my wife's getting some steady on the side, hunh? Well, I respect expert opinion. But, Grace? isn't this risky, even somewhat rude of you? First time you see me in eighteen years and you immediately point out a little flaw like that? I mean, one hour after meeting my wife for the first time ever? I'd be within my rights to get furious at your telling me she's got a lover, Mom. Fact is: it's either her decorator, her hair guy, or the gynecologist. Sounds like some Clyde-joke, doesn't it? 'Hear the one about the wife whose whole staff . . . ?' Just my luck. A spouse that finds the only heterosexual decorator and beautician in New Hampshire. Truth is, I'm a little worried she encouraged our meeting, yours and mine, because she's about to bail on me. She thinks you'll help me with the girls when things get rough. I shouldn't admit all this to you. It sounds weak to, Mom. But everything feels so . . . Bethany's dad's is actually the Lincoln-Cadillac dealership in Buffalo. But her mother's family, well, her mother was a Cushing."

"Whatever that is. Sounds like something we should all be sitting on. Still, beautiful thin nose, great bones. You got her good bones into your girls, that counts. —You got the best from her, whatever finally happens between you two. It's the doctor. That's a gal with too much class to 'do' the decorator or some hair-burner. Has she been going in for extra checkups for something she sorta vaguely calls a female complaint?" I sat very still. "Want a good stiff drink, son? That, I can dish out. Rum's wonderful for the nerves. The darker the better. Your earlier pirates knew that," and Grace rose, moved off without asking what I'd actually like.

"Yes," I said loud to her empty sweat-barred chair. "Yes, Mother. Thank you, Mother. Who is fucking my wife, Mother? I've had suspicions, but you of all people should know. And, hey, *muchas gracias* for sharing. And during our first talk in eighteen motherfucking years!" (And yet I felt relieved. I found I had known, too. It was her OB-GYN. We entertained him and his wife almost monthly. The monthlies. And what about certain "male complaints"?)

I felt self-conscious—why? I turned to see our young navigator at his chromium wheel. He smirked toward my solitary conversation here in sunlight. Luckily, the wind on deck, the thick curved glass kept him from hearing me exactly. Still, he'd seen my bitter gesturing, my chatting myself up and lecturing Mom's deck chair. I now flashed the kid his own fakey salute. He nodded and, smiling, raised one circular-motion finger to his own temple. The international sign for lunacy.

I still don't know if he meant my lunacy, Bethany's, Grace's, or the world's. Till now, he hadn't seemed all that philosophical.

.   .   .

"Tell me about Clyde," I started again, tactless, before she, strad-dling teak, had quite regained the chair between her legs, "since you've just offered me my own wife's history in the stirrups."

Grace now handed me a heavy glass tumbler. Its sides were gilded with this ship's entire ridiculous name, doubtless hand-painted in China. (Some poor piecework family, non-English-speakers. At least not at first.) The tumbler held about a pound of serious liq-uid, smelling good, the darkest, costliest rum. Truth serum. As if I needed it!

"What do you really know about Dad's ancestry?," I began hard. Settled now, she was slathering more coconut essence across her west-erly haunch.

"Clyde's people?"

"Yeah. You did spend a decade with him. You do remember the husband I'm asking about?" Snorting, she gave me such a look. "Sorry," I relented, hands lifting, palms exposed. "Really."

"You're bitchy enough to be gay, Meadows. Know that? It always seemed a possibility. Shouldn't have shipped you to that all-boys school. No tellin what they did to my baby. Maybe that's what's sent your wife off antsy elsewhere. You might not even know your own nature yet. It'd be fine by me. Half my pals are, and one ex. —But Clyde? Never did meet Clyde's folks. We had a quick justice-of-the-peace wedding. He never seemed to hear from them. Wasn't there a sister somewhere? Times, Clyde did act a little ashamed of his family. But, then, who doesn't? —Right, son?"

I gave her one unblinking stare, I took a commensurate swig. "Poor Clyde," she went on grinning, leaned way back, sipping delighted as a child with her first float at a soda fountain. "He always thought my mother was such a great lady, the old sherry swiller. Oh, she could be very la-dee-da, no question. She had a chintzy, Garden Club kinda charm. Always pretended to look down on Clyde's nastier jokes, but I noticed she never forgot one. The minute the War broke out, and I mean December 7, Mom became my jailer. Overnight we all felt very patriotic, us young girls. Every boy looks even better in uniform. And they'd looked damn good to start with. I finally got away from Mom at sixteen. The kid I loved first was killed just a few weeks in. But I lucked out. Other men liked me, and right off. One reason I chose Clyde, scared I was in the family way. False alarm from somebody else. But we stuck. He was my standby, such a strange, sweet thing. Till Buck, the current Buck, nobody ever thought more of me or treated me righter. I just wasn't always up to being worshiped in a house so small in that awful little backbiter town. Oh, but our Clyde himself, now he was something, wasn't he? And, boy, does he grow on you or what? It's gotten even better, looking back. Not that he gets better-looking! But such heart always on tap. Man woke up smiling. —Memory lane, hunh? But why Clyde's people?"

" 'Why?' " I asked, feeling either slightly sick or fairly drunk. "Why didn't you ever even hint to me about Dad's race?"

"What race? I know he lost his drivers' license more than once, but . . ."

"Race. Aren't you being coy now? 'Race' as in 'ethnicity.' You did know that Dad's famous Aunt Sutie was black, right?"

"Was she? Course I never saw her. Why, did you? I never believed you two boys kept sneaking off just to drop off those ole sad-sack Bibles. —But her being black shouldn't come as a surprise. Miss Sutie was his 'mammy,' Meadows. Any idea how many Southern whitemen worship their boyhood mammies? Those poor old gals all seem to be named Hattie or Lutie or worse. They do all the white folks' dirty work for years. Their reward is to later get called 'saints,' usually as soon they're off the family payroll. —Look, son, you want another drink? You haven't finished that one. But it sure looks like you're ready for a li'l picker-upper. I hear your ice clinking, and the ocean's smooth as glass."

She rose, meandered off, brought a whole new one without my having answered. I sat staring at my lap. I should've worn a bathing suit. What did I expect to learn from her this late? In the next long silent minute, I drank most of my old drink, in order to drain the new one.

I wanted to report to her how, not a year ago, while I was trying to trim the hedge, my new electric trimmer got away from me. Took quite a toucan bite out of my pale left wrist. I decided it'd do okay without being stitched. Months later, during my annual physical, our family doctor turned over my arm. "What's all this? Keloid healing? I've never noticed that in you before. You have African or Middle Eastern ancestry? Because some of my Jewish patients show this bumpy, shiny kind of mending. See the gleam on that?"

. . .

The salt air smelled metallic this far out, then its odor went as green as leaves. The scent of a jungle blown out this far. A sailboat passed, its sailors—one bronzed young family—waved, kids and all. From *More Trouble*'s lower deck, a good laugh rose concerning some well-played hand of cards. Buck called, "Grace? We got a couple of unbeatable young con-women down here! I swear these girls'll own your boat before we get the dern thing back ashore."

"So you came with a list, Meadows. That it? Come to grill the elder-hostel tramp? That it?" Grace now offered me a cigarette.

"No," I said. "I like your rum-based drink. And I'm touched you bought my books and kept Clyde's Bible gift. I'm glad you're so happy down here. And I like Buck, I do. And I see why you'd marry a guy like him twice. And you've both been so sweet to the girls (though I could live without more news about my wife's libido), umkay? But surely I deserve a few straight answers. You were there and grown. I was there but really wasn't quite conscious yet. Aren't I entitled to figure out a couple more things about my life before it's over? Did you ever even know our Clyde was half black?"

"Was have-a-what?," she sat up only slightly. She removed her sunglasses. Grace studied me as if my head had just become a smiling dolphin's. "Look, son, you may think I've been married so often I've had a guy from every country. 'United Nations Gracie.' Not to sound too prejudiced but, like you, I grew up in the Old South. And to my knowledge I have not yet married me a colored fellow. Never say never, of course. But if so, you'd be the first to hear. I'd sure tell you if your own dad was black or 'African-American' or whatever we're supposed to call them this year. . . ."

"So—do you want to maybe hint now who my father really was? Because I'd have preferred Clyde over any other flavor."

"Meadows, Meadows. This why you came? Look, you little prick, who your actual father is, that's one question. And apart from this new DNA testing, I don't know if even the FBI could go back and determine that exactly. I always thought of you as Clyde's. *He* sure as hell did. It's true you never were his dead-ringer. But you two were so like each other then. In temperament. You didn't need to talk. The two of you could just sit there, smiling and humming, for hours. Drove me mad. And you neither could see why I felt more restless than you boys did. But you were little, new here, so I can't really blame you for that.

"In most all the ways that count, you're still so damn much his. Even sound like him. Man had the most beautiful voice. —But all that's on one side. The other is whether our sweet Clyde Delman was a black guy. And maybe whether you are? That why you're finally bothering to track me down? Look, I saw him naked, saw him dressed. Clyde and I clocked lots of very happy racktime. Whatever your memories tell you about it. He could be a circus in bed, game for anything, an absolute monkey. So—I knew the kind ole thing pretty thoroughly for going on ten years. And to my knowledge he was as white as . . . well, started to say, as you are. No, as I am. (Which is harder to prove than you might guess.)

"Now, to me right now, you appear to be many things, my Meadows—but several I'm sure of. One: you came out of me down here. And two: you're at least a good bit of you Caucasian, son. You may not want to be. It's out of fashion, I know. But, hey, I worked with what was available to Presbyterian white girls, even 'fast' ones, back in '46. Platinum-blonds do tend toward being white people! When you were two, your eyelashes were so blond they were white. What the hell's your problem, son?"

I explained about visiting Sutie; I told how I'd found Clyde's older sister in D.C. Definitely not Scotch-Irish, his next of kin.

"Look," Grace grew testier. Unwowed by my legal brief, she canted forward—her face nearer, over, all but in mine. I could see our crewman at his wheel, watching us far harder. And I, influenced by her to-hell-with-it spirit, now held a pre-emptive middle finger up behind my head, generally clearing the area: protection, privacy, agent orange.

"Meadows? Have you ever known me to lie? You of all people should remember, I'm a real bad liar. Couldn't keep a secret if my life depended on it. Which it did. Several times. Funny, I figure that's why I've lived so long. I basically don't give two shits about most of the things most people do. Seems I have a different kind of pride from others. So, if Clyde had horns and a tail and could play organ music out his butthole, wouldn't have bothered me a bit. If I loved him. And I did. In my own way and time, I was nuts for the guy. As mad for him as you were. And I saw how mad you were for him. I know. . . ." She faltered around something, coughed once, proceeded through it. "And I know, son, nobody ever loved anybody the way he loved you. Ev-er. Got so I felt jealous. Even when I had my lover in the house. Jealous of you two being out loose in the world without me. Those motels, you made them sound like early Disneyland. All the news you two came home with. All those loonies you collected. Remember the one that brought the plant by taxi clear from the coast? And you think I'd now be scared to admit marrying a husband who had one type blood or other? Grow the fuck up. You're still basically such a squirt. I was afraid of that. Look, you—my father's family is the one rumored to've had somebody frisky in the woodpile. And not too many generations back. Have you noticed how I take the sun? Never had a bit of 'surgery,' I've never shriveled up like most the old Naugahyde white-broads down here. And it ain't 'Cherokee,' honey. If you'd ever seen my dad's youngest sister's hair and features, you'd believe the rumors. Meadows, their family'd walk into stores and clerks would always hand her the heavy parcels. Got so she wised up, stayed home, upstairs. She's not in any of the photographs. And nobody begged her, either. I don't know many 'good' old Southern families don't have some of this. So if you're a black, it's probably likelier on my side, Mr. Bean Counter Professor!

"And now you fly south with your federal case all plotted out up north. Your father is a Negro. Come to think of it, you might not be Clyde's. Tightass like you. I wasn't much older than your daughters when I had you. Three weeks past nineteen when you were born. I was somewhat of a mess as a parent, I know. But, hey, I tried to be a mother for a while there. I really did, Meadows. I never bragged about how it all turned out. Maybe I gave up on you by sending you away so soon. But one thing I'll say for me in the self-knowledge department: I never chanced motherhood again. Live and learn. Your later little half-siblings all got nipped in the bud pretty early. You were—how can I put it?—an experiment. All we can do is learn from our bigger goof-ups.

"I have no talent at mothering anybody except grown men. And nobody needs it more or pays better rates! But, hey, I've kept on keeping in touch. With you. Which ain't easy after years of your not answering me once. Arguing's easy—silence is the killer, Christmas to birthday to Christmas. You should know from having kids of your own. And no matter how bad at it a parent is, the kids're always your particular mistakes, nobody else's. So, now, let's us make a little peace, kiddo, umkay? What say?

"There are piles of things I need to answer for, but the race of the late Clyde Delman ain't one. I will tell you this: I have never seen anybody love anybody the way that man loved you. When he couldn't sleep? He'd get up, tiptoe in and refold your whole sock drawer! Living around you two, sometimes, I felt so left out."

"Dolphins!" the youngest deckhand shouted. He knew my girls would come running above deck wearing cocked cute caps. And sure enough. Each still held a fan of playing cards. They'd been playing what? "Go Fish"? And something about their dashing aloft into the freshness of the daylight this far out at sea, something about the beauty of those horizontally striped black-white French sailor shirts, some element of spectacle in the way Deirdre now pointed toward eight heavy leaping silver fish and cried, "*Per*-fect!"

And our oldest, then her sister threw their playing cards aloft. We all laughed to see paper scatter, hearts, clubs, turning, aces, spades, suddenly meaningless and fluttering, somehow joyful, lost, but beautiful, wasted behind us.

Soon we were tied up again; soon we drove off to a five-course dinner in a private room. It was a costly club called The Thunderbird. Mother first stopped off at their underfurnished stucco hacienda; upstairs she slid into a cream-colored silk dress with a Chinese collar and frogs all down its tailored front. The wrought-iron staircase was spiral and, descending, she took full advantage. Mom had put on lipstick and maybe a little eye-stuff. Now night was here, sixty-four started looking forty-two. Mother, ashore, acted gracious and overconfident, even tony. The staff at the T-bird seemed genuinely glad to see her, and the maître d' nodded my way. "You must be Grace's author."

We were led to a white leather banquette; it featured table settings for seven. One more than we, the living, required. I kept casting an eye on the revolving door, expecting some surprise guest. Hoping.

Mostly Grace interviewed my girls about what foods they liked and what were their favorite colors and what young folks read these days; she asked them both to map out all they really hoped for in a boyfriend. And I heard things from them I'd never guessed. This woman kept pressing up against everything held in common with two granddaughters she'd never met, girls of a mystery race Grace would never know or care to guess.

Cold cucumber soup sprinkled with chopped mint and dill. Soon as we finished, three waiters appeared. They changed the unused silver-ware and plates at table position number seven, too. As if Mom had given instructions: someone, slotted to arrive late, mustn't feel left out; keep the meal going till he gets here. No one else seemed to find this spare chair odd. I didn't like to mention it or stare. I recalled a Seder dinner, one honored chair reserved for the prophet Elijah.

As I drank excellent Burgundy, as I marveled at the beauty of these all-ages women, I felt a presence come to occupy that chair. Some column of humidity, not quite a mist. But if you put your hand in it, you'd know! It took slow, fond possession of that chair, that one-seventh of our white tablecloth. I loomed closer into mutual candle-light. I said less and less but sat safe behind my half-smile that nobody noticed. And I sensed its enjoying us even more than we remembered just now to enjoy ourselves. Museums, I swear, museums should be phoned.

After Buck secretly slipped our waiter a platinum card, preventing my "getting this," as our chatter wound warmly down, I excused myself. I was headed into the chrome-and-granite crypt of a Men's Room when I heard some big swamp bird's cry. Across the narrow hall, one screen door stood open. It showed a trash-canned dock over-looking the weedy canal out back.

I slid into night air. I wandered clear to the end of half-lit planking. Shielded from valet parking by ramshackle wooden lath, I whipped mine out and took a leak into the black canal. Wild-creature sounds so near the restaurant seemed both a relief and contradiction. Through the open door, behind me, I could still hear the knife-to-plate clatter, and there was Mother laughing with a hoot.

Here at dock's end rested an an antique aluminum beach chair, frayed green-white woven strips. So many cigarettes had been smoked here, the woodgrain reeked. One nicotine-addicted waiter at a time must slouch here during wealthy older people's salad courses. Some kid inhaling, thinking his own horny and ambitious thoughts.

Tobacco smelled evocative for once, almost healthful. It made Clyde seem alive and quite nearby. Back at the dim table, he'd presided as a force invisible. But out here, as I reeled in and zipped up, I swear I could feel him press. Knobbed kneecaps just at the back joints of my legs. Some memory of "driving" in his lap. Thanks to peripheral vision, some animal sense of what's where, I knew that Clyde himself was standing just in back of me.

All my life I had been learning, scrounging, preparing one phrase. I'd wanted to instruct my savior dad: how to meet his Saviour in His native tongue. Clyde should offer the greeting in Aramaic Hebrew, a "middle" or "Rabbinic" form. Dad's must be the very accent spoken by a dusty wandering Nazarene, Himself something of a Bible-route traveling salesman. His people had used weak gutturals, a certain singsong quite easy to imitate in other parts of the empire. It felt so right to me that Jesus' twang should've been considered—a hick's.

I'd known these words, first phonetically and then for real—by heart—nearly forty years. I'd carried them around, awaiting the one big ear to whisper into. Practicing, I'd muttered them to walls, by heart, to trees, to shopwindows but never once felt heard. I always told myself I'd know the truest chance for transfer when I finally met it.

Far across this dark swift-moving channel, that heron kept crying, waiting, repeating—soliciting the last of its kind to offer some romantic mirroring response. No answer. Only the one large bird sang, paused, then cried again into the dark. As I—methodical, depending on the rickety chair, half conscious that my family must be wondering where I'd gone—as I eased down onto my knees here at the pier's murky end. Planking still felt warm from the day's heat. I expected boards to be all splintery; instead I knelt on suede.

"It's this," I whispered.

> "'*Anoki aleka*' is how He would've said it.
> 'I belong to you, Lord, sir.' "

And at that moment, my oldest daughter's voice called down the bathroom corridor, "Dad, you fall in or what?," just then the distant heron got answered by his same song only half a mile away. And right that minute, on the word "belong," some great fish (invisible but breaking water very loud) leapt clear of current, hung one second midair—an arc of silver underbelly glinting overhead—then splashed back, flinging such wet all across me. I laughed surprise. The bilge tasted like shrimp, like rust, a life: my dry mouth savoring each drop. It is He who hath made us and not we ourselves.